"In a novel that is beautiful, engrossing and fascinating, Kelhmann succeeds in exploring how hard it is to explain the world when a thousand theories, all superstitions, compete. Lucid, limpid, savage. *Tyll* quietly intrudes on our present crisis of European identity. This novel is a masterly achievement, a work of imaginative grandeur and complete artistic control" Ian McEwan

"This is a brilliant and unputdownable novel. Kehlmann is the true inheritor of the German fabulist tradition that stretches back to the Brothers Grimm and even further, and in the legendary prankster figure of Tyll Ulenspiegel he has found his perfect avatar" Salman Rushdie

"*Tyll* proves that Kehlmann is literature's jack-of-all trades. He manages to combine meticulous historical research and virtuoso language mimicry with a frightening exploration of our current sense of dystopia. An incredible educational experience and improbably entertaining" Michael Haneke

"Kehlmann's imagination runs deep and wild. It travels with the currents of history, in its cycles of brutality and violence, it reaches into our own solitude and silence, summoning us, it soars far and high, and echoes with the power of myth" Valeria Luiselli

"Vivid . . . Kehlmann, a confident magician himself, plays his bright pages like cards. But he has a deeper purpose, which is revealed only gradually, as the grand climacteric of his chosen war steadily justifies its presence in the novel . . . Kehlmann is a gifted and sensitive storyteller . . . Despite the grimness of the surroundings and the lancing interventions of history, the novel's tone remains light, sprightly, enterprising. Kehlmann has an unusual combination of talents and ambitions—he is a playful realist, a rationalist drawn to magical games and tricky performances, a modern who likes to look backward" James Wood, *New Yorker*

"Daniel Kehlmann's *Tyll* is a laugh-outloud-then-weep-into-your-beer comic novel about a war. . . Kehlmann is at the top of his game" *The Times*

"A romp through the thirty years' war. . . This energetic historical fiction, featuring a folkloric jester in a violent, superstitious Europe, is the work of an immense talent" *Guardian*

"The narrative moves from myth to historical novel to ballad and back and Ross Benjamin's translation follows it faithfully" *The Spectator*

"*Tyll* is an absorbing and, for a novel about a prankster, remarkably sincere novel" *Literary Review*

"Like a magician, Kehlmann conjures comedy, farce and badinage, even in a blighted time of war" *Financial Times*

"Profoundly enchanting but never sentimental, *Tyll* is a magnificent story . . . Kehlmann is a master of economical, devastating description . . . Chilling . . . In this exquisitely crafted novel, Kehlmann moves just as nimbly through the grimmest of human experiences. The result is a spellbinding memorial to the nameless souls lost in Europe's vicious past, whose whispers are best heard in fables" Irina Dumitrescu, *The New York Times Book Review*

Also by Daniel Kehlmann

TYLL

Daniel Kehlmann

Translated from the German
by Ross Benjamin

riverrun

First published in German in 2017 by Rowohlt Verlag
This English edition first published in the United States in 2020 by Pantheon Books
First published in Great Britain in 2020 by riverrun
This paperback edition published in 2021 by

riverrun

An imprint of

Quercus Editions Limited
Carmelite House
50 Victoria Embankment
London EC4Y 0DZ

An Hachette UK company

A CIP catalogue record for this book is available
from the British Library.

Paperback 978 1 52940 367 1
Ebook 978 1 52940 368 8

10 9 8 7 6 5 4 3 2 1

Typeset by CC Book Production
Printed and bound in Great Britain by Clays Ltd, Elcograf S.p.A.

Papers used by riverrun are from well-managed forests and other responsible sources.

For A

TYLL

Shoes

THE WAR HAD NOT YET COME TO US. WE LIVED IN FEAR
and hope and tried not to draw God's wrath down upon our
securely walled town, with its hundred and five houses and
the church and the cemetery, where our ancestors waited for
the Day of Resurrection.

We prayed often to keep the war away. We prayed to the
Almighty and to the kind Virgin. We prayed to the Lady of the
Forest and to the Little People of Midnight, to Saint Gerwin,
to Peter the Gatekeeper, to John the Evangelist—and to be safe
we also prayed to Old Mela, who during the Twelve Nights,
when the demons are let loose, roams the heavens at the head of
her retinue. We prayed to the Horned Ones of ancient days and
to Bishop Martin, who shared his cloak with the beggar when
the latter was freezing, so that they were then both freezing
and pleasing to God, for what's the use of half a cloak in winter, and of course we prayed to Saint Maurice, who had chosen
death with a whole legion rather than betray his faith in the one
just God.

Twice a year the tax collector came and always seemed
surprised that we were still here. Now and then merchants
came, but since we didn't buy much they soon went on their

way, which was all right with us. We needed nothing from the wide world and gave it no thought until one morning a covered wagon, pulled by a donkey, rolled down our main street. It was a Sunday at the beginning of spring, the stream was swollen with meltwater, and in those fields that weren't lying fallow we had sown the seed.

A red canvas tent was pitched on the wagon. In front of it crouched an old woman. Her body looked like a bag, her face seemed made of leather, her eyes looked like tiny black buttons. A younger woman with freckles and dark hair stood behind her. But on the coach box sat a man we recognized even though he had never been here before, and when the first of us realized who he was and called his name, others too realized, and soon many voices were calling from all directions: "Tyll is here!" "Tyll has come!" "Look, it's Tyll!" It could be no one else.

Leaflets came even to us. They came through the forest, the wind carried them, merchants brought them—out in the world more of them were printed than anyone could count. They were about the Ship of Fools and the great priestly folly and the evil Pope in Rome and the devilish Martinus Luther of Wittenberg and the sorcerer Horridus and Doctor Faust and the hero Gawain of the Round Table and indeed about him, Tyll Ulenspiegel, who had now come to us himself. We knew his pied jerkin, we knew the battered hood and the calfskin cloak. We knew the gaunt face, the small eyes, the hollow cheeks, and the buckteeth. His breeches were made of good material, his shoes of fine leather, but his hands were a thief's or a scribe's hands, which had never done work; his right held the reins, his left the whip. His eyes flashed as he greeted this person and that.

"And what's your name?" he asked a little girl.

She was speechless, unable to fathom that a person of such renown should be addressing her.

"Well, tell me!"

When she stammered that her name was Martha, he only smiled as if he had always known it.

Then he asked intently: "And how old are you?"

She cleared her throat and told him. In the twelve years of her life she had not seen eyes like his. There might be eyes like these in the free cities of the Empire and at the great courts, but never before had anyone with such eyes come to us. Martha hadn't known that such strength, such agility of soul could speak from a human face. One day she would tell her husband and then much later her incredulous grandchildren, who would consider Ulenspiegel a figure of old legends, that she had once seen him in the flesh.

In the meantime the wagon had rolled by and his gaze had glided elsewhere, to others on the roadside. Again there were shouts of "Tyll has come!" along the street and "Tyll is here!" from the windows and "It's Tyll!" from the church square, onto which his wagon now rolled. He cracked the whip and stood up.

With lightning speed the wagon turned into a stage. The two women folded the tent. The young one tied her hair into a knot, put on a little crown, and threw a piece of purple cloth around her, while the old one stood in front of the wagon and began to sing droningly. Her dialect had the sound of the south, of the big cities of Bavaria, and wasn't easy to understand, but we did glean that the song was about a woman and a man who loved each other and were cruelly separated by a body of water. Tyll Ulenspiegel took a blue sheet, kneeled down, flung it, holding on to one end, away from him so that it unfurled with a crackle. He pulled it back and flung it away again, pulled it back, flung it, and the way he kneeled on one end and the woman on the other and the blue billowed between them, there really seemed to be water there, and the waves went up and down so furiously that it seemed no ship could sail them.

When the woman straightened up and looked at the waves, her face rigid with fright, we suddenly noticed how beautiful she was. As she stood there and stretched her arms toward the sky, she all at once no longer belonged here, and none of us could look away. Only out of the corner of our eyes did we see her beloved leaping and dancing and bustling around and brandishing his sword and battling dragons and foes and witches and evil kings, on the difficult journey to her.

The play lasted into the afternoon. But even though we knew the cows' udders were hurting, none of us stirred. The old woman performed hour after hour. It seemed impossible that someone could memorize so many verses, and some of us began to suspect she was making them up as she sang. Tyll Ulenspiegel's body was meanwhile never at rest, his soles seemed hardly to touch the ground; whenever our eyes found him, he was once again elsewhere on the small stage. At the end there was a misunderstanding: The beautiful woman had obtained a potion to feign death and not be forced to marry her evil guardian, but the message to her beloved explaining everything had gone astray and when he, her true bridegroom, the friend of her soul, at last arrived beside her motionless body, the shock struck him like a bolt of lightning. For a long time he stood there as if frozen. The old woman was silent. We heard the wind and the cows mooing for us. No one breathed.

Finally he drew his knife and stabbed himself in the breast. It was astonishing: the blade disappeared in his flesh, a red cloth rolled out of his collar like a stream of blood, and he let out a death rattle, twitched, lay still. Was dead. Twitched once again, sat up, sank back down. Twitched again, lay still again, and this time forever. We waited. So it was. Forever.

Seconds later, the woman woke up and saw the body lying beside her. First she was stunned, then she shook him, then she comprehended and was stunned again, and then she wept as if the world could hold no consolation. Then she took his knife and killed herself in turn, and again we admired the clever device and how deep in her breast the blade disappeared. Now only the old woman remained and spoke a few more verses, which we hardly understood because of the dialect. Then the play was over, and many of us were still weeping long after the dead had stood up and bowed.

But that wasn't all. The cows would have to keep waiting, because after the tragedy came the comedy. The old woman beat a drum, and Tyll Ulenspiegel piped on a flute and danced with the young woman, who now no longer looked especially beautiful at all, to the right and to the left and forward and back again. The two of them threw their arms up, and their movements were in such harmony that they seemed to be not two people but mirror images of each other. We could dance fairly well, we celebrated often, but none of us could dance like them; watching them, you felt as if a human body had no weight and life were not sad and hard. We too could no longer keep still, and we began to bob, jump, hop, and spin.

But suddenly the dance was over. Gasping for breath, we looked up at the wagon, on which Tyll Ulenspiegel was now standing alone; the two women were nowhere to be seen. He sang a mocking ballad about the poor, stupid Winter King, the Elector Palatine, who had thought he could defeat the Kaiser and accept Prague's crown from the Protestants, yet his kingship had melted away even before the snow. He sang about the Kaiser too, who was always cold from praying, the little man trembling before the Swedes in the imperial palace in Vienna, and then he sang about the King of Sweden, the Lion of Midnight, strong as a bear, but of what use had it been to him against the bullets in Lützen that took his life like that of any mere soldier, and out was your light, and gone the little royal soul, gone the lion! Tyll Ulenspiegel laughed, and we laughed too, because you couldn't resist him and because it did us good to remember that these great men were dead and we were still alive, and then he sang about the King of Spain with his bulging lower lip, who believed he ruled the world even though he was broke as a chicken.

In all our laughter we realized only after a while that the music had changed, that it had suddenly lost its mocking tone. He was now singing a ballad of war, of riding together and the clanking of the weapons and the friendship of the men and standing the test of danger and the jubilation of the whistling bullets. He sang of the soldier's life and the beauty of dying in battle, he sang of the whooping joy of each and every man who rode against the enemy on horseback, and we all felt our hearts beat faster. The men among us smiled, the women swayed their heads, the fathers lifted their children onto their shoulders, the mothers looked down at their sons with pride.

Only old Luise hissed and jerked her head and muttered so loudly that those standing near her told her to go home, which, however, only prompted her to raise her voice further and shout: Didn't anyone understand what he was doing here? He was invoking it, he was summoning it!

But as we were hissing and waving dismissively and threatening her, she waddled off, thank God, and by then he was playing the flute again, and the woman was standing next to him and she now looked majestic like a person of rank. She sang with a clear voice of love, which was stronger than death. She sang of the love of parents and the love of God and the love between man and woman, and here something changed again, the beat became faster, the notes sharper and sharper, and suddenly the song was about carnal love, warm bodies, rolling in the grass, the scent of your nakedness, and your big behind. The men among us laughed, and then the women joined in the laughter, and the children laughed loudest of all. Little Martha was laughing too. She had pushed her way forward, and she understood the song very well, for she had often heard her mother and father in bed and the farmhands in the straw and her sister with the carpenter's son the previous year—in the night the two of them had stolen away, but Martha had crept after them and had seen everything.

A broad lewd grin appeared on the face of the famous man. A strong power now stretched between him and the woman. He was impelled toward her and she toward him, so forcefully were their bodies drawn together, and it was hardly bearable that they had not yet touched. Yet the music he played seemed to prevent it, for as if by accident it had changed, and the moment had passed, the notes no longer permitted it. It was the Agnus Dei. The woman folded her hands piously, *qui tollis peccata mundi*, he backed away, and the two of them seemed startled themselves by the wildness that had almost seized them, just as we were startled and crossed ourselves because we remembered that God saw all and condoned little. The two of them sank to their knees. We did the same. He put down the flute, stood up, spread his arms, and asked for payment and food. Because now there would be a pause. And the best would come, if we slipped him good money, thereafter.

In a daze, we reached into our pockets. The two women went around with cups. The coins jingled and jumped. We all gave: Karl Schönknecht gave, and Malte Schopf gave, and his lisping sister gave, and the miller's family, who were usually so stingy, gave too, and toothless Heinrich Matter and Matthias Wohlsegen gave an especially large amount, even though they were craftsmen and thought they were better than everyone else.

Martha walked slowly around the covered wagon.

There sat Tyll Ulenspiegel, leaning his back against the wagon wheel and drinking from a large stein. Next to him stood the donkey.

"Come here," he said.

Her heart pounding, she stepped closer.

He held out the stein to her. "Drink," he said.

She took the stein. The beer tasted bitter and heavy.

"The people here. Are they good people?"

She nodded.

"Peaceful people, help each other, understand each other, like each other, is that the sort of people they are?"

She took another sip. "Yes."

"Well, then," he said.

"We'll see," said the donkey.

In her fright Martha dropped the stein.

"The precious beer," said the donkey. "You damned stupid child."

"It's called ventriloquism," said Tyll Ulenspiegel. "You can learn it too, if you'd like."

"You can learn it too," said the donkey.

Martha picked up the stein and took a step back. The puddle of beer grew and then shrank again, the dry ground soaking up the wetness.

"Seriously," he said. "Come with us. You know me now. I'm Tyll. My sister over there is Nele. She's not my sister. The name of the old woman I don't know. The donkey is the donkey."

Martha stared at him.

"We'll teach you everything," said the donkey. "Nele and the old woman and Tyll and I. And you'll get away from here. The world is big. You can see it. I'm not just called donkey, I have a name too, I'm Origenes."

"Why are you two asking me?"

"Because you're not like them," said Tyll Ulenspiegel. "You're like us."

Martha held out the stein to him, but he didn't take it, so she put it on the ground. Her heart was pounding. She thought of her parents and her sister and the house in which she lived, and the hills out beyond the forest and the sound of the wind in the trees, which she couldn't imagine sounded quite the same anywhere else. And she thought of her mother's stew.

The famous man's eyes flashed as he said with a smile: "Think of the old saying: You can find something better than death everywhere."

Martha shook her head.

"Very well, then," he said.

She waited, but he said nothing more, and it took her a moment to realize that his interest in her had already died away.

And so she walked back around the wagon and to the people she knew, to us. We were now her life; there was no longer any other life for her. She sat down on the ground. She felt empty. But when we looked up, she did too, for we had all noticed at the same time that something was hanging in the sky.

A black line cut through the blue. We squinted. It was a rope.

On one side it was tied to the window grille of the church tower, on the other to a flagpole jutting out of the wall next to the window of the town hall where the reeve worked, which didn't happen often, however, because he was lazy. In the window stood the young woman, who must have just knotted the rope—but how, we wondered, had she stretched it? You could be here or there, in this window or in the other, you could easily knot a rope and drop it, but how did you get it back up to the other window to fasten the other end?

We gaped. For a while it seemed to us as if the rope itself were the trick and nothing more were required. A sparrow landed on it, took a small jump, spread its wings, changed its mind, and stayed perched there.

Then Tyll Ulenspiegel appeared in the church tower window. He waved, jumped onto the windowsill, stepped onto the rope. He did it as if it were nothing. He did it as if it were only a step like any other. None of us spoke, none shouted, none moved. We had stopped breathing.

He neither teetered nor tried to find his balance—he simply walked. His arms swinging, he walked the way you walk on the ground, except it looked a bit mincing how he always set one foot precisely in front of the other. You had to look closely to notice how he absorbed the swaying of the rope with small movements of his hips. He took a leap and bent his knees for only a moment when he landed. Then he strolled, his hands folded behind his back, to the middle. The sparrow took off, but it only beat its wings a few times and perched again and turned its head; all was so quiet that we could hear it cheeping and peeping. And of course we heard our cows.

Above us Tyll Ulenspiegel turned, slowly and carelessly—not like someone in danger but like someone looking around with curiosity. He stood with his right foot lengthwise on the rope, his left crosswise, his knees slightly bent and his fists on his hips. And all of us, looking up, suddenly understood what lightness was. We understood what life could be like for someone who really did whatever he wanted, who believed in nothing and obeyed no one; we understood what it would be like to be such a person, and we understood that we would never be such people.

"Take off your shoes!"

We didn't know whether we had heard him correctly.

"Take them off," he shouted. "Everyone, your right shoe. Don't ask, do it, it will be a lark. Trust me, take them off. Old and young, woman and man! Everyone. Your right shoe."

We stared at him.

"Haven't you been enjoying it so far? Don't you want more? I'll show you more, take off your shoes, everyone, your right shoe, go on!"

It took us a while to get moving. That's how it always is with us, we're unhurried people. The first to obey was the baker, followed by Malte Schopf and then Karl Lamm and then his wife, and then the craftsmen who always thought they were better than everyone else obeyed, and then we all did, every one of us, with the exception of Martha. Tine Krugmann next to her nudged her and pointed to her right foot, but Martha shook her head, and Tyll Ulenspiegel on the rope took another leap, striking his feet together in the air. He jumped so high that he had

13

to spread his arms when he landed to find his balance—only very briefly, but it was enough to remind us that even he had weight and couldn't fly.

"And now throw," he cried with a high, clear voice. "Don't think, don't ask, don't hesitate, this will be a great lark. Do what I say. Throw!"

Tine Krugmann was the first to do it. Her shoe flew, rising higher and disappearing in the crowd. Then the next shoe flew, it was Susanne Schopf's, and then the next, and then dozens flew and then even more and more and more. We all laughed and screamed and shouted: "Watch out!" and "Duck!" and "Heads up!" It was terrific entertainment, and it didn't matter that some of the shoes hit people's heads. Curses rang out, a few women scolded, a few children wept, but it wasn't bad, and Martha even had to laugh when a heavy leather boot only barely missed her, while a woven slipper sailed through the air to land at her feet. He had been right, and some even found it so exhilarating that they threw their left shoes too. And some also threw hats and spoons and jugs, which shattered somewhere, and of course a few threw stones too. But when his voice spoke to us, the noise faded away, and we listened.

"You idiots."

We squinted. The sun was low in the sky. Those at the back of the square could see him clearly, while for the rest he was only a silhouette.

"You half-wits. You crumb-heads. You tadpoles. You good-for-nothing beetle-brained oafs. Now fetch them again."

We stared.

"Or are you too stupid? Is the word fetch too much to penetrate your skulls?" He let out a bleating laugh. The sparrow took off, soared over the roofs, was gone.

We looked at each other. We had been derided, but then again his rude mockery was not so sharp that it couldn't have been meant in jest. He was famous, after all, he could take that liberty.

"Well, what is it?" he asked. "Don't you need them anymore? Don't you want them anymore? Don't you like them anymore? You dolts, fetch your shoes!"

Malte Schopf was the first. He had felt ill at ease the whole time, and so he now ran to where he thought his shoe had flown. He pushed people aside, forcing and jostling his way through the crowd, bending over and rooting around between their legs. On the other side of the square Karl Schönknecht did the same, followed by Elsbeth, the widow of the smith, but old Lembke blocked her and shouted at her to be off, that was his daughter's shoe. Elsbeth, whose forehead was still hurting from being hit by a boot, shouted back that he was the one who should be off, because she could certainly still recognize her own shoe, Lembke's daughter by no means had such beautifully embroidered shoes as she did, whereupon old Lembke screamed at her to get out of his way and not to disparage his daughter, whereupon she in turn screamed that he was a stinking shoe thief. Here Lembke's son intervened: "I'm warning you!" At the same time Lise Schoch and the miller's wife began to quarrel, because their shoes really did look alike, and their feet were the same size, and Karl Lamm and his brother-in-law also exchanged loud words, and Martha suddenly grasped what was happening here, and she crouched down on the ground and started to crawl.

Above her there was now shoving, rebuking, and jostling. A few, who had found their shoes quickly, slipped away, but among the rest of us a rage broke out with the force of long-pent-up grievance. The carpenter Moritz Blatt and the black-smith Simon Kern pummeled each other so ferociously that someone who thought they were fighting over shoes could not have understood, since he would not have known that Moritz's wife had been promised to Simon as a child. Both were bleeding from nose and mouth, both were panting like horses, and no one dared break them up. Lore Pilz and Elsa Kohlschmitt were locked in terrible combat too, but then they had hated each other for so long that even they had forgotten why. It was very well known, however, why the Semmler family and the people from the Grünanger house lashed out at each other; it was because of the disputed field and the unresolved inheritance that went back as far as the days of Prefect Peter, and also because of the Semmler daughter and her child, which was not her husband's but Karl Schönknecht's. The rage spread like a fever—wherever you looked people were shrieking and punching, bodies were rolling, and now Martha turned her head and looked up.

There he stood, laughing. Back arched, mouth wide, shoulders heaving. Only his feet stood steadily, and his hips swung with the swaying of the rope. It seemed to Martha as if she only had to look more carefully, then she would understand why he was so delighted—but then a man ran toward her and didn't see her and his boot struck her chest, and her head hit the ground, and when she inhaled it was as if needles were pricking her. She rolled onto her back. Rope and sky were empty. Tyll Ulenspiegel was gone.

She struggled to her feet. She hobbled past the brawling, rolling, biting, weeping, battering bodies, here and there still recognizing their faces; she hobbled along the street, hunching her shoulders and bowing her head, but just as she reached her front door, she heard the rumble of the covered wagon behind her. She turned around. On the coach box sat the young woman he had called Nele. Next to her the old woman crouched motionless. Why wasn't anyone stopping them? Why wasn't anyone following them? The wagon passed Martha. She stared after it. Soon it would be at the elm, then at the city gate, then gone.

And now, when the wagon had almost reached the last houses, someone was running after it, with effortless long strides. The calfskin of the cloak bristled around his neck like something alive.

"I would have taken you with me!" he cried as he ran past Martha. Shortly before the bend of the street, he caught up with the wagon and jumped aboard. The gatekeeper was with the rest of us on the main square; no one held them back.

Slowly Martha went into the house, closed the door behind her, and bolted it. The billy goat was lying next to the stove and looked up at her questioningly. She heard the cows bellowing, and our shouting rang out from the square.

In the end we recovered our tempers. The cows were milked before sundown. Martha's mother came back, and besides a few scratches not much had happened to her. Her father had lost a tooth, and his ear was torn. Someone had stepped on her sister's foot so hard that she limped for a few weeks. But the next morning and the next evening came, and life went on. In every house there were bumps and cuts and scratches and sprained arms and missing teeth, but by the next day the main square was clean again, and we were all wearing our shoes.

We never spoke about what had happened. Nor did we speak about Ulenspiegel. Without having arranged it, we stuck to this. Even Hans Semmler, who was so severely injured that from now on he was confined to his bed and could eat nothing but thick soup, pretended it had never been otherwise. And even the widow of Karl Schönknecht, whom we buried the next day in the churchyard, acted as if it had been a blow of fate and as if she didn't know exactly whose knife it had been in his back. Only the rope still hung for days over the square, trembled in the wind, and was a perch for sparrows and swallows until the priest, who had been roughed up especially badly during the brawl, because we didn't like his boastfulness and his condescension, could climb up the bell tower again to cut it down.

At the same time, we didn't forget. What had happened remained between us. It was there while we brought in the harvest, and it was there when we bargained over our grain or assembled on Sunday for the Mass, where the priest had a new facial expression, half wonder and half fear. And it was there especially when we held celebrations on the square and when we looked each other in the face while dancing. Then the air seemed heavier, the water different on our tongues, and the sky, where the rope had hung, not quite itself.

It was a good year later before the war came to us after all. One night we heard whinnying, and then there were many voices laughing outside, and soon we heard the crash of doors being smashed in, and before we were even on the street, armed with useless pitchforks or knives, the flames were flickering.

The soldiers were hungrier than usual, and deeper in their cups. It had been a long time since they entered a town that offered them so much. Old Luise, who had been fast asleep and this time had no presentiment, died in her bed. The priest died standing protectively in front of the church portal. Lise Schoch died trying to conceal a stash of gold coins. The baker and the smith and old Lembke and Moritz Blatt and most of the other men died trying to protect their women. And the women died as women do in war.

Martha died too. She saw the ceiling of the room turn into red heat above her, she smelled the thick smoke before it seized her so tightly that she could make out nothing more, and she heard her sister cry for help, while the future that had a moment ago been hers dissolved: the husband she would never have and the children she would never raise and the grandchildren she would never tell about a famous jester one morning in spring, and the children of these grandchildren, all the people who now would not exist. That's how quickly it happens, she thought, as if she had penetrated a great secret. And as she heard the roof beams splintering, it occurred to her that Tyll Ulenspiegel was now perhaps the only person who would remember our faces and would know that we had existed.

Indeed the only survivors were the lame Hans Semmler, whose house had not caught fire and who had been over-looked because he couldn't move, and Elsa Ziegler and Paul Grünanger, who had secretly been in the forest together. When they returned at dawn with rumpled clothes and disheveled hair and found nothing but rubble under curling smoke, they thought for a moment that the Lord God had punished them for their sin by sending them a mad vision. They moved west together, and for a brief time they were happy.

As for the rest of us, we can sometimes be heard here, where we once lived, in the trees. We can be heard in the grass and in the chirping of the crickets, we can be heard when you lean your head against the knothole of the old elm, and at times children think they see our faces in the water of the stream. Our church is no longer standing, but the pebbles polished round and white by the water are still the same, just as the trees are the same. We remember, even if no one remembers us, because we have not yet reconciled ourselves to not being. Death is still new to us, and we are not indifferent to the things that concern the living. For it all happened not long ago.

Lord of the Air

I

HE STRETCHED THE ROPE AT KNEE HEIGHT, FROM THE LINden to the old fir. He had to cut notches for it, which was easy to do in the fir, whereas the knife kept slipping off the linden, but in the end he did it. Now he tests the knots, slowly takes off his wooden shoes, climbs onto the rope, falls.

He climbs on again, spreads his arms out, and takes a step, but he can't keep his balance and falls. He climbs back on, gives it another try, falls once again.

He tries and falls again.

It is not possible to walk on a rope. That is clear. Human feet aren't made for it. Why attempt it at all?

But he keeps trying. He always starts at the linden. Every time he falls immediately. Hours pass. In the afternoon he successfully takes a step, just one, and by the time it grows dark, he hasn't managed another. Yet for one moment the rope held him, and he stood on it as if on solid ground.

The next day it's pouring rain. He stays indoors and helps his mother. "Hold the cloth taut, stop daydreaming, for Christ's sake!" And the rain patters on the roof like hundreds of little fingers.

The next day it's still raining. It's icy cold, and the rope is clammy, making it impossible to take a step.

The next day, rain again. He climbs on and falls and climbs on again and falls, every time. For a while he lies on the ground, his arms spread, his hair so wet that it's only a dark blot.

The next day is Sunday, and so he can't get onto the rope until the afternoon, when the church service is finally over. In the evening he successfully takes three steps, and if the rope hadn't been wet, it could have been four.

Gradually he comprehends how it can be done. His knees understand, his shoulders carry themselves differently. You have to yield to the swaying, have to soften your knees and hips, have to stay one step ahead of the fall. Heaviness reaches for you, but you've already moved on. Tightrope walking: running away from falling.

The following day it's warmer. Jackdaws are cawing. Bugs and bees are buzzing, and the sun is dispelling the clouds. His breath rises in small puffs of mist into the air. The brightness of the morning carries voices; he hears his father shouting at a mill hand in the house. He sings to himself, the song of the Grim Reaper, they call him Death, his power's from God on high— the melody is conducive to walking on the rope, but apparently he was too loud, for all at once Agneta, his mother, is standing next to him and asking why he isn't working.

"I'll be right there."

"Water has to be fetched," she says, "the stove cleaned."

He spreads his arms out and climbs onto the rope, trying to disregard her bulging belly. Is there really a baby inside her, kicking and thrashing around and listening to them? The thought disturbs him. When God wants to make a person, why does he do it in another person? There's something ugly in the fact that all beings emerge in obscurity: maggots in dough, flies in excrement, worms in the brown earth. Only very rarely, as his father explained to him, do children grow out of mandrakes and even more rarely infants out of rotten eggs.

"Shall I send Sepp?" she asks. "Do you want me to send Sepp?"

The boy falls off the rope, closes his eyes, spreads his arms out, climbs on again. The next time he looks, his mother is gone.

He hopes that she doesn't make good on the threat, but after a while Sepp does come. Sepp watches him briefly, then he comes up to the rope and pushes him off: no light nudge, but a push, so hard that the boy falls flat on his face. In his anger he calls Sepp a disgusting ox's arse who sleeps with his own sister.

That wasn't wise. Because first of all he has no idea whether Sepp, who like all mill hands came from some unknown place and will move on to some unknown place, even has a sister; secondly, the fellow was only waiting for something like this. Before the boy can get up, Sepp has sat down on the back of his head.

He can't breathe. Rocks are cutting into his face. He writhes, but it's no help, because Sepp is twice his age and three times his weight and five times his strength. He pulls himself together so that he doesn't use up too much air. His tongue tastes like blood. He inhales dirt, chokes, spits. There's a humming and whistling in his ears, and the ground seems to be rising, sinking, and rising again.

Suddenly the weight is gone. He is rolled onto his back, soil in his mouth, his eyes sticky, a piercing pain in his head. The mill hand drags him to the mill: over gravel and soil, through grass, over even more soil, over sharp pebbles, past the trees, past the laughing female mill hand, the hay shed, the goat stable. Then he yanks him up, opens the door and shoves him in.

"Well, it's about time," says Agneta. "The stove isn't going to clean itself."

To go from the mill to the village you have to pass through a stretch of forest. At the point where the trees thin and you cross the village farmland—meadows and pastures and fields, a third of them lying fallow, two thirds cultivated and protected by wooden fences—you can already see the top of the church tower. Someone is always lying here in the dirt and mending the fences, which are constantly being broken but have to be maintained, otherwise the livestock will escape, or the forest animals will destroy the grain. Most of the fields belong to Peter Steger. Most of the animals too, which is easy to tell, for they have his brand on their necks.

First you pass Hanna Krell's house. She sits—what else is she supposed to do?—on her doorstep and patches clothing; thus she earns her daily bread. Then you walk through the narrow gap between the Steger farm and Ludwig Stelling's smithy, step onto the wooden footbridge that prevents you from sinking into the soft muck, go beyond Jakob Brantner's cowshed on your right, and find yourself on the main street, which is the only street: Here lives Anselm Melker with wife and children, next door his brother-in-law Ludwig Koller, and in the next house Maria Leserin, whose husband died last year, because someone cursed him. Their daughter is seventeen and very beautiful, and she will marry Peter Steger's oldest son. On the other side lives Martin Holtz, who bakes the bread, together with his wife and daughters, and next to him are the smaller houses of the Tamms, the Henrichs, and the Heinerling family, from whose windows you often hear quarrels. The Heinerlings are not good people; they have no honor. Besides the smith and the baker, they all have a little land outside, everyone has a few goats, but only Peter Steger, who's rich, has cows.

Then you're on the village square with the church, the old village linden, and the well. Next to the church is the priest's house, next to the priest's house the house where the steward lives, Paul Steger, Peter Steger's cousin, who twice a year walks the fields and every third month brings the taxes to the lord.

On the far end of the village square is a fence. After you open the gate and cross the large field, which also belongs to Steger, you're in the forest again, and if you're not too afraid of the Cold Woman and keep going, in three hours you will be in the next village, which is not much bigger.

There, however, the boy has never been. He has never been elsewhere. And although several people who have been elsewhere before have told him that it's exactly the same there as here, he can't stop wondering where you would end up if you just kept going on and on, not merely to the next village, but farther and farther still.

At the head of the table the miller is speaking about the stars. His wife and his son and the mill hands are pretending to listen. There are groats. There were groats yesterday too, and there will be groats again tomorrow, boiled now in more and now in less water; there are groats every day, except on worse days when instead of groats there's nothing. In the window a thick pane keeps the wind out. Under the stove, which doesn't emit enough warmth, two cats are scuffling. In the corner of the room lies a goat, which should actually be over in the stable, but no one wants to throw it out, because they're all tired, and its horns are sharp. Next to the door and around the window pentagrams are carved, to ward off evil spirits.

The miller is describing how, exactly ten thousand seven hundred and three years, five months, and nine days ago, the maelstrom in the heart of the world caught fire. And now the thing that is the world is spinning like a spindle and eternally giving birth to stars, for since time has no beginning it has no end either.

"No end," he repeats and stops short, having realized that he said something unclear. "No end," he says softly, "no end."

Claus Ulenspiegel is from Mölln, up in the Lutheran north. A decade ago, even then no longer young, he arrived in this place, and because he wasn't from here, he could only be a mill hand. The miller's trade is not dishonorable like that of the renderer, who disposes of animal remains, or that of the night watchman or even the hangman, but it's also no better than day labor and far worse than the trade of the craftsmen in their guilds or that of the farmers, who wouldn't have offered someone like him so much as a handshake. But then the miller's daughter married him, and soon the miller died, and now he is the miller himself. On the side he heals the farmers, who still won't shake his hand, for what is not proper is not proper; but when they're suffering, they come to his door.

No end. Claus can't go on speaking, it preoccupies him too much. How could time cease? On the other hand . . . He rubs his head. It must have begun. For if it had never begun, how would we have reached this moment? He looks around. An infinite amount of time cannot be over. Therefore it simply must have begun. But before that? A before before time? It makes you dizzy. Just like in the mountains when you look into a ravine.

Once, he now says, he looked into one, in Switzerland. A herdsman had taken him along on the cattle drive up to the alpine pastures. The cows had worn large bells, and the name of the herdsman had been Ruedi. Claus pauses. Then he remembers what he actually wanted to say. So he looked into the ravine, and it was so deep that you couldn't see the ground. He asked the herdsman, who by the way was named Ruedi—a strange name—well, he asked Ruedi: "How deep is it, then?" In a voice of the greatest weariness, Ruedi replied: "It has no bottom!"

Claus sighs. The spoons scrape in the silence. At first, he continues, he thought it wasn't possible and the herdsman must be a liar. Then he wondered whether the gorge was perhaps the entrance to hell. But suddenly he realized that it didn't matter at all: Even if this gorge happened to have a bottom, there was a bottomless gorge overhead, you only had to look up. With a heavy hand he scratches his head. A gorge, he murmurs, that just keeps going, farther and farther still, perpetually farther, in which, therefore, all the things in the world fit without filling even the tiniest fraction of its depth, a depth that nullifies everything . . . He eats a spoonful of groats. This makes you very queasy, he says, just as you also feel ill as soon as you realize that numbers never end! The fact that to every number you can add another, as if there were no God to stem such a tide. Always another! Counting without end, depth without bottom, time before time. Claus shakes his head. And if—

At this moment Sepp cries out. He presses his hands over his mouth. Everyone looks at him, baffled, but above all grateful for the interruption.

Sepp spits out a few brown pebbles that look exactly like

the lumps of dough in the groats. It wasn't easy to smuggle them into his bowl unnoticed. For something like that you have to wait for the right moment, and if necessary, you have to create a diversion yourself. That was why the boy a short while ago kicked Rosa, the female mill hand, in the shin, and when she cried out and told him that he was a stinking rat and he told her she was an ugly cow, and she in turn told him that he was filthier than filth, and his mother told both of them to hush, for God's sake, or there wouldn't be any food today, he quickly leaned forward and at the precise moment when everyone was looking at Agneta plopped the stones into Sepp's bowl. The right moment is quickly missed, but if you're attentive, you can sense it. Then a unicorn could run through the room without the others noticing.

Sepp feels around in his mouth with his finger, spits a tooth onto the table, lifts his head, and looks at the boy.

That's not good. The boy was fairly certain that Sepp wouldn't see through it, but apparently he's not so stupid after all.

The boy jumps up and runs to the door. Unfortunately, Sepp is not only big but also fast, and he gets hold of him. The boy wants to break free, but he can't. Sepp draws back his arm and punches him in the face. The blow absorbs all other noises.

He squints. Agneta has jumped up. Rosa is laughing; she likes it when there are beatings. Claus is sitting there with a furrowed brow, caught up in his thoughts. The other two mill hands are wide-eyed with curiosity. The boy hears nothing. The room is spinning. The ceiling is under him. Sepp has thrown him over his shoulder like a sack of flour. Then he carries him out, and the boy sees grass above him. Down below arches the sky, streaked with the evening strands of clouds. Now he hears something again: A high tone hangs trembling in the air.

Sepp holds him by the upper arms and stares into his face from up close. The boy can see the red in the mill hand's beard. Where the tooth is missing it's bleeding. He could punch the mill hand in the face with all his strength. Sepp would probably drop him, and if he could get to his feet again quickly enough, he could put some distance between them and reach the forest.

But what would be the point? They live in the same mill. If Sepp doesn't catch him today, he'll catch him tomorrow, and if not tomorrow, then the day after. It would be better to get it over with now, while everyone's watching. Before the eyes of the others Sepp probably won't kill him.

They've all come out of the house: Rosa is standing on tiptoe to be able to see better, she's still laughing, and the two mill hands next to her are laughing too. Agneta is shouting something; the boy sees her opening her mouth wide and waving her hands, but he can't hear her. Next to her Claus still looks as if he were thinking about something else.

Now the mill hand has lifted him high over his head. Afraid that Sepp will hurl him onto the hard ground, the boy raises his hands protectively over his forehead. But Sepp takes a step forward, then another and a third, and suddenly the boy's heart begins to race. His blood throbbing in his ears, he begins to scream. He can't hear his voice. He screams louder, but he still doesn't hear it. He knows what Sepp is planning. Do the others know too? They could still intervene, but—not anymore. Sepp has done it. The boy is falling.

He's still falling. Time seems to be slowing down, he can look around, he feels the plunge, the gliding through the air, and he can even think that the very thing is happening against which he has been warned all his life: Do not step into the stream in front of the wheel, never go in front of it, don't go in front of the mill wheel, under no circumstances, never go, never, never, never go into the stream in front of the mill wheel! And now, after this has been thought, the plunge still isn't over, and he's still falling and falling and still falling, but just as he is forming another thought, namely, that possibly nothing at all will happen and the plunge will last forever, he hits the water with a slap and sinks, and again it takes a moment before the icy cold bites. His chest constricts. Everything goes black.

He feels a fish brush his cheek. He feels the current, feels it flowing faster and faster, feels the suction between his fingers. He knows that he has to hold on to something, but what? Everything is in motion, nothing solid anywhere. Then he feels a movement above him, and he can't help thinking that he has imagined this all his life, with horror and curiosity, the question of what he should do if he ever really did fall into the stream in front of the mill wheel. Now everything is different, and he can't do anything at all, and he knows that he will soon be dead, crushed, ground, mashed, but he does remember that he must not come to the surface, there's no escape up there, up there is the wheel. He has to go down.

But where is that, down?

With all his strength, he makes swimming strokes. Dying is nothing, he understands that. It happens so quickly, it's no big thing: take one false step, one leap, make one movement, and you're no longer alive. A blade of grass snaps, a bug is stepped on, a flame goes out, a person dies—it's nothing! His hands dig into the mud; he made it to the bottom.

And suddenly he knows that he won't die today. Threads of

long grass caressing him, dirt getting in his nose, he feels a cold grasp on the nape of his neck, hears a crunching sound, feels something on his back, then on his heels; he has passed under the mill wheel.

He pushes off from the bottom. As he rises, he briefly sees a pale face. The eyes large and empty, the mouth open, it glows faintly in the darkness of the water, probably the ghost of a child who was at some point less fortunate than he. He makes swimming strokes. Now he has reached the surface. He breathes in and spits mud and coughs and claws at the grass and crawls, gasping, onto the bank.

A dot is moving on thin little legs in front of his right eye. He squints. The dot comes closer. It tickles his eyebrow. He presses his hand against his face, and the dot disappears. Up above, roundly shimmering, hovers a cloud. Someone bends down over him. It's Claus. He kneels, reaches out his hand and touches his chest, murmurs something that the boy doesn't understand because the high tone is still hanging in the air and drowning out everything else. But as his father speaks, the tone grows softer and softer. Claus stands up. The tone has gone silent.

Now Agneta's there too. And Rosa next to her. Every time someone reappears, it takes the boy a moment to recognize the face; something in his head slowed down and is not yet working again. His father is making circles with his hands. He feels his strength returning. He tries to speak, but all that comes out of his throat is croaking.

Agneta strokes his cheek. "Twice," she says. "You've now been baptized twice."

He doesn't understand what she means. That's probably due to the pain in his head, a pain so intense that it fills not only him but also the world itself—all visible things, the earth, the people around him, even the cloud up there, which is still as white as fresh snow.

"Well, come into the house," says Claus. His voice sounds reproving, as if he had caught him doing something forbidden.

The boy sits up, leans forward, and vomits. Agneta kneels beside him and holds his head.

Then he sees his father draw his arm far back and slap Sepp's face. Sepp's upper body pitches forward. He holds his cheek and straightens up again, when the next blow hits him. And then a third, another big swing, the force almost hurling him to the ground. Claus rubs his sore hands together as Sepp staggers. It's clear to the boy that he's only pretending: it didn't hurt him very much; he is substantially stronger than the miller. But even he knows that you have to be punished when you almost kill the child of your employer, just as the miller and everyone else know that they can't just chase him off, for Claus needs three mill hands, fewer won't do, and when one of them is missing, it can take weeks before a new wandering mill hand turns up—the farmhands don't want to work in the mill, it's too far away from the village, and the trade is not quite honorable, only the desperate are willing to do it.

"Come into the house," Agneta now says too.

It's almost dark. Everyone is in a hurry, because no one wants to be outside any longer. Everyone knows what roams the forests at night.

"Baptized twice," Agneta says again.

He is about to ask her what she means when he realizes that she's no longer with him. The stream is murmuring behind him. Some light leaks out through the thick curtain of the mill window. Claus must have already lit the tallow candle. Apparently no one took the trouble to drag him inside.

Freezing, the boy stands up. Survived. He survived. The mill wheel. He survived the mill wheel. He feels indescribably light. He takes a leap, but when he lands, his leg gives way, and he falls to his knees with a groan.

A whisper is coming from the forest. He holds his breath and listens. Now it's a growl, now a hiss, then it stops for a moment, then it begins again. He feels that if only he listened closer, he would make out words. But that's the last thing he wants. He hobbles hastily to the mill.

Weeks pass before his leg allows him to get back on the rope. On the very first day, one of the baker's daughters appears and sits down in the grass. He knows her by sight; her father often comes to the mill, because ever since Hanna Krell cursed him after a quarrel he has been plagued by rheumatism. The pain won't let him sleep, which is why he needs Claus's protective magic.

The boy considers whether to chase her away. But first of all it wouldn't be nice, and secondly he hasn't forgotten that she won the stone-throwing contest at the last village festival. She must be very strong, whereas his whole body aches. So he tolerates her presence. Although he sees her only out of the corner of his eye, he notices that she has freckles on her arms and face and that in the sun her eyes are as blue as water.

"Your father," she says, "told my father there's no hell."

"He did not." He manages four whole steps before he falls. "Did so."

"Never," he says firmly. "I swear."

He's fairly certain that she's right. Although his father could also have said the opposite: we are in hell, forever, and will never get out. Or he could have said that we're in heaven. He has heard his father say everything that can be said.

"Have you heard?" she asks. "Peter Steger slaughtered a calf at the old tree. The smith said so. It was the three of them. Peter Steger, the smith, and old Heinerling. They went to the willow at night and left the calf there, for the Cold Woman."

"I was there once too," he says.

She laughs. She doesn't believe him, of course, and she's right, of course, he wasn't there; no one goes to the willow if he doesn't have to.

"I swear!" he says. "Believe me, Nele!"

He climbs onto the rope again and stands there without holding on. He can do it now. To strengthen the oath he has sworn he places two fingers of his right hand on his heart. But then he takes the hand away again quickly, because he remembers that little Käthe Leser swore falsely to her parents last year, and two nights later she died. To escape the embarrassment, he pretends to lose his balance and lets himself fall flat on his face in the grass.

"Keep doing it," she says calmly.

"What?" His face contorted with pain, he stands up.

"The rope. Being able to do something no one else can. That's good."

He shrugs. He can't tell whether she's mocking him.

"Have to go," she says, jumps up, and runs off.

As he watches her leave, he rubs his sore shoulder. Then he climbs back onto the rope.

The next week they have to bring a cart of flour to the Reutter farm. Martin Reutter brought the grain three days ago, but he can't fetch the flour because his drawbar broke. His farmhand Heiner came yesterday to let them know.

The situation is complicated. They can't just send the farmhand with the flour, because he could abscond with it, never to be seen again; you cannot trust a farmhand an inch. But Claus can't leave the mill, because there's too much work, so Agneta has to go with Heiner, and because she shouldn't be alone with him in the forest, since farmhands are capable of anything, the boy comes too.

They set off before sunrise after a night of heavy rain. Fog hangs between the tree trunks, the high branches seem to disappear in the still-dark sky, the meadows are waterlogged. The donkey takes dragging steps, it's all the same to him. The boy has known him as long as he can remember. He has spent many hours sitting with him in the stable, listening to his soft snorting, stroking him and taking pleasure in the way the animal pressed his always damp muzzle against his cheek. Agneta holds the reins. The boy sits next to her on the box, his eyes half closed, and snuggles up to her. Behind them Heiner is lying on the sacks of flour; sometimes he grunts, and sometimes he laughs to himself; you couldn't say whether he's asleep or awake.

If they had taken the wide road, they could have been at their destination already this afternoon, but it passes too close to the clearing with the old willow. No unborn child may come close to the Cold Woman. Therefore, they have to take the detour by way of the narrow overgrown path that leads much deeper through the forest, past Maple Hill and the large Mouse Pond.

Agneta is talking about the time when she was not yet Ulenspiegel's wife. One of baker Holtz's two sons wanted to marry her. He threatened to join the soldiers if she didn't take him. He would march east, to the Hungarian plains, to fight against the Turks. And she almost would have taken him—why not, she thought, in the end they're all the same. But then Claus came to the village, a Catholic from the north, which was in itself strange enough, and when she married him, because she couldn't resist him, young Holtz didn't march east after all. He stayed and baked bread, and when two years later the plague spread through the village, he was the first to die, and when his father too died, his brother took over the bakery.

Agneta sighs and strokes the boy's head. "You don't know what he used to be like. Young and lithe and completely different from the others."

It takes the boy a moment to understand whom she's talking about.

"He knew everything. He could read. And he was beautiful too. He was strong, and he had bright eyes, and he could sing and dance better than anyone else." She reflects for a while. "He was . . . awake!"

The boy nods. He would rather hear a fairy tale.

"He's a good person," says Agneta. "You must never forget that."

The boy can't help yawning.

"Only, his mind is never there. I didn't understand it at the time. I didn't know that such people existed. How should I have known, I who have never been anywhere but here, that he would never truly live among us? In the beginning his mind was elsewhere only now and then. Most of the time he was with me. He carried me in his arms. We laughed. His eyes were so bright. Only sometimes did he read his books or do his experiments, igniting something or mixing powders. Then he began spending more time with his books and less with me, and then even less, and now? Well, you see. Last month, when the mill wheel stopped. Only after three days did he repair it, because first he wanted to test something out in the meadow. He didn't have time for the mill, the miller himself. And then he repaired the wheel poorly too, and the axle got stuck, and we had to get Anselm Melker's help. But he didn't care!"

"Can you tell me a fairy tale?"

Agneta nods. "A long time ago," she begins. "When the stones were still young and there were no dukes and no one had to pay a tithe. A long time ago, when even in winter no snow fell . . ."

She hesitates, touches her belly, and shortens the reins. The path is now narrow and runs over broad roots. One false step by the donkey and the wagon could overturn.

"A long time ago," she begins anew, "a girl found a golden apple. She wanted to share it with her mother, but then she cut her finger, and from a drop of her blood a tree grew. It bore more apples, though not golden ones, but shriveled ugly nasty apples. Whoever ate them died a hard death. For her mother was a witch. She guarded the golden apple like her most treasured possession, and she tore to pieces and devoured every knight who went up against her to free her daughter, laughing and asking: Is there no hero among you, then? But when winter finally came and covered everything with snow, the poor daughter had to clean and cook for her mother, day in, day out and without end."

"Snow?"

Agneta falls silent.

"You said there was no snow in winter."

Agneta remains silent.

"Sorry," says the boy.

"The poor daughter had to clean and cook for her mother, day in, day out and without end, and this even though she was so beautiful that no one could look at her without falling in love."

Agneta is silent again. Then she groans softly.

"What's wrong?"

"And so the daughter ran away in the depth of winter, for she heard that far, far, far away, at the edge of the great sea, there lived a boy who was worthy of the golden apple. But first she had to flee, and this was hard, for her mother, the witch, was watchful."

Agneta falls silent once again. The forest is now very dense; only high up between the treetops are there still flashes of light blue sky. Agneta pulls on the reins. The donkey stops. A squirrel jumps onto the path, looks at them with cold eyes. Then, as quickly as an illusion, it is gone. The farmhand behind them stops snoring and sits up.

"What's wrong?" the boy asks again.

Agneta doesn't reply. She's suddenly deathly pale. And now the boy sees that her skirt is full of blood.

For a moment he is surprised that he didn't notice such a big spot until now. Then he understands that just a moment ago the blood wasn't there yet.

"It's coming," says Agneta. "I have to go back."

The boy stares at her.

"Hot water," she says, her voice cracking. "And Claus. I need hot water, and I need Claus too with his spells and herbs. And the midwife from the village, I need her too, Lise Köllerin."

The boy stares at her. Heiner stares at her. The donkey stares ahead.

"Because I'll die otherwise," she says. "It has to happen. It can't be helped. I can't turn the wagon around here. Heiner will support me, we'll walk, and you stay."

"Why don't we keep driving?"

"We won't be at the Reutter farm until evening. To get back to the mill on foot will be faster." Panting, she climbs down. The boy tries to reach for her arm, but she pushes him away. "Do you understand?"

"What?"

Agneta is struggling for air. "Someone has to stay with the flour. It's worth as much as half the mill."

"Alone in the forest?"

Agneta groans.

Heiner looks dully back and forth between them.

"I'm here with two idiots." Agneta places both hands on the boy's cheeks and looks him in the eyes so hard that he can see his reflection. Her breath whistles and rattles in her throat. "Do you understand?" she asks softly. "My heart, my little boy, do you understand? You wait here."

The pounding in his chest is so loud that he thinks she must be able to hear it. He wants to tell her that she's not thinking straight, that the pain has clouded her mind. She won't make it on foot, it will take hours, she's bleeding too heavily. But his throat is dried out; the words get stuck in it. Helplessly he watches her hobble away, leaning on Heiner. The farmhand is half supporting her, half dragging her. With each step she lets out a groan. For a short time he can still see them. Then he hears the groaning fading away, and then he is alone.

For a while he distracts himself by pulling on the donkey's ears. Right and left and right, each time the animal makes a sad noise. Why is he so patient, why so good-natured, why doesn't he bite? He looks him in the right eye. It sits in its socket like a glass ball, dark, watery, and empty. It doesn't blink, it just twitches a little when he touches it with his finger. He wonders what it's like to be this donkey. Imprisoned in a donkey soul, a donkey head on your shoulders, with donkey thoughts inside it—what does it feel like?

He holds his breath and listens. The wind: Noises within noises behind other noises, buzzing and rustling, squeaking, moaning and creaking. The whispering of the leaves over the whispering of voices, and again it seems to him as if he would only have to listen for a while, then he could understand. He begins to hum to himself, but his voice sounds foreign to him.

At this moment he notices that the flour sacks are knotted with a rope—a long one, which runs from one sack to the next. With relief he pulls out his knife and sets to work cutting notches into tree trunks.

As soon as he has fastened the rope at chest height between two trees, he feels better. He tests the firmness. Then he takes off his shoes, climbs on, and walks with outspread arms to the middle. There he stands, in front of the cart and donkey, over the loamy path. He loses his balance, jumps down, immediately climbs back up. A bee rises out of the bushes, descends again, and disappears in the greenery. Slowly the boy starts moving. He almost would have made it to the other end, but then he falls after all.

He stays on the ground for a while. What's the point of standing up? He rolls onto his back. He feels as if time were coming to a halt. Something has changed: the wind is still whispering, and the leaves are still moving, and the donkey's stomach is growling, but all this has nothing to do with time. Earlier was now, and now is now, and in the future, when everything is different and when there are different people and no one but God knows about him and Agneta and Claus and the mill anymore, then it will still be now.

The strip of sky over him has turned dark blue. Now it is clouding over with a velvety gray. Shadows climb down tree trunks, and all at once it's evening down below. The light above ebbs to a trickle. And then it's night.

He weeps. But because no one is there who could help, and because you can actually always weep for only a short while before you run out of strength and tears, he stops.

He is thirsty. Agneta and Heiner took the skin of beer with them. Heiner strapped it on; no one thought of leaving something here for him to drink. His lips are dry. There must be a stream nearby, but how is he supposed to find it?

The noises are different now than during the day: different animal sounds, a different wind, even the creaking of the branches is different. He listens. It must be safer up there. He sets about climbing a tree. But it's hard when you can hardly see anything. Thin branches break, and the cracked bark cuts into his fingers. A shoe slips off his foot; he hears it bang into one branch and then another. Clasping the trunk, he shinnies up and makes it a little higher. Then he can't go on.

For a while he hangs. He imagined that he could sleep on a wide limb, leaning against the trunk, but now he realizes that this is impossible. There's nothing soft on a tree, and you have to cling to it constantly to keep from falling. A branch is pressing against his knee. At first he thinks that it can be endured, yet all at once it's unbearable. Even the limb he's sitting on hurts him. He finds himself thinking of the fairy tale about the evil witch and the beautiful daughter and the knight and the golden apple: will he ever find out how it ends?

He climbs back down. It's difficult in the dark, but he is skillful and doesn't slip off and reaches the ground. Only, he can no longer find his shoe. What a good thing that at least the donkey is there. The boy snuggles up to the soft, slightly stinking animal.

It occurs to him that his mother could come back. If she died on the way home, she could suddenly appear. She could brush past him, whisper something to him, show him her transformed face. The thought makes his blood run cold. Is it really possible to have just a second ago loved a person, but the next moment to die of fright when this person comes back? He thinks of little Gritt, who last year encountered her dead father while gathering mushrooms: he had no eyes and was hovering a hand's breadth over the ground. And he thinks of the head that Grandmother saw many years ago in the boundary stone behind the Steger farm, lift your skirt, little girl, and there was no one hiding behind the stone, rather the stone all at once had eyes and lips, just lift it already and show what's underneath! Grandmother told this story when he was little. Now she is long dead. Her body too must have decayed long ago, her eyes turning to stone and her hair to grass. He forbids himself to think of such things, but his effort fails, and there's one thought above all that he can't put out of his mind: better for Agneta to be dead, better imprisoned in the deepest eternal hell, than to suddenly step as a ghost out of the bushes.

The donkey gives a start. Wood cracks nearby. Something is approaching. His breeches fill up with warmth. A massive body brushes past and departs again. His breeches grow cold and heavy. The donkey growls; he felt it too. What was it? Now there's a greenish gleam between the branches, bigger than a glowworm, yet less bright, and in his fear feverish images come into his head. He is hot, then cold. Then hot again. And despite everything he thinks: Agneta, alive or dead, must not find out that he wet himself, or else there will be blows. And when he sees her lying and whimpering under a bush that is at the same time the ribbon on which the earthly disk hangs from the moon, a remnant of his dissolving rational mind tells him that he must be falling asleep, exhausted by his fear and all the pounding of his heart, mercifully abandoned to his dwindling powers, on the cold ground and in the nocturnal noise of the forest, beside the softly snoring donkey. And so he doesn't know that his mother is actually lying not far from him on the ground, whimpering and groaning, under a bush, which doesn't look very different from the one in his dream, a juniper bush with majestically full berries. There she lies, in the darkness, there.

Agneta and the farmhand took the shortcut because she was too weak for the detour, and so they came too close to the Cold Woman's clearing. Now Agneta is lying on the ground and has no more strength and barely any voice left to scream, and Heiner is sitting beside her, in his lap the newborn being.

The farmhand is considering whether to run away. What's keeping him? This woman will die, and if he is nearby, people will say he is to blame. That's how it always is. If something happens and a farmhand is nearby, then the farmhand is to blame.

He could disappear, never to be seen again. Nothing is keeping him on the Reutter farm. The food is not abundant, and the farmer is not good to him; he hits him as often as he hits his own sons. Why not leave mother and child here? The world is big, say the farmhands, new masters are easy to find, there are enough new farms, and something better than death can be found wherever you look.

He knows that it's ill-advised to be in the forest at night, and he's hungry and searingly thirsty, because somewhere along the way he lost the skin of beer. He closes his eyes. That helps. When you close your eyes, you are by yourself, no one else is there to hurt you, you are inside, you yourself are the only one there. He remembers meadows through which he ran when he was a child, he remembers fresh bread better than any he's had in a long time, and a man who hit him with a stick, perhaps it was his father, he doesn't know. And so he ran away from the man, and then he was elsewhere. Then he ran away again. Running away is a wonderful thing. There's no danger you can't escape when you have fast legs.

But this time he doesn't run. He holds the baby, and he holds Agneta's head too, and when she wants to stand up, he supports her and heaves her upward.

Nonetheless, Agneta would not have gotten to her feet if she hadn't remembered the most powerful of all squares. Memorize it, Claus said, use it only in an emergency. You can write it down, only you must never say it aloud! And so she applied the last remainder of clarity in her head to scratching the letters into the ground. It began with Salom Arepo, but she couldn't recall what came next—writing is triply difficult when you never learned how and it's dark and you're bleeding. But then she defied Claus's instructions and cried hoarsely: "Salom Arepo, Salom Arepo!" And, since even fragments exert power, this was enough to bring back her memory, and she knew the rest too.

```
S A L O M
A R E P O
L E M E L
O P E R A
M O L A S
```

And this alone, she could feel it, drove back the evil forces, the bleeding abated, and, with pain as though from red-hot irons, the baby slid out of her body.

She would have liked so much to keep lying on the ground. But she knows that when you've lost a lot of blood, if you stay on the ground, you'll be lying there forever.

"Give me the baby."

He gives her the baby. It's a girl.

She can't see her, the night is so black that she might as well be blind, but when she holds the little being, she feels that she is still alive.

No one will know about you, she thinks. No one will remember, only I, your mother, and I won't forget, because I must not forget. For everyone else will forget you.

She said the same thing to her other three who died at birth. And she really does still know everything there is to know about each of them: the smell, the weight, the shape—each time a little different—in her hands. They didn't even have names.

Her knees give way. Heiner holds her. For a moment the temptation to simply lie down again is strong. But she has lost too much blood, the Cold Woman is not far, and the Little People might find her too. She hands Heiner the baby and wants to set off, but immediately she falls and lies on roots and sticks and senses how vast the night is. Why resist anyway? It would be so easy. Just let go. So easy.

Instead she opens her eyes. She feels the roots under her. She shivers with cold and grasps that she's still alive.

Again she stands up. Apparently the bleeding has abated. Heiner holds out the baby to her. She takes her and realizes at once that there's no life left in her, so she gives her back, because she needs both hands to hold on to a tree trunk. He lays the baby on the ground, but Agneta hisses at him, and he picks her back up. For of course they can't leave her here: moss would grow over her, plants entwine her, bugs live in her limbs. Her spirit would never rest.

And at this moment it happens that a premonition of something wrong creeps up on Claus in the attic room of his mill. He quickly murmurs a prayer, sprinkles a pinch of crushed mandrake into the flame of his weak, smoky lamp. The bad omen is confirmed: instead of flaring up, the flame immediately goes out. A sharp stench fills the room.

In the darkness Claus writes a square of moderate strength on the wall:

MILON
IRAGO
LAMAL
OGARI

Afterward, to be safe, he says aloud seven times: *Nipson ano-mimata mi monan ospin*. He knows that this is Greek. What it means, he doesn't know, but it reads the same way forward as backward, and sentences of this sort have special power. Then he lies back down on the hard floorboards to continue his work.

Recently he has been observing the course of the moon every night. His sluggish progress is enough to drive him to despair. The moon always rises in a different place than it did the night before; its path never stays the same. And because apparently no one can explain this, Claus decided to clear up the matter himself.

"When there's something no one knows," Wolf Hüttner once said to him, "we have to find it out!"

Hüttner, the man who was his teacher, a chiromancer and necromancer of Konstanz, a night watchman by trade. Claus Ulenspiegel spent a winter in his employ, and not a day goes by that he doesn't think of him with gratitude. Hüttner showed him the squares, spells, and potent herbs, and Claus hung on every word when Hüttner spoke to him of the Little People and the Big People and the Ancient Ones and the People of the Earthly Depths and the Spirits of the Air and the fact that you couldn't trust the scholars, for they knew nothing, but they wouldn't admit it, lest they fall out of favor with their princes, and when Claus moved on after the thaw, he had three books from Hüttner's collection in his bag. At the time he had not yet known how to read, but a pastor in Augsburg whom he cured of rheumatism taught him, and when he moved on, he took with him three books from the pastor's library too. All the books were heavy; a dozen of them filled the bag like lead. Soon it became clear to him that he either had to leave the books behind or else settle down somewhere, ideally in a hidden place away from the big roads, for books are expensive and not every owner had parted with his voluntarily, and by a stroke of ill fortune Hüttner himself could suddenly appear outside his door, put a curse on him, and demand back what belonged to him.

When he had amassed so many books that he actually couldn't remain on the move, fate took its course. A miller's daughter caught his fancy. She was pretty, and she was funny too, and strong, and a blind man could see that she liked him. To win her wasn't hard. He was a good dancer, and he knew the right spells and herbs to bind a heart. On the whole he knew more than anyone else in the village. She found that appealing. At first her father had doubts, but none of the other mill hands seemed capable of taking over the mill, so he gave in. And for a while all was well.

Then he sensed her disappointment. First occasionally, then more often. And then all the time. She didn't like his books, she didn't like his need to solve the mysteries of the world, and besides, she wasn't wrong, it's a huge task, it doesn't leave much strength for other things, especially not for the daily routine of the mill. Suddenly it seemed like a mistake to Claus too: What am I doing here, what do these clouds of flour have to do with me, or these dull farmers who always try to cheat you when they pay, or these slow-witted mill hands who never do what you instruct them to? On the other hand, he tells himself often, life simply leads you somewhere or other—if you weren't here, you would be elsewhere, and everything would be just as strange. What really troubles him, however, is the question of whether a person will go to hell for stealing so many books.

But you must simply snatch knowledge wherever it can be found. People are not meant to languish in ignorance. And when you have no one to talk to, it's not easy. So much preoccupies you, but no one wants to hear it, your thoughts about what the sky is and how stones come into being, and flies, and the teeming life everywhere, and in what language the angels speak with each other, and how the Lord God created himself and still must create himself, day after day, for if he didn't do so, everything would cease from one moment to the next—who, if not God, should prevent the world from simply not existing?

Some books took Claus months, others years. Some he knows by heart and still doesn't understand. And at least once a month he returns in perplexity to the thick Latin work he stole from the burning house of a priest in Trier. He wasn't the one who started the fire, but he was nearby and smelled the smoke and seized the opportunity. Without him the book would have been reduced to ashes. He has a right to it. Yet he cannot read it.

It's seven hundred sixty-six pages long, closely printed, and some pages contain pictures that seem to come from bad dreams: men with bird heads, a city with battlements and tall towers on a cloud from which rain is falling in thin lines, a horse with two heads in a forest clearing, an insect with long wings, a turtle climbing heavenward on a ray of sun. The first leaf, which must have once had the book's title on it, is missing; someone also tore out the leaf with pages twenty-three and twenty-four and the one with pages five hundred nineteen and five hundred twenty. Claus has brought the book to the priest three times and asked for help, but each time the priest sent him away brusquely and declared that only educated people were entitled to concern themselves with Latin writings. At first Claus considered saddling him with a mild curse—rheumatism or an infestation of mice or spoiled milk—but then he realized that the poor village priest who drinks too much and is constantly repeating himself in his sermons in truth hardly understands Latin himself. Thus he has nearly reconciled himself to never being able to read this one book that possibly holds the key to everything. For who could teach him Latin here, in a godforsaken mill?

Nonetheless, in recent years he has found out a great deal. Essentially he now knows where things come from, how the world came into being, and why everything is the way it is: spirits, substances, souls, wood, water, sky, leather, grain, crickets. Hüttner would be proud of him. It won't be long before he has filled in the final gaps. Then he himself will write a book containing all the answers, and then the scholars in their universities will marvel and feel ashamed and tear out their hair.

But it won't be easy. His hands are big, and the thin quill is always breaking between his fingers. He will have to practice a lot before he will be able to fill a whole book with spidery signs in ink. But it has to happen, for he cannot forever retain in his memory everything he has found out. Even now it's too much, it's painful to him, often he feels dizzy from all the knowledge in his head.

Perhaps he will one day be able to teach his son something. He has noticed that the boy occasionally listens to him at meals, almost against his will and trying not to let anything show. He is thin and too weak, but he seems to be clever. Not long ago Claus caught him juggling three stones, very easily and effortlessly—sheer nonsense, but still a sign that the child is perhaps not as dull-witted as the others. Recently the boy asked him how many stars there actually are, and because only a short while ago Claus had counted, he was, not without pride, able to give him an answer. He hopes that the baby Agneta is carrying will be another boy—with some luck even one who is stronger so that he can help him better with the work, and whom he can then teach something too.

The floorboards are too hard. But if he were lying on a softer surface, he would fall asleep and wouldn't be able to observe the moon. Painstakingly Claus made a grid out of thin threads in the slanted attic window. His fingers are thick and ponderous, and the wool spun by Agneta is recalcitrant. Yet in the end he succeeded in dividing the window into small and almost equal-sized squares.

And so he lies and stares. Time passes. He yawns. Tears come to his eyes. You must not fall asleep, he tells himself, no matter what, you must not fall asleep!

And finally the moon is there, silver and nearly round, with spots like those of dirty copper. It appeared in the lowest row, yet not in the first square as Claus would have expected, but in the second. But why? He squints. His eyes hurt. He fights sleep and dozes off and is awake again and dozes off again, but now he is awake and squints, and the moon is no longer in the second but in the third row from the bottom, in the second square from the left. How did that happen? Unfortunately, the squares are not equal-sized, because the wool frays, hence the knots turned out too thick—but why is the moon behaving like this? It is a wicked heavenly body, treacherous and deceitful; it's no accident that in the cards its picture stands for decline and betrayal. To record when the moon is where, one must also know the time, but how, by all the devils, is one supposed to read the time if not from the position of the moon? It can drive you completely mad! On top of this, one of the threads has just come undone; Claus sits up and tries to tie it with intractable fingers. And no sooner has he finally succeeded than a cloud approaches. The light gleams faintly around its edges, but where exactly the moon is can no longer be said. He closes his weary eyes.

When Claus comes to, freezing, early in the morning, he has dreamed of flour. It's unbelievable—this keeps happening to him. He used to have dreams full of light and noise. There was music in his dreams. Sometimes ghosts spoke with him. But that was a long time ago. Now he dreams of flour.

As he sits up in annoyance, it becomes clear to him that it wasn't the flour dream that woke him, it was voices from outside. At this hour? Unsettled, he remembers the omen of the past night. He leans out the window and at the same moment the twilight gray of the forest opens and Agneta and Heiner hobble out.

They really made it, against all odds. At first the farmhand carried both of them, the living woman and the dead baby; then he couldn't go on, and Agneta walked on her own, supported by him; then the baby was too heavy for him and too dangerous too, for one who died unbaptized attracts spirits, both those from above and those from the depths, and Agneta had to carry her herself. Thus they gropingly found their way.

Claus climbs down the ladder, stumbles over the snoring mill hands, kicks a goat aside, flings open the door, and runs out just in time to catch Agneta as she collapses. Carefully, he lays her down and gropes for her face. He feels her breath. He draws a pentagram on her forehead, with the point on top, of course, to bring about healing, and then he inhales deeply and says in a single breath: *Christ was born in Bedlem, baptized in tho flem Jordan. Also tho flem astode, also astond thi blode. In nomine Patris et Filii et Spiritus Sancti.* He knows only roughly what this means, but the spell is ancient and he knows none stronger to stanch bleeding.

Now quicksilver would be good, but he has none left, so instead he makes the sign of quicksilver over her lower body—the cross with the eight that stands for Hermes, the great Mercury; the sign by itself doesn't work as well as real quicksilver, but it's better than nothing. Then he shouts at Heiner: "Go on, to the attic, fetch the orchis!" Heiner nods, staggers into the mill, and climbs up the ladder, gasping for breath. Only when he is up in the room, which smells of wood and old paper, and staring in confusion at the wool mesh in the window does it occur to him that he has no idea what an orchis is. And so he lies down on the floor, lays his head on the hay-stuffed pillow in which the miller has left an imprint, and falls asleep.

Day breaks. After Claus has carried his wife into the mill, the dew rises from the meadow, the sun comes up, the morning haze gives way to the noon light. The sun reaches its zenith and begins its path downward. Next to the mill there's now a mound of earth freshly piled up: there lies the nameless baby who was not baptized and is therefore barred from the cemetery.

And Agneta doesn't die. This surprises everyone. Perhaps it is due to her strength, perhaps to Claus's spells, perhaps to the orchis, although it is not very strong, bryony or monkshood would have been better, but unfortunately he recently gave away the last of his supply to Maria Stelling, whose child was stillborn; there are rumors she helped make it happen, because she was pregnant not by her husband but by Anselm Melker, but this doesn't interest Claus. Agneta, in any case, didn't die, and only when she sits up and looks around wearily and calls a name at first softly, then more loudly, and finally earsplittingly, does everyone realize that in all the excitement they have forgotten the boy and the wagon with the donkey. And the expensive flour.

But the sun will go down soon. It's too late to head out now. And so another night begins.

Early in the morning Claus sets off with Sepp and Heiner. They walk in silence. Claus is absorbed in his thoughts. Heiner never says a word anyway, and Sepp whistles softly to himself. Since they're men and there are three of them, they don't have to take a detour but can cut straight across the clearing with the old willow. The evil tree stands there black and huge, and its branches move in ways branches don't usually move. The men make an effort not to look. When they are in the forest again, they heave a sigh.

Claus's thoughts keep returning to the dead baby. Even though it was a girl, the loss is painful. It is indeed a good custom, he tells himself, not to love your own children too soon. Agneta has given birth so often, but only one of the babies survived, and even he is thin and frail, and they don't know whether he has come through the two nights in the forest.

The love for your children—better to fight against it. You don't get too close to a dog, after all; even if it looks friendly, it can snap at you. You always have to keep a distance between you and your children, they simply die too quickly. But with each year that passes, you get more used to such a being. You begin to trust, you allow yourself to be fond of them—and suddenly they're gone.

Shortly before noon they discover footprints of the Little People. Out of caution they stop, but after a thorough examination Claus determines that they are leading southward, away from here. Besides, the Little People are not yet dangerous in spring. Only in autumn do they become restless and malevolent.

They find the place in the late afternoon. They almost would have passed it, because they veered off the path a little. The underbrush is thick; you hardly know where you're going. But then Sepp noticed the sweetly sharp smell. They pushed branches aside, broke limbs, covered their noses with their hands. With each step the smell grew stronger. And there is the wagon, a cloud of flies swarming around it. The sacks have been torn open. The ground is white with flour. Something is lying behind the wagon. It looks like a heap of old skins. It takes them a moment to realize that it's the remains of the donkey. Only the head is missing.

"It was probably a wolf," says Sepp, flailing his arms to fend off the flies.

"That would look different," says Claus.

"The Cold Woman?"

"She's not interested in donkeys." Claus bends down and gropes around. A smooth cut, no bite marks anywhere. No doubt, it was a knife.

They call for the boy. They listen. They call again. Sepp looks up and goes silent. Claus and Heiner keep calling. Sepp stands as if frozen.

Now Claus too looks up. Horror reaches for him and holds him and grips him even tighter until he thinks he might choke to death. Something is hovering above them, white from head to toe, and staring downward, and even though it's growing dark, they can see the wide eyes, the bared teeth, the contorted face. And as they're gaping upward, they hear a high sound. It sounds like a sob, but it's not one. Whatever is above them there, it's laughing.

"Come down," calls Claus.

The boy, for it's really him, giggles and doesn't budge. He's completely naked, completely white. He must have rolled around in the flour.

"Good Lord," says Sepp. "Great merciful Lord!"

And while Claus is looking up, he sees something else that he just a moment ago didn't see yet, because it's too strange. What the boy is wearing on his head up there, while he is standing giggling and naked on a rope without falling down, is no hat.

"Blessed Virgin," says Sepp. "Help us and don't abandon us."

Even Heiner crosses himself.

Claus draws his knife and, his hand trembling, carves a pentagram into a tree trunk: point on the right, the shape securely closed. To the right of it he engraves an alpha, to the left an omega. Then he holds his breath, counts slowly to seven, and murmurs an incantation—spirits of the upper world, spirits of the lower world, all saints, kind Virgin, stand by us in the name of the triune God. "Get him down," he then says to Sepp. "Cut the rope!"

"Why me?"

"Because I say so."

Sepp stares and doesn't move. Flies land on his face, but he doesn't wave them away.

"Then you," Claus says to Heiner.

Heiner opens and closes his mouth. If he didn't find it so hard to speak, he would now say that he has only just dragged a woman through the forest and saved her; completely on his own he found the way. He would say that everything has its limits, even the tolerance of the most forbearing. But since talking is not in his nature, he crosses his arms and looks stubbornly at the ground.

"Then you," Claus says to Sepp. "Someone has to do it. And I have rheumatism. You climb now or you'll regret it as long as you live." He tries to remember the spell that compels the resistant to obey, but the words slip his mind.

Sepp utters terrible curses and begins to climb. He groans. The branches don't give him a good foothold, and it takes all his strength not to look up at the white apparition.

"What is going on?" Claus calls up. "What has gotten into you?"

"The great, great devil," the boy says cheerfully.

Sepp climbs back down. Hearing this reply was too much for him. Besides, it came back to him that he threw the boy into the stream, and if the boy remembers it and is angry at him, then now is not the moment to confront him. He reaches the ground and shakes his head.

"Then you!" Claus says to Heiner.

But he turns around without a word, walks away, and disappears in the thicket. For a while he can still be heard. Then no longer.

"Go back up," Claus says to Sepp.

"No!"

"*Mutus dedit*," Claus murmurs, now remembering the words of the spell after all, "*mutus dedit nomen*—"

"Makes no difference," says Sepp. "I'm not doing it."

There's a crack in the underbrush, the sound of branches breaking. Heiner is back. It became clear to him that it would soon be night. He can't be alone in the dark forest; he won't be able to stand it again. Angrily he fends off flies, leans against a tree trunk, and hums to himself.

When Claus and Sepp turn away from him, they notice that the boy is standing next to them. Startled, they jump back. How did he get down so quickly? The boy takes off what he was wearing on his head: a piece of fur-covered scalp with two long donkey ears. His hair is encrusted with blood.

"For God's sake," says Claus. "For Mary's and God's and the Son's sake."

"It was a long time," says the boy. "No one came. It was only a joke. And the voices! A big joke."

"What voices?"

Claus looks around. Where is the rest of the donkey's head? The eyes, the jaw with the teeth, the whole huge skull—where is all that?

The boy slowly kneels down. Then, laughing, he tips over sideways and stops moving.

They lift him up, wrap him in a blanket, and make off—away from the wagon, the flour, the blood. For a while they stumble through the darkness, until they feel safe enough to lay the child down. They don't light a fire and they don't talk to each other because they don't want to attract anything. The boy giggles in his sleep. His skin is hot to the touch. Branches crack. The wind whispers. With his eyes closed Claus murmurs prayers and incantations. This helps a little, for they gradually feel better. As he prays, he tries to estimate how much this will cost him: the wagon is wrecked, the donkey dead, above all he will have to replace the flour. Where is he going to get the money?

In the early morning hours the boy's fever subsides. When he wakes up, he asks in confusion why his hair is so sticky and why his body is white. Then he shrugs and doesn't trouble himself further about it, and when they tell him that Agneta is alive, he is happy and laughs. They find a stream. He washes himself. The water is so cold that he trembles all over. Claus wraps him in the blanket again, and they set off. On the way home the boy tells the fairy tale he heard from Agneta. There's a witch in it and a knight and a golden apple, and in the end everything turns out well, the princess marries the hero, the evil old woman is dead as a doornail.

Back in the mill, on his straw sack next to the stove that night, the boy sleeps so deeply that it is as if nothing could ever wake him again. He's the only one who can sleep, for the dead baby returns: only a flicker in the darkness, along with a soft whimpering, more a draft than a voice. For a while she is in the partitioned area in the back where Claus and Agneta are lying, but when she can't reach her parents' bed because the pentagrams on the posts keep her away, she appears in the room where the boy and the mill hands have bedded down around the warm stove. She is blind and deaf and understands nothing and knocks over the milk bucket, whirls the freshly washed cloths off the shelf, and gets tangled in the curtain on the window before she disappears—into the limbo where the unbaptized freeze in the icy cold for a million years before the Lord forgives them.

A few days later Claus sends the boy to Ludwig Stelling, the smith, in the village. Claus needs a new hammer, which must not be expensive, however, because ever since he lost the load of flour, he is deep in debt to Martin Reutter.

On the way the boy picks up three stones. He throws the first up into the air, then the second, then he catches the first and throws it up again, then he throws the third, catches the second and throws it again, then he catches the third and throws it, then the first again—now all three are in the air. His hands make circular movements, and everything takes care of itself. The trick is not to think and not to look sharply at any of the stones. You have to pay close attention and at the same time pretend they aren't there.

Thus he walks, the stones whirling around him, past Hanna Krell's house and across Steger's field. Outside the smithy he drops the stones into the mud and enters.

He places two coins on the anvil. He still has two in his pocket, but the smith doesn't need to know that.

"Much too little," says the smith.

The boy shrugs, takes the two coins, and turns to the door.

"Wait," says the smith.

The boy stops.

"You do have to give more."

The boy shakes his head.

"It doesn't work like that," says the smith. "If you want to buy something, you have to bargain."

The boy walks to the door.

"Wait!"

The smith is gigantic, his naked belly is hairy, he has a cloth tied around his head, and his face is red and full of pores. Everyone in the village knows that he goes into the bushes at night with Ilse Melkerin, only Ilse's husband doesn't know, or maybe he knows and only pretends not to know, for what can anyone do against a smith. When the priest preaches on Sunday about immorality, he always looks at the smith and sometimes at Ilse too. But that doesn't stop them.

"That's too little," the smith says.

But the boy knows that he has won. He wipes his forehead.

The fire radiates scorching heat. Shadows dance on the wall. He puts his hand on his heart and swears: "This is all I was given, by the salvation of my soul!"

With an angry expression the smith gives him the hammer. The boy thanks him politely and walks slowly, so that the coins in his pocket don't jingle, to the door.

He walks past Jakob Brantner's cowshed and the Melker house and the Tamm house to the village square. Might Nele be there? And indeed, she is sitting there, in the drizzle, on the little wall of the well.

"You again," he says.

"Then just go away," she says.

"You go away."

"I was here first."

He sits down next to her. They both grin.

"The merchant was here," she says. "He said the Kaiser is now having all the noblemen of Bohemia beheaded."

"The King too?"

"The Winter King. Him too. That's what they call him, because he was king for only a winter after the Bohemians gave him their crown. He was able to flee and will come back, at the head of a large army, because the English king is his wife's father. He will reconquer Prague, and he will depose the Kaiser and become Kaiser himself."

Hanna Krell comes with a bucket and busies herself at the edge of the well. The water is dirty, it's undrinkable, but it's needed for washing and for the livestock. When they were little, they drank milk, but for a few years now they have been old enough for small beer. Everyone in the village eats groats and drinks small beer. Even the rich Stegers. For Winter Kings and Kaisers there's rose water and wine, but simple people drink milk and small beer, from their first day to their last.

"Prague," says the boy.

"Yes," says Nele. "Prague!"

The two of them think about Prague. Precisely because it's a word, because they know nothing about it, it sounds as full of promise as a place in a fairy tale.

"How far is Prague?" asks the boy.

"Very far."

He nods as if that were an answer. "And England?"

"Also very far."

"It probably takes a year to journey there."

"Longer."

"Shall we go?"

Nele laughs.

"Why not?" he asks.

She doesn't reply, and he knows that they have to be careful now. One wrong word can have consequences. Peter Steger's youngest son gave Else Brantnerin a wooden pipe last year, and because she accepted the gift, the two of them are now engaged, even though they don't like each other that much. The matter went all the way to the reeve in the district seat, who in turn passed it on to the diocese court, where it was decided that there was nothing to be done about it: a gift is a promise, and a promise is binding before God. To invite someone on a journey is not yet a gift, but it is almost a promise. The boy knows this, and he knows that Nele knows it too, and they both know that they have to change the subject.

"How is your father?" asks the boy. "The rheumatism better?"

She nods. "I don't know what your father did. But it helped."

"Spells and herbs."

"Will you learn how to do that? Heal people, will you be able to do it too one day?"

"I'd rather go to England."

Nele laughs.

He stands up. He has the vague hope that she will hold him back but she doesn't budge.

"At the next solstice festival," he says, "I will jump over the fire like the others."

"Me too."

"You're a girl!"

"And this girl is about to smack you."

He sets off without looking back. He knows that this is important, because if he turns around, she has won.

The hammer is heavy. The wooden footbridge ends at the Steger farm. The boy leaves the path and makes his way through tall grass. This is not entirely without danger, due to the Little People. He thinks of Sepp. Ever since the night in the forest the mill hand has been afraid of him and has kept a safe distance, which has been useful. If only he knew what happened in the forest. He knows that he shouldn't think about it. Memory is a peculiar thing: it doesn't simply come and go as it pleases; rather you can light it and extinguish it again like a pitchwood torch. The boy thinks of his mother, who can only just stand up again, and for a moment he thinks of the dead infant too, his sister, whose soul is now in the cold, because she was not baptized.

He stops and looks up. You would have to stretch the rope over the crowns, from one church tower to the next, from village to village. He spreads his arms out and imagines it. Then he sits down on a rock and watches the clouds parting. It has grown warm, and the air is filling with steam. He is sweating, puts the hammer down next to him. Suddenly he feels sleepy, and he's hungry, but it's still many hours until groats. And if you could fly? Flap your arms, leave the rope, rise higher, higher? He plucks a blade of grass and slides it between his lips. It tastes sweet, damp, and a little acrid. He lies down in the grass and closes his eyes so that the sunlight lies warm on his lids. The wetness of the grass penetrates his clothing clammily.

A shadow falls on him. The boy opens his eyes.

"Did I frighten you?"

The boy sits up, shakes his head. There are rarely strangers here. Sometimes the reeve comes from the district capital, and now and then come merchants. But he doesn't know this stranger. He is young, just barely a man. He has a little goatee, and he is wearing a jerkin, breeches made of good gray material, and high boots. His eyes are bright and curious.

"Been imagining what it would be like if you could fly?"

The boy stares at the stranger.

"No," says the stranger, "it wasn't magic. Another person cannot read your thoughts. No one can do that. But when a child spreads his arms and stands on tiptoe and looks up, then he is thinking about flying. He does this because he cannot yet fully believe that he will never fly. That God doesn't permit us to fly. The birds, yes, but not us."

"Eventually we can all fly," says the boy. "When we're dead."

"When you're dead, you're first of all dead. Then you lie in the grave until the Lord returns to judge us."

"When will he return?"

"The priest hasn't taught you that?"

The boy shrugs. The priest speaks often in church about these things, of course, the grave, the judgment, the dead, but he has a monotonous voice, and it's also not rare for him to be drunk.

"At the end of time," says the stranger. "Except that the dead cannot experience time, they're dead, after all, so one can also say: immediately. As soon as you're dead, the Day of Judgment dawns."

"My father said the same thing."

"Your father is a scholar?"

"My father is a miller."

"Does he have opinions? Does he read?"

"He knows a lot," says the boy. "He helps people."

"Helps them?"

"When they're ill."

"Perhaps he can help me too."

"Are you ill?"

The stranger sits down beside him on the ground. "What do you think, will it stay sunny, or will we have more rain?"

"How am I supposed to know?"

"You're from here, aren't you?"

"We'll have more rain," says the boy, because it rains most of the time. The weather is almost always bad. Which is why the harvest is so pitiful, which is why the mill doesn't get enough grain, which is why everyone is hungry. Supposedly it used to be better. The older people remember long summers, but perhaps they're also imagining it, who can know, they are old.

"My father thinks," says the boy, "that angels ride on the rain clouds and look down at us."

"Clouds are made of water," says the stranger. "No one sits on them. The angels have bodies of light and need no conveyance. Nor do demons. They are made of air. That's why the devil is known as the Lord of the Air." He pauses as if to hearken to his own sentences, and gazes with an almost curious expression at his fingertips. "And yet," he then says, "they are nothing but particles of God's will."

"Even the devils?"

"Naturally."

"The devils are God's will?"

"God's will is greater than everything imaginable. It is so great that it is able to negate itself. An old riddle goes: can God make a stone so heavy that he can no longer lift it? It sounds like a paradox. Do you know what that is, a paradox?"

"Yes."

"Really?"

The boy nods.

"What is it?"

"You are a paradox, and your rogue of a pimp father is one too."

The stranger is silent for a moment. Then the corners of his mouth stretch upward into a thin smile. "It's actually not a paradox, for the correct answer is: naturally he can. But the stone that he can no longer lift he can then lift effortlessly. God is too encompassing to be one with himself. That's why the Lord of the Air and his associates exist. That's why everything that is not God exists. That's why the world exists."

The boy raises a hand in front of his face. The sun is now unobstructed by clouds. A blackbird flits past. Yes, of course, he thinks, you should fly like that, it would be even better than walking on the rope. But if you simply cannot fly, then walking on the rope is second best.

"I'd like to meet your father."

The boy nods indifferently.

"You'd better hurry," says the stranger. "It will be raining in an hour."

The boy points to the sun questioningly.

"Do you see the small clouds back there?" asks the stranger. "And the elongated ones over us? The wind is massing together the ones back there, it's coming from the east and bringing cold air, and the ones over us are catching it, and then everything cools even more, and the water grows heavy and falls to the earth. There are no angels sitting on the clouds, but it is nonetheless worthwhile to look at them, for they bring water and beauty. What's your name?"

The boy tells him.

"Don't forget your hammer, Tyll." The stranger turns away and leaves.

Claus is in a gloomy mood this evening. The fact that he cannot solve the grain problem is weighing on his mind at the table.

It's maddening. If you have a heap of grain in front of you and take away one grain, you still have a heap in front of you. Now take another. Is it still a heap? Of course. Now take another away. Is it still a heap? Yes, of course. Now take another away. Is it still a heap? Of course. And so on and so on. It is quite simple: merely by taking a single grain away, you never make a heap of grain into something that is not a heap of grain. Also, by putting on one grain, you never make something that is not a heap of grain into a heap.

And yet: if you remove grain after grain, the heap is at some point no longer a heap. At some point there will be just a few little grains left on the ground, which by no stretch of the imagination can be called a heap. And if you keep going, the moment will eventually come when you take the last one and there's nothing left on the floor. Is one grain a heap? Certainly not. And nothing at all? No, nothing at all is not a heap. For nothing at all is nothing at all.

But which is the grain whose removal causes the heap to cease being a heap? When does it actually happen? Claus has played it through hundreds of times, piling up hundreds of grain heaps in his imagination, then mentally removing individual grains. But he has not found the decisive moment. It has ousted even the moon from his attention and he has no longer been thinking much about the dead baby either.

This afternoon he then tried it in reality. The most difficult part was hauling so much unground grain up to the attic room without losing some in the process, for the day after tomorrow Peter Steger is coming and picking up the flour. Claus had to shout and threaten the mill hands to make them be careful; he cannot afford any more debts. Agneta called him a furry horned animal, whereupon he told her not to meddle in things that are too difficult for women, whereupon she smacked him, whereupon he told her to watch herself, whereupon she slapped him so hard that he had to sit down for a while. This is how it often goes between them. In the beginning he sometimes hit Agneta back, but it never went well for him, he may be stronger, but she is usually angrier, and in every fight whoever is angrier wins, and so he long ago gave up hitting her, for as quickly as her anger comes, it fortunately evaporates just as quickly.

Then he began to work in his attic room. At first deliberate and scrupulous, examining the heap with each grain, but gradually sweating and morose and by late afternoon in sheer despair. On the right side of the room there was eventually a new heap and on the left side something that could perhaps still be called a heap, but perhaps not. And a little while later there was on the left only a handful of grains.

And where, then, was the dividing line? It's enough to make you cry. He spoons his groats, sighs, and listens to the pelting rain. The groats taste bad as always, but for a while the sound of the rain soothes him. Then it occurs to him that it's similar with rain: How many drops fewer would have to fall for it to no longer be rain? He groans. Sometimes it seems to him as if it were God's goal in the way he made the world to confound a poor miller.

Agneta puts her hand on his arm and asks whether he'd like more groats.

He doesn't want more, but he understands that she feels sorry for him and that it's a peace offering because of the slaps. "Yes," he says softly. "Thank you."

Then there's a thump at the door.

Claus crosses his fingers for protection. He murmurs a spell, makes signs in the air; only then does he call: "Who's there, in the name of God?" Everyone knows never to say come in before whoever is outside has said his name. The evil spirits are powerful, but the vast majority of them cannot cross the threshold unless they are invited.

"Two wanderers," calls a voice. "In Christ's name, open the door."

Claus stands up, goes to the door, and unbolts it.

A man enters. He is no longer young, but he looks strong. His hair and his beard are dripping wet. Rainwater forms pearls on the thick gray linen of his cloak. He is followed by a second, much younger man. This man looks around, and when he sees the boy, a smile passes over his face. It's the stranger he encountered at noon.

"I am Dr. Oswald Tesimond of the Society of Jesus," says the older man. "This is Dr. Kircher. We were invited."

"Invited?" asks Agneta.

"Society of Jesus?" asks Claus.

"We are Jesuits."

"Jesuits," Claus repeats. "Real, true Jesuits?"

Agneta brings two stools to the table; the others move closer together.

Claus bows awkwardly. "I am Claus Ulenspiegel," he says, "and this is my wife and this is my son and these are my mill hands. We rarely receive distinguished visitors. It's an honor. There's not much, but what we have is at your disposal. Here are the groats, there is the small beer, and there's still some milk in the jug." He clears his throat. "May I ask whether you are scholars?"

"I should say so," replies Dr. Tesimond, taking a spoon gingerly. "I am a doctor of medicine and of theology, in addition a chemicus specializing in dracontology. Dr. Kircher concerns himself with occult signs, crystallography, and the nature of music." He eats some groats, screws up his face, and puts down the spoon.

For a moment it is silent. Then Claus leans forward and says, "May I be permitted to ask a question?"

"With certainty," says Dr. Tesimond. Something about the way he speaks is unusual: some words in his sentences are not where you would expect them, and he also emphasizes them differently; it sounds as if he had little stones in his mouth.

"What is dracontology?" asks Claus. Even in the weak light

of the tallow candle the others can tell that his cheeks have turned red.

"The study of the nature of dragons."

The mill hands raise their heads. Rosa's mouth hangs open. The boy feels hot. "Have you seen any?" he asks.

Dr. Tesimond furrows his brow as if an unpleasant noise had disturbed him.

Dr. Kircher looks at the boy and shakes his head.

"My apologies," says Claus. "This is a simple house. My son doesn't know how to behave and sometimes forgets that a child is to be quiet when adults are speaking. But the question did occur to me too. Have you seen any?"

"It is not the first time I've heard this amusing question," says Dr. Tesimond. "Indeed every dracontologist is met with it regularly among the simple people. But dragons are rare. They are very . . . what's the word again?"

"Shy," says Dr. Kircher.

"German is not my native tongue," says Dr. Tesimond. "I must apologize, sometimes I fall into the idiom of my beloved native land, which I will never see again in my life: England, the island of apples and of morning fog. Yes, dragons are inconceivably shy and capable of astounding feats of camouflage. You could search for a hundred years and yet never get close to a dragon. Just as you can spend a hundred years in immediate proximity to a dragon and never notice it. That is precisely why dracontology is necessary. For medical science cannot do without the healing power of their blood."

Claus rubs his forehead. "Where do you get the blood, then?"

"We don't have the blood, of course. Medicine is the art of . . . what's the word?"

"Substitution," says Dr. Kircher.

"Yes, indeed," says Dr. Tesimond, "dragon blood is a substance of such power that you don't need the stuff itself. It's enough that the substance is in the world. In my beloved native land there are still two dragons, but no one has tracked them down in centuries."

"Earthworm and grub," says Dr. Kircher, "look like the dragon. Crushed into a fine substance their bodies can achieve astonishing things. Dragon blood has the power to make a person invulnerable, but as a substitute pulverized cinnabar can still cure skin diseases due to its resemblance. Cinnabar is itself hard to obtain, yet all herbs with surfaces that are scaly like dragons can in turn be substituted for cinnabar. The art of healing is substitution according to the principle of resemblance—crocus cures eye afflictions because it looks like an eye."

"The better a dracontologist knows his trade," says Dr. Tesimond, "the better he can make up for the absence of the dragon through substitution. The pinnacle of the art, however, lies in using not the body of the dragon, but its . . . what is it called?"

"Knowledge," says Dr. Kircher.

"Its knowledge. As early a writer as Pliny the Elder reports that dragons know an herb by means of which they bring dead members of their species back to life. To find this herb would be the Holy Grail of our science."

"But how do we know that dragons exist?" asks the boy.

Dr. Tesimond furrows his brow. Claus leans forward and slaps his son's face.

"Because of the efficacy of the substitutes," says Dr. Kircher. "How would such a puny insect as the grub have healing power if not by its resemblance to the dragon! Why can cinnabar heal, if not because it is dark red like dragon blood!"

"Another question," says Claus. "While I am speaking with learned men . . . while I have the opportunity . . ."

"Go on," says Dr. Tesimond.

"A heap of grains. If you always take away only one. It's driving me mad."

The mill hands laugh.

"A well-known problem," says Dr. Tesimond. He makes an encouraging gesture in Dr. Kircher's direction.

"Where one thing is, no other thing can be," says Dr. Kircher, "but two words do not exclude each other. Between a thing that is a grain heap and a thing that is not a grain heap there is no sharp dividing line. The heap nature fades little by little, comparable to a cloud dispersing."

"Yes," Claus says as if to himself. "Yes. No, no. Because . . . No! You can't make a table out of a fingernail of wood. Not one you could use. It's not enough. It's impossible. Nor out of two fingernails of wood. Not enough wood to make a table never becomes enough wood just because you add a tiny bit!"

The guests are silent. Everyone listens to the rain and the scratching of the spoons and the wind rattling the windows.

"A good question," says Dr. Tesimond, looking encouragingly at Dr. Kircher.

"Things are what they are," says Dr. Kircher, "but vagueness is embedded deep within our concepts. It is simply not always clear whether a thing is a mountain or not a mountain, a flower or not a flower, a shoe or not a shoe—or, indeed, a table or not a table. That is why, when God wants clarity, he speaks in numbers."

"It's unusual for a miller to take an interest in such questions," says Dr. Tesimond. "Or in things like that." He points to the pentagrams engraved over the doorframe.

"They keep away demons," says Claus.

"And one just engraves them? That's sufficient?"

"You need the right words."

"Hold your tongue," says Agneta.

"But it's difficult with the words, isn't it?" says Dr. Tesimond. "With the . . ." He looks questioningly at Dr. Kircher.

"Spells," says Dr. Kircher.

"Exactly," says Dr. Tesimond. "Isn't it dangerous? They say that the same words that banish demons under certain conditions also lure them."

"Those are different spells. I know them too. Don't worry. I know the difference."

"Be quiet," says Agneta.

"And in what else, then, does a miller like you take an interest? What occupies his mind, what does he want to know? How else can one . . . help you?"

"Well, with the leaves," says Claus.

"Hold your tongue!" says Agneta.

"A few months ago I found two leaves near the old oak on Jakob Brantner's field. Actually it's not Brantner's field, it has always belonged to the Lesers, but in the inheritance dispute the prefect decided that it's a Brantner field. No matter, the leaves, in any case, looked exactly alike."

"It most certainly is Brantner's field," says Sepp, who was a hand on Brantner's farm for a year. "The Lesers are liars, devil take them."

"If there's a liar here," says Rosa, "then it's Jakob Brantner. You need only see how he looks at the women in church."

"But it really is his field," says Sepp.

Claus pounds on the table. Everyone goes silent.

"The leaves. They looked alike, every vein, every crack. I dried them, I can show them to you. I even bought a magnifying glass from a merchant when he came through the village, to be able to view them better. The merchant doesn't come often, his name is Hugo, he has only two fingers on his left hand, and when you ask him how he lost the others, he says: Miller, they're only fingers!" Claus stops and thinks briefly, astounded at where the stream of his speech has carried him. "Well, when they were lying there in front of me, the two leaves, I suddenly wondered whether it doesn't mean that they are actually one. If the difference consists only in the fact that the one leaf is on the left and the other on the right—well, all you need to do is make a hand movement." He demonstrates it with such an awkward gesture that a spoon flies in one direction and a bowl in the other. "Imagine someone says now that the two leaves are one and the same—what can you reply? He would be right!" Claus thumps on the table, but all except Agneta, who is looking at him fixedly and beseechingly, are following with their eyes the rolling bowl, which goes around in a circle once, twice, and then comes to rest. "These two leaves, then," Claus says into the silence. "If they are only in appearance two leaves and in truth one, doesn't that mean that . . . all this here and there and elsewhere is only a web that God has woven so that we won't penetrate his mysteries?"

"You must be silent now," says Agneta.

"And speaking of mysteries," says Claus, "I have a book that I can't read."

"No two leaves in all Creation are alike," says Dr. Kircher.

"Nor even two grains of sand. No two things between which God doesn't distinguish."

"The leaves are upstairs, I can show them to you! And I can show you the book too! And what you said about the grub is not true, honorable sir, crushed grub cannot heal, but causes back pain and cold joints." Claus gives his son a sign. "Fetch the big book, the one without binding, the one with the pictures!"

The boy stands up and runs to the ladder that leads upstairs. He climbs with lightning speed, disappearing through the hatch.

"You have a good son," says Dr. Kircher.

Claus nods distractedly.

"Be that as it may," says Dr. Tesimond. "It's late, and we must be in the village before nightfall. Are you coming, miller?"

Claus looks at him uncomprehendingly. The two guests stand up.

"You idiot," says Agneta.

"Where?" asks Claus. "Why?"

"No reason to worry," says Dr. Tesimond. "We just want to talk, at length and in peace. That's what you wanted, isn't it, miller? In peace. About everything that occupies your mind. Do we look like bad people?"

"But I can't," says Claus. "Steger is coming the day after tomorrow and wants his grain. It is not yet ground. I have it up in the room. Time is pressing."

"These are good mill hands," says Dr. Tesimond. "One can rely on them. The work will be done."

"He who refuses to follow his friends," says Dr. Kircher, "must be prepared to deal with people who are not his friends.

We supped together, sat together in the mill. We can trust each other."

"This Latin book," says Dr. Tesimond. "I want to see it. If you have questions, we can answer them."

Everyone is waiting for the boy, who is groping through the dark attic room above. It takes a while before he has found the right book next to the heap of grain. By the time he climbs back down, his father and the guests are standing in the doorway.

He hands the book to Claus, who strokes his head, then bends down and kisses him on the forehead. In the last light of day the boy sees the thin wrinkles chiseled into his father's face. He sees the flicker in his restless eyes, which can always only briefly look at one thing, he sees the white hairs in the black beard.

And as Claus looks down at his son, it amazes him that so many of his children have died at birth but that of all his children this one survived. He didn't take enough interest in the boy, he was simply too accustomed to all of them immediately disappearing again. But that will change, Claus thinks, I will teach him what I know, the spells, the squares, the herbs, and the course of the moon. Cheerfully he takes the book and steps out into the evening. The rain has stopped.

Agneta clasps him. They embrace for a long time. Claus wants to let go, but Agneta keeps holding him. The mill hands titter.

"You'll be back soon," says Dr. Tesimond.

"There you have it," says Claus.

"You idiot," says Agneta, weeping.

Suddenly all this is embarrassing to Claus—the mill, the sobbing wife, the scrawny son, his whole poor existence. Res-

olutely he pushes Agneta away from him. It pleases him that
he will now have the chance to make common cause with the
learned men, to whom he feels closer than to these mill people,
who know nothing.

"Don't worry," he says to Dr. Tesimond. "I'll find the way in
the dark too."

Claus sets off with long strides. The two men follow him.
Agneta watches them until the twilight swallows them.

"Go inside," she says to the boy.

"When is he coming back?"

She closes and bolts the door.

II

Dr. Kircher opens his eyes. Someone is in the room. He listens.
No, there's no one here except Dr. Tesimond, whose snoring
he hears from the bed over there. He throws back the blanket,
crosses himself, and gets up. The time has come. The day of the
trial.

To crown it all he dreamed again of Egyptian signs. A clay-
yellow wall, in it little men with dog heads, lions with wings,
axes, swords, lances, wavy lines of all sorts. No one understands
them. The knowledge of them has been lost, until a divinely
gifted intellect will appear to decipher them again.

That will be he. One day.

His back hurts as it does every morning. The straw sack
on which he has to sleep is thin, the floor icy cold. There's only
one bed in the priest's house, and his master is sleeping in it;
even the priest must lie on the floor in the next room. At least

his master didn't wake up last night. Often he screams in his sleep, and sometimes he pulls out the knife hidden under his pillow and thinks his life is in danger. When this happens, he has again been dreaming of the great conspiracy, in England, when he and a few brave people almost succeeded in blowing up the King. The attempt failed, but they didn't give up: for days they searched for Princess Elizabeth in order to kidnap her and place her on the throne by force. It could have succeeded, and had it succeeded, the island would today again be in possession of the true faith. For weeks Dr. Tesimond lived in the forests, on roots and spring water. He was the only one to escape and make his way across the sea. Later he will be canonized, but at night one shouldn't lie near him, for the knife is always under his pillow, and his dreams are swarming with Protestant oppressors.

Dr. Kircher throws his cloak over his shoulders and leaves the priest's house. In a daze, he stands in the pale light of the early morning. On his right is the church, in front of him the main square with the well and the linden and the platform erected yesterday, next to it the houses of the Tamms, the Henrichs, and the Heinerlings. He now knows all the inhabitants of this village, he has interrogated them, he knows their secrets. Something is moving on the roof of the Henrich house. Instinctively he recoils, but it is probably only a cat. He murmurs a protective blessing and crosses himself three times, go away, evil spirit, desist, I stand under the protection of the Lord and the Virgin and all the saints. Then he sits down, leans against the wall of the priest's house, and waits with chattering teeth for the sun.

He realizes that someone is sitting next to him. He must

have approached soundlessly, sat down soundlessly. It's Master Tilman.

"Good morning," Dr. Kircher mutters and gives a start. That was a mistake; now Master Tilman might return the greeting.

To his horror it happens too. "Good morning!"

Dr. Kircher looks around in all directions. Fortunately there's no one to be seen, the village is still asleep, no one is observing them.

"This cold," says Master Tilman.

"Yes," says Dr. Kircher, because he has to say something. "Bad."

"And gets worse every year," says Master Tilman.

They're silent.

Dr. Kircher knows that it would be best not to reply, but the silence is oppressive, so he clears his throat and says: "The world is ending."

Master Tilman spits on the ground. "And how much longer?"

"Probably about a hundred years," says Dr. Kircher, still looking around uneasily. "Some think a bit sooner, while others believe that it will be around a hundred and twenty."

He falls silent, feels a lump in his throat. This happens to him whenever he speaks of the apocalypse. He crosses himself. Master Tilman does the same.

The poor man, thinks Dr. Kircher. Actually, no hangman need fear the Last Judgment, since the condemned must forgive their executioners before death, but now and then there are stubborn ones who refuse, and occasionally it even happens that someone summons his hangman to the Valley of Josaphat.

Everyone knows this curse: I summon you to the Valley of Josaphat. Whoever says that to the hangman accuses him of murder and denies him forgiveness. Has this ever happened to Master Tilman?

"You're wondering whether I'm afraid of the Judgment."

"No!"

"Whether anyone has summoned me to the Valley of Josaphat."

"No!"

"Everyone wonders that. You know, I didn't choose this. I am what I am because my father was what he was. And he was what he was because of *his* father. And my son will have to be what I am, for a hangman's son becomes a hangman." Master Tilman spits again. "My son is a gentle boy. I look at him, he is only eight and very kind, and killing doesn't suit him. But he has no choice. It didn't suit me either. And I learned how, and not badly at all."

Dr. Kircher is now really worried. By no means may anyone see how he is chatting peacefully with the hangman here.

Whitish brightness spreads in the sky. On the walls of the houses the colors can now be distinguished. Even the platform is clearly visible over there in front of the linden. Nearby, only a blur in the dawn, stands the horse-drawn wagon of the balladeer who arrived two days ago. So it always happens: when there's something to see, the traveling people gather.

"Thank God there's no tavern in this hole," says Master Tilman. "Because when there is one, I go there in the evening, but then I sit alone, and everyone peers over and whispers. And even though I know this beforehand, I still go to the tavern, for where else am I supposed to go? I can't wait to get back to Eichstätt."

"Do they treat you better there?"

"No, but there I'm at home. To be treated badly at home is better than to be treated badly elsewhere." Master Tilman raises his arms and stretches with a yawn.

Dr. Kircher jerks sideways. The hangman's hand is only a few inches away from his shoulder; there must not be any contact. Anyone touched by a hangman, even if only fleetingly, loses his honor. But of course you must not arouse his hostility either. If you anger him, he could grasp you intentionally and accept the punishment. Dr. Kircher curses himself for his own good nature—he never should have let himself be drawn into this conversation.

Now, to his relief, he hears from inside the house the dry cough of his master. Dr. Tesimond has awoken. With an apologetic gesture he stands up.

Master Tilman smiles wryly.

"God be with us on this great day," says Dr. Kircher.

But the hangman doesn't reply. Dr. Kircher goes quickly into the priest's house to help his master get dressed.

With a measured step and clad in the red robe of the judge, Dr. Tesimond moves toward the platform. Up there stands a table with stacks of paper, weighed down with stones from the millstream, lest the wind carry away a sheet. The sun is approaching its zenith. The light falls shimmering through the crown of the linden. Everyone is here: in front all the members of the Steger family and the smith Stelling with his wife and the farmer Brantner with his family, behind them the baker

Holtz with his wife and two daughters and Anselm Melker with his children and wife and sister-in-law and old mother and old mother-in-law and old father-in-law and aunt and next to them Maria Leserin with her beautiful daughter and behind them the Henrichs and the Heinerlings along with their hands and at the very back the mouselike round faces of the Tamms. Master Tilman stands apart, leaning on the trunk of the tree. He is wearing a brown cowl, his face is pale and swollen. Behind the tree the balladeer stands on his wagon, scribbling in a little book.

Light-footedly, Dr. Tesimond springs onto the platform and stands behind a chair. Despite his youth, Dr. Kircher has a less easy time of it; the platform is high and the robe hampers his climbing. When he is up there, Dr. Tesimond looks at him encouragingly, and Dr. Kircher knows that he is now supposed to speak, but as he looks around, he grows dizzy. The feeling of unreality is so great that he has to hold on to the edge of the table. It's not the first time this has happened to him. It's one of the things he must keep secret at all costs. He has only just received the minor orders, he is still far from a full Jesuit, and only men of the best health in body and mind may be members of the Society of Jesus.

Above all, however, no one must know how muddled time keeps becoming for him. Sometimes he finds himself in a strange place without knowing what has happened in the interim. Recently he forgot for a good hour that he is already grown up; he thought he was a child playing near his parents' house in the grass, as if the fifteen years since then and the difficult studies in Paderborn were merely the fantasy of a boy wishing to finally be grown up. How fragile the world is. Almost every night he sees Egyptian signs, and increasingly the worry grows in him that he might one day no longer awake from one of these dreams, that he might be imprisoned forever in the colorful hell of a godless land of Pharaohs.

Hastily he rubs his eyes. Peter Steger and Ludwig Stelling, the assistant judges, have climbed up in black robes to join them, followed by Ludwig von Esch, the administrator and chairman of the local court district, who must deliver the verdict so that it has validity. Spots of sunlight dance on the grass and the well. Despite the brightness it's so cold that your breath turns into little clouds of vapor. Linden crown, thinks Dr. Kircher. Linden crown, a word like that can get stuck in your head, but this must not happen now, he must not let himself be distracted, he must direct all his strength at the ceremony. Linden king, linden crone, linden crow. No! Not now, no confusion now, everyone is waiting! As the scribe he opens the trial, no one else can do it, it is his duty, he must fulfill it. To calm himself he looks into the faces of the spectators in front and in the middle, but no sooner has he grown calmer than his gaze meets that of the miller's boy. He is standing at the very back, next to his mother. His eyes are narrow, cheeks hollow, lips a bit pursed as if he were whistling to himself.

Try to expunge him from your thoughts. You haven't taken part in so many spiritual exercises for nothing. It's the same with the mind as with the eyes: they see what lies in front of them, but you can determine where you direct them. He squints. Only a spot, he thinks, only colors, only a play of light. I don't see a boy, I see light. I don't see a face, I see colors. Only colors, light, and shadows.

And indeed, the boy is no longer of consequence. He simply must not look at him. Their gazes must not meet. As long as that doesn't happen, everything is all right.

"Is the judge here?" he asks hoarsely.

"The judge is here," replies Dr. Tesimond.

"The administrator here?"

"I'm here," Ludwig von Esch says in an annoyed tone. Under normal circumstances he would be the one leading the trial, but these are not normal circumstances.

"The first assistant judge here?"

"Here," says Peter Steger.

"The second?"

Silence. Peter Steger gives Ludwig Stelling a nudge. He looks around in surprise. Peter Steger gives another nudge.

"Yes, here," says Ludwig Stelling.

"The tribunal is assembled," says Dr. Kircher.

Inadvertently, he looks at Master Tilman. The hangman is leaning almost casually against the trunk of the linden, rubbing his beard and smiling, but at what? His heart pounding, he looks elsewhere. The impression must by no means be given that he has a mutual understanding with the executioner. So he looks at the balladeer. The day before yesterday he heard him singing. The lute was poorly tuned, the rhymes were rickety, and the outrageous events about which he sang were not so outrageous: a child murder by the Protestants in Magdeburg, a miserable song mocking the Elector Palatine in which *bread* was rhymed with *bent* and *quivering* with *belligerents*. With unease he thinks about the likelihood that in the ballad that the singer will sing about this trial he too will appear.

"The tribunal is assembled," he hears himself saying once again. "Gathered to dispense justice and see justice done before the community, which is to maintain order and peace, from the beginning of the trial until the end, in the name of God." He clears his throat. Then he calls: "Bring out the condemned!"

For a while it is so quiet that the wind can be heard, the bees, all the bleating and mooing and yapping of the animals. Then the door of the Brantner cowshed opens. It squeaks because it has just recently been reinforced with iron; the window shutters too have been boarded up. The cows, for whom there is now no more room inside, have been housed in the Steger shed, which caused a quarrel because Peter Steger wanted payment for it and Ludwig Brantner said it wasn't his fault. In a village nothing is ever simple.

A pikeman steps outside, yawning, followed by the two accused, blinking, and behind them another two pikemen. They're elderly warriors on the cusp of withdrawal from service. One of them limps, the other is missing his left hand. Nothing better was sent from Eichstätt.

And from the appearance of the accused, it can seem as if no more was necessary. With their shorn heads on which, as always when you cut off a person's hair, all sorts of bumps and dents are visible, they look like the most harmless and weakest of people. Their hands are wrapped in thick bandages so that the crushed fingers cannot be seen, and bloody imprints stretch around their foreheads where Master Tilman applied the leather band. How easily, Dr. Kircher thinks, pity could overcome you, but you must not permit yourself to believe the appearance, for they are in league with the greatest power of the fallen world, and their lord is with them at every moment. That's why it is so dangerous: during the trial, the devil can always intervene. At any time he can show his strength and free them. Only the courage and purity of the judges can prevent it. Again and again his superiors impressed this on him in the seminary: do not underestimate those who have made a pact with the devil! Never forget that your compassion is their weapon and that they have means at their disposal of which your mind has no inkling.

The spectators clear a path. The two accused are led to the platform: in front old Hanna Krell, behind her the miller. Both of them walk stooped. They appear abstracted. It remains unclear whether they know who they are or what is happening.

Don't underestimate them, Dr. Kircher tells himself, that's the important thing. Not to underestimate them.

The tribunal sits down: in the middle Dr. Tesimond, to his right Peter Steger, to his left Ludwig Stelling. And to Stelling's left—at a slight distance because the court scribe, while responsible for the smooth course of the trial, is not himself part of the tribunal—is the chair for him.

"Hanna," says Dr. Tesimond, raising a sheet of paper. "Here is your confession."

She is silent. Her lips don't move, her eyes seem extinguished. She looks like an empty shell, her face a mask that no one is wearing, her arms as if hung wrong at the joints. Better not to think about it, thinks Dr. Kircher, who at the same moment naturally cannot help thinking about what Master Tilman did to those arms to make them hang so wrong. Better not to imagine it. He rubs his eyes and imagines it.

"You are silent," says Dr. Tesimond, "so we will read your words from the interrogation. They are written on this sheet of paper. You spoke them, Hanna. Now everyone shall hear them. Now everything shall come to light." His words seem to echo as if they were spoken in a stone room and not outside under a linden, in whose linden crown the lingering wind—no! Not for the first time Dr. Kircher finds himself thinking about how fortunate he can consider himself and how favored by God he is that Dr. Tesimond chose him as his famulus. He himself did nothing, didn't volunteer and didn't thrust himself forward on the occasion when the legendary man came from Vienna to Paderborn, a guest of the superior, an admired traveler passing through, a witness to the true faith, who during an exercise in the church of the order suddenly stood up and approached him. I will question you, my boy, answer quickly. Don't think about what I want to hear, you cannot guess it, just say what is correct. Whom does God love more—the angels who are without sin or the man who has sinned and repented? Answer more quickly. Are the angels of God's substance and thus eternal or are they created as we are? Even more quickly. And sin, is it God's creation, and if so, can he love it as he does all his creatures, and if not, how is it possible that the punishment of the sinner is without end, his pain without end, and his suffering in the fire without end? Speak quickly!

It went on like this for an hour. He heard himself giving answers, to ever-new questions, and when he didn't know an answer, he made something up and sometimes even quotations and sources for it. Thomas Aquinas wrote over a hundred volumes, no one knows them all, and he had always been able to rely on his inventiveness. So he spoke and spoke as if someone else were talking through him, and gathered all his strength and didn't permit his memory to withhold answers, sentences, or names from him, and he was even able to add and subtract and divide the numbers without paying attention to the beating of his heart or the dizziness in his head, and the whole time his brother in faith was looking him in the face with such intensity that to this day it sometimes seems to him as if the questioning were still going on and would go on forever, as if everything since then were a dream. Yet in the end Dr. Tesimond took a step back and said with his eyes closed and as if to himself: "I need you. My German is not good, you must help. I am traveling back to Vienna, holy duties call, you will come with me."

And so they have now been on their way for a year. The journey to Vienna is long when there are so many urgent matters on the way; a man like Dr. Tesimond cannot simply move on when he discovers machinations. In Lippstadt they had to exorcise a demon. Then in Passau a dishonorable priest had to be chased away. They steered clear of Pilsen because the especially raging Protestants there might have arrested Jesuits passing through, and this detour brought them to a little village where the arrest, torture, and condemnation of an evil witch took them six months. Then they received tidings of a dracontological colloquium in Bayreuth. Naturally, they had to travel there to prevent Erhard von Felz, the doctor's greatest rival, from spouting unchallenged nonsense. The debate between the two of them lasted seven weeks, four days, and three hours. Afterward he fervently hoped that they would now finally reach the imperial city, but when they spent the night at the Collegium Willibaldinum in Eichstätt, the Prince-Bishop summoned them to an audience: "My people are sleepy, Dr. Tesimond, the administrators don't report enough offenses in the villages, there are more and more witches, no one does anything, I can hardly finance my own Jesuit seminary, because the cathedral canon is against it. Will you help me? I will appoint you ad hoc commissarius of witches, and I will grant you permission to administer capital supplicium to malefactors on the spot, if you will only help me. You will receive every authority."

That was why Dr. Kircher hesitated for an entire afternoon when a conversation with a strange boy aroused in him the suspicion that they had once again crossed paths with a warlock. I don't have to report it, he thought, I can keep silent, I can forget it, it was not at all necessary for me to talk to the boy, after all, it was a chance encounter. But the voice of conscience returned: Talk to your master. There is no such thing as chance, there is only God's will. And as expected Dr. Tesimond immediately decided that the miller had to be paid a visit, and as expected everything that followed took its usual course. Now they have spent weeks already in this godforsaken village, and Vienna is more distant than ever.

He realizes that everyone is looking at him, only the accused are looking down at the ground. It happened again: he was absent. He can only hope that it didn't last too long. Hastily he looks around and finds his bearings: In front of him lies Hanna Krell's confession. He recognizes the handwriting, it is his own, he wrote it himself, and now he has to read it out. With unsteady fingers he reaches for it, but at the very moment his fingers touch the paper, a wind stirs. Dr. Kircher grasps the paper, fortunately quickly enough. It is firmly in his hand. It doesn't bear thinking about what would have happened if it had flown away from him. Satan is powerful, the air his realm. It would suit him perfectly if the tribunal made a mockery of itself.

As he reads Hanna's confession aloud, he thinks back helplessly to the interrogation. To the dark room in the back of the priest's house, once the broom closet, now the interrogation room in which Master Tilman and Dr. Tesimond worked day after day on luring the truth out of the old woman. Dr. Tesimond has a kind soul and would have preferred to stay away from the harsh interrogation, but the Procedure for the Judgment of Capital Crimes of Kaiser Charles obliges a judge to be present at every torture he orders. And it also prescribes a confession. No trial may end without a confession; no sentence may be imposed if the defendants have not admitted anything. The actual trial takes place in the locked closet, but on the day of the tribunal, when the confession is publicly confirmed and the verdict delivered, all are present.

While Dr. Kircher is reading, cries of horror come from the crowd. People gasp, people whisper, people shake their heads, people bare their teeth in fury and disgust. His voice trembles as he hears himself speaking of nocturnal flights and exposed flesh, of traveling on the wind, of the great Sabbath of the night, of blood in the cauldrons and naked bodies, lo, they are rolling, the huge billy goat with never-flagging lust, he takes you from in front and takes you from behind, to songs sung in the language of Orcus. Dr. Kircher turns the page and comes to the curses: cold and hail on the fields, spoiling the crop of the pious, and hunger visited on the heads of the God-fearing and death and disease on the weak and pestilence on the children. Several times his voice almost fails, but he thinks of his sacred ministry and admonishes himself, and thank God he is prepared. None of these horrible things is new to him. He knows every word, has written it not only once but again and again, outside the closet, while the interrogation took place inside and Master Tilman brought to light everything that must be confessed in a witchcraft trial: And did you not fly too, Hanna? All witches fly. Do you mean to tell me that you of all people did not fly, will you deny it? And the Sabbath? Did you not kiss Satan, Hanna? If you speak, you will be forgiven, but if you keep silent, then look what Master Tilman has in his hand, he will use it.

"This has happened." Dr. Kircher reads the last lines aloud. "In this way I, Hanna Krell, daughter of Leopoldina and Franz

Krell, have renounced the Lord, betrayed the community of Christians, visited harm upon my fellow citizens and upon the holy church and my authorities too. In deep shame I confess and accept the just punishment, so help me God."

He falls silent. A fly buzzes past his ear, flies in an arc, settles on his forehead. Should he drive it away or pretend he doesn't notice it? What is more appropriate to the dignity of the tribunal, what is less ridiculous? He glances at his master inquisitively, but he doesn't give him any sign.

Instead Dr. Tesimond leans forward, looks at Hanna Krell, and asks: "Is this your confession?"

She nods. Her chains rattle.

"You have to say it, Hanna!"

"That is my confession."

"You have done all this?"

"I've done all that."

"And who was the leader?"

She is silent.

"Hanna! Who was your leader? Who brought all of you to the Sabbath? Who taught you how to fly?"

She is silent.

"Hanna?"

She raises her hand and points to the miller.

"You have to say it, Hanna."

"He did."

"Louder!"

"It was he."

Dr. Tesimond makes a hand movement. The guard pushes the miller forward. Now the main part of the trial begins. They came upon old Hanna only incidentally. A warlock almost always has followers. Nonetheless, it took a while before Ludwig Stelling's wife admitted under threat of punishment that her rheumatism had been plaguing her only since she had quarreled with Hanna Krell, and again only after a week of interrogation did it also occur to Magda Steger and Maria Leserin that storms always came when Hanna was supposedly too ill to attend church. Hanna herself didn't deny it long. As soon as Master Tilman showed her the instruments, she began to confess her crimes, and when he set to work in earnest, their full magnitude was very quickly revealed.

"Claus Ulenspiegel!" Dr. Tesimond holds three sheets of paper in the air. "Your confession!"

Dr. Kircher sees the sheets of paper in his master's hand, and immediately his head hurts. He knows every sentence on them by heart. He rewrote it again and again, outside the locked door of the interrogation room through which you could hear everything.

"May I say something?" asks the miller.

Dr. Tesimond looks at him disapprovingly.

"Please," says the miller. He rubs the red imprint of the leather band on his forehead. The chains rattle.

"What, then?" asks Dr. Tesimond.

This was how it went the whole time. Never before, Dr. Tesimond repeated often, had he encountered such a difficult case as this miller! And this is still so, despite all of Master Tilman's efforts—despite blade and needle, despite salt and fire, despite leather loop, wet shoes, thumbscrew, and steel countess—all unclear. An executioner knows how to loosen tongues, but what does he do with someone who talks and talks and has absolutely no qualms about contradicting himself as if Aristotle had written nothing on logic? At first Dr. Tesimond took it for a perfidious ruse, but then he realized that the miller's confusions always also contained fragments of truths—indeed, even astonishing insights.

"I've been thinking," says Claus. "Now I understand. About my errors. I ask for forgiveness. I ask for mercy."

"Did you do what this woman said? Lead the Witches' Sabbath, did you do that?"

"I thought I was clever," the miller says with downcast eyes. "I overestimated myself. Expected too much of my mind, my stupid intellect. I'm sorry. I ask for mercy."

"And the black magic? The ruined fields? The cold, the rain—was that you?"

"I helped the sick according to the old way. There were some I couldn't help. The old remedies are not so reliable. I always did my best. I was paid only if it helped, of course. I read the future of those who wanted to know it in water and bird flight. Peter Steger's cousin, not Paul Steger, the other one, Karl, I told him not to climb the beech tree, not even to find treasures, don't do it, I said, and the Steger cousin asked: A treasure in my beech tree? And I said: Don't do it, Steger, and Karl said: If there's a treasure there, I'm going up, and then he fell and smashed his head. And I can't figure out, even though I think about it all the time, whether a prophecy that would not have come true if I hadn't made it is actually a prophecy or something else."

"Did you hear the witch's confession? That she called you the leader of the Sabbath, did you hear that?"

"If there's a treasure in the beech tree, then it's still there."

"Did you hear the witch?"

"And the two birch leaves I found."

"Not again!"

"They looked like a single leaf."

"Not the leaves again!"

Claus is sweating, he is breathing heavily. "The matter confused me so." He reflects, shakes his head, scratches his shorn head, rattling his chains. "May I show you the leaves? They must still be in the mill, in the attic, where I pursued my foolish studies." He turns around and points with a chain-rattling arm over the heads of the spectators. "My son can fetch them!"

"There are no more magic materials in the mill," says Dr. Tesimond. "There's a new miller there now, and he won't have kept that junk."

"And the books?" Claus asks softly.

Dr. Kircher is unsettled to see a fly land on the paper in his hands. Its little black legs follow the course of the letters. Is it possible that it's trying to tell him something? But it's moving so quickly that you can't read what it's writing, and he must not let himself be distracted once again.

"Where are my books?" asks Claus.

Dr. Tesimond gives his assistant a sign, and Dr. Kircher stands up and reads out the miller's confession.

His thoughts turn again to the investigations. The mill hand Sepp readily told how often he found the miller in a deep sleep during the day. Without a witness to such states of unconsciousness, no one can be convicted of witchcraft, there are strict rules about that. The servants of Satan leave their bodies behind, and their spirits fly out to distant lands. Even shaking him, shouting at him, and kicking him wouldn't have done any good, Sepp testified, and the priest too heavily incriminated the miller: I curse you, he cried as soon as anyone in the village angered him, I'll burn you to death, I'll cause you pain! He demanded obedience from the whole village, everyone feared his wrath. And the baker's wife once saw the demons he invoked after dark on the Steger field: she spoke of throats, teeth, claws, and large genitals, slimy figures of midnight. Dr. Kircher could hardly bring himself to write it down. And then four, five, six villagers, and then another three and then another two, and more and more, described in detail how often he brought bad weather down upon their fields. Black magic is even more important than unconsciousness—if it is not witnessed, an accused can be condemned only of heresy but not of witchcraft. To ensure that there was no error, Dr. Kircher explained to the witnesses for days the gestures and words they must have noticed. Their minds work slowly, you have to repeat everything, the curses, the old spells, the Satanic invocations, before they remember. Indeed it turned out thereafter that they all heard the correct words and saw the correct gestures of invocation. Only the baker, who was also questioned, was suddenly no longer certain, but then Dr. Tesimond took him aside and asked him whether he really wanted to protect a warlock and whether his life was so pure that he had nothing to fear from a thorough investigation. Then the baker remembered after all that he saw everything the others saw, and then nothing more was needed to lead the miller to a confession in a severe interrogation.

"I sent the hail onto the fields," Dr. Kircher reads aloud. "I carved my circles into the earth, summoned the powers below and the demons above and the Lord of the Air, brought ruin to the crops, ice onto the earth, death to the grain. In addition, I acquired a forbidden book, written in Latin . . ."

At this point he notices a stranger and goes silent. Where did he come from? Dr. Kircher didn't see him approaching, but if the man had already been among the spectators before, with his broad-brimmed hat and the velvet collar and the silver cane, he would surely have caught Dr. Kircher's eye! Yet there he stands, next to the balladeer's wagon. What if he alone could see him? His heart begins to pound. If the man were here only for him and invisible to the others, what then?

But as the stranger now comes forward with slow strides, the people step aside to let him pass. Dr. Kircher heaves a sigh of relief. The man's beard is cut short, his cloak is made of velvet, a feather bobs on his felt hat. With a solemn gesture he takes off the hat and bows.

"Greetings. Vaclav van Haag."

Dr. Tesimond stands up and bows himself. "An honor," he says. "A great pleasure!"

Dr. Kircher too stands up, bows, and sits back down. So it is not the devil, but the author of a well-known work on crystal formation in limestone caves—Dr. Kircher read it at some point and retained little in his memory. Questioningly he looks at the linden: The light wavers as if everything were an illusion. What is this expert on crystallization doing here?

"I'm writing a treatise on witchcraft," says Dr. van Haag as he straightens up again. "Word has spread that you have apprehended a warlock in this village. I ask permission to defend him."

A murmur goes through the spectators. Dr. Tesimond hesitates. "I'm certain," he then says, "a man of your erudition has better things to do with his time."

"Perhaps, but nonetheless I am here and ask you for this favor."

"The Procedure for the Judgment of Capital Crimes prescribes no advocate for the condemned."

"Nor does it forbid advocacy, however. Administrator, will you permit me—"

"Address the judge, dear colleague, not the administrator. He will announce the verdict, but I will judge."

Dr. van Haag looks at the administrator, who is white with rage, but it's true, he has no say here. Van Haag briefly tilts his head and speaks to Dr. Tesimond: "There are numerous precedents. Trials with advocates are becoming more and more common. Many a condemned man doesn't speak as well for himself as he would certainly do if he could only speak well. For example, the forbidden book that was just mentioned. Wasn't it said that it was written in Latin?"

"Correct."

"Has the miller read it?"

"Well, for God's sake, how could he have read it?"

Dr. van Haag smiles. He looks at Dr. Tesimond, then Dr. Kircher, then the miller, then Dr. Tesimond again.

"So what?" asks Dr. Tesimond.

"If the book is written in Latin!"

"Yes?"

"And if the miller doesn't speak Latin."

"Yes?"

Dr. van Haag spreads his arms and smiles again.

"Can I ask a question?" says the miller.

"A book that one is forbidden to possess, dear colleague, is a book that one is forbidden to possess, not a book that one is merely forbidden to read. The Holy Office speaks deliberately of having, not of knowing. Dr. Kircher?"

Dr. Kircher swallows, clears his throat, blinks. "A book is a possibility," he says. "It is always prepared to speak. Even someone who does not understand its language can pass it on to others who can read it very well, so that it may do its wicked work on them. Or he could learn the language, and if there's no one to teach it to him, he might find a way to teach it to himself. That's not unheard of either. It can be achieved purely by examining the letters, by counting their frequency, by contemplating their pattern, for the human mind is powerful. In this way Saint Zagraphius learned Hebrew in the desert, merely out of the strong yearning to know God's word in its primordial sound. And it's reported that Taras of Byzantium comprehended Egyptian hieroglyphs solely by examining them for years. Unfortunately, he left us no key, and so we must undertake anew the task of deciphering them, but the problem will be solved, perhaps even soon. And lest we forget, there's always the possibility that Satan, whose vassals understand all languages, endows one of his servants overnight with the ability to read the book. For these reasons the question of understanding is to be left to God and not his servants. To that God who will look into our souls on the Day of Judgment. The task of the human judges is to clear up the simple circumstances. And the simplest of them is this: if a book is forbidden, one is not permitted to have it."

"Besides, it's too late for a defense," says Dr. Tesimond. "The trial is over. Only the verdict remains to be delivered. The accused confessed."

"But evidently under torture?"

"Yes, of course," cries Dr. Tesimond. "Why else should he have confessed? Without torture no one would ever confess anything!"

"Whereas under torture everyone confesses."

"Thank God, yes!"

"Even an innocent man."

"But he is not innocent. We have the testimony of the others. We have the book!"

"The testimony of the others who would have been subjected to torture if they had not testified?"

Dr. Tesimond is silent for a moment. "Dear colleague," he says softly. "Naturally, someone who refuses to testify against a warlock must himself be investigated and charged. Where would we be if we did things differently?"

"Very well, another question: What does the unconsciousness of the warlocks actually mean? In the past it was said the unconscious ones had congress with the devil in their dreams. The devil has no power in God's world, as even Institoris writes, therefore he must use sleep to instill in his allies the delusion he is giving them wild pleasure. Now, however, we condemn warlocks for the very acts we formerly declared illusions inspired by the devil, but we still indict them for the sleep and the delusional dreams. Well, is the evil deed real or imagined? It cannot be both. That doesn't make sense, dear colleague!"

"It makes perfect sense, dear colleague!"

"Then explain it to me."

"Dear colleague, I will not allow the trial to be debased by drivel and doubt."

"May I ask a question?" the miller calls out.

"Me too," says Peter Steger, smoothing his robe. "This is taking a long time, can we take a break? The cows' udders are full, you can hear it yourselves."

"Arrest him," says Dr. Tesimond.

Dr. van Haag takes a step back. The guards stare at him.

"Take him away and bind him. It's true that the Procedure for the Judgment of Capital Crimes permits the condemned an advocate, but nowhere does it say that it is decent to set oneself up as the advocate of a servant of the devil and to disrupt the trial with stupid questions. With all due respect to a learned colleague, I cannot tolerate that, and we will clear up in a rigorous interrogation what induces an esteemed man to conduct himself in this fashion."

No one moves. Dr. van Haag looks at the guards; the guards look at Dr. Tesimond.

"Perhaps it is thirst for glory," says Dr. Tesimond. "Perhaps something worse. Time will tell."

Laughter goes through the crowd. Dr. van Haag takes another step back and puts his hand on the hilt of his sword. He really could have escaped, for the guards are neither fast nor brave, but now Master Tilman is standing beside him and shaking his head.

That's all it takes. Master Tilman is very tall and very broad, and his face all at once looks different than it did just a moment ago. Dr. van Haag lets go of the sword. One of the guards grasps him by the wrist, takes the sword, and leads him to the shed with the iron-reinforced door.

"I protest!" says Dr. van Haag, as he goes along without resistance. "A man of rank must not be treated like this."

"Permit me, dear colleague, to promise you that your rank will not be forgotten."

While walking, Dr. van Haag turns around once more. He opens his mouth, but he seems suddenly to have no strength. He has been completely taken by surprise. Now the door is opening with a creak, and he disappears into the shed along with the guard. A short time passes. Then the guard comes back out, closes the door, and secures the two bolts.

Dr. Kircher's heart is pounding. He feels dizzy with pride. It's not the first time he has watched someone underestimate his master's determination. You are not the sole survivor of the Gunpowder Plot for no reason; you do not become one of the most famous religious witnesses in the Society of Jesus just like that. Time and again there are people who don't know whom they are dealing with. But without fail they find out.

"This is the great trial," Dr. Tesimond says to Peter Steger. "This is not the time for milking cows. If your cattle's udders are hurting, then they are hurting for God's cause."

"I understand," says Peter Steger.

"Do you really understand?"

"Really. Yes, yes, I understand."

"And you, miller. We have read out your confession. Now we want to hear it, loud and clear: Is it true? Did you do it? Do you repent?"

It grows quiet. Only the wind can be heard and the mooing of the cows. A cloud has drifted in front of the sun; to Dr. Kircher's relief, the play of light in the crown of the tree has ceased. Now, however, the branches are rustling and whispering and hissing in the wind. It has grown cold. Probably it will soon rain again. Even the execution of this warlock won't do any good against the bad weather, for there are too many evil people, all of whom together are to blame for the cold and the failed harvests and the scarcity of everything in these final years before the end of the world. But one does what one can. Even if one is fighting a losing battle. One holds out, defends the remaining positions and waits for the day when God will return in glory.

"Miller," Dr. Tesimond repeats. "You must say it, before all the people here. Is it true? Did you do it?"

"May I ask a question?"

"No. You shall only answer. Is it true? Did you do it?"

The miller looks around like someone who doesn't know exactly where he is. But this too is probably a feint. Dr. Kircher knows well that one mustn't fall for it, for behind these apparently lost people the old adversary is hiding, ready to kill and to destroy wherever he can. If only the branches would quit making their noises. The rustling wind is suddenly even worse than the flickering light was. And if only the cows would be quiet!

Master Tilman steps beside the miller and puts his hand on his shoulder as if they were old friends. The miller looks at him. Since he's shorter than the executioner, his gaze goes upward like that of a child. Master Tilman bends down and says something in his ear. The miller nods as if he understood. There's an intimacy between the two of them that confuses Dr. Kircher. This is probably due to the fact that he is not paying attention and is looking in the wrong direction, directly into the eyes of the boy.

The boy has climbed onto the balladeer's wagon. There he stands, elevated above everyone, on the edge of the wagon, and it's strange that he doesn't fall. How is he keeping his balance up there? Dr. Kircher can't help smiling tensely. The boy doesn't smile back. Involuntarily Dr. Kircher wonders whether the child too has been touched by Satan, yet in the interrogation there was no sign of it. The wife wept a great deal, the boy was withdrawn into himself, but both of them said everything that was necessary. All at once Dr. Kircher is no longer certain. Were they too careless? The feints of the Lord of the Air are manifold. What if the miller is not the worst warlock at all? Dr. Kircher feels a suspicion stirring in him.

"Did you do it?" Dr. Tesimond asks once again.

The executioner backs away. All listen attentively, stand on tiptoe, lift their heads. Even the wind subsides for a moment as Claus Ulenspiegel draws a breath to finally answer.

III

He didn't know such good food existed. Never in his life has he encountered anything like it: first a hearty chicken soup with freshly baked wheat bread, then a leg of lamb, spiced with salt and even pepper, then the loin of a fat pig with sauce, finally sweet cherry cake, still warm from the oven, with a strong red wine rising like fog to his head. They must have brought a cook from somewhere. As Claus eats at his small table in the cowshed and feels his stomach filling up with warm, fine things, he thinks that a meal like this is ultimately even worth dying for.

He believed the hangman's meal was only a figure of speech, never suspecting that a cook was actually called to prepare you food better than any you'd had in your whole life. With your arms chained together it's hard to hold the meat, the iron chafes, your wrists are sore, but at the moment it doesn't matter, so good does it taste. And on the whole his hands no longer hurt as much as a week ago. Master Tilman is also a master of healing; Claus has to admit without envy that the executioner knows herbs he has never heard of. Nonetheless, the feeling hasn't returned to his crushed fingers, and so the meat keeps falling to the ground. He closes his eyes. He hears the chickens scratching in the coop next door, he hears the snoring of the man with the expensive clothing who wanted to be his advocate and is now lying chained up in the straw. As he chews the wonderful pork, he tries to conceive of the fact that he will never learn the outcome of this man's trial.

For he will be dead by then. Nor will he learn what the

weather will be like the day after tomorrow. He will be dead by then. Or whether it will rain again tomorrow night. But it doesn't matter anyway, who cares about the rain.

Only it really is odd: Now you're still sitting here and can rattle off all the numbers between one and a thousand, but the day after tomorrow you will be either an ethereal being or else a soul that returns to the world in a person or animal and hardly remembers the miller you still are—but when you are some weasel or a chicken or a sparrow on a branch and don't even know that you were once a miller who concerned himself with the heavenly course of the moon, indeed, when you are hopping from branch to branch and thinking only about seeds and of course the buzzards you have to escape, what meaning does it actually still have that you were formerly a miller whom you have now completely forgotten?

He remembers that Master Tilman told him he could have more at any time. Just call, let me know, you can have as much as you want, because afterward there won't be anything else.

So Claus tries it. He calls. He calls while chewing, for he still has meat on his plate, and there's still cake too, but when you can have more, why wait until everything is gone and until the people outside might change their minds? He calls again, and the door really does open.

"Can I have more?"

"Of everything?"

"Of everything please."

Master Tilman walks out silently, and Claus tucks into the cake. And while he is chewing up the warm, soft, sweet mass, it suddenly becomes clear to him that he has always been hungry: day and night, evening and morning. Only he no longer knew it was hunger—that feeling of dissatisfaction, the hollowness in everything, the never-abating weakness of the body, which makes the knees and the hands limp and confuses the head. It wasn't necessary, it didn't have to be like that, it was just hunger!

The door opens with a creak, and Master Tilman carries in a tray with bowls. Claus sighs with pleasure. Master Tilman, misunderstanding the sigh, sets down the tray and puts his hand on his shoulder.

"It will be all right," he says.

"I know," says Claus.

"It happens very quickly. I can do that. I promise you."

"Thank you," says Claus.

"Sometimes the condemned anger me. Then it doesn't happen quickly. Believe me. But you haven't angered me."

Claus nods gratefully.

"These are better days. In the past you were all burned to death. That takes time, it's not pleasant. But hanging is nothing. It happens quickly. You climb onto the scaffold and before you know it, you're standing before the Creator. You're incinerated afterward, but by then you're dead, it doesn't bother you at all, you'll see."

"Good," says Claus.

The two of them look at each other. Master Tilman seems not to want to go. You might think he liked it in the shed.

"You're not a bad fellow," says Master Tilman.

"Thank you."

"For a servant of the devil."

Claus shrugs.

Master Tilman walks out and laboriously bolts the door.

Claus continues to eat. Again he tries to imagine it: the houses out there, the birds in the sky, the clouds, the brownish green ground with grass and fields and all the molehills in spring, for you'll never get rid of the moles, not with any herb or spell, and the rain, of course—all this going on without him.

Only he can't imagine it.

For whenever he pictures a world without Claus Ulenspiegel, his imagination smuggles back in the very Claus Ulenspiegel it is meant to remove—as an invisible man, an eye without a body, a ghost. But when he really thinks himself utterly away, then the world he would like to imagine without Claus Ulenspiegel vanishes with him. However often he tries it, it's always the same thing. May he conclude from this that he is safe? For he cannot be gone at all, because the world ultimately must not vanish and because without him it would have to vanish?

The pork still tastes wonderful, but, he notices now, Master Tilman didn't bring more cake, and because the cake was the best of all, Claus gives it a try and calls once again.

The executioner comes in.

"Can I have more cake?"

Master Tilman doesn't reply and goes out. Claus chews the pork. Now that his hunger is sated, he realizes all the more how good it tastes, how fine and rich, how warm and salty, and a bit sweet too. He contemplates the wall of the shed. If you paint a square on it shortly before midnight and also draw two double circles with some blood on the ground and invoke three times the third of the secret names of the Almighty, then a door will appear, and you can slip away. The only problem would be the chains, for to cast them off you would need horsetail extract; and so he would have to flee in chains and find horsetail on the way, but Claus is tired, and his body hurts, and it's also not the season for horsetail.

And it's difficult to begin anew elsewhere. In the past it would have been possible, but now he is older and no longer has the strength to be a dishonorable traveling journeyman again, a despised day laborer on the outskirts of some village, a stranger shunned by everyone. You couldn't even work as a healer, because that would attract attention.

No, it's easier to be hanged. And if it should be that after death you can remember what was before, then this could advance your knowledge of the world further than any ten years of research and exploration. Perhaps afterward he will understand the principles behind the course of the moon, perhaps also grasp at which grain a heap ceases to be a heap, possibly even see what distinguishes two leaves between which there's no difference but the fact that they are indeed two and not one. Perhaps it's due to the wine and the warm comfort enveloping Claus for the first time in his life—whatever the reason, he no longer wants out. Let the wall stay where it is.

The door is unbolted. Master Tilman brings cake. "But that's it now, I'm not coming again." He pats Claus on the shoulder. He likes to do that, probably because he is forbidden ever to touch people outside. Then he yawns, walks out, and slams the door so loudly that the sleeping man wakes up.

He sits up, stretches, and looks around in all directions. "Where's the old woman?"

"In a different shed," says Claus. "Fortunately. She moans incessantly, it's unbearable."

"Give me wine!"

Claus looks at him in fright. He wants to reply that this is his wine, all his alone, that he has honestly earned it, for he must die for it. But then he feels sorry for the man, who doesn't have it easy either, after all, and so he passes him the jug. The man grabs it and takes big gulps. Stop, Claus wants to cry, I won't get any more! Yet he cannot bring himself to do it, for this is a man of rank; you don't give someone like that commands. The wine runs down his chin and makes stains on his velvet collar, but it doesn't seem to trouble him, so thirsty is he.

Finally he puts down the jug and says: "My God, that's good wine!"

"Yes, yes," says Claus, "very good." He fervently hopes that the man doesn't want the cake too.

"Now that no one can hear us, tell me the truth. Were you in league with the devil?"

"I don't know, sir."

"How can someone not know that?"

Claus reflects. It's obvious that he did something wrong in his stupid head, or else he wouldn't be here. But he doesn't really know what it was. He was interrogated for so long, again and again, in so much pain, he had to retell his story so many times, each time something else was missing, he always had to add something, another demon that had to be described, another conjuration, another dark book, another Sabbath, so that Master Tilman would let him be, and then he had to retell these new details too again and again, so that he no longer really knows what he had to make up and what actually happened in his short life, where there had not been much order anyhow: now he was here, now there, then somewhere else, and then he was suddenly in the flour dust, and his wife was dissatisfied, and the mill hands had no respect, and now he is in chains, and that was everything already. Just as the cake is about to be finished—three or four more bites, perhaps five, if he has only very little each time.

"I don't know," he says again.

"Damned misfortune," the man says, looking at the cake.

In fright Claus takes all that's left and swallows it without chewing. The cake filling his throat, he swallows as hard as he can: it's gone. So that was it with food. Forever.

"Sir," says Claus, to show that he knows what is proper. "What's going to happen to you now?"

"Hard to predict. Once you're in, it's not easy to get out. They will bring me to the city, then they will interrogate me. I will have to confess something." With a sigh, he gazes at his hands. He is obviously thinking of the executioner; everyone knows that he always starts with the fingers.

"Sir," Claus says again. "If you imagine a heap of grain."

"What?"

"You keep taking one away and putting it to the side."

"What?"

"Always just one. When is it no longer a heap?"

"After twelve thousand grains."

Claus rubs his forehead. His chains rattle. He feels the imprint of the leather band on his forehead. It was hellish agony, he still remembers every second he howled and begged, but Master Tilman loosened it only when he invented and described another Witches' Sabbath. "Twelve thousand exactly?"

"Naturally," says the man. "Do you think I can get a meal like that too? There must be something left. This is all a great injustice. I shouldn't be here. I only wanted to defend you to write about it in my book. I finished the study of crystals. Now I wanted to take up law. But my situation has nothing to do with you. Perhaps you are in league with the devil, what do I know, perhaps you really are! Perhaps you're not." He is silent for a short time. Then he calls Master Tilman in an imperious tone.

This won't go well, thinks Claus, who knows the executioner fairly well by now. He sighs. Now he would like to have some more wine to keep the sadness from returning, but he was clearly told there was no more.

The door is unbolted. Master Tilman looks in.

"Bring me some of this meat," the man says without looking at him. "And wine. The jug is empty."

"Will you be dead tomorrow too?" asks Master Tilman.

"This is a misunderstanding," the man says hoarsely, acting as if he were speaking to Claus, for it's better even to talk to a condemned warlock than to an executioner. "And it's a nasty affront too, for which some people are going to pay."

"If you will be alive tomorrow, you don't get a hangman's meal," says Master Tilman. He puts his hand on Claus's shoulder. "Listen," he says softly. "When you're standing under the gallows tomorrow—don't forget that you have to forgive everyone."

Claus nods.

"The judges," says Master Tilman. "And you have to forgive me too."

Claus closes his eyes. He still feels the wine—a warm, soft dizziness.

"Loud and clear," says Master Tilman.

Claus sighs.

"It is proper," says Master Tilman. "It is what's done: the condemned forgives his hangman loud and clear so that everyone can hear. You know that?"

Claus can't help thinking of his wife. Earlier Agneta was there and talked to him through the cracks between the wall boards. She was so sorry, she whispered. She had no choice but to say what they demanded of her. Could he forgive her?

Of course, he replied. He forgave everything. But he kept to himself that it was not quite clear to him what she was even talking about. There was nothing to be done about it; since his interrogations, his mind was no longer as reliable as it used to be.

Then she wept again and spoke of her hard life and also of the boy, who worried her, and she didn't know what to do with him.

Claus was happy to hear about the boy, because he hadn't thought about him for a long time, and at bottom he really was fond of him. But there was something odd about him, it was hard to explain, the boy seemed not to be made of the same stuff as other people.

"You have it easy," she said. "You don't have to trouble your head about anything anymore. But I can't stay here in the village. They won't let me. And I've never been anywhere else—what am I supposed to do?"

"Yes, certainly," he replied, still thinking about the boy. "That's true."

"Maybe I could go to my family in Pfünz."

"You have family in Pfünz?"

"The wife of my uncle's nephew. Franz Melker's cousin. You didn't know my uncle; he died when I was a child. But before he died, he said he heard that she is now in Pfünz. Maybe it's true. Where else am I supposed to go?"

"I don't know."

"But what about the boy? Maybe she'll help me, if she remembers, who knows. If she's still alive. But two hungry people at the same time? That's too many."

"Yes, that's too many."

"Maybe I can get the boy work as a day laborer. He's small and not a good worker, but it might be possible. What else am I supposed to do? I'm not allowed to stay here."

"No, you're not allowed."

"You stupid creature, you have it easy now. But just tell me, should I go looking for her? Maybe it wasn't Pfünz at all. You always know everything, tell me, what do I do?"

Fortunately, at that moment the hangman's meal came, and Agneta withdrew so that the executioner wouldn't see her, for no one is permitted to talk to a condemned man. And then the wine and food were so good that the sobbing had completely passed from his mind.

"Miller!" Master Tilman shouts. "Are you listening to me?"

"Yes, yes."

Master Tilman's hand is lying heavily on his shoulder. "You have to say it loud tomorrow! That you forgive me! Do you hear? In front of everyone, did you hear? It's what's done!"

Claus wants to reply, but his mind keeps wandering, especially now that he finds himself thinking about the boy once again. Recently he saw him juggling. It was between two interrogations, in the empty time in which the world consists of nothing but throbbing pain—he looked through the cracks and saw his son passing by and making stones whirl above him as if they had no weight, as if it were happening of its own accord. Claus called his name to warn him. Someone who can do something like that must be careful; for that too you can be accused of witchcraft. But the boy didn't hear him—perhaps also because Claus's voice was too weak. That is now always the case, he can't help it, it's due to the interrogation.

"Listen," says Master Tilman. "You will not summon me to the Valley of Josaphat!"

"The curse of a dying man is the most powerful," says the man in the straw. "It clings to the soul, you can never get rid of it."

"You won't do that, miller, curse the executioner, you won't do that to me, will you?"

"No," says Claus. "I won't."

"You might think it doesn't matter. You're going to hang anyway, you think, but I'm the one who stands with you on the ladder, and I'm the one who puts on the noose, and I have to pull on your legs so that your neck breaks, or else it will take a long time!"

"That's true," says the man in the straw.

"You won't summon me to the Valley of Josaphat? You won't curse me, you'll forgive the hangman, as is proper?"

"Yes, I will," says Claus.

Master Tilman takes his hand off his shoulder and gives him a friendly pat. "I don't care if you forgive the judges. That's not my concern. You can handle that as you please."

Suddenly Claus can't help smiling. It must still be due to the wine, but it's also because he realized that he can now finally try out the great Key of Solomon. There has never been an opportunity for it. He learned the many long sentences from old Hüttner. At the time it came easily to him. Probably he could still find them in his memory. They will see when he is standing on the ladder tomorrow and all at once the chains break as if they were made of paper. They will goggle when he spreads his arms and rises and hovers in the air above their stupid faces—above that idiotic Peter Steger and his even stupider wife and his relatives and children and grandparents, each one stupider than the next, above the Melkers and the Henrichs and the Holtzes and the Tamms and all the others. How they will goggle when he doesn't fall but rises and keeps rising, how their mouths will hang open. For a brief time he sees them shrinking, then they are dots, and then the village itself is a spot in the middle of the dark green forest, and when he lifts his head he will see the white velvet of the clouds and their inhabitants, some with wings, some made of white fire, some with two or three heads, and there he is, the Prince of the Air, the King of the Spirits and Flames. Have mercy, my great devil, take me into your realm, set me free, and now Claus hears him reply: See my land. See how vast it is, and see how far below. Fly with me.

Claus laughs out loud. For a moment he sees mice swarming around his feet, some with the tails of snakes, others with the feelers of caterpillars, and it seems to him as if he felt their bites, but the pain is prickly and almost pleasant, and then he sees himself flying again, so light am I when my Lord permits it. All you have to do is remember the words. None may be wrong, none missing, or else the Key of Solomon will not unlock, or else it is in vain. If you find the words, however, everything will fall away from you, the heavy chains, the distress, the miller's existence of cold and hunger.

"That's due to the wine," says Master Tilman.

"I won't be imprisoned for long," the man says without looking at him. "Tesimond will be sorry."

"He said he'll forgive me," says Master Tilman. "He said he won't curse me."

"Don't talk to me!"

"Say whether you heard it," says Master Tilman. "Or I'll hurt you. Did he say it?"

Both of them look at the miller. He has closed his eyes and leaned his head against the wall, and he won't stop giggling.

"Yes," says the man. "He said it."

IV

Nele noticed at the very outset that he was not good. But only now, hearing Gottfried perform the song about the devilish miller in front of the crowd in the market town, does it become clear to her that they have stumbled on the worst balladeer of all.

He sings much too high, and sometimes he clears his throat in the middle of a line. When he speaks, his voice still sounds all right, yet when he sings, it cracks and squeaks. The voice by itself would not be bad if he could only carry a tune. Just as the poor singing would not be so bad if he could at least play the lute—Gottfried incessantly plays the wrong notes, and sometimes he forgets how the rest of the song goes. But even this would not be so unbearable if only his verses were better. They tell of the wicked miller and the village he had under his thumb, of his witcheries and tricks, yet although they are as rich in grisly stories and bloody details as people expect, they are jumbled and hard to understand, and the rhymes are so awkward that it must bother even a child.

Still, the people listen. Balladeers don't come often, and people want to hear ballads about witch trials even when they're terrible. But after four verses Nele can see that their expressions are changing, and by the time he has arrived at the twelfth and last, many have left. Now there's an urgent need for something that will go over better. This much he must know, thinks Nele, this much he must be able to sense!

Gottfried starts the song from the beginning.

He notices the restlessness in the people's faces, and in his desperation he sings louder, which makes his voice even shriller. Nele looks over at Tyll. He rolls his eyes. Then he spreads his arms in a resigned gesture. Light-footedly he leaps beside the singer and begins to dance on the wagon.

The improvement is immediate. Gottfried is singing as badly as before, but suddenly it no longer matters. Tyll is dancing as if he had been trained, he is dancing as if his body had no weight and as if there were no greater pleasure. He leaps and spins and leaps again as if he hadn't just lost everything, and it's so infectious that a few members of the audience and then another few and then more and more begin to dance too. Now coins are flying over. Nele gathers them up.

Gottfried sees it too, and in his relief he now manages better to keep the rhythm; Tyll is dancing with such abandon and such light determination that watching him Nele could almost forget that the song is about his father. *Miller* is rhymed with *dealer*, *devil* with *shovel*, *fire* with *fear*, and *night* with *night*, for this word is constantly repeated: dark night, black night, Witches' Night. From the fifth verse on it's about the trial: the stern and virtuous judges, God's mercy, the punishment that in the end befalls every evildoer, despite all Satan's maneuvers, under the eyes of his accusers, and the gallows on which the wicked miller must breathe his last, while the devil stands aghast. Tyll doesn't stop dancing during all this, for they need the coins, they have to eat.

It still seems like a dream to her. That this village is not her village, that people live here whose faces she doesn't know, and there are houses in which she has never been. Who could have foreseen that she would ever leave her home? It was not in store for her, and she half expects that in a moment she will wake up at home, next to the large oven, from which the bread's warmth wafts. Girls don't go to other places. They stay where they were born. So it has always been: you're little, you help in the house; you get bigger, you help the female hands; you grow up and marry a Steger son, if you're pretty, or else a relative of the smith or, if things go badly, a Heinerling. Then you have a child and another child and more children, most of whom die, and you continue to help the hands and in church sit somewhat farther toward the front, next to your husband and behind your mother-in-law, and then, when you're forty and your bones ache and your teeth are gone, you sit in your mother-in-law's old seat.

Because she didn't want that, she went with Tyll.

How many days ago was it now? She couldn't say; in the forest time is muddled. But she remembers well how Tyll stood before her, the evening after the trial, thin and somewhat lopsided, in the billowing grain of the Steger meadow.

"What's going to happen to you now?" she asked.

"My mother says I have to become a day laborer. She says it will be hard because I'm too small and weak to be a good worker."

"And that's what you'll do?"

"No, I'm going."

"Where?"

"Far away."

"When?"

"Now. One of the Jesuits, the younger one, was staring at me so."

"But you can't just go away!"

"Yes, I can."

"And if they catch you? You're alone, and they are many."

"But I have two feet, and a judge with a robe or a guard with halberds, they also have only two. Each of them has the same number of feet as I do. No one has more. They can't run faster together than we can."

Suddenly she felt a wondrous excitement, and her throat seemed constricted, and her heart pounded. "Why do you say *we*?"

"Because you're coming with me."

"With you?"

"That's why I was waiting."

She knew that she must not think, or else she would lose her courage, or else she would stay here, as was in store for her; but he was right, you really could leave. The place where everyone thought you had to stay—in actuality nothing was keeping you there.

"Now go home," he said, "and fetch as much bread as you can carry."

"No!"

"You're not coming with me?"

"Yes, I am coming with you, but I'm not going home first."

"But the bread!"

"If I see my father and Mama and the oven and my sister, then I won't leave anymore, then I'll stay!"

"We need bread."

She shook her head. And it's true, she thinks now, while she collects coins on the market square of a strange village—if she had gone to the bakery again, she would have stayed and soon would have married the Steger son, the middle one, whose two front teeth are missing. There are only a few moments when two things are possible, one path as much as another. Only a few moments when you can decide.

"Without bread we can't go," he said. "We should also wait until morning. The forest at night, you don't know what it's like. You've never experienced it."

"Are you afraid of the Cold Woman?"

Now she knew that she had won.

"I'm not afraid," he said.

"Well, then let's go!"

She will never forget that night for the rest of her life, never forget the giggling will-o'-the-wisps, the voices out of the blackness, never forget the animal noises or the sparkling face that appeared in front of her for a moment, only to vanish again before she was even certain that she had seen it at all. For the rest of her life she will think of the fear, her heart in her mouth, the blood pounding in her ears, and the whimpering murmur of the boy in front of her, who was talking either to himself or to the beings of the forest. When morning came, they found themselves trembling with cold at the edge of a loamy clearing. The dew was dripping from the trees. They were hungry.

"You really should have fetched bread."

"I could bash you in the face."

As they walked onward, in the clammy morning air, Tyll wept a little, and Nele felt like sobbing too. Her legs were heavy, the hunger was hardly bearable, and Tyll was right, without bread they would surely die. Yes, there were berries and roots, and even the grass should be edible, but that was not enough, it didn't fill your stomach. In the summer it might do, but not in this cold.

And now they heard behind them the rumble and squeal of

a carriage. They hid in the bushes until they saw that it was only the balladeer's wagon. Tyll jumped out and stood in the middle of the road.

"Oh," said the singer. "The miller's son!"

"Take us with you?"

"Why?"

"Because we'll die if you don't, for one thing. But also because we'll help you. Don't you want company?"

"They're probably already searching for you," said the singer.

"Yet another reason. Or do you maybe want me to get caught?"

"Climb on."

Gottfried explained the essentials to them: If you ride with a balladeer, you belong to the traveling people. No guild protects you, no authorities. If you're in a city and there's a fire, you have to slip away, for people will think you started it. If you're in a village and something is stolen, slip away then too. If you're ambushed by robbers, give them everything. Most of the time, however, they don't take anything but demand a song—then sing for them, as well as you can, for robbers often dance better than the dullards in the villages. Always keep your ears open, so that you know where it's market day, for when it's not market day they won't let you into the villages. At a market people come together, they want to dance, they want to hear songs, they part with their money easily.

"Is my father dead?"

"Yes, he is dead."

"Did you see?"

"Of course I saw it, that's why I was there. First he forgave the judges, as is proper, then the hangman, then he climbed onto the ladder, then the noose was put around his neck, and then he began to murmur, but I was standing too far back, I couldn't understand him."

"And then?"

"It went the way it goes."

"So he is dead?"

"My boy, when someone is hanging from the gallows, what else is supposed to happen? Of course he's dead! What do you think?"

"Did it go quickly?"

Gottfried was silent for a while before he answered: "Yes, very quickly."

For some time they rode without speaking. The trees were no longer so dense; rays of light fell through the canopy of leaves. A fine haze rose from the grass of the clearings. The air was filled with insects and birds.

"How do you become a singer?" Nele finally asked.

"You train. I had a master. He taught me everything. You've heard of him, it's Gerhard Vogtland."

"No."

"The one from Trier!"

The boy shrugged.

"The Great Litany of the Campaign of Duke Ernest Against the Treacherous Sultan."

"What?"

"That's his most famous song: The Great Litany of the Campaign of Duke Ernest Against the Treacherous Sultan. You really don't know it? Shall I sing it?"

Nele nodded, and so they became acquainted for the first time with Gottfried's paltry talent. "The Great Litany of the Campaign of Duke Ernest Against the Treacherous Sultan" had thirty-three verses, and although Gottfried could do little else, he did have an outstanding memory and had forgotten not a single one.

Thus they traveled for a long time. The singer sang, the horse grunted from time to time, and the wheels rumbled and squealed as if they were carrying on a conversation with each other. Nele saw out of the corner of her eye that tears were running down the boy's face. He had turned his head away so that no one would notice.

When Gottfried was finished with his song, he started from the beginning. Next he sang them a ballad about the handsome Elector Friedrich and the Bohemian estates, next he sang about the evil dragon Kufer and the knight Robert, next about the wicked king in France and the great king in Spain, his enemy. Then he told stories from his life. His father was an executioner, so he was supposed to become an executioner too. But he ran away.

"Like us," said Nele.

"Many people do it, more than you think! It is part of an upstanding life to stay put, but the land is full of people who didn't stay put. They have no protection, but they are free. They don't have to string anyone up. They don't have to kill anyone."

"Don't have to marry the Steger son," said Nele.

"Don't have to be day laborers," said the boy.

They heard how Gottfried had fared in earlier days with his master. Vogtland had often struck him and kicked him and once even bit him in the ear because he didn't hit the right notes and could also hardly play the lute with his thick fingers. Poor idiot, Vogtland exclaimed, didn't want to be a hangman, now you torture people ten times over with your music! But then

Vogtland didn't drive him away after all, and so he improved more and more, Gottfried said proudly, until he himself finally became a master. He discovered, however, that people want to hear about executions, everywhere, all the time. No one is indifferent to executions.

"I know all there is to know about executions. How to hold the sword, how to position the knot, how to stack a pyre, and the best place to apply the hot tongs—I know everything about that. Other singers might have smoother rhymes, but I can tell which hangman knows his trade and which doesn't, and my ballads are the most accurate."

When it grew dark, they lit a fire. Gottfried shared his provisions with them: dry flatbread, which Nele immediately recognized as having been made by her father. Her eyes briefly welled up with tears too, for at the sight of this bread with the cross pressed into the middle and the crumbling edges it became clear to her that she was in the same situation as the boy. He would never see his father again because he was dead, but she wouldn't see hers either, because she couldn't go back. Both of them were now orphans. But the moment passed. She stared into the fire and all at once felt as free as if she could fly.

The second night in the forest was not as bad as the first. They were now used to the sounds; besides, warmth emanated from the embers, and the singer had given them a blanket. As she was falling asleep, she noticed that Tyll was still awake next to her. He was so wakeful, so attentive, he was thinking so hard that she could feel it. She didn't dare turn her head in his direction.

"Someone who carries fire," he said softly.

She didn't know whether he was talking to her. "Are you ill?"

He seemed to have a fever. She snuggled up to him. Waves of warmth radiated from him, which was pleasant and kept her from freezing so. Thus she fell asleep after a short time and dreamed of a battlefield and thousands of people marching over a hilly landscape, and then the cannons began to hammer. When she woke up, it was morning, and it was raining again.

The singer was sitting hunched under his blanket, a small writing calendar in one hand and the pencil in the other. He wrote in tiny signs, almost illegibly, for he had only this calendar, and paper was expensive.

"Versifying is the hardest," he said. "Do you know a word that rhymes with *rogue*?"

But finally he did finish the song of the evil miller, and now they are in the market town, while Gottfried sings and Tyll dances to it, with such lightness and elegance that it surprises even Nele.

Other wagons are standing here too. On the opposite side of the square is the wagon of a cloth merchant, next to two scissors grinders, next to a fruit merchant, a kettle mender, another scissors grinder, a healer who is in possession of theriac, which can cure any illness, another fruit merchant, a spice merchant, another healer who unfortunately has no theriac and hence is left empty-handed, a fourth scissors grinder, and a barber. All these people are in the traveling trades. Anyone who robs or kills them is not prosecuted. That is the price of freedom.

At the edge of the square are another few dubious figures. These are the dishonest people, including musicians with fife, bagpipes, and fiddle. They stand far away, yet it seems to Nele as if they were grinning across at her and whispering jokes about Gottfried to each other. Next to them sits a storyteller. You can recognize him by the yellow hat and the blue jerkin and by the sign around his neck on which something is written in big letters that must mean "storyteller," for only storytellers have signs—senseless though it is, since his audience consists of people who cannot read. You can recognize musicians by their instruments and merchants by their wares, but to recognize a storyteller all it takes is a sign. And then there's also a man of small stature in the widely recognizable clothing of traveling entertainers: motley jerkin, puffed breeches, fur collar. With a thin smile he too looks across, something worse than mockery is in it, and when he notices that Nele is looking at him, he raises an eyebrow, shows his tongue in the corner of his mouth, and winks.

Gottfried has reached the twelfth verse for the second time, he concludes his ballad for the second time, considers for a moment, and then starts again from the beginning. Tyll gives Nele a sign. She stands up. She has danced before, of course—at the village festivals, when musicians came and the young people jumped over the fire, and often she also danced with the female hands, just like that, without music, during breaks from work. But she has never done it in front of an audience.

Yet as she spins first in one direction and then in the other, she realizes that it doesn't make a difference. She only has to follow Tyll. Whenever the boy claps his hands, she claps too, when he raises his right foot, she raises her right foot, and the left when he raises the left, at first with a slight delay, but soon simultaneously, as if she knew beforehand what he was going to do, as if they were not two people but in dancing became one—and now all at once he pitches forward and dances on his hands, and she spins around him, again and again and again, so that the village square turns into a smear of colors. Dizziness rises in her, but she fights against it and keeps her gaze directed into empty space, it's getting better already, and she can keep her balance without teetering while she spins.

For a moment she is confused when the music swells and the tones grow richer, but then she realizes that the musicians have joined in. Playing their instruments, they approach, and Gottfried, who cannot keep their rhythm, helplessly lowers the lute, so that now finally everything sounds right. The people applaud. Coins leap over the wood of the wagon. Tyll is again standing on his feet. Nele stops spinning, suppresses her dizziness, and watches as he knots a rope—where did he get it from so quickly?—to the wagon and then casts it from him so that it unwinds. Someone catches it, she can't tell who it is because everything is still swaying, someone has fastened it, and now Tyll is standing on the rope and jumping forward and back and bowing, and more coins are flying, and Gottfried can hardly pick them up fast enough. Finally Tyll jumps down and takes her hand, the musicians play a fanfare, the two of them bow, and the people clap and howl. The fruit merchant throws them apples. She catches one and bites into it. She hasn't eaten an apple in an eternity. Next to her Tyll catches one too and another and another and then another and juggles them. Again a cheer goes through the crowd.

When evening falls, they are sitting on the ground and listening to the storyteller. He is speaking of poor King Friedrich of Prague, whose reign lasted only a winter, before the Kaiser's mighty army drove him out. Now the proud city has been laid low and will never recover. He speaks in long sentences in a liltingly beautiful melody, without moving his hands; with his voice alone he ensures that you won't look elsewhere. All this is true, he says, even what has been made up is true. And Nele, without understanding what that's supposed to mean, claps.

Gottfried scrawls in his calendar. He didn't know, he mutters, that Friedrich was deposed again already; now he has to rewrite his song about him.

On Nele's right the fiddler tunes his instrument with his eyes closed in concentration. Now we belong here, she thinks. Now we are among the traveling people.

Someone taps her on the shoulder. She wheels around.

Behind her crouches the traveling entertainer who winked at her earlier. He's no longer so young, and his face is very red. Heinrich Tamm had such a red face shortly before he died. Even his eyes are shot through with red. But they are also sharp and alert and shrewd and unkind.

"You two," he says softly.

Now the boy too turns around.

"Do you want to come with me?"

"Yes," the boy says without hesitation.

Nele stares at him uncomprehendingly. Didn't they want to travel with Gottfried, who is good to them, gives them food, led them out of the forest? Gottfried, who could really use the two of them?

"I can really use two people like you," the entertainer says. "You could use someone like me. I'll teach you everything."

"But we're with him." Nele points to Gottfried, whose lips are moving as he writes in his little book. The pencil in his hand breaks. He curses softly, keeps scrawling.

"Then you won't go far," says the entertainer.

"We don't know you," says Nele.

"I am Pirmin," says the entertainer. "Now you know me."

"My name is Tyll. This is Nele."

"I won't ask again. If you're not sure, never mind. Then I'll be gone. Then you can go on with him."

"We're coming with you," says the boy.

Pirmin extends his hand. Tyll grasps it. Pirmin chuckles, his lips twisting, his thick, moist tongue again becoming visible in the corner of his mouth. Nele is loath to travel with him.

Now he extends his hand to her.

She doesn't move. Behind her the storyteller is speaking of the flight of the Winter King from the burning city—now he is a burden to Europe's Protestant princes, roams the land with his silly court, still wears purple as if he were one of the great, but the children laugh at him, and the wise men shed tears because they see in him the frailty of all greatness.

Now Gottfried too has noticed it. With a furrowed brow he looks at the fool's extended hand.

"Come on," says the boy. "Shake his hand."

But why should she do what Tyll says? Did she run away in order to obey him instead of her father? What does she owe him, why should he be in charge?

"What's wrong?" asks Gottfried. "What's going on here, what is this?"

Pirmin's hand is still extended. His grin too is unchanging, as if her hesitation didn't mean anything, as if he had long known what she will decide.

"Well, what's this all about?" Gottfried asks again.

The hand is fleshy and soft. Nele doesn't want to touch it. It's true, of course, that Gottfried can't do much. But he has been good to them. And she doesn't like this fellow. There is something not right about him. On the other hand, it's true, of course: Gottfried will not be able to teach them anything.

On the one hand, on the other hand. Pirmin winks as if he were reading her thoughts.

Tyll jerks his head impatiently. "Come on, Nele!"

She need only extend her arm.

Zusmarshausen

HE COULD NOT HAVE KNOWN, OF COURSE, THE FAT COUNT wrote in his life's chronicle, penned in the early years of the eighteenth century, when he was already an old man, plagued by gout, syphilis, and the quicksilver poisoning that the treatment of the syphilis brought him—he could not have known, of course, what awaited him when His Majesty dispatched him in the final year of the war to find the famous jester.

At that time Martin von Wolkenstein was not yet twenty-five but already corpulent. As a descendant of the minnesinger Oswald, he had grown up at the Viennese court. His father had once been chief chamberlain under Kaiser Matthias, his grandfather second key bearer of the mad Rudolf. Whoever knew Martin von Wolkenstein liked him; there was something bright surrounding him, a confidence and a friendliness that never failed him, even in the face of adversity. The Kaiser himself had shown him his favor several times, and he had also understood it as a show of favor when Count Trauttmansdorff, the President of the Privy Council, had summoned him and informed him that the Kaiser had heard that the most famous jester in the Empire had found refuge in the half-destroyed Abbey of Andechs. They had seen so much go to ruin, had been forced to allow so much destruction, invaluable things had been lost, but that someone like Tyll Ulenspiegel should simply waste away, whether Protestant or Catholic—for what he actually was, no one seemed to know—that was out of the question.

"I congratulate you, young man," said Trauttmansdorff. "Take advantage of the occasion, who knows what could come of it."

Then, as the fat count described it more than fifty years later, he had held out his gloved hand to him for the kiss that was at the time still prescribed by court ceremony—and that was exactly how it had been, he had made up none of it, even though he gladly made things up when there were gaps in his memory, and there were a lot of those, for all this was, by the time he was writing it down, a lifetime ago.

The very next day we ventured forth, he wrote. I rode in good spirits and full of hope, yet not without melancholy, because, for reasons that even now remain obscure unto my understanding, I could not look upon the path before me as one foreordained, eager though I was to behold the undisguised countenance of the red god Mars.

It was not true about the haste; in actuality more than a week had passed. After all, he had still had to write letters conveying his plans, had to say his goodbyes, visit his parents, be blessed by the bishop; he had to drink with his friends once more, had to call once more on his favorite among the court prostitutes, the dainty Aglaia, whom he still remembered decades later with a remorse he himself could not fathom; and of course he had to select the right companions. He chose three battle-tested men from the Lobkowitz dragoon regiment along with a secretary of the Imperial Court Council, Karl von Doder, who had seen the famous jester twenty years earlier at a market near Neulengbach, where the man, as was his way, played a very dirty trick on a woman in the audience and afterward provoked a bad knife fight, to the delight, naturally, of those who were not affected by it, for so it always was when he appeared: Some fared badly, but those who got away enjoyed themselves immensely. At first the secretary didn't want to come with him. He argued and begged and pleaded and cited an unconquerable abhorrence of violence and of bad weather, but all to no avail. An order was an order; he had to do as he was told. Slightly over a week after the mission was assigned, the fat count thus set off westward with his dragoons and the secretary from the capital city and imperial residence of Vienna.

In his life's chronicle, the style of which was still beholden to the fashionable tone of his youthful days, that is, of erudite arabesque and florid ornamentation, the fat count depicted in sentences that, precisely due to their exemplary tortuousness, have since found their way into many a schoolbook, the leisurely ride through the green of the Vienna Woods: At Melk we reached the wide blue of the Danube, alighting there at the magnificent abbey to pillow our weary heads for the night.

Once again this was not entirely true; in reality they stayed for a month. His uncle was the prior, and so they ate splendidly and slept well. Karl von Doder, who had always been interested in alchemy, spent many days in the library, absorbed in a book by the sage Athanasius Kircher, the dragoons played cards with the lay brothers, and with his uncle the fat count completed several chess games of such sublime perfection as he would never again attain; it almost seemed to him later as if his subsequent experiences stifled his gift for playing chess. Only during the fourth week of their stay did a letter find him, sent by Count Trauttmansdorff, who believed him to be already at the destination and asked whether they had found Ulenspiegel in Andechs and when their return was to be expected.

His uncle blessed him in parting. The abbot gave him a vial of consecrated oil. They followed the course of the Danube to Pöchlarn, thence turning southwest.

At the beginning of their journey they encountered a steady stream of merchants, vagabonds, monks, and travelers of all sorts. But now the land seemed empty. Even the weather was no longer congenial. Cold winds blew, trees spread bare limbs, almost all the fields lay fallow. The few people they saw were old: hunched women at wells, old men who crouched haggard outside huts, hollow-cheeked faces on the roadside. Nothing indicated whether these people were only resting or rather waiting for their end.

When the fat count spoke to Karl von Doder about it, he only wanted to talk about the book he had been studying in the abbey library, *Ars magna lucis et umbrae*. You became quite dizzy, you gazed, so to speak, into an abyss of erudition—and no, he had no idea where the younger people were, but if he might venture to surmise, then anyone who could still run had long since run away. But that book expatiated upon lenses and how one could magnify things and moreover upon angels, their form, their color, and upon music and the harmonies of the spheres, and finally upon Egypt too—by God, it was a very peculiar work.

The fat count used this sentence verbatim in his account. But because things became confused for him, he claimed there that it had been he himself who read the *Ars magna*, and indeed on their journey. He mentioned having tucked the work into his saddlebag, which, to be sure, clearly revealed, as the annotators later noted with mocking objectivity, that he had never held this gigantic book in his hands. The fat count, however, ingenuously described how he had studied Kircher's memorable descriptions of light, lenses, and angels on various evenings in front of meager campfires, the subtle reflections of the great scholar appearing to him in the strangest contrast to their advance into the more and more ravaged land.

At Altheim the wind became so biting that they had to put on their lined cloaks and pull their hoods down low over their foreheads. At Ranshofen the weather cleared again. In a vacant farmhouse they watched the sunset. No people far and wide. Only a goose that must have fled from someone stood ragged next to a well.

The fat count stretched and yawned. The land was hilly, but there was not another tree to be seen; everything had been cut down. A distant rumble could be heard.

"Oh my," said the fat count, "not that too, a thunderstorm."

The dragoons laughed.

The fat count recognized his mistake. He had already realized what it was, he said awkwardly, only compounding his embarrassment. He had spoken in jest.

The goose stared at them with uncomprehending goose eyes. It opened and closed its bill. The dragoon Franz Kärrnbauer aimed his carbine and fired. And although the fat count would soon thereafter witness much more, he would not forget for the rest of his days what horror pierced him to the core when the head of the bird burst. Something about it was almost incomprehensible—how quickly it happened, how from one moment to the next a solid small head was transformed into a spray and into nothing and how the animal took another few waddles and then collapsed into a white mound, in a spreading pool of blood. As he rubbed his eyes and tried to breathe calmly so that he wouldn't faint, he decided that he had to forget it at all costs. But of course he did not forget it, and when he recalled this journey half a century later while composing his life's chronicle, it was the image of the bursting goose head that outshone everything else in clarity. In an utterly honest book he would have had to include it, but he couldn't bring himself to do so and took it with him to the grave, and no one learned with what inexpressible disgust he had watched the dragoons dress the bird for dinner: cheerfully, they scraped off the feathers, cut and tore, took out the guts, and roasted the meat over the fire.

That night the fat count slept badly. The wind howled through the empty window frames. He shivered with cold. The dragoon Kärrnbauer snored loudly. Another dragoon, named Stefan Purner, or perhaps it was Konrad Purner—the two of them were brothers, and the fat count mixed them up so often that they later merged into a single figure in the book—gave him a nudge, but he only snored louder.

In the morning they rode on. The village of Markl was completely destroyed: walls full of holes, cracked beams, rubble in the road, a few old people begging for food next to the filthy well. The enemy had been here and had taken everything, and the little that they had been able to hide had been taken afterward by friendly troops, that is, the Elector's soldiers, and no sooner had these soldiers withdrawn than what the villagers had managed to conceal even from them was in turn taken by more enemy forces.

"Which enemies, then?" the fat count asked worriedly. "Swedes or Frenchmen?"

It was all the same to them, they said. They were so hungry.

The fat count hesitated for a moment. Then he gave the command to ride onward.

It had been quite right not to leave them anything, said Karl von Doder. The travelers didn't have enough provisions and had to carry out orders from the highest authority. You simply could not help everyone, only God had that power, and he would certainly look after these Christians in his infinite mercy.

All the fields lay fallow; some were in ashes, from great fires. The hills cowered under a leaden sky. In the distance columns of smoke stood against the horizon.

It would be best, said Karl von Doder, to head southward past Altötting, Polling, and Tüssling, far from the country road, in the open field. Whoever had not abandoned the villages by now was armed and mistrustful. A group of riders bearing down on a village could be shot from cover without further ado.

"All right," said the fat count, who didn't understand why an Imperial Court Council secretary suddenly had such clear ideas about the conduct required in a war zone. "Agreed!"

"If we're lucky and don't encounter any soldiers," said Karl von Doder, "then we'll make it to Andechs in two days."

The fat count nodded and tried to imagine someone seriously shooting at him, aiming over the iron sights. At him, Martin von Wolkenstein, who had never done anyone wrong, with a real bullet made of lead. He looked down at himself. His back hurt, his bottom was sore from the days in the saddle. He stroked his belly and imagined a bullet, he thought of the burst goose head, and he also thought of the metal magic about which Athanasius Kircher had written in his book on magnets: if you carried a magnetic stone of sufficient strength in your pocket, you could deflect the bullets and make a man invulnerable. The legendary scholar himself had tried it. Unfortunately, such strong magnets were very rare and expensive.

When he attempted to reconstruct their journey half a century later, the course of time grew muddled in his mind. To disguise his uncertainty, a florid digression is found at this point, seventeen and a half pages long, about the camaraderie of the men, who go to meet danger in the knowledge that this very danger will either kill them or bind them in friendship for life. The passage became famous, irrespective of the fact that it was fabricated, for in truth none of the men had become his friend. One conversation or another with the Imperial Court Council secretary remained in his memory in fragments, but as for the dragoons, he hardly remembered their names, much less their faces. One of them had been wearing a broad-brimmed hat with a grayish red plume—this he remembered. Above all he saw loamy paths in front of him and felt, as if it had been yesterday, the patter of the rain on his hood. His cloak had been heavy with water. At the time it struck him that nothing had ever been so wet, that it could not get any wetter.

Some time ago there had been forests here. But when he thought about it while riding, with aching back and sore bottom, he became aware that this knowledge meant nothing to him. The war didn't seem to him like something manmade, but like wind and rain, like the sea, like the high cliffs of Sicily that he had seen as a child. This war was older than he was. It had at times grown and at times shrunk, it had crept here and there, had laid waste to the north, turned west, had extended one arm eastward and one southward, then heaved its full weight into the south, only to settle again for a while in the north. Naturally, the fat count knew people who still remembered the time before, chief among them his father, who, coughing and good-humored, awaited death in the family's country seat, Rodenegg in Tyrol, as the fat count himself would await it almost sixty years later, coughing and writing, in the same place and at the same stone table. His father had once spoken with Albrecht von Wallenstein. The tall and dark man had complained about the damp weather in Vienna. His father had responded that one got used to it, to which Wallenstein had replied that he did not want to and would not get used to such foul weather—a statement that his father had been about to parry with an especially witty remark, but Wallenstein had already turned away brusquely. Scarcely a month went by in which his father did not find a reason to talk about it, just as he never forgot to mention that he had several years earlier also encountered the unfortunate Elector Friedrich, who shortly thereafter had accepted the Bohemian crown and provoked the great war, only to be chased off in disgrace after a single winter and finally to perish somewhere on the roadside, without so much as a grave.

That night they found no shelter. They curled up on a bare field and wrapped themselves in their wet cloaks. The rain was too heavy for a fire. Never had the fat count felt so miserable. The wet cloak, which kept getting wetter, was now indescribably sodden, and his body was gradually sinking deeper into the soft loam. Could the mire simply swallow you? He tried to sit up but couldn't; the loam seemed to hold him down.

Eventually the rain stopped. Coughing, Franz Kärrnbauer piled a few sticks and struck the flints together, again and again, until finally sparks flew, and then he bustled around for another half an eternity and blew on the wood and murmured magic spells until little flames flickered in the darkness. Shivering, they held their hands in the warmth.

The horses shied and whinnied. One of the dragoons stood up, the fat count couldn't make out which, but he saw that he was leveling the carbine. The fire made their shadows dance.

"Wolves," whispered Karl von Doder.

They stared into the night. Suddenly the fat count was filled with the conviction that all this must be a dream, indeed this was how he remembered it later, as a dream from which he had awoken in the bright morning, dry and well rested. It could not have happened like that, but instead of grappling with his memory, he inserted twelve pages of artfully nested sentences about his mother. Most of it was pure invention, for he merged his distant and coldhearted mother with the figure of his favorite governess, who had been gentler to him than any other person, except perhaps the thin and beautiful prostitute Aglaia. When his account after this long and fabricated recollection found its way back to the journey, they had already passed Haar, and behind him the dragoons were carrying on a conversation about magic spells that protected you from stray bullets.

"Can't do anything about a well-aimed one," said Franz Kärrnbauer.

"Unless you have a really strong spell," said Konrad Purner. "One of the very secret ones. They can even do something about cannonballs, I've seen it myself, at Augsburg. A man next to me used one like that, I thought he was dead, but then he stood up again as if nothing had happened. I couldn't quite hear the spell, alas."

"Yes, it can be done with a spell like that," said Franz Kärrnbauer. "A really expensive one. But the simple spells that you buy at the market, they're useless."

"I knew a fellow," said Stefan Purner, "he fought for the Swedes, and he had an amulet; with it he survived first Magdeburg, then Lützen. Then he drank himself to death."

"But the amulet," asked Franz Kärrnbauer. "Who got it, where is it?"

"Yes, if I only knew." Stefan Purner sighed. "If you had that, then everything would be different."

"Yes," Franz Kärrnbauer said prayerfully. "If only you had that!"

At Baierbronn they found the first dead man. He must have been lying there awhile already, for his clothes were covered with a layer of earth, and his hair seemed to have become intertwined with the blades of grass. He was lying facedown, his legs spread, with bare feet.

"That's normal," said Konrad Purner. "No one leaves a corpse his boots. If you're unlucky, you get killed just for the shoes."

The wind carried small, cold raindrops. All around them were tree stumps, hundreds of them; a whole forest had been cut down here. They passed through a village that had been burned down to its foundation walls, and there they saw a heap of corpses. The fat count averted his eyes and then looked after all. He saw blackened faces, a torso with only one arm, a hand clenched into a claw, two empty eye sockets over an open mouth, and something that looked like a sack but was the remains of a body. An acrid smell hung in the air.

In the late afternoon they reached a village in which there were still people. Yes, Ulenspiegel was in the abbey, said an old woman, he was still alive. And when they encountered a feral-looking man and a small boy pulling a cart together shortly before sunset, they received the same information. "He's in the abbey," said the man, staring up at the fat count's horse. "Keep heading west, past the lake, then you can't miss it. Do you have food for me and my son, sirs?"

The fat count reached into his saddlebag and gave him a sausage. It was his last, and he knew that it was a mistake, but he couldn't help it, he felt so sorry for the child. In a daze, he asked why they were pulling the wagon.

"It's all we have."

"But it's empty," said the fat count.

"But it's all we have."

Again they slept in the open field; to be safe they didn't light a fire. The fat count was freezing, but at least it wasn't raining, and the ground was solid. Shortly after midnight they heard two shots nearby. They listened. In the first morning light Karl von Doder swore he had seen a wolf observing them from not too far away. Hastily they mounted their horses and rode onward.

They encountered a woman. It was hard to tell whether she was old or whether life had just treated her badly, so furrowed was her face, so stooped her gait. Yes, in the abbey, he was still there. No sooner had she spoken of the famous jester than she had to smile. And so it always was, the fat count wrote fifty years later: word of him had reached whomsoever we met; at the mere mention of his name, they indicated the way to his abode; every soul remaining in this wasteland seemed to know his whereabouts.

Toward midday soldiers approached them. First a group of pikemen: feral people with shaggy beards. Some had open wounds, others were dragging sacks full of booty. A smell of sweat, disease, and blood hung over them, and they gazed with small, hostile eyes. They were followed by covered wagons, on which their women and children were sitting. A few of the women were holding infants tight. We saw only the devastation of the bodies, the fat count wrote later, but whether friend or foe could not be discerned, for they carried no standard.

After the pikemen came a good dozen horsemen.

"Godspeed," said a man who was apparently their leader. "Where are you bound?"

"For the abbey," said the fat count.

"We're just coming from there. Nothing to eat there."

"We're not looking for food. We're looking for Tyll Ulenspiegel."

"Yes, he's there. We saw him, but we had to make off when the Kaiser's men came."

The fat count turned pale.

"Don't worry, I won't hurt you. I'm Hans Kloppmess from Hamburg. I was once one of the Kaiser's men too. And maybe I'll be one again, who knows? A soldier has a trade, no less than a carpenter or baker. The army is my guild. There in the wagon I have a wife and children. I have to feed them. At the moment the French aren't paying anything, but when they do pay, then it will be more than you get from the Kaiser. In Westphalia the great lords are negotiating peace. When the war ends, all the men will get their outstanding pay, you can count on that, because without the pay we would refuse to go home, the lords are afraid of that. Nice horses you have there!"

"Thank you," said the fat count.

"Could really use them," said Hans Kloppmess.

Worriedly the fat count turned to look at his dragoons.

"Where are you coming from?" asked Hans Kloppmess.

"Vienna," the fat count said hoarsely.

"I was almost in Vienna once," said the horseman next to Hans Kloppmess.

"What, really?" asked Hans Kloppmess. "You, in Vienna?"

"Only almost. Didn't make it there."

"What happened?"

"Nothing happened, I didn't make it to Vienna."

"Keep away from Starnberg," said Hans Kloppmess. "It would be best to head south past Gauting, then toward Herrsching, then from there to the abbey. The road is still open to foot travelers. But hurry. Turenne and Wrangel have already crossed the Danube. Soon sparks will be flying."

"We're no foot travelers," said Karl von Doder.

"Just wait and see."

No command was necessary, no consultation. All of them spurred their horses. The fat count bent down over the neck of the animal and held on tight, clinging to both reins and mane. He saw the earth spraying under the hooves, he heard shouts behind him, he heard the report of a shot, he resisted the temptation to look back.

They rode and rode, and kept on riding and riding. His back ached unbearably, he had no strength left in his legs, and he didn't dare turn his head. Alongside him rode Franz Kärrnbauer, in front of him rode Konrad Purner and Karl von Doder, behind him rode Stefan Purner.

Finally they stopped. The horses were steaming with sweat. Everything went black before the fat count's eyes. He slid out of the saddle. Franz Kärrnbauer supported him and helped him dismount. The soldiers hadn't followed them. It had begun to snow. Whitish gray flakes drifted in the air. When he caught one of them on his finger, he recognized that it was ash.

Karl von Doder patted his horse's neck. "South past Gauting, he said, then toward Herrsching. The horses are thirsty, they need water."

They mounted again. Silently they rode through the falling ash. They no longer encountered anyone, and in the late afternoon they saw above them the tower of the abbey.

Here Martin von Wolkenstein's life's chronicle makes

a leap: he doesn't say a word about the steep ascent beyond Herrsching, which cannot have been easy for the horses, nor is there anything about the half-destroyed abbey building and no description of the monks. This was due to his memory, of course, but it was probably due even more to the nervous impatience that came over him while writing. And so readers find him two turbid lines later already opposite the abbot, in the early morning hours of the next day.

They sat on two stools in an empty hall. The furniture had been looted, destroyed, or burned. There had been tapestries too, said the abbot, silver candleholders and a large cross made of gold above the door arch over there. Now the light came from a single pitchwood torch. Father Friesenegger spoke matter-of-factly and tersely; nonetheless, the fat count's eyes fell shut several times. Again and again he started, only to notice that the gaunt man had meanwhile gone on talking. The fat count would have liked to take a rest, but the abbot wanted to tell him about the past years, he wanted the Kaiser's envoy to know exactly what the abbey had undergone. When the fat count would write his life's chronicle in the days of Leopold I, by which time he was constantly mixing up things, people, and years, he would recall with envy Father Friesenegger's flawless memory.

The hard years had failed to harm the abbot's mind, he wrote. His eyes had been sharp and attentive, his words well chosen, his sentences long and well formed, yet veracity was not everything: he had been unable to shape the welter of events into stories, and so it had been difficult to follow him. Over the years soldiers had overrun the abbey time and time again: the imperial troops had taken what they needed, then the Protestant troops had come and had taken what they needed. Then the Protestants had withdrawn, and the imperial troops had come back and had taken what they needed: animals and wood and boots. Then the imperial troops had withdrawn, but they had left a contingent of guards there, and then marauding soldiers who belonged to no army had come, and the guards had driven them away, or they had driven the guards away, either one or the other or perhaps one first and the other later, the fat count wasn't certain, nor did it matter, for the guards had withdrawn again, and either the imperial troops or the Swedes had come to take what they needed: animals and wood and clothes and above all, naturally, boots, if there had been any boots left. The wood too was already gone. The next winter the peasants of the surrounding villages had taken refuge in the abbey. People had lain in all the halls, in all the closets, in even the smallest corridor. The hunger, the contaminated wells, the cold, the wolves!

"Wolves?"

They had penetrated the houses, the abbot said, at first only at night, but soon during the day too. The people had fled into the woods and there had killed and eaten the smaller animals and then cut down the trees to keep from freezing to death— this had made the wolves so hungry that they lost all fear and timidity. Like nightmares come to life they descended on the villages, like monsters out of old fairy tales. With hungry eyes they appeared in rooms and stables, without the slightest fear of knives or pitchforks. On the worst winter days they had even found their way into the abbey. One of the animals had attacked a woman with an infant and torn the child from her hands.

No, this was not exactly what had happened; the abbot had spoken only of the fear for the small children. But for some reason the idea that an infant could be devoured by a wolf before its mother's eyes had so captivated the fat count, who at this time already had five grandchildren and three great-grandchildren, that he believed the abbot might well have told him this too, which was why, amid eloquent apologies for the fact that he did not have the right to spare the reader what followed, he inserted a profoundly gruesome description including cries of pain, horror, the growling of the wolf, sharp teeth, and blood.

And so, the abbot said in his calm voice, it had gone on and on, day after day, year after year. So much hunger. So much disease. The alternation of the armies and marauders. The land had been depopulated. The forests had disappeared, the villages had burned down, the people had fled, God knows where. The past year even the wolves had made off. He leaned forward, put a hand on the fat count's shoulder, and asked whether he could memorize all that.

"All of it," said the fat count.

It was important that the court learn of this, said the abbot. The Bavarian Elector as the supreme commander of the imperial troops was, in his wisdom, interested only in the big picture, not in the details. Often they had appealed to him for help, but the truth was that his own troops had wreaked worse havoc than the Swedes. Only if this was remembered had all the suffering had meaning.

The fat count nodded.

The abbot looked him intently in the face.

Composure, he said, as if he had read the mind of the man opposite him. Discipline and inner will. The welfare of the abbey rested on his shoulders, the survival of the brothers.

He crossed himself. The fat count did the same.

This helped a great deal, the abbot said, reaching into the collar of his cowl. And with a horror such as he knew only from fever visions the fat count saw a jute fabric, into which had been woven metal spikes and shards of glass with dried blood.

You got used to it, said the abbot. The first years had been the worst; at that time, he had sometimes taken off the sackcloth and cooled his suppurating upper body with water. But then he had felt ashamed of his weakness, and time after time God had given him the strength to put it back on. There had been moments when the pain had been so intense, had pierced and seared him with such diabolical power, that he had thought he was losing his mind. But prayer had helped. Habit had helped. And his skin had grown thicker. From the fourth year on the constant pain had transformed itself into a friend.

At that moment, the fat count later wrote, sleep must have overpowered him, for when he yawned and rubbed his eyes and took a few moments to remember where he was, someone else was sitting opposite him.

It was a scrawny man with hollow cheeks and a scar that ran from his hairline down to the root of his nose. He was wearing a cowl, and yet it was clearly discernible—even if it couldn't be said how—that he was not a monk. Never before had the fat count seen such eyes. When he described this conversation, he could not quite remember whether it had really taken place as he had recounted it over the years to friends, acquaintances, and strangers. But he decided to stick with the version that by now too many had heard for him to revise it.

"Here you are at last," the man had said. "I've been waiting for a long time."

"Are you Tyll Ulenspiegel?"

"One of us is. You're here to fetch me?"

"On behalf of the Kaiser."

"Which one? There are many."

"No, there aren't! What are you laughing at?"

"I'm not laughing at the Kaiser, I'm laughing at you. Why

are you so fat? After all, there's nothing to eat, how do you do it?"

"Hold your tongue," said the fat count, immediately annoyed that nothing wittier had occurred to him. And even though for the rest of his days he thought about a better response and even found a whole string of them, he deviated in not a single account from this embarrassing phrase. For these very words seemed to seal the truth of his memory. Would anyone invent something that made him look so bad?

"Or else you'll hit me? But you won't do that. You're soft. Gentle and soft and kindhearted. All this is not for you."

"War is not for me?"

"It certainly is not."

"But it is for you?"

"It certainly is."

"Will you come of your own free will, or do we have to force you?"

"Of course I'll come. There's nothing left to eat here, everything is falling apart, the abbot won't last much longer—that's why I sent for you."

"You didn't send for me."

"I sent for you, you big dumpling."

"His Majesty heard—"

"Well, why did His Majesty hear that, then, you giant ball of flesh? His Majesty, His Idiotic Majesty with his golden crown on his golden throne, heard about me because I sent for you. And don't smack me, I'm allowed to say that, you have heard of fool's license, haven't you? If I don't call His Majesty an idiot, who will? Somebody has to. And you're not allowed."

Ulenspiegel grinned. It was a terrible grin, wicked and mocking, and since the fat count couldn't remember how their conversation had gone on, he used half a dozen sentences to describe this grin, then rhapsodized for a page about the deep, sound, and refreshing sleep he had enjoyed on the floor of an abbey cell until noon the following day: O Morpheus, merciful god of slumbers, bringer of peace, holy guardian of sweet oblivion, in this the night of my most dire need thou didst not fail thy servant but broughtest rest to mine eyelids, and I awoke renewed in flesh and spirit, rejoicing in thy blessings.

This last phrase reflects less the feelings of the young man than the religious doubts of the old, on which he expatiated in moving words in another passage. Out of shame, however, he withheld a detail that even at a distance of fifty years made him blush. For when they met toward noon in the courtyard to take leave of the abbot and three emaciated monks who looked more like ghosts than like real people, they realized that they had forgotten to bring a horse for Ulenspiegel.

Indeed, none of them had thought about what the man they were to bring to Vienna would actually ride on. For of course there were no horses here to buy or borrow, there weren't even donkeys. All the animals had been eaten or run away.

"Well, then he'll just mount behind me," said Franz Kärrnbauer.

"That doesn't suit me," said Ulenspiegel. In the light of day he looked even thinner in his monk's cowl. He stood bent forward, his cheeks were hollow, his eyes were set deep in their sockets. "The Kaiser is my friend. I want a horse of my own."

"I'll knock your teeth out," Franz Kärrnbauer said calmly, "and I'll break your nose. I'll do it. Look at me. You know I'll do it."

Ulenspiegel looked up at him reflectively for a moment. Then he climbed into the saddle behind Franz Kärrnbauer.

Karl von Doder put a hand on the fat count's shoulder and whispered: "That's not him."

"Pardon me?"

"That's not him!"

"What's not whom?"

"I don't think that's the man I have seen."

"What?"

"That time at the fair. I can't help it. I don't think it's him."

The fat count looked at the secretary for a long moment. "Are you certain?"

"Not completely certain. It was years ago, and he was above me on a rope. Under such circumstances, how can one be certain?"

"Let's not speak of it again," said the fat count.

With trembling hands the abbot blessed them and advised them to avoid the cities. The royal seat of Munich had closed its gates against the onslaught of people seeking help, no one else was allowed in, the streets were overflowing with the hungry, the wells were filthy. Things were similar around Nuremberg, where the Protestants were encamped. It was claimed that Wrangel and Turenne were coming with detachments from the northwest; therefore it would be best to steer clear of them by heading northeast in a wide loop, between Augsburg and Ingolstadt. At Rottenburg they could head straight east; from there the way to Lower Austria was clear. The abbot fell silent and scratched his chest—a seemingly ordinary movement, but now that the fat count knew about the sackcloth, he could hardly watch. Rumor had it that both sides were bent on battle before the armistice could be proclaimed in Westphalia. Each side wanted to improve its position first.

"Many thanks," said the fat count, having hardly absorbed

anything. Geography had never been his forte. In his father's library there were several volumes of Matthäus Merian's *Topographia Germaniae*; a few times he had leafed through them with a shudder. What was the point of memorizing all this? What was the point of visiting all these places when you could also just stay in the middle, in the center of the world, in Vienna?

"Go with God," the abbot said to Ulenspiegel.

"Stay with God," the fool replied from the horse. He had put his arms around Franz Kärrnbauer and looked so thin and weak that it was hard to imagine how he would keep himself on the horse.

"One day you stood outside our gates," said the abbot. "We took you in, we didn't ask your denomination. For more than a year you were here, now you're leaving again."

"Nice speech," said Ulenspiegel.

The abbot made the sign of the cross. The entertainer moved to do the same, but apparently got muddled—his arms got tangled, his hands didn't end up where they were supposed to go. The abbot turned away. The fat count had to suppress his laughter. Two monks opened the gate.

They didn't get far. After a mere few hours they found themselves in a downpour such as the fat count had never before experienced. Hurriedly they dismounted and crouched under the horses. The rain poured, pelted, roared around them as if the sky were dissolving.

"But if it's not Ulenspiegel?" whispered Karl von Doder.

Two things that could not be distinguished were the same thing, said the fat count. Either this man was Ulenspiegel, who had sought refuge in the Abbey of Andechs, or this was a man who had sought refuge in the abbey and called himself Ulenspiegel. God knew, but as long as he didn't intervene, what was the difference?

At that moment they heard shots nearby. Hastily they mounted their horses, spurred them, and thundered across the open field. The fat count wheezed, his back ached. Raindrops struck his face. It seemed to him an eternity before the dragoons reined their horses.

With unsteady legs he dismounted and patted his horse's neck. The animal pursed its lips and snorted. To their left was a small river; on the other side the slope rose toward a forest such as the fat count hadn't seen since Melk.

"That must be Streitheim Forest," said Karl von Doder.

"Then we're too far north," said Franz Kärrnbauer.

"There's no way that's Streitheim Forest," said Stefan Purner.

"It most certainly is," said Karl von Doder.

"Absolutely not," said Stefan Purner.

Then they heard music. They held their breath and listened: trumpets and drums, a cheerful march that made you want to dance. The fat count noticed that his shoulders were moving up and down to the beat.

"Let's get out of here," said Konrad Purner.

"Not on the horses," hissed Karl von Doder. "Into the forest!"

"Careful," said the fat count, trying to at least keep up the pretense that he was the one giving orders here. "Ulenspiegel must be protected."

"You poor idiots," the scrawny man said softly. "You cattle. It is I who must protect you."

The treetops soon closed over them. The fat count could

see his horse's reluctance, but he held the reins tight and patted its damp nostrils, and the animal complied. Before long the underbrush was so dense that the dragoons drew their sabers to clear a path.

They listened again. An indistinct murmur could be heard. Where was it coming from, what was it? Gradually the fat count realized that it was countless voices, an intermingling of singing and shouting and talking from many throats. He sensed his horse's fear. He stroked its mane. The animal snorted.

Later he could no longer say how long they had walked like this, and so he claimed that it had been two hours. The voices behind us died away, he wrote, the loud silence of the forest enveloped us, birds shrieked, branches broke, and the wind whispered to us from the treetops.

"We have to head east," said Karl von Doder, "toward Augsburg."

"The abbot said the cities aren't letting anyone in," said the fat count.

"But we are envoys of the Kaiser," said Karl von Doder.

It occurred to the fat count that he was carrying no paper that proved it: no identification, no charter, no document of any sort. He hadn't requested papers, and apparently no one in the administration of the imperial palace had felt responsible for issuing such a thing.

"Where's east?" asked Franz Kärrnbauer.

Stefan Purner pointed somewhere.

"That's south," said his brother.

"You really are half-wits," Ulenspiegel said cheerfully. "You're utterly incompetent nobodies! West is where we are, thus east is everywhere."

Franz Kärrnbauer drew back his arm, but Ulenspiegel

ducked with a speed of which no one would have thought him capable, and leaped behind a tree trunk. The dragoons followed him, yet Ulenspiegel glided like a shadow around the trunk and disappeared behind another and was no longer to be seen.

"You won't get me," they heard him say with a giggle, "I know the forest. I became a forest spirit when I was a small boy."

"A forest spirit?" the fat count asked uneasily.

"A white forest spirit." Ulenspiegel stepped out of the bushes with a laugh. "For the great devil."

They took a rest. Their provisions were almost used up. The horses were nibbling on tree bark. They passed around the bottle of small beer, each of them taking a sip. When it arrived at the fat count, nothing was left.

Wearily they went on. The forest thinned. The trees stood at wider intervals. The underbrush was no longer impassable; the horses could walk without the path having to be cleared. It struck the fat count that no more birds could be heard: not a sparrow, not a blackbird, not a crow. They mounted and rode out of the forest.

"My God," said Karl von Doder.

"Merciful Lord," said Stefan Purner.

"Blessed Virgin," said Franz Kärrnbauer.

When he later tried to depict what they had seen, the fat count discovered that he could not do it. It was beyond his abilities as a rational person: Even at a distance of half a century he found himself incapable of putting it into sentences that had any actual meaning. Naturally, he described the sight nonetheless. It was one of the most important moments of his life, and the fact that he had witnessed the final battle of the Thirty Years' War defined from then on who he was and what people thought of him—the Lord Steward of the Household experienced firsthand the Battle of Zusmarshausen, it had been said ever since when he was introduced to someone. He fended this off with practiced modesty: "Let's drop it, it's not an easy story to tell."

What sounded like a commonplace was the truth. It was not an easy story to tell. Not for him, at least. From the instant he rode out of the forest on the hill and looked across the river valley and saw the Kaiser's army stretching to the horizon with its cannon emplacements, entrenched musketeers, and the pikemen standing in orderly groups of a hundred, whose pikes seemed to him a second forest, he felt as if he were experiencing something that did not belong in reality. The fact that so many people could come together in formation seemed so weighty that everything was thrown off balance. The fat count had to seize the mane of the horse to keep from sliding off.

Only then did it become clear to him that he had not only the imperial army before his eyes. To their right the slope fell away sharply. Below it was a wide road on which, silent and without music, so that only the hooves on the stone could be heard, the cavalry of the united crowns of France and Sweden was approaching: one rank behind the other, heading toward a single small bridge.

And at that moment it happened that this very bridge, which had just a second ago still stood there so solidly, dissolved into a small cloud. The fat count almost had to laugh at this magic trick. Bright smoke rose, the bridge was gone, and only now, when the smoke had already begun to drift away in the wind, did the bang reach them. How beautiful, the fat count thought and immediately felt ashamed and a moment later thought again, as if in defiance: No, that was beautiful.

"Let's get out of here," said Karl von Doder.

Too late. Time, like rapids, was carrying them along. Over on the other side of the river, small clouds were rising, a few dozen, white and shimmering. Our cannons, thought the fat count, that's them, our Kaiser's artillery, yet even before he had finished the thought, more clouds rose from where the musketeers were standing, tiny but countless ones, for a moment still sharply divided from each other, then quickly mixing together into a single cloud, and now the noise came rolling, and the fat count heard the shots ring out, the steam of which he had just seen, and next he saw the enemy's horsemen, who were still advancing on the river, perform the strangest trick. Swaths were all at once cut in their ranks, one here, another right next to it, one at some distance. While he was still straining his eyes to grasp what he was seeing, he heard a noise like nothing he had ever heard before, a screaming from the air. Franz Kärrnbauer threw himself from his horse; surprised, the fat count watched him rolling through the grass and wondered whether he shouldn't do the same, but the horse was high and the ground was covered with hard stones. Now Karl von Doder did it first. Only he didn't jump in one direction but in two, as if he hadn't been able to decide and had taken both opportunities.

At first the fat count thought that he must have been dreaming, yet then he saw that Karl von Doder was indeed lying in two places: one part to the right of his horse, the other to the left, and the one on the right was still moving. A disgust of monstrous proportions overcame the fat count, and then, to crown it all, he remembered the goose that Franz Kärrnbauer had shot dead days ago; he thought of how he had seen its head explode, and comprehended that he had been so shocked because that event had heralded this one, against the current of time. In the meantime the question of whether he should get off his horse or not had been rendered irrelevant; his horse had lain down, just like that, and when he hit the ground sideways, he noticed that it had begun to rain again, but it was not the usual rain, not water, that made the earth spray, rather invisible flails were threshing the ground. He saw Franz Kärrnbauer crawling on his belly, he saw a horse's hoof lying in the grass with no horse attached to it, he saw Konrad Purner riding down the slope, he saw that the smoke was now coiling around the ranks of imperial soldiers on the other side of the river too, which he had just a moment ago still been able to make out so clearly. They were gone. In just one place the wind swept away the thick smoke and revealed the men crouching between their pikes, who now stood up, all at the same moment, and with raised weapons walked backward like a single man—how did they make their movements correspond so perfectly? Apparently they were backing away from the cavalry, which was now coming through the water after all. The river seemed to be boiling, horses were rearing, horsemen were falling, but other horsemen reached the riverbank. The water had turned red, and the pikemen walking backward disappeared in thick smoke.

He looked around. The grass stood calmly. The fat count struggled to his feet. His legs obeyed him, only he couldn't feel his right hand. When he held it in front of his face, he noticed that a finger was missing. He counted again. Indeed, four fingers, something was wrong, one was missing, it was supposed to be five, it was four. He spat blood on the ground. He had to go back into the forest. Only in the forest was there cover, only in—

Shapes assembled themselves, colorful surfaces emerged, and as it became clear to the fat count that he must have fainted and was now coming to, a painful memory seized him, rising as if out of the void. He thought of a girl he had loved at the age of nineteen; at that time she had laughed at him, yet here she was again, and the knowledge that they would never be reunited filled every fiber of his being with sadness. Above him he saw the sky. Far and full of frayed clouds. Someone bent down over him. He didn't know him—yes, he did know him, now he recognized him.

"Stand up!"

The fat count squinted.

Ulenspiegel drew back his arm and slapped his face.

The fat count stood up. His cheek hurt. His hand hurt even more. The missing finger hurt most of all. Over there lay what was left of Karl von Doder, next to that lay two horses, and nearby was the dead Konrad Purner. Fog hung in the distance, flashes flaring in it. Horsemen were still trotting closer, a swath opened up and closed again—that must have been the work of the twelve-pounder. Horsemen were swarming along the river and impeding each other and brandishing whips, horses were splashing into the water, men were bellowing—but he could tell only by the fact that their mouths were moving, he could not hear them. The river was full of horses and people, more and more of them made it to the riverbank and disappeared in the thick smoke.

Ulenspiegel set off, the fat count following him. The forest was only a few paces away. Ulenspiegel began to run. The fat count ran after him.

The grass sprayed up beside him. Again he heard the scream from earlier, ringing through the air, ringing next to him. Something hit the ground and rolled toward the river with a roar. How can anyone live, he thought, how can anyone stand it when the air is full of metal? At that moment Ulenspiegel threw his arms outward and hurled himself, chest first, onto the meadow.

The fat count bent down over him. Ulenspiegel lay motionless. The back of his cowl was torn, blood was flowing out, he was already lying in a pool of it. The fat count backed away and started to run, but he stumbled and fell down. He struggled to his feet, ran again. Someone was running next to him, the grass was again sprayed up by bullets—why were they shooting in this direction, why not at the enemy, why so wide of the mark, and who was running here at his side? The fat count turned his head.

"Don't stop," Ulenspiegel hissed.

They ran into the forest. The trees stifled the thunder. The fat count wanted to stop, he had stabbing pains in his chest, but Ulenspiegel grabbed him and pulled him deeper into the underbrush. There they crouched down. For a while they listened to the cannons. Ulenspiegel carefully took off the torn cowl. The fat count looked at his back: the shirt was smeared with blood, but there was no wound to be seen.

"I don't understand it," said the fat count.

"You have to tie off your hand." Ulenspiegel tore a strip from the cloak and wrapped it around the fat count's arm.

Even then he sensed that all this would have to be told differently in his book one day. He would not succeed in any description, for everything would elude him, and the sentences he would be able to form would not match the pictures in his memory.

And indeed: that which had happened did not even appear in his dreams. Only occasionally did he recognize in what seemed utterly different dream events a distant echo of those moments when he had come under fire at the edge of Streit-heim Forest near Zusmarshausen.

Years later he questioned the unfortunate Count Gronsfeld, whom the Bavarian Elector had had summarily arrested after the defeat. Toothless, weary, and coughing, the former com-mander of the Bavarian troops named the names and places, he described the strength of the various units and drew deploy-ment maps so that the fat count managed to some extent to account for roughly where he had been and what had befallen him and his companions. Yet the sentences refused to fall into line. And so he stole others.

In a popular novel he found a description he liked, and when people urged him to recount the last battle of the great German war, he told them what he had read in Grimmelshau-sen's *Simplicissimus*. It didn't quite fit, because that passage was about the Battle of Wittstock, but it didn't bother anyone, no one ever raised any questions. What the fat count could not have known, however, was that Grimmelshausen, though he did experience the Battle of Wittstock firsthand, had himself been unable to describe it and instead had stolen the sentences of an English novel translated by Martin Opitz, the author of which had never witnessed a battle in his life.

In his book the fat count then also briefly depicted the night in the forest, when the fool, all at once becoming talkative, had told him about his time at the court of the Winter King in The Hague and about how he had been buried alive three years ago during the Siege of Brno. First he had been in the town commandant's bad graces because of a remark about his face, so that the man had stuck him with the miners, and then the shaft had caved in over his unit—here, the scar on his forehead, he got it there. He had been confined in the darkness, deep down, no way out, no air, yet then wondrously saved. It had been an incredible and wild story, the fat count wrote, and the fact that he then abruptly changed the subject, and did not elaborate on how the miraculous salvation under Brno had actually taken place, would later arouse the bewilderment and anger of many a reader.

Ulenspiegel, in any case, was a good storyteller, better than the abbot and better than the fat count too, and his stories distracted the fat count from the throbbing pain in his hand. Don't worry, said the fool, that night the wolves would find enough to eat.

At the first morning light they set off. They avoided the battlefield, from which a smell wafted to them that the fat count never could have imagined. Then they traversed Schlipsheim, Hainhofen, and Ottmarshausen. Ulenspiegel knew his way around, and he was calm and collected and never once insulted the fat count again.

The empty landscape had filled up with people. Peasants were pulling their possessions in carts. Scattered soldiers were searching for their units and families. The wounded were squatting on the roadside, in makeshift bandages, staring motionless into space. The two of them passed burning Oberhausen to the west and arrived in Augsburg, where the remnants of the Kaiser's army had assembled. After the defeat, it was no longer large.

The camp outside the city stank even worse than the battlefield. Like visions of hell, the deformed bodies, the festering faces, the open wounds, the heaps of excrement burned themselves into the fat count's memory. I will never be the same again, he thought, as they pushed their way to the city gate, and:

they're only images, they can't hurt me, they can't touch me—only images. And he imagined he was someone else who walked invisibly alongside them and didn't have to see what he saw.

In the afternoon they reached the gates of the city. Fearfully, the fat count revealed his identity to the guards, and it surprised even him when they believed all he said and let them in without hesitation.

Kings in Winter

I

IT WAS NOVEMBER. THE WINE SUPPLY WAS EXHAUSTED, and because the well in the garden was filthy, they drank nothing but milk. Since they could no longer afford candles, the whole court went to bed in the evening with the sun. The state of affairs was not good, yet there were still princes who would die for Liz. Recently, one of them had been here in The Hague, Christian von Braunschweig, and had promised her to have POUR DIEU ET POUR ELLE embroidered on his standard, and afterward, he had sworn fervently, he would win or die for her. He was an excited hero, so moved by himself that tears came to his eyes. Friedrich had patted him reassuringly on the shoulder, and she had given him her handkerchief, but then he had burst into tears once again, so overwhelmed was he by the thought of possessing a handkerchief of hers. She had given him a royal blessing, and, deeply stirred, he had gone on his way.

Naturally, he would not accomplish it, neither for God nor for her. This prince had few soldiers and no money, nor was he particularly clever. It would take men of a different caliber to defeat Wallenstein, someone like the Swedish king, say, who had recently come down on the Empire like a storm and had so far won all the battles he had fought. He was the one she should have married long ago, according to Papa's plans, but he hadn't wanted her.

It was almost twenty years ago that she had instead married her poor Friedrich. Twenty German years, a whirl of events and faces and noise and bad weather and even worse food and completely wretched theater.

She had missed good theater more than anything else, from the beginning, even more than palatable food. In German lands real theater was unknown; there, pitiful players roamed through the rain and screamed and hopped and farted and brawled. This was probably due to the cumbersome language. It was no language for theater, it was a brew of groans and harsh grunts, it was a language that sounded like someone struggling not to choke, like a cow having a coughing fit, like a man with beer coming out his nose. What was a poet supposed to do with this language? She had given German literature a try, first that Opitz and then someone else, whose name she had forgotten; she could not commit to memory these people who were always named Krautbacher or Engelkrämer or Kargholzsteingrömpl, and when you had grown up with Chaucer, and John Donne had dedicated verses to you—"fair phoenix bride," he had called her, "and from thine eye all lesser birds will take their jollity"—then even with the utmost politeness you could not bring yourself to find any merit in all this German bleating.

She often thought back to the court theater in Whitehall. She thought of the small gestures of the actors, of the long sentences, their ever-varying, nearly musical rhythm, now swift and clattering along, now dying gradually away, now questioning, now bristling with authority. There had been theater performances whenever she came to the court to visit her parents.

People stood on the stage and dissembled, but she had grasped at once that this was not so at all and that the dissembling too was merely a mask, for it was not the theater that was false, no, everything else was pretense, disguise, and frippery, everything that was *not* theater was false. On the stage people were themselves, completely true, fully transparent.

In real life no one spoke in soliloquies. Everyone kept his thoughts to himself, faces could not be read, everyone dragged the dead weight of his secrets. No one stood alone in his room and spoke aloud about his desires and fears, but when Burbage did so on the stage, in his rasping voice, his very thin fingers at eye level, it seemed unnatural that men should forever conceal what transpired within them. And what words he used! Rich words, rare, shimmering like cloth of gold—sentences so perfectly constructed that they were beyond anything you yourself could ever have managed. This is how things should be, the theater told you, this is how you should talk, how you should hold yourself, how you should feel, this is what it would be like to be a true human being.

When the performance was over and the applause faded, the actors returned to the state of paltriness. After taking their bows, they stood like extinguished candles. Then they approached, bending down low, Alleyn and Kemp and the great Burbage himself, to kiss Papa's hand, and if Papa asked them something, they answered like people whom language resisted and to whom no clear sentences occurred. Burbage's face was waxy and weary, and there was nothing special anymore about his now rather ugly hands. Hard to believe how quickly the spirit of lightness had abandoned him.

That spirit had itself appeared in one of the plays, which had been performed on Allhallows. It was about an old duke on a magical island, who captured his enemies only to spare them in the end. At the time she had been unable to understand why he had been lenient, and when she thought about it today, she still didn't understand. If she had Wallenstein or the Kaiser in her power, she would handle things differently! At the conclusion of the play the duke had simply released his ministering spirit, so that he might pass into the clouds, the air, the sunlight, and the blue of the sea, and had remained behind like an old sack of flour, a wrinkly actor who now briefly apologized that he had no more lines. The leading dramatist of the King's Men had taken on the role himself at the time. He was not one of the great actors, not Kemp and certainly not Burbage. You could even tell by looking at him that he struggled to remember his lines, which none other than he himself had written. After the performance he had kissed her hand with soft lips, and because it had been impressed on her that at such moments she must always ask some question, she had inquired whether he had any children.

"Two daughters living. And a son."

She waited, for now it would be Papa's turn to say something. But Papa was silent. The dramatist looked at her. She looked at him, her heart beginning to pound. All the people in the room were waiting, all the lords with their silk collars, all the ladies with diadems and fans—they were looking at her. And she realized that she had to keep talking. This was just how Papa was. When you were counting on him, he left you in the lurch. She cleared her throat to gain time. But you don't gain much time by clearing your throat. You can't clear your throat for very long, it hardly gets you anywhere.

And so she said that she was very sorry to hear of the death of his son. The Lord gave and the Lord took away, his will passed our understanding, and his trials made us strong.

For the blink of an eye, she was proud of herself. It takes quite a bit to manage something like that before the whole court, you have to be well-bred and quick-witted too.

The dramatist had smiled and bowed his head, and suddenly she had the feeling that she had made a fool of herself in a manner difficult to describe. She sensed herself turning red, and because she felt ashamed of this too, she turned even redder. She cleared her throat once again and asked him the name of his son. Not that it interested her. But nothing else occurred to her.

He answered in a soft voice.

"Really?" she asked in surprise. "Hamlet?"

"Hamnet." He drew a breath, then said pensively and as if to himself that, although he could not pretend to have borne his trial with that fortitude she praised, yet today, when it was his great fortune to behold the future's maiden face, he would swear that such a life as his, comprising such currents as had brought him to this sea, could not be counted among the worst, and that thanks to this moment in her gracious presence, he was disposed to accept with gratitude every pain and tribulation that lay in his past or, indeed, in days to come.

Here she couldn't think of anything else to say for the time being.

All well and good, Papa finally said. But shadows were cast on the future. There were more witches than ever. The Frenchman was treacherous. The recent unity of England and Scotland was still untested. Doom was lurking everywhere. But worst of all were the witches.

Doom might well lurk, the dramatist replied, that was the nature of doom, yet the hand of a mighty ruler held it off, as the mantle of the air held off the heavy cloud and dissolved it into gentle rain.

Now it was Papa who couldn't think of anything to say. This was funny, because it didn't happen often. Papa was looking at the dramatist, everyone was looking at Papa, no one said anything, and the silence had already lasted too long.

Finally Papa turned away—just like that, without a word. He did this often, it was one of his tricks to unsettle people. Normally they wondered for weeks afterward what they had done wrong and whether they had fallen out of favor. But the dramatist seemed to see through it. Bowing as he walked backward, he departed, a faint smile on his face.

"Do you think you're better than everyone else, Liz?" her fool had recently asked her when she had told him about it. "Have seen more, know more, come from a better land than we do?"

"Yes," she had said. "I do."

"And do you think your father will save you? At the head of an army, is that what you think?"

"No, I don't think that anymore."

"Yes, you do. You still believe that one fine day he will turn up and make you into a queen again."

"I *am* a queen."

At that he laughed derisively, and she had to swallow and push back tears and remember that it was his very duty—to tell her what no one else dared. That was why you had fools, and even if you didn't want a fool, you had to consent to one, for without a court jester a court was not a court, and if she and

Friedrich no longer had a country, at least their court had to be in order.

There was something strange about this fool. She had sensed it at once when he had first appeared, last winter, when the days had been especially cold and life even more impoverished than usual. At that time, the two of them had suddenly stood outside her door, the scrawny young man in the motley jerkin and the tall woman.

They had looked exhausted and haggard, ill from traveling and from the dangers of the wilderness. But when they had danced for her, there was a harmony, a consonance of the voices and bodies, such as she had not witnessed ever since she had left England. Then he had juggled, and she had pulled out the flute, and then the two of them had performed a play about a guardian and his ward, and she had feigned death, and he had found her lifeless, and in his grief he had killed himself, whereupon she had awoken and, her face contorted with horror, had seized his knife to now take her life too. Liz knew the story; it was from a play of the King's Men. Moved by the memory of something that had once had great significance in her life, she had asked the two of them whether they wouldn't stay. "We don't yet have a jester."

He had made his debut by giving her a painting. No, it was not a painting, it was a white canvas with nothing on it. "Have it framed, little Liz, hang it up. Show it to the others!" Nothing gave him the right to address her like that, but at least he pronounced her name correctly, complete with the English z—he did it as well as if he had been there. "Show it to your husband, the beautiful picture, let the poor king see it. And everyone else!"

She had done so. She had a green landscape painting, which she didn't like anyhow, taken out of its frame and replaced with the white canvas, and then the fool had hung up the painting in the large room that she and Friedrich called their throne room.

"It's a magic picture, little Liz. No one born out of wedlock can see it. No one stupid can see it. No one who has stolen money can see it. No one up to no good, no one who cannot be trusted, no one who's a gallows bird or a thievish knave or an arsehole with ears can see it—for him, there's no picture there!"

She hadn't been able to help laughing.

"No, really, little Liz, tell the people! Bastards and dolts and villains and men ripe for the gallows, none of them can see anything, neither the blue sky nor the castle nor the wonderful woman on the balcony letting down her golden hair nor the angel behind her. Tell them, watch what happens!"

What had happened still astonished her, every single day, and it would never cease to astonish her. The visitors stood helplessly before the white picture and didn't know what they were supposed to say. For it was complicated, after all. They knew that nothing was there, of course, but they weren't sure whether Liz knew it too, and thus it was also conceivable that she would take someone who told her that nothing was there for illegitimate, stupid, or thieving. They racked their brains. Had a spell been cast on the picture, or had someone fooled Liz, or was she playing a joke on everyone? The fact that by then almost everyone who came to the court of the Winter King and Queen was either illegitimate or stupid or a thief or a person with ill intentions didn't make matters easier.

In any case, not many visitors came these days. In the past people had come to see Liz and Friedrich with their own eyes, and some had also come to make promises, for even if scarcely anyone believed that Friedrich would rule over Bohemia again, it was nonetheless not completely impossible either. To promise something cost little: as long as the man was out of power, you didn't have to keep your word, but if he reascended, he would remember those who had stuck by him in dark times. By this time, however, promises were all they received; no one brought presents anymore that were valuable enough to be turned into money.

With an impassive face she had shown Christian von Braunschweig the white canvas, too. Stupid, deceitful, and illegitimate people, she had explained, could not see the magnificent painting, and then she had observed with a pleasure difficult to describe how her tearful admirer had kept looking helplessly across at the wall where the picture, mocking and blank, withstood his pathos.

"This is the best gift anyone has ever given me," she said to her fool.

"That's not saying much, little Liz."

"John Donne wrote me an ode. *Fair phoenix bride,* he called—"

"Little Liz, he was paid, he would have called you a stinking fish too if he had been given money for it. What do you think I would call you if you paid me better!"

"And I got a ruby necklace from the Kaiser, a diadem from the King of France."

"Can I see it?"

She was silent.

"Did you have to sell it?"

She was silent.

"And who is John Dung anyway? What sort of fellow is that, and who is fearful Nick's bride supposed to be?"

173

She was silent.

"Had to give it to the pawnbroker, your diadem? And the necklace from the Kaiser, little Liz, who is wearing it now?"

Not even her poor king had dared to say anything about the picture. And when she had explained to him that it was only a joke and the canvas was not enchanted, he had merely nodded and gazed at her uneasily.

She had always known that he wasn't the cleverest. From the beginning it had been obvious, but for a man of his rank it wasn't important. A prince did nothing, and if he happened to be unusually clever, it was nearly a blot on his honor. Subordinates had to be clever. He was himself—that was enough, nothing more was necessary.

This was the way of the world. There were a few real people, and then there were the rest: a shadowy army, a host of figures in the background, a swarm of ants crawling over the earth and having in common with each other that they were lacking something. They were born and died, were like the flecks of fluttering life that made up a flock of birds—if one disappeared, you hardly noticed it. The people who mattered were few.

The fact that her poor Friedrich was not the cleverest and also somewhat sickly, with a tendency to stomach pain and earaches, had already become apparent when he had come to London at the age of sixteen, in white ermine, with a court of four hundred attendants. He had come because the other suitors had stolen away or had at the decisive moment made no offer; first the young King of Sweden had declined, then Maurice of Orange, then Otto of Hesse. For a while, there had then been the positively foolhardy plan of marrying her to the Prince of Piedmont, who may not have had any money but was the nephew of the Spanish king—Papa's old dream of a reconciliation with Spain—but the Spaniards had remained skeptical, and all at once there was no one left but the German Electoral Prince Friedrich and his brilliant prospects. The Palatine chancellor had spent months negotiating in London before they reached an agreement: a forty-thousand-pound dowry from Papa to Germany in exchange for ten thousand pounds a year from the Palatinate to London.

After the signing of the contract Friedrich himself had arrived, rigid with trepidation. He had begun by garbling the words of his speech; it was noticeable how pitiful his French was, and to forestall keener embarrassment, Papa had simply walked up to him and embraced him. Then, with pursed, dry lips, the poor fellow had given her the kiss prescribed by protocol.

The next day they had taken a boat ride on the largest vessel of the court; only Mama hadn't wanted to come with them, because she found a prince Palatine beneath their station. Although the Palatine chancellor had claimed with the help of silly official opinions by his court jurists that an elector had the rank of a king, everyone knew that this was sheer nonsense. Only a king was a king.

On the boat ride, Friedrich had leaned on the railing and tried not to let his seasickness show. He had had the eyes of a child, but he had held himself perfectly erect as only those taught by the best court tutors could. You must be a good fencer, she had thought, and: you're not ugly. Don't worry, she would have liked best to whisper to him, I am with you now.

And now, so many years later, he still had impeccable posture. Whatever else had happened, however much he had been humiliated and made the laughingstock of Europe—to stand up straight was something he could still do as before, his head tilted back slightly, his chin raised, his hands clasped behind him, and he even still had his beautiful calf eyes.

She was fond of her poor king. She couldn't help it. She had spent all these years with him, borne him more children than she could count. They called him the Winter King, her the Winter Queen—their fates were indissolubly bound together. That day on the Thames she had had no such foreboding, she had merely thought that she would have to teach the poor boy a few things, for when two people were married, they had to talk to each other. With this fellow here it could become difficult; he had no idea about anything.

He must have been utterly overwhelmed, so far away from his Heidelberg castle, from the cattle of his native land, from the pointed houses and little German people, in a city for the first time. And here he stood right in front of all the shrewd, fearsome lords and ladies and, to top it all, in front of Papa, who frightened everyone anyhow.

The evening after the boat ride, she and Papa had had their longest talk of her life. She hardly knew her father. She had not grown up with him but with Lord Harington at Coombe Abbey; families of rank didn't raise their children themselves. Her father had been a shadow in her dreams, a figure in paintings, a character who appeared in fairy tales—the ruler of the two kingdoms of England and Scotland, the hunter of godless witches, the terror of Spain, the Protestant son of the beheaded Catholic queen. When you met him, you were always surprised that he had such a long nose and such swollen bags under his eyes, which always seemed to be pensively looking inward. He always gave you the feeling that you had said something wrong. But this was on purpose; it had become a habit.

It had been their first real conversation. How do you, my

dear daughter? That was how he had usually greeted her when she came to Whitehall. Excellent, I thank you, my dear father. It pleases your mother and me to see you faring well. Hardly as much as it pleases me to see you in good health, my dear father. In her mind she called him Papa, but she would not have dared to address him like that.

That evening they had been alone together for the first time. Papa stood by the window, his hands behind his back. For quite a while he didn't say a word. And because she didn't know what to say, she too was silent.

"The oaf has a great future," he finally said.

Again he was silent. He took some marble thing from the shelf, gazed at it, and put it back.

"There are three Protestant electors," he said, so softly that she had to lean forward, "and the Elector Palatine—that is, yours—is the highest in rank, the head of the Protestant Union in the Empire. The Kaiser is ill, soon there will be a new imperial election in Frankfurt. If our side has grown even stronger by then . . ." He scrutinized her. His eyes were so small and set so deep in their sockets that it seemed as if he were not even looking at you.

"A Calvinist Kaiser?" she asked.

"Never. Unthinkable. But a formerly Calvinist elector who has found his way to the Catholic faith. Just as France's Henry once became Catholic or"—he tapped himself with a gentle gesture on his chest—"we became Protestants. The House of Habsburg is losing influence. Spain has almost forfeited Holland. The Bohemian nobility has extorted religious tolerance from the Kaiser." He fell silent once again. Then he asked: "Do you like him, then?"

The question came as such a surprise that she didn't know

what to say. With a faint smile she tilted her head. This gesture usually worked; people were then satisfied without your having had to commit yourself to anything. But it had no effect on Papa.

"It's a risk," he said. "You didn't know her, my aunt, the virgin, the old dragon. When I was young, no one thought that I would be her successor. She had my mother beheaded, and she didn't like me very much. They thought that she would have me killed too, but it didn't happen. She was your godmother, you bear her name, but she didn't come to the baptism, a sign of her aversion to us. And nonetheless I came after her in the line of succession to the throne. No one thought that she would permit a Stuart king. I didn't think so either. I will die before this year is over, that's what I thought every year, but then, at the end of every year, I was still alive. And here I am, and she is rotting in the grave. So, then, do not shy from risk, Liz. And never forget that the poor fellow will do what you tell him. He doesn't measure up to you." He reflected. Then he added as if out of nowhere: "The gunpowder under the Parliament, Liz. We could all be dead. But we are still here."

That was the longest speech she had ever heard him give. She waited, but instead of continuing to speak, he folded his hands behind his back again and without another word left the room.

And she remained behind alone. She looked out the window he had just been looking out as if she could in this way better understand her father, and thought of the gunpowder. It was only eight years ago that the assassins had tried to kill Papa and Mama and make the country Catholic again. Deep in the night Lord Harington had shaken her awake and cried: "They're coming!"

At first she hadn't known where she was and what he was talking about, and when her consciousness had gradually freed itself from the mists of sleep, it occurred to her how improper it was that this grown man was standing in her bedroom. Nothing of the sort had ever happened before.

"Do they want to kill me?"

"Worse. First you must convert, and then they will put you on the throne."

Then they had journeyed, a night, a day, another night. Liz had sat beside her lady's maid in a coach that had jerked so much that she had to vomit out the window several times. Behind the coach rode half a dozen armed men. Lord Harington rode in front. When they took a rest in the early morning hours, he explained to her in a whisper that he himself knew almost nothing. A messenger had come and had reported that a band of murderers under the command of a Jesuit was searching for Mary Stuart's granddaughter. They wanted to kidnap her and make her queen. Her father was probably dead, her mother too.

"But there are no Jesuits in England. My great-aunt drove them out!"

"There are still a few. They conceal themselves. One of the worst is named Tesimond. We have been searching for him a long time, but he has always escaped, and now he is searching for you." Lord Harington stood up with a groan. He was no longer the youngest, and it was hard for him to ride for hours. "We must go on!"

Then they had hidden in a small house at Coventry, and Liz had not been permitted to leave her room. She had had only a doll with her, no books, and from the second day on the boredom had been so agonizing that she would have preferred even the Jesuit Tesimond to the desolation of the room: always the same chest of drawers, the same floor tiles she had already counted so often—the third in the second row, counting from the window, had cracked, as had the seventh in the sixth row—and then the bed and the chamber pot, which one of the men emptied outside twice a day, and the candle that she was not permitted to light, lest someone see the glow through the window, and on a chair next to the bed her lady's maid, who had already told Liz the whole story of her life three times, though nothing interesting had ever happened in it. The Jesuit couldn't be so bad. He didn't want to hurt her, after all, he wanted to make her queen!

"Your Royal Highness misunderstands," Harington said. "You wouldn't be free. You would have to do whatever the Pope says."

"And now I have to do whatever you say."

"Correct, and later you will be grateful."

By that time the danger had passed. But none of them had known. The powder under the Parliament had been found before the conspirators had been able to ignite it, her parents had survived unscathed, the Catholics had been caught, and the hapless kidnappers were now themselves hunted and were hiding in the forests. But because they didn't know this, Liz stayed another seven endless days in the room with the two cracked tiles, seven days next to her lady's maid telling her about her uninteresting life, seven days without books, seven days with only a doll that as of the third day she had already hated more than she ever could have hated the Jesuit.

She hadn't known that Papa had meanwhile dealt with the conspirators. He summoned not only the best torturers of his two kingdoms but also three pain experts from Persia and the Emperor of China's most learned tormentor. He commanded them to cause the prisoners every kind of agony that was known to be possible for a person to cause other people, and in addition he had tortures invented that no one had yet envisioned. All the specialists were ordered to devise procedures more refined and dreadful than anything the great painters of the inferno had dreamed. The one condition was that the light of the soul not be extinguished and that the prisoner not go mad: the perpetrators still had to name their confidants, after all, and they should have time to ask God's forgiveness and to repent. For Papa was a good Christian.

In the meantime the court had sent a troop of one hundred soldiers to protect Liz. But her hiding place was so good that the soldiers could no more find it than the conspirators might have done. So the days passed. And even more days passed and then even more, and all at once the boredom had abated, and it seemed to Liz in her room as if she now understood something about the nature of time that she had not grasped before: Nothing passed. Everything was. Everything remained. And even if things changed, it always happened in the one, same, never-changing now.

During the flights that came later she often thought back to this first flight. After the defeat at White Mountain it seemed to her as if she had prepared for it early and as if fleeing were familiar to her from time immemorial. "Fold the silk," she exclaimed, "leave the dishes behind, better to take the linen, it's worth more on the road! And as for the paintings, take the Spanish ones and leave the Bohemian, the Spaniards are better painters!" And to her poor Friedrich she said: "Pay it no mind.

You run away, you hunker down for a while in a hiding place, and then you come back."

For that was how it had been in Coventry. Eventually, they had learned that the danger had been averted, and had come back to London just in time for the great service of thanksgiving. The streets between Westminster and Whitehall were filled with cheering crowds. Then the King's Men performed a play that their leading dramatist had written specially for the occasion. It was about a Scottish king who was killed by a rogue, a man with a black soul, spurred on by witches, who lied by telling the truth. It was a black play, full of fire and blood and diabolical power, and when it was over, she knew that she never wanted to see it again, even though it had been perhaps the best play she had seen in her life.

But her poor stupid husband wouldn't listen to her when they were fleeing Prague. He was too horrified by the loss of his army and of his throne and only muttered again and again that it had been a mistake to accept the Bohemian crown. Everyone who mattered had told him that it was a mistake, everyone, time and again, but in his stupidity he had listened to the wrong people.

By which he meant her, of course.

"I listened to the wrong people!" he said again, just loud enough that she could hear it, as the coach—the least conspicuous one they had—left the capital.

At that moment she realized that he would not forgive her for this. But he would still love her, just as she loved him. The nature of marriage consisted not only in the fact that you had children, it also consisted of all the wounds you had inflicted on each other, all the mistakes you had made together, all the things you held against each other forever. He would not forgive her for persuading him to accept the crown, just as she would not forgive him for having always been too stupid for her. Everything would have been simpler if only he had been somewhat quicker-witted. In the beginning she had thought she would be able to change this, but then she had recognized that nothing could be done. That disappointment had never entirely faded, and whenever he entered a room with his well-bred firm steps or she looked into his beautiful face, she felt at the same time as love a slight pang.

She raised the curtain and looked out the coach window. Prague: the second capital of the world, the center of scholarship, the old seat of the Kaiser, the Venice of the East. Despite the darkness, the contours of the castle could be made out, illuminated by the glow of countless tongues of fire.

"We shall return," she said, although even now she no longer believed it. But she knew that the only way to endure a flight was to cling to a promise. "You are the King of Bohemia, as God wills. You shall return."

And as awful as it was, there was still something about this moment that pleased her. It reminded her of the theater: acts of state, a crown changing heads, a great lost battle. All that was missing was a speech.

For here too Friedrich had failed. When he had hastily taken leave of his followers, who were pale with worry, that would have been the moment for a speech; he would have had to climb onto a table and speak. Someone would have committed it to memory, someone taken it down and passed it on. A great speech would have made him immortal. But naturally nothing had occurred to him, he had mumbled something unintelligible, and then he and she were out the door, on the way into exile. And all the noble Bohemian lords whose names she had never been able to pronounce, all the Vrshvitshkys, Prtshkatrts, and Tshrrkattrrs that the court tutor responsible for the Czech language had whispered in her ear at every reception without her ever being able to repeat them, would no longer live to see the dawn of the new year. The Kaiser was not playing games.

"It's all right," she whispered in the coach, without meaning it, for it was not all right. "It's all right, it's all right."

"I should not have accepted the damned crown!"

"It's all right."

"I listened to the wrong people."

"It's all right!"

"Is it still possible to go back?" he whispered. "To make a change? With an astrologer? It would have to work, wouldn't it, with the help of the stars, what do you think?"

"Yes, perhaps," she replied, without knowing what he meant. And when she stroked his tearstained face, she thought, strangely enough, of their wedding night. She had known nothing, no one had deemed it necessary to explain such things to a princess, whereas someone had apparently told him that it was quite simple, you just had to take the woman, she would be shy at first, but then you seized her; you had to meet her with strength and determination like an adversary in battle. He must have been trying to follow this advice. But when suddenly he grabbed hold of her, she thought he had gone mad, and since he was a head shorter than she, she shook him off and said: "Stop this nonsense!" He made another attempt, and she pushed him away so hard that he staggered into the sideboard: A carafe shattered, and for the rest of her life she remembered the puddle on the stone inlays, on which three rose petals floated like little ships. There had been three—that she remembered clearly.

He straightened up and tried again.

And since she had noticed that she was stronger, she didn't cry for help, but only held him firmly by the wrists. He could not break free. Gasping, he pulled; gasping, she held him; their eyes wide with fear, they stared at each other.

"Stop it," she said.

He began to weep.

And as she would later in the coach, she whispered: "It's all right, it's all right!" and sat down on the edge of the bed and stroked his head.

He pulled himself together, tried one last time and grabbed at her breast. She slapped his face. Almost with relief he gave up. She gave him a kiss on the cheek. He sighed. Then he curled up, slipped so deep under the blanket that even his head could no longer be seen, and fell asleep immediately.

Only a few weeks later they conceived their first son.

He was a kind child, alert and as if suffused with light, he had bright eyes and a clear voice, and he was beautiful like his father and clever like Liz, and she remembered distinctly his rocking horse and a little castle he built out of little wooden blocks and how with a high, strong voice he had sung English songs, instructed by her. At the age of fifteen he drowned under a capsized ferryboat. They had lost children before, but never so late. When the children were little, you expected it almost daily, but they had become accustomed to this one for fifteen years, he had grown up before their eyes, and then, all at once, he was gone. She found herself thinking about him all the time, and always about the moments when he was trapped under the overturned vessel, yet when she managed to put him out of her mind, he only haunted her dreams all the more vividly.

But she knew nothing about this yet on their wedding night; nor did she know it later in the coach when they were fleeing Prague; only now did she know it, in the house at The Hague that they called their royal residence, even though it was only a villa with two floors: downstairs the sitting room, which they called the reception hall and sometimes even the throne room, and a kitchen, which they called the servants' wing, and the little annex, which they called the stables, and on the second floor their bedroom, which they called their apartments. In front was a garden, which they called the park, surrounded by a hedge too infrequently trimmed.

She could never keep track of how many people were living with them. There were lady's maids, there was a cook, there was Count Hudenitz—an old idiot who had fled Prague with them and whom Friedrich had without further ado appointed chancellor—there was a gardener, who was also the stable master, which didn't mean much, since they had barely any animals in the stable, and there was a lackey, who announced the guests with a loud voice and afterward served the food. One day she realized that the lackey and the cook didn't merely resemble each other, as she had previously thought, but were one and the same—how had she not noticed it before? The servants lived in the servants' wing, except for the cook, who slept in the foyer, and the gardener, who spent the night in the throne room with his wife, if she was his wife, Liz was not sure, it was beneath the dignity of a queen to concern herself with such things, but the woman was round and winsome and a dependable minder of the children. Nele and the fool slept upstairs in the corridor, or perhaps they didn't sleep at all; Liz never saw them sleep. Housekeeping not being her forte, she left it to the majordomo, who, incidentally, also cooked.

"Can I take the fool with me to Mainz?" asked Friedrich.

"What do you want with the fool?"

He had to appear there like a ruler, he explained in his awkward way. A court simply required a fool.

"Well, if you think it will help."

And so they departed, her husband and the fool and Count Hudenitz and then also, so that the retinue wouldn't look too small, the cook. She saw them receding against the gray November sky. From the window she watched them until they were out of sight. Some time passed. The movement of the trees in the wind was scarcely perceptible. Nothing else stirred.

She sat down in her old favorite spot, the chair between window and fireplace, in which there had not been a fire in a long time. She would have liked to ask her lady's maid for another blanket, but unfortunately her lady's maid had run away the day before yesterday. A new one would be found. There were always some commoners who wanted their daughter to serve a queen—even if it was a mocked queen, of whom funny little pictures circulated. In Catholic lands it was claimed that she had slept with every nobleman of Prague; she had long been aware of this, and she could do nothing about it but be especially dignified and kind and queenly. She and Friedrich had been placed under the imperial ban, and anyone who wanted to kill them could do so without any priest denying him blessing and salvation.

It began to snow. She closed her eyes and whistled softly to herself. People called her poor Friedrich the Winter King, but when it grew cold, he froze quite terribly. Soon the snow in the garden would be knee-deep, and no one would shovel the path, for her gardener too had disappeared. She would write to Christian von Braunschweig and ask him for a few men to shovel snow *pour Dieu et pour elle*.

She thought of the day that had changed everything. The day when the letter had come and, with it, doom. All the signatures: in sweeping strokes, one name as unpronounceable as the next. Lords she had never heard of were offering the Elector Friedrich the crown of Bohemia. They no longer wanted their old king who, in personal union, was also the Kaiser; their new ruler should be a Protestant. To seal their decision, they had thrown the imperial governors out the window of Prague Castle.

Only they had fallen into a pile of shit and had survived. There was always a lot of shit below castle windows due to all the chamber pots being emptied every day. The stupid thing was that thereupon in all the land the Jesuits preached that an angel had caught the governors and set them gently on the ground.

No sooner had the letter arrived than Friedrich wrote to Papa.

Dearest Son-in-Law, Papa replied by mounted courier, don't do it under any circumstances.

Then Friedrich asked the princes of the Protestant Union. For days messengers came, breathless men on steaming horses, and every letter said the same thing: don't be stupid, Your Serene Electoral Highness, don't do it.

Friedrich asked anyone he could find. One must think it through carefully, he explained time and again. Bohemia was not part of the Empire's territory; to accept the crown was thus, according to the opinion of authoritative legal scholars, not a violation of the oath of allegiance to the Imperial Majesty.

Don't do it, Papa wrote again.

Only now did he ask Liz. She had been waiting for it; she was prepared.

It was late in the evening, and they were in the bedroom, surrounded by little flames standing motionless in the air—only the most expensive wax candles burned so still.

"Don't be stupid," she said too. Then she let a moment pass and added: "How often is one offered a crown?"

That was the moment that had changed their lives, the moment for which he never forgave her. For the rest of her life she would see it before her eyes: their four-poster bed with the coat of arms of the House of Wittelsbach on the canopy, the candle flames reflected in the carafe on the bedside table, the enormous painting of a woman with a little dog on the wall. Later she couldn't remember who had painted it—it didn't matter, they hadn't taken it with them to Prague, it was lost.

"How often is one offered a crown? How often does it happen that it is a deed pleasing to God to accept it? The Bohemian Protestants were given the letter of tolerance, then it was taken back, the noose keeps tightening. You alone can help them."

All at once she felt as if this bedroom with the four-poster bed, wall painting, and carafe were a stage and as if she were speaking before a hall full of spectators in spellbound silence. She thought of the great dramatist, the hovering magical power of his sentences; she felt as if she were surrounded by the shades of future historians, as if it weren't she who spoke but the actress who later, in a play in which this moment occurred, had the task of portraying Princess Elizabeth Stuart. The play was about the future of Christendom and a kingship and a Kaiser. If she persuaded her husband, the world would take one course, and if she didn't persuade him, it would take another course.

She stood up, walked up and down with measured steps, and delivered her speech.

She spoke of God and of duties. She spoke of the faith of the simple people and of the faith of the wise. She spoke of Calvin, who had taught all humanity not to take life lightly but as a test that one could fail every day, and once you had failed, you were a failure forever. She spoke of the obligation to take risks with pride and courage. She spoke of Julius Caesar, who, with the words "The die is cast," had crossed the Rubicon.

"Caesar?"

"Let me finish!"

"But I wouldn't be Caesar, I would be his enemy. At best I'd be Brutus. The Kaiser is Caesar!"

"In this analogy you are Caesar."

"The Kaiser is Caesar, Liz. Caesar *means* Kaiser! It's the same word."

Perhaps it was the same word, she exclaimed, but that didn't change the fact that in this analogy Caesar was not the Kaiser, even if Caesar meant Kaiser, rather he was the man who crossed the Rubicon and cast the die, and looking at it that way, Caesar was he, Friedrich, because he wanted to defeat his enemies, and not the Kaiser in Vienna, even if he bore the title Caesar!

"But Caesar didn't defeat his enemies. His enemies stabbed him to death!"

"Anyone can stab anyone, that doesn't mean anything! But they are forgotten, and Caesar's name lives on!"

"Yes, and do you know where? In the word Kaiser!"

"When you're King of Bohemia and I'm Queen, Papa will

send us help. And when the Union of Protestant Princes sees that the English are protecting Prague, they will rally around us. The crown of Bohemia is the drop that makes the ocean—"

"The barrel! A drop makes the barrel overflow. A drop in the ocean, that stands for futility. You mean the barrel."

"For God's sake, this language!"

"That has nothing to do with German, that's logic."

At that point she had lost her patience and shouted at him to be quiet and listen, and he had murmured an apology and gone silent. And she had said everything once again: Rubicon, the die, God with us, and she noticed with pride that it sounded better the third time; now she had strung the right sentences together.

"Your father will send soldiers?"

She looked him in the eyes. This was the moment, now everything was up to her: everything that would happen as of now, all the centuries, the whole immeasurable future, everything hinged on her answer.

"He is my father, he won't abandon me."

And even though she knew that they would have the same conversation again the next day and the day after that, she also knew that the decision had been made and that she would be crowned in Prague's cathedral and that she would have a court theater with the best players in the world.

She sighed. Unfortunately, she had never made it that far. She hadn't had the time, she thought between the window and the cold fireplace as she watched the flakes falling. The one winter had not been enough. To build a court theater took years. Still, their coronation had been as sublime as she had imagined, and afterward her portrait had been painted by the best artists of Bohemia, Moravia, and England, and she had eaten from golden plates and led parades through the city, and boys dressed as cherubim had carried her train.

Meanwhile Friedrich had sent letters to Papa: the Kaiser will come, dear Father, he will come without doubt, we need protection.

Papa had written back and wished them strength and fortitude, he had summoned God's blessing down upon them, he had given them advice on health, on the decoration of the throne room, and on reigning wisely, he had assured them of his eternal love, he had promised always to stand by them.

But he had not sent any soldiers.

And when Friedrich had finally written him beseechingly that he needed help for God's and Christ's sake, Papa had replied that never would even a second go by in which his dearest children were not the content of all his hope and trepidation.

But because he hadn't sent any soldiers, the Protestant Union hadn't sent any either, and thus all that remained to them was the Bohemian army, which had gathered outside the city in splendor and steel.

From the castle she saw them marching, and with cold horror it became clear to her that those flashing lances, those swords and halberds were not simply any mere shiny things but blades. They were knives, sharpened for the sole purpose of cutting human flesh, penetrating human skin, and shattering human bones. The people marching in step down there so beautifully would thrust these long knives into others' faces, and they themselves would have knives thrust into their bellies and necks, and quite a few of them would be struck by lumps of cast iron flying fast enough to tear off heads, crush limbs, smash through bellies. And hundreds of buckets of blood that was still flowing in these men would soon no longer be in them, it would spray, spill, finally seep away. What did the earth actually do with all that blood, did the rain leach it out, or was it a fertilizer that made special plants grow? A doctor had told her that the last sperm of the dying begat little mandrake men, root creatures trembling with life, which screamed like infants when you pulled them out of the ground.

And all at once she knew that this army would lose. She knew it with an assurance that made her dizzy. Never before had she seen into the future, nor did she manage to do so ever again, but at that moment it was not a presentiment but the clearest certainty: these men would die, almost all of them, except for those who would be crippled and those who would simply run away, and then Friedrich and she and the children would flee westward, and a life in exile would lie ahead of them, for they wouldn't be able to return to Heidelberg either, the Kaiser would not allow it.

And that was exactly what had happened.

They moved from one Protestant court to the next, with a dwindling retinue and dwindling money, under the shadow of the imperial ban and the revoked electoral dignity, for Friedrich's Catholic cousin in Bavaria was according to the Kaiser's will now Elector instead of Friedrich. Under the Golden Bull the Kaiser did not even have the authority to make such a decree, but who was supposed to prevent him? The Kaiser's commanders won every battle. Papa could probably have helped, and indeed he wrote full of goodwill and concern, regularly and in the finest style. But he didn't send soldiers. He also advised them not to come to England. Due to the negotiations with Spain the situation was not favorable at the moment. After all, Spanish troops were now stationed in the Palatinate to continue the war against Holland from there—keep waiting patiently, my children, God is with the righteous and fortune with the decent, don't lose heart, not a day goes by when your father James is not praying for you.

And still the Kaiser won battle after battle. He defeated the Union, he defeated the King of Denmark, and for the first time it seemed possible that Protestantism would vanish again from God's world.

But then the Swede Gustav Adolf, who had not wanted to marry Liz, landed and won. He won every battle, and now he was in winter quarters outside Mainz, and after long hesitation Friedrich had written to him, in a sweeping hand and with a royal seal, and only two months later a letter with an equally large seal had arrived at The Hague: We are pleased to know that you are well and hope that you will visit.

It was not the best moment. Friedrich had a cold, his back ached. But there was only one person who could get them back to the Palatinate and perhaps even back to Prague, and when he summoned you, you had to go.

"Do I really have to?"

"Yes, Fritz."

"But he cannot give me orders."

"Of course not."

"I am a king as he is."

"Of course, Fritz."

"But do I have to go?"

"Yes, Fritz."

And so he had set off, with the fool, the cook, and Hudenitz. It was about time too that things changed; the day before yesterday there had been groats for lunch and bread for dinner and yesterday bread for lunch and nothing for dinner. The

Dutch States General were so weary of them that they hardly gave them enough money to survive anymore.

She squinted into the snowstorm. It had grown cold. Here I sit, she thought, Queen of Bohemia, Electress of the Palatinate, daughter of the King of England, niece of the King of Denmark, grandniece of the Virgin Queen Elizabeth, granddaughter of Mary, Queen of Scots, and can't afford firewood.

She noticed that Nele was standing next to her. For a moment this surprised her. Why hadn't she gone with her husband, if indeed that's what he was?

Nele curtsied, placed one foot pointed in front of the other, spread her arms, and splayed her fingers.

"There won't be dancing today," said Liz. "Today we will talk."

Nele nodded submissively.

"We'll tell each other things. I'll tell you, you'll tell me. What do you want to know?"

"Madame?"

She was somewhat unkempt, and she had the coarse build and the crude face of her lowly station, but she was actually pretty: clear, dark eyes, silky hair, curved hips. Only, her chin was too broad, and her lips a bit too thick.

"What do you want to know?" Liz repeated. She felt a pang in her chest, half fear, half excitement. "Ask whatever you want."

"It's not my place, madame."

"If I say so, it's your place."

"It doesn't bother me that people laugh at me and Tyll. For that's our job."

"That's not a question."

"The question is, does it hurt Your Majesty?"

Liz was silent.

"That everyone is laughing, madame, does that hurt?"

"I don't understand."

Nele smiled.

"You have decided to ask me something that I don't understand. As you wish. I have given you an answer. Now it's my turn. Is the fool your husband?"

"No, madame."

"Why not?"

"Does there need to be a reason?"

"There does need to be one, yes."

"We ran away together. His father was condemned for witchcraft, and I didn't want to stay, I didn't want to marry a Steger—that's why I went away with him."

"Why didn't you want to marry?"

"Always filth, madame, and in the evening no light. Candles are too expensive. You sit in the dark and eat groats. Always groats. And I didn't like the Steger son either."

"But Tyll?"

"I'm telling you, he isn't my husband."

"Now it's your turn again to ask a question," said Liz.

"Is it bad to have nothing?"

"How should I know? You tell me!"

"It's not easy," said Nele. "No protection, through the land without a home, no house to keep the wind at bay. Now I have one."

"If I send you away, you won't have one anymore. So, then, you fled together, but why isn't he your husband?"

"A balladeer took us along. In the next market town we met a traveling entertainer, Pirmin. We learned the trade from him, but he was cruel and didn't give us enough to eat, and he hit us too. We headed north, away from the war, almost made it to the sea, but then the Swedes landed, and we turned west to avoid them."

"You and Tyll and Pirmin?"

"By then it was the two of us again."

"Did you run away from Pirmin?"

"Tyll killed him. May I ask a question again now, madame?"

Liz was silent for a moment. Nele spoke a strange peasant German; perhaps she had misunderstood something. "Yes," she then said, "now you may ask a question again."

"How many maids did you used to have?"

"Under my marriage contract I had forty-three servants for myself alone, among them six noble ladies-in-waiting, each of whom had four maids."

"And today?"

"Now it's my turn again. Why isn't he your husband? Don't you like him?"

"He is like a brother and parents. He is all I have. And I am all he has."

"But you don't want him as a husband?"

"Is it my turn again, madame?"

"Yes, it is."

"Did you want him as a husband, madame?"

"Whom?"

"His Majesty. Did Your Majesty want His Majesty as a husband to Your Majesty when Your Majesty married him?"

"That's different, child."

"Why?"

"It was an affair of state. My father and two ministers negotiated for months. And therefore I wanted him before I had ever seen him."

"And when Your Majesty saw him?"

"Then I wanted him all the more," Liz said with a furrowed brow. She was no longer enjoying this conversation.

"His Majesty is indeed a very majestic gentleman."

Liz looked her sharply in the face.

Nele returned her gaze with eyes wide open. It was impossible to tell whether she was making fun of her.

"Now you can dance," said Liz.

Nele curtsied. Then she began. Her shoes clacked on the parquet floor, her arms swung, her shoulders rolled, her hair flew. It was one of the most difficult dances in the latest style, and she did it so gracefully that Liz regretted not having musicians anymore.

She closed her eyes, listened to the clatter of Nele's shoes, and thought about what she should sell next. There were a few paintings left, among them her portrait, painted by that kind man from Delft, and the one by the self-important wretch with the large mustache who had brandished his brush with such pomp; she found his painting somewhat clumsy, but it was probably worth a great deal. She had already given away her jewelry, yet there was still a diadem and two or three necklaces; the situation wasn't hopeless.

The clatter had stopped. She opened her eyes. She was alone in the room. Where had Nele gone? How could she be so presumptuous? No one was permitted to leave the presence of a sovereign without having been dismissed.

She looked outside. On the lawn there was already a thick layer of snow, the branches of the trees bent—but hadn't it just begun to snow? All at once she was no longer certain how long she had been sitting here, in this chair by the window beside the cold fireplace, the patched blanket on her knees. Had Nele been here just now, or was that a while ago? And how many people had Friedrich taken with him to Mainz? Who had remained with her?

She tried to count: The cook was with him, the fool too, the second lady's maid had asked for a week's leave to visit her ailing parents, she probably would not come back. Perhaps there was still someone in the kitchen, perhaps not, how was one supposed to know, she had never been in the kitchen before. There was a night watchman too—so she assumed, but since she didn't leave her bedroom at night, she had never seen him. The cupbearer? He was a fine elderly gentleman, very distinguished, but now all at once it seemed to her as if he hadn't appeared in a long time; either he had remained in Prague or died somewhere on their way from exile to exile—just as Papa too had died without her having seen him again, and suddenly her brother reigned in London, whom she hardly knew and from whom there was even less reason to expect anything.

She listened. In the next room something rustled and clicked, but when she held her breath to hear better, she could no longer make it out. It was completely silent.

"Is someone there?"

No one answered.

Somewhere there was a bell. When she rang it, someone appeared. So it had always been, as was proper, so it had been her whole life. But where was it, this bell?

Perhaps everything would change soon. If Gustav Adolf and Friedrich, that is, the man she had almost married and the one she then actually had, came to an agreement, then there would again be celebrations in Prague, then they could return to the high castle, at the end of the winter, when the war resumed. For that was what happened every year: when snow fell, the war took a break, and when the birds came back and the flowers sprouted and the ice released the streams, the war too got going again.

A man was standing in the room.

That was odd—for one thing, because she hadn't rung, and for another, because she had never seen this man before. For a moment she wondered whether she ought to be afraid. Assassins were cunning, they could sneak in anywhere, nowhere was safe. But this man didn't look dangerous, and he bowed as was proper, and then he said something that was far too strange for a murderer.

"Madame, the donkey is gone."

"What donkey? And who is that?"

"Who is the donkey?"

"No, who is that. Who is . . . that there?" She pointed to him, but the idiot didn't understand. "Who are you?"

He spoke for a while. She found it hard to understand him, for her German was still not good, and his was especially coarse. Only gradually did it dawn on her that he was trying to explain that he was responsible for the stable and that the fool had returned and taken the donkey. The donkey and Nele—he had taken her too. The three of them had departed together.

"Just a donkey? The other animals are still there?"

He answered, she didn't understand, he answered again, and she comprehended that there were no other animals. The stable was now empty. Which was why, the man explained, he was standing here before her: he needed a new job.

"But why did the fool come back at all, what about His Majesty? Did His Majesty come back too?"

Only the fool had come back, said the man who due to the empty stable was no longer a stable master, and then he had gone again, with the woman and the donkey. He had left the letter behind.

"A letter? Let me see it!"

The man reached into his right pants pocket, reached into the left, scratched himself, reached into the right again, found a folded piece of paper. He was sorry about the donkey, he said. It had been an unusually clever animal. The fool had had no right to take it. He had tried to prevent him from doing so, of course, but the fellow had played a nefarious prank on him. It was very embarrassing, and he didn't want to talk about it.

Liz unfolded the piece of paper. It was crumpled and stained, the black letters were smudged, but she recognized the handwriting at one glance.

For a moment, in which she had skimmed it with one part of her mind already and with another part not yet, she was inclined to tear the letter up and simply forget that she had ever received it. But she couldn't do that, of course. She gathered her strength, clenched her fists, and read.

II

Gustav Adolf had no right to keep him waiting. Not only because it was impolite. No, he literally wasn't permitted to do it. How one behaved toward other royal personages was not at one's discretion, it was governed by strict rules. The crown of Saint Wenceslas was older than the crown of Sweden, and Bohemia was the older and richer of the two lands, thus the ruler of Bohemia enjoyed seniority over a king of Sweden—not to mention the fact that an elector too had royal rank, the Palatine court had once had an official opinion issued on it, it was proven. Now, it was true, he had been placed under the imperial ban, but the Swedish king had declared war on the Kaiser who had imposed the ban, and the Protestant Union had never accepted the revocation of the electoral dignity, therefore the King of Sweden was obliged to treat him as an elector and as such he had equal status to him—an equal status in general princely rank, and if one took into account how far back the family traced its lineage, the Palatine House clearly outranked the House of Vasa. Thus, however you looked at it, it wouldn't do that Gustav Adolf was keeping him waiting.

The king had a headache. He had difficulty breathing. He had not been prepared for the smell of the camp. He had known that cleanliness didn't prevail when thousands upon thousands of soldiers along with their supply train were camping in one place, and he still remembered the smell of his own army, which he had commanded outside Prague before it disappeared, seeping away into the ground, dispersing like smoke, but that had been nothing like this—this was unimaginable. You smelled the camp even before it came into view, a whiff of sourness and acridity hovering over the depopulated landscape.

"God, how it stinks," the King had said.

"Awful," the fool had replied. "Absolutely awful. Winter King, it's time you took a bath."

The cook and the four soldiers the Dutch States General had reluctantly given him for protection had laughed stupidly, and the King had considered for a moment whether he should put up with it, but that's what fools were for, in the end, such conduct was proper when you were a king. The world treated you with respect, but this one person was permitted to say anything.

"The King needs a bath," said the cook.

"He needs to wash his feet," cried a soldier.

The King looked at Count Hudenitz riding next to him, but since the count's face remained impassive, he could pretend he hadn't heard it.

"And behind his ears," said another soldier, and again everyone laughed except the count and the fool.

The King didn't know what he ought to do. It would have been appropriate to strike at the shameless fellow, but he didn't feel well, for days he had had a cough, and what if the man struck back? The soldier was ultimately answerable to the States General, not to him. On the other hand, he certainly couldn't let people insult him who were not his court jesters.

Then they had seen the camp from a hilltop, and the King had forgotten his anger, and the soldiers had no longer thought to mock him. Like a white city wavering in the wind it had lain at their feet—a city with a gentle movement going through its houses, a back and forth, a gliding and undulating. Only at second glance did you realize that this city consisted of tents.

The closer they came, the stronger the smell grew. It stung your eyes, it pierced your chest, and when you held a cloth over your face, it penetrated the fabric. The King squinted, he gagged. He tried to take shallow breaths, but in vain, there was no escape, he gagged more violently. He noticed that Count Hudenitz wasn't doing any better, and the soldiers too were pressing their hands over their faces. The cook was deathly pale. Even the fool no longer had his usual impudent expression.

The earth was churned up. The horses sank in, trudging as if through deep mire. Muck was heaped up dark brown on the roadside. The King tried to tell himself that it probably wasn't what he suspected, but he knew it was precisely that: the excrement of a hundred thousand people.

That wasn't all it stank of. It also stank of wounds and sores, of sweat and of all diseases known to man. The King blinked. It seemed to him as if you could even see the smell, a poisonous yellow thickening of the air.

"Where are you heading?"

A dozen cuirassiers were blocking their way—tall, composed-looking men with helmets and breastplates, such as the King hadn't seen since his days in Prague. He looked at Count Hudenitz. Count Hudenitz looked at the soldiers. The soldiers looked at the King. Someone had to speak, had to announce him.

"His Bohemian Majesty and Serene Highness Elector and Count Palatine," the King finally said himself. "On the way to your supreme commander."

"Where is His Bohemian Majesty?" asked one of the cuirassiers. He spoke Saxon dialect, and the King had to remind himself that only a small number of Swedes fought on the Swedish side—just as there were hardly any Danes in the Danish army and merely a few hundred Czechs had stood outside Prague during the battle.

"Here," said the King.

The cuirassier gave him an amused look.

"It's me. His Majesty. That's me."

The other cuirassiers grinned too.

"What's so funny?" asked the King. "We have a letter of safe conduct, an invitation from the King of Sweden. Bring me to him at once."

"All right, all right," said the cuirassier.

"I will tolerate no disrespect," said the King.

"Very well," said the cuirassier. "Come along now, Majesty."

And then he had led them through the outskirts of the camp into the interior. As the stench, which had already been so pestilential that you might have thought it couldn't grow any stronger, grew ever stronger, they passed the covered wagons of the supply train: drawbars jutted into the air, sick horses lay on the ground, children played in the filth, women nursed infants or washed clothes in tubs of brown water. These were the buyable soldiers' brides, but they were also the wives with whom many a soldier traveled. A man who had a family brought them with him to war; where else should they have stayed?

Here the King saw something horrible. He looked at it, didn't realize at first what it was, it defied recognition, but when you looked at it longer, it took shape, and you understood. He quickly looked elsewhere. He heard Count Hudenitz groaning next to him.

It was dead children. Probably none of them older than five, most of them not even a year old. They lay there heaped up and discolored, with blond, brown, and red hair, and when you looked closely, many pairs of eyes were open, forty or more, and the air was dark with flies. When they had passed, the King was tempted to turn around, because even though he didn't want to see it, he did want to see it, but he resisted the temptation.

Now they were in the interior of the camp, among the soldiers. Tents stood beside tents, men sat around fires, roasted meat, played cards, slept on the ground, drank. Everything would have been normal if you hadn't seen so many sick men: sick men in the mud, sick men on sacks of straw, sick men on wagons—not merely wounded men, but men with sores, men with bumps on their faces, men with watering eyes and drooling mouths. Not a few lay there motionless and bent; you couldn't have said whether they were dead or dying.

The stench was now hardly bearable. The King and his escorts pressed their hands over their noses. They all tried not to breathe. Only when there was no other choice did they gasp for breath behind their palms. The King gagged again, he gathered all his strength, but he gagged even more violently, and then he had to vomit off his horse. Immediately Count Hudenitz and the cook and then even one of the Dutch soldiers had the same reaction.

"Are you finished?" asked the cuirassier.

"It's Your Majesty," said the fool.

"Your Majesty," said the cuirassier.

"He's finished," said the fool.

As they rode on, the King closed his eyes. This helped a little, for you actually smelled less when you didn't see anything. Still, you smelled enough. He heard someone saying something, then he heard shouts, then he heard laughter from all sides, but it didn't matter; let them make fun of him. All he wanted was not to have to endure this stench anymore.

And so he had been brought with his eyes closed to the royal tent, in the center of the camp, guarded by a dozen Swedes in full uniform, the king's bodyguard, who stood here to fend off dissatisfied soldiers. The Swedish crown was always behind in its payments. Even if you won all the battles and took everything the defeated land offered, war was not a business that paid for itself.

"I bring a king," said the cuirassier who had led them.

The guards laughed.

The King heard his own soldiers join in the laughter. "Count Hudenitz!" he said in his sharpest authoritative tone. "This insolent behavior must come to an end."

"Yes, Your Majesty," the count muttered, and strangely enough it worked and the stupid swine went silent.

The King dismounted. He was dizzy. He bent forward and

coughed for a while. One of the guards folded back the tent flap, and the King entered with his escorts.

That had been half an eternity ago. Two hours, perhaps three, they had been waiting, on low little benches without backrests, and the King no longer knew how he was supposed to go on overlooking the fact that he was being left sitting here; but he absolutely had to overlook it, because otherwise he would have had to stand up and leave, yet no one but this Swede could bring him back to Prague. Might it have had to do with the fact that the fellow had wanted to marry Liz? He had written dozens of letters, swearing his love countless times, again and again he had sent his portrait, but she hadn't wanted him. That was probably the reason. This pettiness was his revenge.

Still, perhaps his need for retaliation would now be sated. Perhaps this was a good sign. Possibly the waiting meant that Gustav Adolf would help him. He rubbed his eyes. As always when he was agitated, his hands felt clammy, and in his stomach was a burning that no herbal tea could assuage. During the battle outside Prague it had been so strong that he had had to remove himself from the battlefield due to his attacks of colic; at home, surrounded by servants and courtiers, he had waited for the outcome, the worst hour of his life up to that point—except that everything that was to follow, every single hour, every moment, had been far worse.

He heard himself sigh. The wind above them rustled the tent. He heard men's voices outside. Somewhere someone was screaming, either a wounded man or a man dying of the plague. In all camps there were plague victims. No one spoke of it, for no one wanted to think about it; there was nothing anyone could do.

"Tyll," said the King.

"King?" said the fool.

"Do something."

"Is time going by too slowly for your liking?"

The King was silent.

"Because he's keeping you waiting so long, because he's treating you like his renderer, like his barber, like his stool groom, that's why you're bored, and I'm supposed to offer you some entertainment, right?"

The King was silent.

"I'd be happy to." The fool leaned forward. "Look me in the eyes."

Hesitantly, the King looked at the fool. The pursed lips, the thin chin, the pied jerkin, the calfskin cap; once he had asked him why he wore this costume, whether he was perhaps trying to dress up as an animal, to which the fool had replied: "Oh no, as a person!"

Then he did as he was told and looked him in the eyes. He blinked. It was unpleasant, because he wasn't accustomed to holding another person's gaze. But anything was better than having to talk about the fact that the Swede was keeping him waiting, and he had asked the fool for entertainment, after all, and now he was also a little curious what he was up to. Suppressing the desire to close his eyes, he stared at the fool.

He thought of the white canvas. It hung in his throne room and had at first given him much pleasure. "Tell the visitors that stupid people don't see the picture, tell them only the highborn see it, just say it, and you will witness a miracle!" It had been hilarious how the visitors had pretended, looking at the white picture discerningly and nodding. Of course they hadn't claimed to actually see the picture, no one was so maladroit, and almost all of them were very well aware that there was nothing but a white canvas hanging there. But first of all they simply were not completely sure whether some magic wasn't at work, and secondly they didn't know whether Liz and he perhaps believed in it—and to be suspected by a king of stupidity or lowly origins was, in the end, just as bad as being stupid or of lowly origins.

Even Liz had said nothing. Even she, his wonderful, beautiful, but ultimately not always very clever wife, had looked at the picture and remained silent. Even she had not been sure, of course not, she was only a woman.

He had wanted to speak to her about it. Liz, he had wanted to say, stop this nonsense, don't put on an act for me! But suddenly he hadn't dared. Because if she believed in it, only a little bit, if she too thought a spell had been cast on the canvas, then what would she think of him?

And if she spoke of it to others? If she said something like: His Majesty, my husband, the King, he has seen no picture on the canvas, then how would he appear in their eyes? His status was fragile, he was a king without a country, he was an exile, he was utterly dependent on what people thought of him—what should he do if word went around that in his throne room hung a magic picture that only the highborn could see, but he couldn't? Of course there was no picture there, it had been one of the fool's jokes, but now that the canvas hung there, it had developed its own power, and the King had realized with horror that he could neither take it down nor say anything about it. Neither could he claim that he saw a painting where there was no painting, for there was no surer way to prove himself an idiot, nor could he declare that the canvas was white, for if the others believed that an enchanted picture hung there with the power to expose the lowly and stupid, then that was enough to disgrace him completely. He couldn't even speak of it to his poor, sweet, dull-witted wife. It was maddening. The fool had done all this to him.

How long had the fool been staring at him now? He wondered what the fellow might be planning. Tyll's eyes were completely blue. They were very bright, almost watery, they seemed to glow faintly of their own accord, and in the middle of the eyeball was a hole. Behind it was—well, what? Behind it was Tyll. Behind it was the soul of the fool, that which he was.

Again the King wanted to close his eyes, but he held the fool's gaze. It became clear to him that what was happening on one side was happening on the other too: just as he was looking into the fool's innermost depths, so the fool was now looking into him.

Completely incongruously he thought of the moment he had looked his wife in the eye for the first time, the evening after their marriage. How shy she had been, how fearful. She had held her hands in front of the bodice he had been about to unlace, but then she had looked up and he had seen her face in the candlelight, up close for the first time, and at that moment he had sensed what it's like to truly be one with another person; but when he had spread his arms to pull her to him he had struck the carafe of rose water on the bedside table, and the tinkling of the shards had broken the spell: The puddle on the ebony parquet floor, he could still see it before his eyes, and drifting on it, like little ships, the rose petals. There had been five petals. That he remembered clearly.

Then she had begun to weep. Apparently no one had explained to her what had to happen on a wedding night, and so he had let her be, because although a king had to be strong, he had above all always been gentle, and they had fallen asleep side by side like brother and sister.

In another bedroom, at home in Heidelberg, they had later discussed the great decision. Night after night, again and again, she had dithered and cautioned, in the age-old manner of women, and he had repeatedly explained to her that one didn't receive an offer like this without the will of God and that one had to accept one's fate. But the Kaiser, she had cried time and again, what about his wrath, no one rose up against the Kaiser, and he had patiently explained to her the argument his jurists had so persuasively presented to him: that the acceptance of the Bohemian crown would not be a breach of the imperial peace because Bohemia wasn't part of the Empire.

And so he had finally persuaded her, as he had persuaded everyone else. He had made clear to her that Bohemia's throne rightfully belonged to whomever the estates of Bohemia wanted as king, and therefore they had left Heidelberg and moved to Prague, and he would never forget the day of the coronation, the vast cathedral, the huge choir, and to this day it echoed within him: You are now a king, Fritz. You are one of the great.

"Don't close your eyes," said the fool.

"I'm not," said the King.

"Be quiet," said the fool, and the King wondered whether he could let that pass, never mind fool's license, that went too far.

"What's going on with the donkey anyway?" he asked, to annoy the fool. "Can he do anything yet?"

"He will soon speak like a preacher," said the fool.

"And what does he say?" asked the King. "What can he do now?"

Two months ago he had spoken in the fool's presence about the wondrous birds of the Orient that could form complete sentences so that you'd think people were talking to you. He had read about them in Athanasius Kircher's book on God's animal world and he had not been able to get the thought of talking birds out of his head ever since.

But the fool had said that it was nothing to teach a bird to talk; all it took was a little skill to make any animal chatty. Animals were smarter than people, which was why they kept quiet: they were determined not to land themselves in trouble over trivialities. But as soon as you offered an animal good reasons for speaking, it broke its silence. He could prove this at any time in exchange for good food.

"Good food?"

Not for himself, the fool had protested, but for the animal. That's how you do it: you stick food in a book and put it in front of the animal again and again and again, with patience and strength. In its voraciousness it turns the pages and in the process picks up more and more of human language. After two months you get results.

"What kind of animal?"

"It can be done with any kind. As long as it's not too small, otherwise you won't hear its voice. With worms you won't get far. Insects aren't good either; they're always flying away before they've finished a sentence. Cats are always argumentative, and colorful Oriental birds like the ones the wise Jesuit describes aren't found here. So that leaves dogs, horses, and donkeys."

"We have no more horses, and the dog has run away."

"He's no great loss. But the donkey in the stable. Give me a year, then I can—"

"Two months!"

"That's not much time."

Not without gloating, the King had reminded the fool that he himself had just spoken of two months. That was how much time he'd have, no more, and if there was no result to be seen in two months, he could brace himself for a thrashing of biblical proportions.

"But I need food to put in the book," the fool had replied almost sheepishly. "And not a small amount."

The King was indeed aware that they never had enough food. But he had gazed at the wretched white canvas on the wall and with sly anticipation promised his fool, who had for a while now loomed larger in his mind than was reasonable, that he could have as much food as he needed for the undertaking, provided that the donkey would speak in two months.

The fool had actually kept up the pretense. Every day he had disappeared into the stable with oats, butter, and a bowl of honey-sweetened groats along with a book. Once, the King's curiosity had become overwhelming and against all seemliness he had gone to take a look and had found the fool sitting on the floor, the book open on his knees, while beside him the donkey stared good-naturedly into space.

Things were progressing quite well, the fool had immediately asserted, they had already done I and A, and by the day after tomorrow the next sound was to be expected. Then he had let out a bleating laugh, and the King, now feeling ashamed of his interest in all this nonsense, had withdrawn without a word to devote himself to affairs of state, which in dismal reality meant that he had drafted a further request for military support from his brother-in-law in England and a further request for money from the Dutch States General, as always without hope.

"Well, what does he say," the King repeated while looking into the fool's eyes, "what can he say now?"

"The donkey speaks well, but what he says doesn't make much sense. He has little knowledge, he's seen nothing of the world—give him time."

"Not a day more than agreed!"

The fool giggled. "In the eyes, King, look me in the eyes, and now tell everyone what you see!"

The King cleared his throat to reply, but then he found it hard to speak. It was dark. Colors and shapes assembled themselves. He saw himself standing before the English family again: the pale James, his feared father-in-law; his Danish mother-in-law, Anne, rigid with arrogance; and his bride, whom he hardly dared to look at. Then a whirling and swaying grew stronger and abated again, and he no longer knew where he was.

He had to cough, and when he recovered his breath, he realized that he was lying on the ground. There were men standing around him. He saw them only blurrily. There was something white above them—it was the tent, held up by poles, rippling slightly in the wind. Now he recognized Count Hudenitz, pressing his plumed hat against his chest, his face furrowed with worry, next to him the fool, then the cook, then one of the soldiers, then a grinning fellow in a Swedish uniform. Had he fainted?

The King reached his hand out. Count Hudenitz grasped it and helped him to his feet. He staggered, his legs gave way again, the cook held him from the other side until he was standing. Yes, he had fainted. At the most inappropriate time, in the tent of Gustav Adolf, whom he had to persuade with strength and shrewdness that their fortunes were linked, he had fallen over like a woman in a tight bodice.

"Gentlemen!" he heard himself saying. "Applaud the fool!"

He noticed that his shirtfront was soiled, his collar, his jacket, the decorations on his chest. Had he been sick too?

"Clap for Tyll Ulenspiegel!" he cried. "What a feat! What an amazing thing!" He grabbed the fool by the ear. It felt soft and sharp and unpleasant. He let go of it again. "But watch out that we don't give you to the Jesuits. That borders on witchcraft— what a trick!"

The fool was silent. He had a crooked smile on his face. As always the King couldn't interpret the expression.

"He is a magician, my fool. Fetch water, clean my garments, don't stand around." The King forced a laugh.

Count Hudenitz set to work on his shirtfront with a cloth; as he wiped and rubbed, his wrinkled face hovered much too close to the King's.

"One must be careful of the fellow!" the King exclaimed. "Clean faster, Hudenitz. One must be careful! No sooner has he looked me in the eyes than I've fallen over—what a magician, what a trick!"

"You fell over on your own," said the fool.

"You must teach me the trick!" the King cried. "As soon as the donkey has learned to speak, I want to learn the trick too."

"You're teaching a donkey to speak?" one of the Dutchmen asked.

"If someone like you can speak and if even the stupid King is constantly speaking, then why shouldn't a donkey speak?"

The King would have liked to slap the fool's face, but he felt too weak, so he joined in the soldiers' laughter, and then he was overcome with dizziness again. The cook supported him.

And just at this completely inopportune moment someone folded back the flap to the adjacent room, and a man in the red uniform of the majordomo stepped out and scrutinized the King with a look of condescending curiosity.

"His Majesty will see you now."

"Finally," said the King.

"Excuse me?" asked the master of ceremonies. "What was that?"

"It's about time," said the King.

"That's no way to speak in the anteroom of His Majesty."

"This creature shall not talk to me!" The King pushed him away and entered the neighboring room with a firm step.

He saw a map table, he saw an unmade bed, he saw gnawed bones and bitten apples on the ground. He saw a short, fat man—round head with a round nose, round belly, scrubby beard, thinning hair, shrewd little eyes. The man went straight up to the King, seized him by the arm with one hand and struck him so hard in the chest with the other that he would have fallen over if the man hadn't pulled him to him and embraced him.

"Dear friend," he said. "Old dear good friend!"

"Brother," gasped the King.

Gustav Adolf was pungent, and his strength was astonishing. Now he pushed the King away and eyed him.

"At last we meet, dear brother," said the King.

He could see that Gustav Adolf didn't like the form of address, and this confirmed his fears: the Swede didn't regard him as his equal.

"After all these years," the King went on with as much dignity as he could, "after all the letters, all the messages, finally face-to-face."

"I'm glad too," said Gustav Adolf. "How goes it, my friend, how are you faring? What about money? Have enough to eat?"

It took the King a moment to realize that he was being

greeted in the familiar form. Was this really happening? It must have been due to this man's poor German; perhaps it was even a Swedish quirk.

"Concern for Christendom weighs heavily on me," said the King. "As it does on . . ." He swallowed, then brought himself to use the familiar form. "As it does on you, my friend."

"Yes, right," said Gustav Adolf. "Something to drink?"

The King reflected. The thought of wine nauseated him, but it probably wasn't wise to decline.

"That's the spirit!" Gustav Adolf exclaimed, clenching his fist, and even as the King was hoping that he wouldn't be subjected to it this time, Gustav Adolf struck.

The King couldn't breathe. Gustav Adolf handed him a cup. He took it and drank. The wine tasted disgusting.

"It's terrible wine," said Gustav Adolf. "We got it from some cellar, can't be choosy, that's war."

"I think it's turned," said the King.

"Better turned than none," said Gustav Adolf. "What do you want, my friend, why are you here?"

The King looked into the bearded, shrewd, round face. So this was the savior of Protestant Christendom, the great hope. And yet once it had been he himself. How had it come to pass that it was now this fellow here, this fat-gutted man with the scraps of food in his beard?

"We're winning," said Gustav Adolf. "Is that why you're here? Because we're defeating them, at every encounter? Up in the north we defeated them and then during the advance and then down in Bavaria. We've been victorious every time, because they're weak and disorganized. Because they don't know how to drill the men. But I do. How is it with your men, I mean, how *was* it when you had some, did they like you, your soldiers, there outside Prague, before the Kaiser killed them? Only yesterday I tore the ears off one who wanted to desert with the cashbox."

The King laughed uncertainly.

"Really. That's what I did, it's not so hard. You grab, then you tear. Something like that gets around. The soldiers find it funny, because it happened to someone else, but at the same time they take care from then on not to do anything of that sort. I have barely any Swedes with me. Most of them out there are Germans, a few Finns too, along with Scotsmen and Irishmen and who knows what. They all love me. That's why we win. Do you want to join me? Is that why you're here?"

The king cleared his throat. "Prague."

"What about Prague? Drink!"

The king looked into the cup in disgust. "I require your support, brother. Give me troops, then Prague will fall."

"I don't need Prague."

"The old seat of the Kaiser, restored to the true faith. It would be a great sign!"

"I don't need signs. We've always had good signs and good words and good books and good songs, we Protestants, but then we lost on the battlefield, and it was all for nothing. I need victories. I must prevail against Wallenstein. Have you ever met him, do you know him?"

The King shook his head.

"I need reports. I think about him all the time. Sometimes I dream about him." Gustav Adolf went to the other side of the tent, bent down, rummaged in a chest, and held up a wax figure. "This is what he looks like! This is Friedland. I always look at him and think: I will defeat you. You're shrewd, I'm shrewder. You're strong, I'm stronger. Your troops love you, mine love me more. You have the devil on your side, but I have God. Every day I tell him that. Sometimes he replies."

"He replies?"

"He has diabolical powers. Of course he replies." With a suddenly morose expression Gustav Adolf pointed to the whitish face of the wax figure. "Then his mouth moves, and he mocks me. He has a soft voice because he's small, but I understand everything. Stupid Swede, he calls me, Swedish scum, Gothic brute, and he says that I can't read. I can read! Shall I show you? I read in three languages. I will defeat that swine. I'll tear his ears off. I'll sever his fingers. I'll burn him to death."

"This war began in Prague," said the King. "Only when we take back—"

"We're not doing it," said Gustav Adolf. "It's decided, we're done talking about it." He sat down on a chair, drank from his cup, and looked at the King with moistly gleaming eyes. "But the Palatinate."

"What about the Palatinate?"

"You have to get it back."

It took the King a moment to grasp what he had heard. "Dear brother, you will help me reclaim my hereditary land?"

"The Spanish troops in the Palatinate, that won't do, they have to go. Either Wallenstein calls them off or I kill them. They shouldn't flatter themselves, they may have their invincible infantry squares, but you know what? They're not so invincible at all, the invincible squares."

"Dear brother!" The King reached for Gustav Adolf's hand.

He leaped to his feet, squeezing the King's fingers so tight that the King had to suppress a yelp, put his hand on his shoulder, pulled him to him. The two of them embraced. And they were still doing it, and now that it was still going on, it had been going on for so long that the King's emotion had disappeared. Finally Gustav Adolf let go of him and began to walk up and down in the tent.

"When the snow is gone, we'll come across Bavaria and at the same time from above, a pincer movement, crushing them. Then we'll make the advance to Heidelberg and drive them out. If all goes well, we won't even need to fight a big battle before we have the Electoral Palatinate, and then I'll give it to you as a fief, and then the Kaiser will kick himself."

"As a fief?"

"Yes, how else?"

"You want to give me the Palatinate as a fief? My own hereditary land?"

"Yes."

"That won't do."

"Sure it will."

"The Palatinate doesn't belong to you."

"When I conquer it, it will belong to me."

"I thought you had come to the Empire for God and the cause of faith!"

"I could smack you, of course I have! What do you think, you mouse, you pebble, you trout! But I want something out of it too. If I simply hand over the Palatinate to you, what's in it for me?"

"You want money?"

"I do want money, but money isn't all I want."

"I'll bring you the support of England."

"Because of your wife? Hasn't done you any good so far. They've left you in the lurch. Do you think I'm stupid? Do I look like someone who believes the English are suddenly going to come running now just because you call them?"

"When I reclaim the Electoral Palatinate, I'll be the head of the Protestant faction in the Empire, and then they'll come."

"You'll never again be the head of anything."

"How dare—"

"Quiet down, poor fellow, listen. You played for high stakes, that's good, I like that. Then you lost, and in the process you set off this whole terrific war. These things happen. Some play for high stakes and win. Like me. A small country, a small military, over in the Empire the Protestant cause seems lost, and who advised me to stake everything on one card, to raise the army and march to Germany? Everyone advised against it. Don't do it, let it be, you can't win—but I did it, and I won, and soon I'll be in Vienna and will tear off Wallenstein's ears, and the Kaiser will kneel before me, and I'll say: Do you still want to be Kaiser? Then do what Gustav Adolf tells you! But it could have turned out differently. I could be dead. I could be sitting in a boat and rowing back across the Baltic Sea in tears. It doesn't do any good to be a real man, strong and clever and fearless, because you can lose anyway. Just as someone can be a fellow like you and can win all the same. Anything is possible. I took a risk and won, you took a risk and lost and then what were you supposed to do? Yes, you could have hanged yourself, but that's not for everyone, and besides, it's a sin. That's why you're still here. Because you have to do something. And so you write letters and make requests and demands and come to audiences and speak and negotiate as if you still had any relevance, but you don't! England isn't sending you any troops. The Union isn't coming to your aid. Your brothers in the Empire have abandoned you.

There's only one person who can give you back the Palatinate, and that's me. And I'll give it to you as a fief. When you kneel before me and swear allegiance to me as your lord. So what do you say, Friedrich? What's it going to be?"

Gustav Adolf crossed his arms and looked the King in the face. His bristly beard trembled. His chest rose and sank. The King could hear his breathing clearly.

"I need time to think," the King stammered.

Gustav Adolf laughed.

"You can't expect . . ." The King cleared his throat, didn't know how to continue the sentence, rubbed his forehead, implored himself not to lose consciousness again, not now of all times, not now at any price, and started over: "You can't expect me to make a decision like that without—"

"That's exactly what I expect. When I called together my generals to intervene in the war for better or worse, do you think I mulled it over endlessly? Do you think I consulted with my wife? Do you think I prayed first? I shall decide now, I said, and then I decided, and immediately forgot why, but that didn't matter either, because it was decided! And now the generals were standing in front of me and shouting 'Vivat!' and I said: I am the Lion of Midnight! That just occurred to me." He tapped himself on the forehead. "Things like that just come. I'm not thinking about anything, and suddenly it's there. The Lion of Midnight! That's me. So accept the Lion's offer or decline it, but don't waste my time."

"My family has had sovereignty over the Electoral Palatinate as well as imperial immediacy since—"

"And you think you can't be the first of your family to be given the Palatinate by the Swede as a fief. But you'll see, I'm not a bad fellow. I'll tax you lightly, and if you don't feel like coming to Sweden for my birthday, send your chancellor. I won't hurt you. Take my hand, put it there, don't be a shoe!"

"A shoe?" The King wasn't sure whether he'd heard correctly. Where had this man learned German?

Gustav Adolf had stretched out his arm, and his small, fleshy hand was hovering in front of the King's chest. All he had to do was clasp it, and he would see Heidelberg Castle again, see the hills and the river again, see the thin rays of sun again that fell through the ivy in the colonnades, see the halls again in which he had grown up. And Liz would be able to live in a manner befitting her again, with enough lady's maids and soft linen and silk and wax candles that didn't flicker and devoted people who knew how to speak to royalty. He could go back. It would be like before.

"No," said the King.

Gustav Adolf tilted his head as if he were having trouble hearing.

"I am the King of Bohemia. I am Elector of the Palatinate. I won't take what belongs to me as a fief from anyone. My family is older than yours, and it is not proper for you, Gustav Adolf Vasa, to speak to me like this or to make me such a despicable offer."

"Well, I'll be damned," said Gustav Adolf.

The King turned away.

"Wait!"

The King, already on his way out, stopped. He knew that in doing so he was destroying any effect he had, and yet he couldn't help it. A spark of hope flared in him and couldn't be smothered: it was actually possible that he had so impressed this man with his strength of character that he would now make him a new offer. You're a real man after all, he might say, I was wrong about you! But no, the King thought, nonsense. And nonetheless he stopped and turned around and hated himself for it.

"You're a real man after all," said Gustav Adolf.

The King swallowed.

"I was wrong about you," said Gustav Adolf.

The King suppressed a fit of coughing. There was a pain in his chest. He was dizzy.

"Go with God, then," said Gustav Adolf.

"What?"

Gustav Adolf punched him in the upper arm. "You have it in the right place. You can be proud. Now shove off, I have a war to win."

"Nothing else?" the King asked with a strained voice. "That was the last word, that's all: Go with God?"

"I don't need you. I'll get the Palatinate either way, and England will probably even stand by my side sooner if you're not with me; you only remind them of the old disgrace and the lost battle outside Prague. It's better for me if we don't do it. It's also better for you—you keep your dignity. Come!" He put his arm around the King's shoulders, led him to the exit, and pulled the flap aside.

When they stepped into the waiting room, everyone stood up. Count Hudenitz took off his hat and bowed deeply. The soldiers stood at attention.

"What sort of fellow is that?" asked Gustav Adolf.

It took the King a moment to realize that he meant the fool.

"What sort of fellow is that?" the fool repeated.

"I like you," said Gustav Adolf.

"I don't like you," said the fool.

"He's funny. I need someone like that," said Gustav Adolf.

"I find you funny too," said the fool.

"What do you want for him?" Gustav Adolf asked the King.

"I wouldn't recommend that," said the fool. "I bring misfortune."

"Really?"

"Look who I came with."

Gustav Adolf stared at the King for a while. The King returned his gaze and fell into a fit of coughing, which he had been suppressing the whole time.

"Go," said Gustav Adolf. "Go quickly, shove off, hurry up. I don't want you in this camp a moment longer." He backed away as if suddenly afraid. The flap fluttered shut; he was gone.

The King wiped away the tears that the coughing had brought to his eyes. His throat hurt. He took off his hat, scratched his head, and tried to understand what had happened.

This had happened: It was over. He would never see his home again. And he would never return to Prague either. He would die in exile.

"Let's go," he said.

"How did it turn out?" asked Count Hudenitz. "What was the outcome?"

"Later," said the King.

Despite everything he was relieved when the army camp was finally behind them. The air was better. The sky was high and blue above them. Hills arched in the distance. Count Hudenitz asked him twice more what the results of the discussion had been and whether a return to Prague was to be expected, but when the answer never came, he gave up.

The King coughed. He asked himself whether it had been reality: that fat man with the fleshy hands, the horrible things he had said, the offer he had wanted to accept, with all his strength, and yet had had to decline. And why, why had he declined it? He no longer knew. The reasons, just a short while ago so compelling, had dissolved into mist. And he could even see this mist; bluish, it filled the air and blurred the hills.

He heard the fool telling stories from his life, yet all at once it seemed to him as if the fool were speaking inside him, as if he weren't riding next to him, as if he were rather a feverish voice in his head, a part of himself he had never wanted to know. He closed his eyes.

The fool was talking about how he had run away with his sister: their father had been burned for witchcraft, their mother had moved to the Orient with a knight, to Jerusalem perhaps or to distant Persia, who could know.

"But she's not your sister at all," the King heard the cook saying.

He and his sister, said the fool, had at first wandered around with a bad balladeer, who had been good to them, and then with a traveling entertainer from whom he had learned everything he knew—an eminent jester, a good juggler, an actor who needn't have feared comparison with anyone on the stage, but above all he had been a wicked man, so cruel that Nele had thought he was the devil. But then they came to understand that every traveling entertainer was a little bit devil and a little bit animal and a little bit harmless too, and as soon as they understood this, they no longer needed Pirmin, that was his name, and the next time he was especially nasty, Nele cooked him a mushroom dish that he did not soon forget, or rather, he forgot it immediately, that is, he died from it, two handfuls of chanterelles, one fly agaric, a piece of a black death cap, that was all you needed. The art consisted in using fly agaric *and* death cap, because although each of the two was deadly, individually they tasted bitter and attracted attention. Cooked together, their flavors merged into a fine, pleasant-tasting sweetness, arousing no suspicion.

"So you two killed him?" asked one of the soldiers.

Not he, said the fool. His sister had killed him. He himself couldn't hurt a fly. He let out a ringing laugh. There had been no choice. The man had been so terrible that even in death they weren't rid of him. For quite a while his ghost had trailed them, had snickered behind them at night in the forest, had appeared in their dreams and offered them one sort of bargain or another.

"What do you mean, bargain?"

The fool was silent, and when the King opened his eyes, he noticed that snowflakes were falling around them. He took a deep breath. The memory of the pestilential stench of the army camp was already dissolving. He licked his lips, thinking of Gustav Adolf, and had to cough again. Were they perhaps riding backward? The idea didn't strike him as particularly odd, he just didn't want to go back to that stinking camp, not among those soldiers again and to the Swedish king, who was only waiting to mock him. The meadows around them were now covered with a thin layer of white, and over the tree stumps— the advancing army had felled all the trees—mounds of snow were forming. He tilted his head back. The sky was flickering with flakes. He thought of his coronation, he thought of the five hundred singers and the eight-part chorale, he thought of Liz in the jeweled cloak.

Hours had passed, perhaps even days, when he found his way back into time—at least the terrain had once again changed. There was now so much snow that the horses could barely proceed. They lifted their hooves carefully and set them down slowly into the high mass of white. Cold wind lashed his face. When he looked around coughing, it struck him that the

Dutch soldiers were no longer there. Only Count Hudenitz, the cook, and the fool were still riding alongside him.

"Where are the soldiers?" he asked, but the others took no notice of him. He repeated the question louder. Now Count Hudenitz looked at him uncomprehendingly, squinted, and turned his face back into the wind.

Must have run off, thought the King. "I have the army I deserve," he said. Then, coughing, he added: "My court jester, my cook, and my chancellor of a court that no longer exists. My army of air, my last faithful!"

"At your command," said the fool, who had apparently understood him despite the wind. "Now and forever. You're ill, Majesty?"

The King realized almost with relief that it was true: hence the coughing, the dizziness, his weakness in the face of the Swede, the confusion. He was ill! It made so much sense that he had to laugh.

"Yes," he cried joyfully. "I'm ill!"

As he bent forward to cough, he thought for some reason of his parents-in-law. He had known from the outset that they didn't like him. But he had won them over, with his elegance and his chivalrous demeanor, with his German clarity, his inner strength.

And he thought of his eldest. The beautiful boy everyone had loved so much. If I don't return, he had told him, the child, then you will return in my stead to the principality and to the high status of our family. Then the boat had capsized and he had drowned, and now he was with the Lord God.

Where I'll soon be too, thought the King, touching his burning forehead. In eternal glory.

He turned his head sideways and adjusted the pillow. His

breath felt hot. He pulled the blanket over his head. It was dirty and didn't smell good. How many people had slept in this bed?

He kicked the blanket away and looked around. Apparently he was in a room at an inn. On the table stood a jug. On the floor lay straw. There was only one window, with thick glass; outside whirled snow. On a stool sat the cook.

"We must go on," said the King.

"Too ill," said the cook. "Your Majesty cannot, you are —"

"Balderdash," said the King. "Nonsense, foolishness, piffle. Liz is waiting for me!"

He heard the cook reply, but before he could understand him, he must have fallen asleep again, for he found himself back in the cathedral, on the throne, facing the high altar, and he heard the choir and thought of the fairy tale about the spindle that his mother had once told him. Suddenly it seemed important, but his memory wouldn't put it in the correct order: when you unwound thread from the spindle, a piece of life was unwound too, and the quicker you turned it, say, because you were in a hurry or because something was hurting you or because things were not the way you wanted, the quicker life went by too, and the man in the fairy tale had already come to the end of the thread, and everything was over and yet had hardly even begun. But what had happened in the middle the King could not remember, and so he opened his eyes and gave the command that they now had to go onward, onward to Holland, where his palace was and his wife was waiting with the court, attired in her silks and diadem, where the festivities never ended, where every day there were the theatrical productions she liked so much, performed by the best players from all over the world.

To his surprise he was on the horse again. Someone had

wrapped a cloak around his shoulders, but he still felt the wind. The world seemed white—the sky, the ground, even the huts to the right and left of the road.

"Where's Hudenitz?" he asked.

"The count is gone!" exclaimed the cook.

"We had to go on," said the fool. "We had no more money. The innkeeper threw us out. King or not, he said, everyone has to pay!"

"Yes," said the King, "but where's Hudenitz?"

He tried to count how large his army still was. There was the fool, and there was the cook, and there was himself, and there was the fool as well, that made four, yet when he counted a second time to be safe he came up with just two, namely the fool and the cook. Because that couldn't be right, however, he counted once again and came up with three, but the next time it was four again: the King of Bohemia, the cook, the fool, himself. And at that point he gave up.

"We have to dismount," said the cook.

And indeed, the snow was too high; the horses could bear them no farther.

"But he can't walk," the King heard the fool say, and for the first time his voice didn't sound derisive but like that of an ordinary person.

"But we have to dismount," said the cook. "You see, don't you? We can't go on."

"Yes," said the fool. "I see."

While the cook held the reins, the King, propped up on the fool, dismounted. He sank into the snow up to his knees. The horse snorted with relief when it was rid of the weight, warm breath rising from its nostrils. The King patted its muzzle. The animal looked at him with dull eyes.

"We can't just abandon the horses," said the King.

"Don't worry," said the fool. "Before they have frozen to death, someone will eat them."

The King coughed. The fool supported him from the left, the cook from the right, and they trudged on.

"Where are we going?" asked the King.

"Home," said the cook.

"I know," said the King, "but today. Now. In the cold. Where are we going now?"

"Half a day's march westward there's supposed to be a village where there are still people," said the cook.

"No one knows for sure," said the fool.

"Half a day's march is a whole day's march," said the cook. "With so much snow."

The King coughed. He trudged while he coughed, he coughed while he trudged, he trudged and trudged, and he coughed, and he marveled at the fact that his chest hardly hurt anymore.

"I think I'm getting better," he said.

"Definitely," said the fool. "It shows. You are indeed, Majesty."

The King could tell that he would have fallen down if the two of them hadn't been supporting him. The snowdrifts grew higher and higher. It became harder and harder for him to keep his eyes open in the cold wind. "Where's Hudenitz, then?" he heard himself asking for the third time. His throat hurt. Snowflakes everywhere, and even when he closed his eyes he saw them: gleaming, dancing, whirling dots. He sighed. His legs buckled. No one was holding him. The soft snow received him.

"Can't leave him behind," he heard someone saying above him.

"What should we do?"

Hands reached for him and pulled him up. A hand stroked his head almost tenderly, which reminded him of his favorite nursemaid, who had raised him, in those days in Heidelberg when he was only a prince and not a king and all was still well. His feet trudged in the snow, and when he briefly opened his eyes, he saw next to him the contours of cracked roofs, empty windows, a destroyed well, but people were nowhere to be seen.

"We can't go inside any of them," he heard. "The roofs are broken. Besides, there are wolves."

"But we'll freeze to death out here," said the King.

"The two of us won't freeze to death," said the fool.

The king looked around. And indeed, the cook was no longer to be seen; he was alone with Tyll.

"He tried a different way," said the fool. "Can't be held against him. Everyone fends for himself in a storm."

"Why won't we freeze to death?" asked the King.

"You're burning too hot. Your fever is too high. The cold can't do anything to you, you'll die first."

"Of what, then?" asked the King.

"Of the plague."

The King was silent for a moment. "I have the plague?"

"Poor fellow," said the fool. "Poor Winter King, yes, that's what you have. You've had it for days now. You haven't noticed the lumps on your neck? You don't feel it when you inhale?"

The King inhaled. The air was icy. He coughed. "If it's the plague," he said, "then you'll get infected too."

"It's too cold for that."

"Can I lie down now?"

"You're a king," said the fool. "You can do what you want, when and wherever you like."

"Then help me. I'm going to lie down."

"Your Majesty," said the fool, supporting him by the back of the neck and helping him onto the ground.

The King had never before lain on such a soft surface. The snowdrifts seemed to be glowing faintly, the sky was already darkening, but the flakes were still a bright shimmer. He wondered whether the poor horses might still be alive. Then he thought of Liz. "Can you deliver a message to her?"

"Of course, sire."

It didn't suit him that the fool was speaking so respectfully to him, it wasn't proper—that was why you had a court jester, after all, so that your mind wasn't lulled to sleep by all the adulation. A fool was expected to be impertinent! He cleared his throat to scold him, but then he had to cough once again, and he found it too difficult to speak.

But hadn't there been something else? Ah, yes, the message to Liz. She had always loved the theater, the appeal of which he had never understood. People standing on the stage and pretending to be someone else. He had to smile. A king without a country in a storm, alone with his fool—something like this would never happen in a play, it was too absurd. He tried to sit up, but his hands sank into the snow and he slumped back again. What was it he had wanted to do? Oh, yes, the message to Liz.

"The Queen," he said.

"Yes," said the fool.

"Will you tell her?"

"I will."

The King waited but the fool still made no move to mock him. And yet it was his duty! Annoyed, he closed his eyes. To his surprise, this didn't change anything at all: he still saw the fool, and he saw the snow too. He felt paper in his hands—apparently the fool had slid it between his fingers—and he felt something firm, probably a piece of coal. *We shall see each other again before God*, he wanted to write, *in my life I have loved only you*, but then everything became muddled and he was no longer certain whether he had already written it or had only wanted to write it, and he also didn't remember clearly to whom the message was to be sent. Therefore he wrote with a shaky hand: "Gustav Adolf will soon be dead, I know that now, but I will die first." Yet that wasn't the message at all, it was completely beside the point, hence he added: "Take good care of the donkey, I give him to you," but no, he hadn't wanted to say that to Liz but to the fool, and the fool was here, he could say it to him personally, while the message was for Liz. And so he started over and was about to write, but it was too late, it was no longer possible. His hand went limp.

He could only hope that he had already written down everything that was important.

Effortlessly he stood up and walked. When he looked back once more, he noticed that they were again three: the fool, kneeling in his calfskin cloak, the King on the ground, whose body was already half covered with white, and he. The fool looked up. Their eyes met. The fool raised his hand to his forehead and bowed.

He lowered his head in parting, turned, and walked away. Now that his feet no longer sank into the snow, the going was swift and easy.

Hunger

"ONCE UPON A TIME," SAYS NELE.

It's already their third day in the forest. Now and then light filters through the canopy of leaves, and despite this ceiling of foliage above them they get wet from the rain. They wonder whether the forest will ever end. Pirmin, who walks ahead of them and from time to time scratches the semicircle of his bald head, never turns around to look at them. Sometimes they hear him muttering, sometimes singing in a foreign language. They now know him well enough not to speak to him, for that could make him angry, and once he's angry, it won't be long before he hurts them.

"A mother had three daughters," Nele goes on. "They owned a goose. It laid a gilded egg."

"A what egg?"

"A golden one."

"You said gilded."

"It's the same thing. The daughters were very different from each other. Two were evil, they had black souls, but they were beautiful. The youngest, on the other hand, was good, and her soul was white as snow."

"Was she beautiful too?"

"The most beautiful of the three. As beautiful as the dawning day."

"The dawning day?"

"Yes," she said in annoyance.

"Is that beautiful?"

"Very."

"The dawning day?"

"Very beautiful. And the evil sisters forced the youngest to work, day and night without cease, and she chafed her fingers bloody, and her feet became sore lumps, and her hair turned gray before its time. One day the golden egg hatched, and a thumbling stepped out and asked: Maiden, what is your wish?"

"Where was the egg the whole time before?"

"I don't know, it was lying someplace."

"The whole time?"

"Yes, it was lying someplace."

"An egg made of gold? And nobody took it?"

"It's a fairy tale!"

"Did you make it up?"

Nele is silent. The question seems senseless to her. The boy's silhouette in the forest twilight looks very thin—he walks with a slight stoop, his neck craned forward over his chest, his body scrawny, as if he were a wooden figure brought to life. Did she invent this fairy tale? She herself doesn't know. She has heard so many told, by her mother and her two aunts and her grandmother, so many about thumblings and golden eggs and wolves and knights and witches and good as well as evil sisters, that she doesn't have to think; once you have begun, it continues of its own accord, and the parts assemble themselves, sometimes one way and sometimes another, and you have a fairy tale.

"Well, go on," says the boy.

As she tells him about how the thumbling grants the beautiful sister's wish and transforms her into a swallow so that she can fly away to the land of milk and honey, where all is well and no one goes hungry, Nele notices that the forest is growing denser and denser. They are supposed to be approaching the city of Augsburg. But that doesn't appear to be the case.

Pirmin stops. He spins around, sniffing. Something has attracted his attention. He leans forward and contemplates the trunk of a birch, the white-and-black bark, the cavity of a knothole.

"What is it?" Nele asks, startled at the same moment by her thoughtlessness. She feels the boy stiffen beside her.

Slowly Pirmin turns his large, unshapely head to them. His eyes glint with hostility.

"Go on," he says.

On her arms and legs she still feels exactly where he has pinched her, and the pain in her shoulder is still almost as bad as it was four or five days ago when he twisted her arm behind her back in a skillful hold. The boy tried to help her, but then he kicked him so hard in the stomach that he couldn't stand upright for the rest of the day.

And yet Pirmin has never gone too far. He has hurt them, but not too badly, and as often as he has touched Nele, it has never been above the knee or below the navel. Since he knows that the two of them could run away at any time, he keeps them the only way he can: he teaches them what they want to learn.

"Go on," he says again. "I won't ask again."

And Nele, who is still wondering what he might have seen in the knothole, tells them how the thumbling and the swallow reach the gate of the land of milk and honey, where a guard, as tall as a tower, keeps watch. He says: Here you will never be hungry and never thirsty, but you may not enter! They implore him and beg and plead, yet he knows no mercy, the guard has a heart of stone, which weighs heavily in his breast and doesn't beat, and so he always says: You may not enter! You may not enter!

Nele falls silent. The two of them are looking at her and waiting.

"And?" asks Pirmin.

"They didn't enter."

"Never?"

"His heart was made of stone!"

Pirmin stares at her for a moment. Then he laughs out loud and continues walking. The two children follow him. Soon it will be night, and unlike Pirmin, who hardly ever shares, they have nothing left to eat.

Normally Nele bears the hunger better than the boy. At those times she imagines that the pain and the weakness inside her are something that belongs elsewhere and has nothing to do with her. But today it is the boy who manages better. His hunger feels like something light, a throbbing and hovering; it almost seems to him as if he could rise into the air. As the two of them walk along behind Pirmin, his thoughts are still with the lesson from this morning: How do you impersonate someone? How do you go about taking a brief glance at someone's face and then becoming him—holding your body as he holds his, making your voice sound like his, having the same look in your eyes that he has?

There's nothing people love as much as this, there's nothing they laugh at as readily, but you have to get it right, for if you do it wrong, you're pitiful. To imitate someone, you idiot, you stupid child, you stubborn, talentless stone, it is not enough merely to resemble him, you must resemble him more than he resembles himself, for he can afford to be any which way, but you must be utterly him, and if you can't do that, then give up, quit, go back to Papa's mill and don't waste Pirmin's time!

It's about looking, do you understand? That's the most important thing: Look! Understand people. It's not so hard. They're not complicated. They don't want anything unusual, everyone just wants what he wants in a somewhat different way. And once you understand in what way someone wants something, then you only have to want as he does, and your body will follow, then your voice will change of its own accord, then you will have the correct look in your eyes.

You have to practice, of course. Everything takes practice. Practice and practice and practice. Just as you have to practice dancing on the tightrope or walking on your hands, or as you still have to practice for a long time before you will manage to keep six balls in the air: you always, always have to practice, and to do so with a teacher who doesn't let you get away with anything, for people always let themselves get away with a great deal, people are not strict with themselves, which is why it is up to the teacher to kick you and hit you and laugh at you and tell you that you're a wretch who will never be able to do it.

And now the boy is so lost in reflection on how to imitate people that he has almost forgotten his hunger. He imagines the Stegers and the smith and the priest and old Hanna Krell, who he didn't know was a witch, but now that he knows, many things make new sense. One after another he summons them and imagines how each of them holds himself and speaks; he stoops his shoulders, draws in his chest, moves his lips soundlessly: Help me with the hammer, boy, drive in the nail, and his hand trembles slightly when he raises it, due to rheumatism.

Pirmin stops and orders them to gather dry branches. They know it's hopeless: after three days of rain the wetness has crept into everything, sparing nothing, leaving nothing dry. But because they don't want to make Pirmin angry, they bend over and crawl this way and that and reach into the bushes and pretend to be searching.

"How does it end?" the boy whispers. "Do they get into the land of milk and honey?"

"No," she whispers. "They find a castle in which an evil king reigns, they kill him, and the girl becomes queen."

"Does she marry the thumbling?"

Nele laughs.

"Why not?" asks the boy. He himself is surprised that he wants to know, but at the end of a fairy tale there must be a marriage, otherwise it's not over, otherwise things are not right.

"How is she supposed to marry the thumbling?"

"Why not!"

"He's a thumbling."

"If he can do magic, he can make himself big."

"Well, fine, then he casts a spell on himself and turns into a prince, and they get married, and if they have not died, they are still alive today. Good?"

"Better."

But when Pirmin sees the damp branches that they bring him, he begins to shout, to hit and to pinch. His hands are quick and strong, and just when you think you have escaped one of them by a leap, the other has already seized you.

"Rats," he shouts, "sloths, stupid, good-for-nothing filthy slugs, you are useless, no wonder your parents drove you away!"

"Not true," says Nele. "We ran away."

"Yeah, yeah," Pirmin shouts, "and his father was incinerated by the executioner, I know, I've heard it often."

"Hanged," says the boy. "Not incinerated."

"Did you see it?"

The boy is silent.

"Quite right!" Pirmin laughs. "Bite fight plight, you have no inkling, your brow is wrinkling! When someone is hanged for witchcraft, the corpse is incinerated afterward—that's what happens, that's how it's done. So he was incinerated, and he was hanged as well."

Pirmin squats down, hums as he fiddles with the wood, rubs sticks together, while saying words under his breath. The boy recognizes a few spells, angel of fire, bring a spark, set this wood alight, kindle the sacred fire, make the flames burn bright; it is an old spell that Claus used too. And indeed it is not long before the boy smells the familiar aroma of burning wood. He opens his eyes and claps his hands. Grinning, Pirmin gives the hint of a bow. He puffs his cheeks and blows air into the fire. The glow of the flames plays on his face. Behind him his shadow, gigantically enlarged, dances on the tree trunks.

"And now perform something for me!"

"We're tired," says Nele.

"If you want to eat, perform. That's how it is now. That's how it will be until you kick the bucket. You belong to the traveling people, no one protects you, and when it rains, you have no roof. No home. No friends but others like you, who will not like you very much, because food is scarce. That is the price you pay to be free. Not to have to listen to anyone's rules. The only rules are that you run when you have to run, and that when you're hungry, you perform."

"Will you give us food?"

"No, crow, oh woe, no, no!" Laughing, Pirmin shakes his head, then he sits down behind the fire. "Nothing more, not a crumb, not a thumb, and don't be too loud, for there are soldiers in the forest. Around this time they are very drunk, and they will also be angry because the peasants near Nuremberg have banded together. If they find us, we're in trouble."

The two of them hesitate for a moment, for they really are very tired. But in the end that's why they are here, that's why they went with Pirmin—to perform, to learn tricks.

First the boy does his tightrope walk. He doesn't stretch the rope very high up, even though by now he no longer falls down—but you never know what Pirmin will do; he could suddenly throw something or shake the rope. The boy takes a few careful steps to test the tautness of the rope, which he can hardly see anymore in the twilight. Then he gains confidence and walks faster. Then he runs outright. He leaps, spins in the air, lands, and runs backward to the end. He runs back again, bends forward, suddenly is running on his hands, reaches the other end again, somersaults, gets back on his feet, flails his arms only briefly, finds his balance, and bows. He jumps down.

Nele claps her hands wildly.

Pirmin spits. "That was ugly at the end."

The boy bends down, picks up a stone, throws it into the air, catches it again without looking, and throws it into the air again. While the stone is in the air, he picks up a second one and throws it, catches the first, throws it, picks up a third with lightning speed, catches the second, throws it again, throws the third after it, catches and throws the first and goes down on his knees to take a fourth stone. Ultimately he has five whirling around his head, an up-and-down in the evening light. Nele is holding her breath. Pirmin sits motionless and stares, his eyes narrow slits.

The difficulty lies in the fact that the stones are not the same shape or weight. Hence the hand must adapt to each one, must change its grasp slightly each time. In the case of the heavy ones the arm must yield somewhat more, in the case of the light ones throw harder, so that they all fly at the same speed and on the same course. This is possible only when you have practiced a great deal. But it is also possible only when you forget that it's you yourself who is throwing the stones. You must to some extent only watch them flying. As soon as you are too involved, you lose the rhythm and can't do it anymore.

For a little while the boy still manages it. He doesn't think, keeping himself inwardly on the edge, looking up and seeing the stones above him. Between the leaves he perceives the last light of the darkening sky. He feels drops on his forehead and his lips, he hears the crackling of the flames, and now he senses that it will not be possible for much longer, that in a moment everything will get muddled—and to forestall this, he lets the first stone whirl into the underbrush behind him, then the second, the third, the fourth, and finally the last, and he looks at his empty hands in astonishment: Where did they go? In feigned perplexity he bows.

Nele claps again. Pirmin makes a disparaging hand gesture—but from his silence the boy can tell that he did a good job. Naturally, he would be able to juggle better if Pirmin would lend him his juggling balls. He has six of them, made of thick leather, smooth and easy to handle, each in a different color, so that they turn into a shimmering fountain of hues when you make them fly fast enough. Pirmin has them in the jute sack that he always carries over his shoulder and that the children don't dare to touch: Try it, just reach in, I'll break your fingers. The boy has seen Pirmin juggling, in this or that market town. He does it very skillfully but no longer quite as agilely as he must have in the past, and if you pay attention, you can see that due to all the strong beer he is gradually losing his sense of balance. With those balls the boy could probably do it even better. But for that very reason Pirmin will never permit him to use them.

Now it's time for the play. The boy nods to Nele, she bounds over and begins to narrate: Once two armies assembled outside golden Prague, trumpets blare, the warriors' armor flashes, and here is the young King, full of courage, in the company of his English wife. Yet nothing is sacred to the Kaiser's generals. They beat their drums, do you hear them? The doom of Christendom is brewing.

The children change from one role to the next, they alter intonation, voice and language, and since they can speak neither Czech nor French nor Latin, they speak the most exquisite gibberish. The boy is an officer in the Kaiser's army, he gives the command, he hears the cannons roaring behind him, he sees the Bohemian musketeers aim their weapons at him, he hears the order to retreat, yet he casts it to the wind, you don't win by retreating! And he advances, the danger is great, but fortune is with him, the musketeers yield to the courage of his regiment, the victory fanfares blare, he can hear them more clearly than the rain, and now he is in the golden throne room of the Kaiser. The sovereign sits mildly on the throne. With a soft hand he drapes a sash of medals over his shoulder: Today you have saved my Empire, Generalissimo! He sees the faces of the noblemen, he inclines his head, they bow in humility. Then a noblewoman comes up to him: A word, I have a mission! He speaks calmly:

Whatever it may be, and even if it costs me my life, for I love you. That I know, distinguished lord, she replies, yet you must forget it. Listen to my mission. I want you to—

Something hits his head, there's a spray of sparks, the boy's knees give way. It takes him a moment to realize that Pirmin has thrown something. He touches his forehead. He leans forward—there lies the stone. Once again he is impressed how well Pirmin can aim.

"You rats," says Pirmin. "Bunglers. Do you think anyone wants to see this? Who wants to stare at playing children? Are you doing this for yourselves? Then go back to your parents, the ones who haven't been incinerated. Or are you doing it for spectators? Then you have to be better. Better story, better acting, quicker, more power, more wit, more of everything! Then you have to have rehearsed it!"

"His forehead!" Nele cries. "He's bleeding!"

"But not enough. He should bleed much more. Someone who can't do his job should bleed all day."

"You swine!" Nele cries.

Absently Pirmin picks up another stone.

Nele ducks.

"We'll begin again," the boy says.

"I've had enough for today," says Pirmin.

"No," says the boy. "No, no. One more time."

"I've had enough, let it be," says Pirmin.

So they sit down with him. The fire has burned down to a faint glow. A memory comes to the boy, which he doesn't know whether he lived or dreamed: nocturnal noise from the thicket, buzzing and cracking and crunching coming from everywhere, and a large animal, the head of a donkey, its eyes open wide, a scream unlike any he has ever heard, and hot streaming blood.

He shakes his head, pushes the memory away, reaches for Nele's hand. Her fingers squeeze his.

Pirmin chuckles. Once again the boy wonders whether this man can read his thoughts. It's not so hard, Claus explained it to him, you only have to know the right spells.

Actually Pirmin is not a bad fellow. Not entirely bad, in any case, not as thoroughly bad as it would seem at first glance. Sometimes there's something soft about him, which could almost turn into mildness, if he didn't have to lead the hard life of the traveling people. He is actually too old to still be moving from place to place, braving the rain and sleeping under trees, but somehow due to bad luck all opportunities for employment with room and board have passed him by, and now no more will arise. Either his knees will hurt so much in a few years that he won't be able to roam anymore and will have to stay in the first village he comes to, with some farmer who has enough sympathy to take him on as a day laborer, for which, however, he will need a great deal of luck, for no one wants traveling people with them, it brings misfortune and bad weather and causes the neighbors to speak ill of them. Or Pirmin will have to beg, outside the wall of Nuremberg, Augsburg, or Munich, for beggars are not let into the cities. People throw food to the unfortunate, but it's never enough for all of them, the stronger ones take it. Thus Pirmin will starve.

Or it won't even come to that. For example, because he stumbles somewhere along the way—damp roots are so treacherous, it's hard to believe how slippery wet wood can be; or a stone on which he steps while climbing is not as stable as it seems. Then he will lie on the roadside with a broken leg, and anyone passing by will steer clear of the foul fellow in the muck, for what are they supposed to do, carry him? Give him warmth and nourishment, provide for him like a brother? Things like that occur in legends of the saints, not in real life.

What, then, is the best thing that can happen to Pirmin? For his heart to stop. For a pang to shoot through his chest and his innards, during a show on the market square: he looks up at the balls, then an instant of the utmost torment, then it's all over.

He could bring it about himself. It wouldn't be hard. Many traveling people do it—they know the mushrooms that guide you gently into sleep. Only, Pirmin confessed to them in a weak moment that he doesn't have the courage. God opposed it with his severest commandment: he who kills himself may escape the adversity of this world, but he does so at the price of eternal torment in the next. And eternal—that doesn't mean just a long time. It means that the longest time you can imagine, even if it were a thousand times as many years as it would take a bird to grind away the Brocken mountain with its beak, is merely the very tiniest fraction of the tiniest fraction of it. And even though it lasts so long, you don't get used to the horror, to the loneliness, to the pain. That's the system. So who can hold it against Pirmin that he is the way he is?

And yet everything could have turned out differently. He has seen good times too. Once upon a time he had a future. In his heyday he made it to London, and whenever the strong beer makes him drunk, that is what he talks about. Then he tells them about the Thames, so wide in the glow of sunset, about the taverns and the bustle on the streets—the city was so huge that you could walk for days and not reach its end! And there were theaters on every corner. He didn't understand the language, but the grace of the players and the truth in their faces moved him in a way that nothing later did.

He was young in those days. He was one of the many traveling performers who crossed the Channel with the retinue of the young Electoral Prince. The Electoral Prince came to England to marry Princess Elizabeth, and since the English have a high regard for performers, he brought along all his country had to offer: ventriloquists, fire eaters, belchers, puppeteers, pugilists, hand walkers, hunchbacks, picturesque cripples, and indeed also him, Pirmin. On the third day of festivities, in the house of a certain Bacon, Pirmin threw his balls in front of all the great lords and ladies. The tables were bedecked with flowers. The host stood with a clever, wicked smile at the entrance to the hall.

"I can still see them before my eyes," Pirmin says. "The straitlaced Princess, the bridegroom who doesn't know what's hit him. We should hunt him down!"

"What should we do?"

"Hunt him down! It's said that he moves from land to land and eats the Protestant nobility out of house and home. It's said that he still acts as if he were king. It's said that he drags his own little court along with him. But does he have a fool? Perhaps an old court jester is just the thing for a king without a country."

Pirmin has said this often. It's another effect of all the beer: he repeats himself, and he doesn't care. But now by the fire he is chewing on his last piece of dried meat while the children sit hungrily beside him listening to the forest noises. They hold hands and try to think of things that distract them from the hunger.

With some practice it works very well. When you really know hunger, then you also know how to go about stifling it for a while. You must banish every image of edible things, you must clench your fists and pull yourself together and simply not permit it. Instead you can think about juggling, for it can be practiced in your head too—in this way you improve. Or you imagine yourself moving across the rope, wondrously high up, over peaks and clouds. The boy squints into the embers. Hunger makes you lighter. And as he gazes into the red glow, it seems to him as if he were seeing below him the bright vast day, as if the sun were blinding him.

Nele puts her head on his shoulder. My brother, she thinks. He is now all she has left. She thinks about the home she will never see again, about her mother who was usually sad, about her father who hit her worse than Pirmin, and about her siblings and the hands. She thinks about the life that lay ahead of her: the Steger son, the work in the bakery. She doesn't permit herself to think about the bread, of course—but now that she has thought about how she must not think about it, it has happened after all, and she sees the soft loaf of bread before her eyes, and she can smell it, and she feels it between her teeth.

"Cut it out!" says the boy.

And now she can't help laughing and wonders how he knows what she was thinking. But it worked; the bread is gone.

Pirmin has sunk forward. He is lying on the ground like a heavy sack, his back is rising and falling, and he is snoring like an animal.

The fearful children look around.

It is cold.

Soon the fire will be out.

The Great Art
of Light and Shadow

AT MOST TIMES, ADAM OLEARIUS, THE GOTTORF COURT
mathematician, curator of the ducal cabinet of curiosities
and author of an account of a grueling mission to Russia and
Persia, from which he had returned a few years earlier nearly
unscathed, had a quick tongue, yet today in his nervousness he
found speaking difficult. For before him, ringed by half a dozen
secretaries in black cowls, deliberate, attentive, and bearing his
incomprehensible wealth of learning like a light burden, stood
none other than Father Athanasius Kircher, professor of the
Collegium Romanum.

Although it was their first meeting, they treated each other
as if they had known each other for half their lives. This was cus-
tomary among scholars. Olearius inquired what had brought his
venerable colleague here, intentionally leaving unclear whether
he meant the Holy Roman Empire of the German Nation or
Holstein or Gottorf Castle towering behind them.

Kircher reflected for a while as if he had to retrieve the
answer from the depths of his memory before he replied with a
soft and somewhat too-high voice that he had left the Eternal
City for the sake of various undertakings, the most important
of which was to find a cure for the plague.

"God help us," said Olearius, "is it in Holstein again?"

Kircher was silent.

Olearius was disconcerted by how young the man standing opposite him was: it was hard to conceive that this head with the soft features had solved the mystery of magnetic force, the mystery of light, the mystery of music, and supposedly even the mystery of the writing of ancient Egypt. Olearius was aware of his own significance and was not known for his modesty. But in the presence of this man his voice threatened to fail.

It went without saying that no religious enmity reigned between scholars. Almost twenty-five years ago, when the great war had begun, it would have been different, but things had changed. In Russia the Protestant Olearius had befriended French monks, and it was no secret that Kircher corresponded with many Calvinist scholars. Except that a short while ago, when Kircher mentioned in passing the death of the Swedish king at the Battle of Lützen and in this connection spoke of the grace of the good Lord, Olearius had to inwardly force himself not to reply that Gustav Adolf's death had been a catastrophe in which any reasonable person had to recognize the hand of the devil.

"You say that you want to cure the plague." Olearius, still without an answer, cleared his throat. "And you say that you have come to Holstein for this purpose. So, then, has the plague come back to us?"

Kircher let another moment pass and, as was apparently his wont, contemplated his fingertips before he replied that he naturally would not have come here to find a cure for the plague if the plague were raging in this region, for where it raged was precisely not where to find the means to hinder its spread. God's goodness had so splendidly decreed that the searcher for a remedy, instead of exposing his life to the danger, should visit the very places to which the disease had not spread. For only there was that which countered it by the force of nature and the will of God to be found.

They were sitting on the only stone bench of the castle park that had not been destroyed and dipping candy canes in diluted wine. Kircher's six secretaries stood at a respectful distance and observed spellbound.

It was not good wine, and Olearius knew that the park and the castle were not exactly impressive either. Marauders had felled the old trees, the lawn was covered with scorch marks, and the hedges were as damaged as the façade of the building, which was even missing part of its roof. Olearius was old enough to remember days when the castle had been a jewel of the north, the pride of the Jutish dukes. At the time he had still been a child and his father a simple craftsman, but the duke had recognized his talent and allowed him to become a student, and later he had sent him as an envoy to Russia and to distant, dazzling Persia, where he had seen camels and griffins and towers of jade and talking snakes. He would have liked to stay there, but he had sworn allegiance to the duke, and his wife too was waiting at home, or so he believed at least, for he hadn't known that she had died in the interim. Thus he had returned to the cold Empire, to the war, and to the sad existence of a widower.

Kircher pursed his lips, took another sip of wine, almost imperceptibly screwed up his face, wiped his lips with a red-stained little handkerchief, and went on to explain why he was here.

"An experiment," he said. "The new way of achieving certainty. One does tests. For example, one ignites a ball of sulfur, bitumen, and coal, and immediately one senses that the sight of the fire provokes anger. If one stays in the same room, one reels with rage. This is due to the fact that the ball reflects qualities of the red planet Mars. In a similar way one can use the watery qualities of Neptune to calm excited tempers or the confusing qualities of the treacherous moon to poison the mind. A sober man need only stay close to a moonlike magnet for a short time to get as drunk as if he had emptied a skin of wine."

"Magnets make you drunk?"

"Read my book. In my new work there will be even more about it. It's called *Ars magna lucis et umbrae* and answers the open questions."

"Which ones?"

"All of them. As for the ball of sulfur: The experiment gave me the idea of having a decoction of sulfur and snail's blood administered to a plague victim. For on the one hand the sulfur drives the Martian components of the disease out of him, while on the other hand the snail's blood as a dracontological substitution sweetens that which sours the humors."

"Excuse me?"

Kircher again contemplated his fingertips.

"Snail's blood is a substitute for dragon's blood?" asked Olearius.

"No," Kircher said forbearingly, "dragon's bile."

"And what brings you here now?"

"The substitution has its limits. The plague victim in the experiment died despite the decoction, which clearly proves that real dragon's blood would have cured him. Thus we need a dragon, and one of the last dragons of the north lives in Holstein."

Kircher looked at his hands. His breath formed little vapor

clouds. Olearius shivered. Inside the castle it was no warmer, there were no trees left far and wide, and the duke used what little firewood there was for his bedroom.

"Has it been sighted, then, the dragon?"

"Of course not. A dragon that had been sighted would be a dragon that did not possess the most important quality of dragons—that of making itself undetectable. For this very reason one must treat all reports by people of having sighted dragons with extreme skepticism, for a dragon that let itself be sighted would be recognized a priori as a dragon that is no real dragon."

Olearius rubbed his forehead.

"In this region, evidently, a dragon has never before been witnessed. Hence I am confident that there must be one here."

"But none have been witnessed in many other places too. So why here in particular?"

"First of all, because the plague has withdrawn from this area. That is a strong sign. Secondly I used a pendulum."

"But that's magic!"

"Not if one uses a magnetic pendulum." Kircher looked at Olearius with gleaming eyes. The slightly disparaging smile disappeared from his face as he leaned forward and asked with a simplicity that astounded Olearius: "Will you help me?"

"Help you do what?"

"Find the dragon."

Olearius pretended he had to think. Yet it wasn't a difficult decision. He was no longer young, he had no children, and his wife was dead. He visited her grave every day, and it still happened that he would wake up and begin to weep, so much did he miss her and so heavily did the loneliness weigh on him.

Nothing held him here. If, then, the most significant scholar in the world was inviting him on a shared adventure, there was not much to mull over. He drew a breath to reply.

But Kircher beat him to it. He rose and brushed dust off his cowl. "Very well, then we will set off tomorrow morning."

"I would like to bring my assistant along," Olearius said, slightly annoyed. "Magister Fleming is knowledgeable and helpful."

"Yes, excellent," said Kircher, evidently already thinking about something else. "Tomorrow morning, then, that's good, we can manage that. Can you take me to the duke now?"

"He is not receiving visitors at the moment."

"Don't worry. When he learns who I am, he will consider himself fortunate."

Four coaches rumbled through the countryside. It was cold, morning haze rose pale from the meadows. The rearmost coach was filled from top to bottom with books that Kircher had acquired recently in Hamburg; in the next sat three secretaries copying manuscripts as well as they could in motion; in the next two secretaries were sleeping; and in the front coach Athanasius Kircher, Adam Olearius, and Magister Fleming, Olearius's traveling companion of many years, were carrying on a conversation that a further secretary, quill and paper on his knees to take it down, was following attentively.

"But what do we do if we find it?" asked Olearius.

"The dragon?" asked Kircher.

For a moment Olearius forgot his reverence and thought: I can't stand him any longer. "Yes," he then said. "The dragon."

Instead of answering, Kircher turned to Magister Fleming. "Do I understand correctly that you are a musician?"

"I am a doctor. Above all, I write poems. And I studied music in Leipzig."

"Latin poems or French?"

"German."

"German? Whatever for?"

"What do we do if we find it?" Olearius repeated.

"The dragon?" asked Kircher, and now Olearius would have liked nothing more than to slap his face.

"Yes," said Olearius. "The dragon!"

"We will soothe it with music. I may presume that the gentlemen have studied my book *Musurgia universalis*?"

"*Musica?*" asked Olearius.

"*Musurgia.*"

"Why not *Musica?*"

Kircher frowned at Olearius.

"Naturally," said Fleming. "Everything I know about harmony I learned from your book."

"I hear that often. Almost all musicians say that. It is an important work. Not my most important, but indisputably important all the same. Several princes want to have a water organ constructed according to my design. And in Braunschweig there are plans to build my cat piano. It astounds me a little. Really I presented the idea mainly as an intellectual game, and I doubt that the results will please the ear."

"What is a cat piano?" asked Olearius.

"You haven't read it, then?"

"My memory. I'm no longer so young. Since our arduous journey it does not always obey me."

"God knows," said Fleming. "Do you remember what it was like when the wolves surrounded us in Riga?"

"A piano that produces sounds by torturing animals," said Kircher. "One strikes a note, and instead of a hammer hitting a string, well-dosed pain is inflicted on a small animal—I propose cats, but it would work with voles too, dogs would be too big, crickets too small—so that the animal makes a noise. When one releases the key, the pain stops too, the animal falls silent. By arranging the animals according to their pitches, the most extraordinary music can be produced."

For a little while it was quiet. Olearius looked into Kircher's face. Fleming chewed on his lower lip.

"Why, then, do you write your poems in German?" Kircher finally asked.

"I know, it sounds strange," said Fleming, who had been waiting for this question. "But it can be done! Our language is only just being born. Here we sit, three men from the same country, and we're speaking Latin. Why? Now German may still be awkward, a boiling brew, a creature still in the midst of development, but one day it will be grown up."

"Back to the dragon," Olearius said, to change the subject. He had experienced it often: Once Fleming got on his hobbyhorse, no one else would have a chance to speak for a long time. And it always ended with Fleming, red-faced, reciting poems. They were not bad at all, his poems, they had melody and power. But who wanted to hear poems without warning, and in German to boot?

"Our language is still a confusion of dialects," said Fleming. "If one is faltering in a sentence, one avails oneself of the appropriate word from Latin or Italian or even French, and one somehow bends the sentences into shape in Latin fashion. But this will change! One must nurture a language, one must help it thrive! And to help it, that means: write poetry." Fleming's cheeks had turned red, his mustache was bristling slightly, his eyes were staring. "He who begins a sentence in German should force himself to finish it in German!"

"Isn't it against God's will to inflict pain on animals?" asked Olearius.

"Why?" Kircher furrowed his brow. "There's no difference between God's animals and God's things. Animals are finely assembled machines that consist of even more finely assembled machines. Whether I elicit a sound from a column of water or from a kitten, what's the difference? You surely wouldn't claim that animals have immortal souls—what a teeming mass that would be in Paradise. One wouldn't be able to turn around without stepping on a worm!"

"I was a choirboy in Leipzig," said Fleming. "Every morning at five we stood in the Saint Thomas Church and had to sing. Each voice was supposed to follow its own melodic punctus, and whoever sang out of tune got the switch. It was hard, but one morning, I remember, I understood for the first time what music is. And when later I learned the art of counterpoint, I understood what language is. And how one writes poetry in it—namely, by letting it prevail. *Being* and *seeing, breath* and *death*. The German rhyme: a question and an answer. *Pain, rain,* and *again*. Rhyme is no accident of sounds. It exists where ideas fit together."

"It's good that you are well acquainted with music," said Kircher. "I have sheet music for melodies with which a dragon's blood can be cooled and a dragon's spirit calmed. Can you play the horn?"

"Not well."

259

"Violin?"

"Passably. Where did you get these melodies?"

"I have composed them in accordance with the strictest science. Don't worry, you won't need to fiddle anything for the dragon, we will find musicians for that. For reasons of rank alone, it would be unseemly if one of us played the instruments."

Olearius closed his eyes. For a moment he saw in his head a lizard rising from the field, its head as high as a tower against the sky: this, then, could be the end of me, he thought, after all the dangers I have survived.

"With all due respect to your zeal, young man," said Kircher, "German has no future. First of all, because it's an ugly language, viscous and unclean, an idiom for unlearned people who don't bathe. Secondly, there is no time at all left for such a prolonged period of development. In seventy-six years the Iron Age will end, fire will come over the world, and our Lord will return in glory. One need not be a great astrologer to foresee it. Simple mathematics suffices."

"What sort of dragon is it anyway?" asked Olearius.

"Probably a very old lindworm. My expertise in dracontology falls short of that of my late master Tesimond, but on a day trip to Hamburg little coiled fly clouds gave me the necessary sign. Have you ever been to Hamburg? It is astonishing, the city has not been destroyed at all."

"Clouds?" asked Fleming. "How does the dragon cause—"

"Not causality, analogy! As above, so below. The cloud resembles a fly, hence the name fly cloud; the lindworm resembles an earthworm, hence the name lindworm. Worm and fly are insects! Do you see?"

Olearius propped his head up on his hands. He was feeling somewhat queasy. In Russia he had spent thousands of hours in coaches, but that was some time ago now, and he was no longer young. Of course, it could also have had to do with Kircher, who had, in a way that he could not have explained, become hard for him to bear.

"And when the dragon is tranquilized?" asked Fleming. "When we have found it and caught it, what then?"

"We draw its blood. As much as our leather skins can hold. I will bring it to Rome and with my assistants manufacture it into a cure for the Black Death, which will then be administered to the Pope and the Kaiser and the Catholic princes . . ." He hesitated. ". . . As well as perhaps to those Protestants who deserve it. To whom exactly will have to be negotiated. In this way, perhaps, we can end the war. It would indeed be fitting if it were I of all people who, with God's help, put an end to this slaughter. I will duly mention the two of you in my book. Strictly speaking, I have done so already."

"You have already mentioned us?"

"To save time I have already written the chapter in Rome. Guglielmo, do you have it here?"

The secretary bent down and rummaged, groaning, under his bench.

"As for musicians," said Olearius, "I would propose that we look for the traveling circus on the Holstein heath. There's a great deal of talk about it, people come from far away to see it. There will certainly be musicians there."

His face flushed, the secretary straightened up and produced a stack of paper. He leafed through it for a moment, blew his nose in a no-longer-clean handkerchief with which he then wiped his bald head, apologized softly, and began to read aloud. His Latin had a distinctly Italian melody, and he beat time in a somewhat affected way with his quill. "Thereupon I embarked on the search in the company of German scholars of outstanding merit. The circumstances were unfavorable, the weather rough, the war had withdrawn from the region but still sent this or that squall of adversity, so that one had to be prepared for marauders as much as for bands of robbers and degenerate animals. I did not let it chagrin me, however, having commended my soul to the Almighty who had until now always protected this his humble servant, and erelong I found the dragon, which was at length soothed and defeated by skillful measures. Its warm blood served me as the basis for many an undertaking that I depict elsewhere in this work, and the most terrible pestilence, which had long kept Christendom in distress, could finally be fended off from the great, mighty, and worthy men, so that in the future it may torment only the simple people. And when one day I—"

"Thank you, Guglielmo, that's enough. I will, of course, insert your names after the words 'German scholars of outstanding merit.' No need to thank me. I insist. It's the least I can do."

And perhaps, Olearius thought, this really was the immortality meant for him—a mention in Athanasius Kircher's book. His own travelogue would vanish almost as quickly as the poems poor Fleming now and then had printed. Time devoured almost everything, but it would be powerless against this. About one thing there was no doubt: as long as the world existed, people would read Athanasius Kircher.

The next morning they found the circus. The keeper of the inn where they had spent the night had pointed them west; keep following the field path, he had said, then you can't miss it.

And since there were no hills here and all the trees were cleared, they soon saw a flagpole in the distance, on which fluttered a colorful scrap of cloth.

Soon they could make out tents and a semicircle of wooden benches, above which two posts were erected, the thin line of a rope stretching between them—the circus people must have brought along all the timber themselves. Between the tents stood covered wagons. Horses and donkeys were grazing, a few children were playing, a man was sleeping in a hammock, an old woman was washing clothes in a tub.

Kircher squinted. He wasn't feeling well. He wondered whether it was due to the rocking of the coach or actually due to these two Germans. They were unfriendly, overserious, narrow-minded, they had thick heads, and besides, it was hard to ignore it, they smelled bad. He had not been in the Empire in a long time; he had almost forgotten what a headache it was to be among Germans.

The two of them underestimated him, that was obvious. He was used to it. Even as a child he had been underestimated, first by his parents, then by the teacher in the village school, until the priest had recommended him to the Jesuits. They had let him study, but then he had been underestimated by his fellow seminarians, who had seen in him only a zealous young man. No one had noticed how much more he could achieve— only his master Tesimond had recognized something in him and plucked him from the crowd of the slow-thinking. They had traveled across the land, he had learned a great deal from the old man, but he too had underestimated him, had believed him capable merely of an existence as a famulus, so that he had had to break away from Tesimond, step by step and with the greatest caution, for you should not antagonize someone like that. He had had to act as if the books he wrote were a harmless whim, but secretly he had sent them with letters of dedication to the important people in the Vatican. And indeed Tesimond had not gotten over the fact that his secretary had suddenly been summoned to Rome; he had fallen ill and had refused to give him a parting blessing. Kircher could still see it clearly before his eyes: the room in Vienna, his master wrapped tight in his blanket. The old wreck had mumbled something and pretended not to understand him, and so Kircher had gone unblessed to Rome, where the staff of the great library had welcomed him, only to underestimate him in turn. They had thought he would be good for mending books, cataloging books, studying books, but they had not grasped that he could write a book faster than it took another man to read it, and so he had had to prove it to them, again and again and again, until the Pope finally appointed him to the most important chair of his university and vested him with all the special authorities.

It would always be like this. The confusion of the past lay behind him; he no longer lost himself in time. And yet people didn't recognize what power dwelled in him, what determination, or what a memory he had. Even now, when he was famous all over the world and no one could study the sciences without being acquainted with the works of Athanasius Kircher, he could not leave Rome without experiencing it: No sooner did he encounter his countrymen than he was scrutinized with the same old disparaging looks. What a mistake to have set off on this journey! One should stay in one place, should work, concentrate one's powers and disappear behind one's books. One had to be an incorporeal authority—a voice that the world heeded without wondering what the body looked like from which it came.

He had again given in to a weakness. Actually he had not even been so very concerned with the plague, he had above all needed a reason to search for the dragon. They are the most ancient and intelligent of creatures, Tesimond had said, and when you stand before one, you will be changed, indeed when you hear its voice, nothing will ever be the same again. Kircher had found out so much about the world, but a dragon was still lacking, without a dragon his work was not complete, and if it should really become dangerous, he could still use the last and strongest defense—that magic to which one was permitted to resort only once in one's life: when the danger is greatest, Tesimond had impressed on him, when the dragon stands before you and all else fails, you can do it once, only once, one single time, so think carefully, *only once*. First you picture the strongest of the magic squares.

```
S A T O R
A R E P O
T E N E T
O P E R A
R O T A S
```

This is the oldest of all, the most secret, which holds the most power. You must see it before you, close your eyes, see it clearly and speak it with your lips closed, without your voice, letter by letter, and then say aloud, clearly enough for the dragon to hear you, a truth that you have never before disclosed, not to your closest friend, not even in confession. This is the most important thing: it must never have been uttered before. Then a mist will arise, and you can flee. Weakness afflicts the monster's limbs, leaden oblivion fills its mind, and you run away before it can seize you. When it awakes, it won't remember you. But don't forget: you can do it only once!

Kircher contemplated his fingertips. Should the music fail to soothe the dragon, he was resolved to turn to this last resort and flee on one of the coach horses. The dragon would then presumably devour the secretaries—it would be a shame about them, especially Guglielmo, who was very quick and eager to learn—and probably the two Germans too. But he himself would escape, thanks to science; he had nothing to fear.

This journey would be his last. He would not subject himself to travel again. He was simply not suited for such exertions. While traveling he was always queasy, the food was always dreadful, it was always cold, and the dangers were also not to be underestimated: The war may have moved south, but that didn't mean things up here were pleasant. How ravaged everything was, how wretched the people! He had, it was true, found several books in Hamburg for which he had long been searching—Hartmut Elias Warnick's *Organicon*, an edition of *Melusina mineralia* by Gottfried von Rosenstein, and a few handwritten pages that might have been penned by Simon von Turin—but even this was no consolation for the weeks without his laboratory, where everything was manageable, while everywhere else chaos reigned.

Why did God's Creation prove to be so recalcitrant, whence came its stubborn tendency to confusion and jaggedness? What was clear within the mind revealed itself outside to be a tangle. Kircher had grasped early on that one had to follow reason without being flustered by the quirks of reality. When one knew how an experiment had to turn out, then the experiment had to turn out like that, and when one possessed a distinct conception of things, then, when one described them, one had to satisfy this conception and not mere observation.

Only because he had learned to trust entirely the Holy Spirit had he been able to accomplish his greatest work, the deciphering of the hieroglyphs. With the old tablet of signs that Cardinal Bembo had once bought he had gotten to the bottom of the mystery: He had plunged deep into the little pictures until he understood. If one combined a wolf and a snake, it had to mean danger, but if there was a dotted wave under it, then God intervened and protected those who deserved his protection, and these three signs side by side meant mercy, and Kircher had fallen to his knees and had thanked heaven for such inspiration. The half-oval open to the left stood for judgment, and if there was a sun too, then it was the Day of Judgment, but if there was a moon, then this meant the torment of the man praying at night and hence the soul of the sinner and sometimes even hell. The little man must have meant person, but if this person had a staff, then it was the working person or work, and the signs behind it indicated what sort of work he did: if there were dots, then he was a sower; if there were dashes, he was a boatman; and if there were circles, he was a priest, and because priests wrote too, he could just as well be a scribe—it depended on whether he was situated at the beginning or at the end of the line, for the priest was always at the beginning, whereas the scribe came after the events that he recorded. Those had been ecstatic weeks. Soon he no longer needed the tablet; he had written in hieroglyphs as if he had never done otherwise. He had no longer been able to sleep at night, because he dreamed in signs. His thoughts consisted of dashes and dots and wedges and waves. So it was when one felt grace. His book, which he would soon have printed under the title *Oedipus Aegyptiacus*, was the greatest of his achievements: for thousands of years humanity had stood baffled before the mystery, no one had been able to solve it. Now it was solved.

The only irksome thing was that people were so dull-witted. He received letters from brothers in the Orient who informed him of sequences of signs that did not conform to the system described by him, and he had to write back to them that it didn't make a difference what some oaf had carved into a stone ten thousand years ago, some little scribe who, after all, knew less about this script than an authority like him—what, then, was the point of concerning oneself with his errors? Had that little scribe received a letter of thanks from Caesar? But Kircher boasted one. He had sent the Kaiser a hymn of praise in hieroglyphs; he always carried with him the grateful reply from Vienna, folded and sewn into a silk pouch. Involuntarily he placed his hand on his chest, could feel the parchment through his jerkin, and immediately felt somewhat better.

The coaches had stopped.

"Are you unwell?" asked Olearius. "You're pale."

"I'm doing splendidly," Kircher said in annoyance.

He flung open the door and climbed out. The sweat of the horses was steaming. The meadow too was damp. He squinted and propped himself up against the coach. He was dizzy.

"Eminent men," said a voice. "Visiting us!"

Over by the tents there were people, and somewhat closer the old woman sat in front of the washtub, but right next to them there was only a donkey. The animal looked up, lowered its head again, and plucked blades of grass.

"Did you hear that too?" asked Fleming.

Olearius, who had climbed out behind him, nodded.

"It's me," said the donkey.

"There's an explanation for this," said Kircher.

"And what is it?" asked the donkey.

"Ventriloquism," said Kircher.

"Right," said the donkey. "I am Origenes."

"Where is the ventriloquist hiding?" asked Olearius.

"He's asleep," said the donkey.

Behind them Fleming and the secretary had climbed out. The other secretaries followed.

"That's really not bad," said Fleming.

"He rarely sleeps," said the donkey. "But now he is dreaming of you." Its voice sounded deep and strange, as if it were not issuing from a human throat. "Do you want to see the show? The next one is the day after tomorrow. We have a fire eater and a hand walker and a coin swallower, that's me. Give me coins, I'll swallow them. Do you want to see? I'll swallow them all. We have a dancer and a woman to play the female roles and we have a maiden who is buried and remains underground for an hour, and when she is dug up, she is fresh and not suffocated. And we have a dancer, did I say that already? The player and the dancer and the maiden are the same person. And we have a peerless tightrope walker, he is our director. But he is asleep at the moment. We also have a freak—when you look at him, your mind will reel. You can hardly tell where his head is, and not even he himself can find his arms."

"And you have a ventriloquist," said Olearius.

"You are a very shrewd man," said the donkey.

"Do you have musicians?" asked Kircher, who was aware that it could damage his reputation to talk to a donkey before witnesses.

"Certainly," said the donkey. "Half a dozen. The director

and the woman dance, it is the climax, the peak of our performance, how would that be possible without musicians?"

"That's enough," said Kircher. "The ventriloquist shall now show himself!"

"I'm here," said the donkey.

Kircher closed his eyes, exhaled deeply, inhaled. A mistake, he thought, the whole journey, this visit here, all a mistake. He thought of the peace in his study, of his stone desk, of the books on the shelves, he thought of the peeled apple that his assistant brought him every afternoon when the clock struck three, of the red wine in his favorite Venetian crystal glass. He rubbed his eyes and turned away.

"Do you need a barber surgeon?" asked the donkey. "We also sell medicine. Just say the word."

It's just a donkey, thought Kircher. But his fists clenched with rage. Now one was being mocked by even the German animals! "Handle this," he said to Olearius. "Talk to these people."

Olearius looked at him in astonishment.

Kircher was already stepping over a heap of donkey manure to climb back into the coach, without paying further attention to him. He closed the door and drew the curtains. He heard Olearius and Fleming outside talking to the donkey—undoubtedly they were now laughing at him, all of them, but it didn't interest him. He didn't even want to know. To quiet his mind, he tried to think in Egyptian signs.

The old woman at the washtub faced Olearius and Fleming as they approached her. Then she stuck two fingers in her mouth and let out a whistle. Immediately three men and a woman emerged from one of the tents. The men were unusually stocky. The woman had brown hair, and she was no longer young, but her eyes were bright and piercing.

"Distinguished visitors," said the woman. "We don't often have such an honor. Do you want to see our show?"

Olearius tried to answer, yet his voice didn't obey him.

"My brother is the best tightrope walker, he was court jester for the Winter King. Do you want to see him?"

Olearius's voice still failed.

"Can't you talk?"

Olearius cleared his throat. He knew that he was making a fool of himself, but it was no use, he couldn't speak.

"Certainly we want to see something," said Fleming.

"These are our acrobats," said the woman. "Tumblers, show our well-born guests something!"

Without a moment's hesitation one of the three men fell forward and stood on his hands. The second climbed up him with inhuman speed and did a handstand on the first one's feet, and now the third man scaled the two of them, only he remained standing upright on the feet of the second, his arms stretched high in the sky, and now, before you knew it, the woman clambered up, and the third man pulled her to him and lifted her over his head. Olearius stared upward, she was hovering over him, in the air.

"Do you want to see more?" she called down.

"We would like to," said Fleming, "but that's not why we're here. We need musicians, we'll pay well."

"Your distinguished companion is mute?"

"No," said Olearius, "not no. Not mute, I mean."

She laughed. "I'm Nele!"

"I am Magister Fleming."

"Olearius," said Olearius. "Court mathematicus in Gottorf."

"Are you coming back down?" called Fleming. "It's hard to talk like this!"

As if on command, the human tower crumbled. The man in the middle leaped, the man on top rolled forward, the man on the bottom did a somersault, the woman seemed to fall, but somehow the jumble sorted itself out in midair, and they all landed on their feet and stood upright. Fleming clapped his hands. Olearius stood rigid.

"Don't clap," said Nele, "that wasn't an act. If it had been an act, you'd have to pay."

"We would like to pay too," said Olearius. "For your musicians."

"Then you have to ask them yourselves. All who are with us are free. If they want to go with you, then they shall go. If they want to continue with us, then they will continue with us. You are in Ulenspiegel's circus only if you want to be in Ulenspiegel's circus, because there is no better circus. Even the freak is here of his own free will, elsewhere he wouldn't have it so good."

"Tyll Ulenspiegel is here?" asked Fleming.

"People come from all over for him," said one of the acrobats. "I wouldn't want to leave. But ask the musicians."

"We have a flutist and a trumpeter and a drummer and a man who plays two fiddles at the same time. Ask them, and if they want to go, we shall part as friends and find other musicians, that won't be hard, everyone wants to join Ulenspiegel's circus."

"Tyll Ulenspiegel?" Fleming asked again.

"None other."

"And you are his sister?"

She shook her head.

"But you said—"

"I know what I said, sir. He is indeed my brother, but I am not his sister."

"How is that possible?" asked Olearius.

"Amazing, isn't it, sir?"

She looked him in the face, her eyes flashing, the wind playing in her hair. Olearius's throat was dry, and his limbs were weak, as if he had caught an illness along the way.

"You don't understand it, do you?" She pushed one of the acrobats in the chest and said: "Will you fetch the musicians?"

He nodded, flung himself forward, and walked away on his hands.

"One question." Fleming pointed at the donkey, which was calmly plucking grass and now and then raising its head and looking at them with dull animal eyes. "Who taught the donkey to—"

"Ventriloquism."

"But where is the ventriloquist hiding?"

"Ask the donkey," said the old woman.

"Who are you, then?" asked Fleming. "Are you her mother?"

"God forbid," said the old woman. "I am just the old woman. I'm no one's mother, no one's daughter."

"Well, you must be someone's daughter."

"And if grass has already grown over all the people whose daughter I was? I am Else Kornfass from Stangenriet. I was sitting outside my house and digging my little garden without a thought in my head, when Ulenspiegel and she, Nele, and Origenes came with the cart, and I called, Good day, Tyll, because I recognized him, everyone recognizes him, and suddenly he pulls on the reins so that the wagon stops and says: The day doesn't need your praise, just come. I didn't know what he meant, and I told him: Don't play jokes on old women, first of all they are poor and weak, and secondly they can cast a spell on you so you fall ill, but he says: You don't belong here. You are one of us. And me: I might have been once, but now I am old! To which he replies: We are all old. And me: If I drop dead along the way, what will you do? His reply: Then we'll leave you behind, for someone who is dead is no longer my friend. To which I didn't know what else to say, sir, and that's why I'm here."

"Eats us out of house and home," said Nele. "Doesn't work much, sleeps a lot, always has an opinion."

"All true," said the old woman.

"But she can memorize something," said Nele. "She delivers the longest ballads, never forgets a line."

"German ballads?" asked Fleming.

"Certainly," said the old woman. "Never learned Spanish."

"Let's hear," said Fleming.

"If you pay, I'll let you hear."

Fleming rummaged in his pocket. Olearius looked up at the rope. For a moment he thought he saw someone up there, but it was swaying empty in the wind. The acrobat came back, followed by three men with instruments.

"It will cost you," said the first man.

"We'll come with you," said the second, "but we want money."

"Money and gold," said the first.

"And a lot of it," said the third. "Do you want to hear something?"

And without Olearius giving them a command, they struck a pose and began to play. One of them strummed the lute, another puffed his cheeks on the bagpipes, the third whirled two drumsticks, and Nele threw her hair back and began to dance, while the old woman recited a ballad to the rhythm of the music: She didn't sing, she spoke in a monotone, and her rhythm submitted to that of the melody. It was about two lovers who could not reach each other because a sea separated them, and Fleming squatted down in the grass next to the old woman, lest he miss even a single word.

In the coach Kircher held his head and wondered when this horrible noise would finally stop. He had written the most important book on music, but for that very reason his ear was too refined to take pleasure in such popular blaring. All at once the coach seemed to him cramped, the bench hard, and this vulgar music bore witness to a cheerfulness that the whole world shared except him.

He sighed. The sunlight cast thin, cold flames through the gaps in the curtains. For a moment what he saw seemed to him a spawn of his headache and his sore eyes. Only then did he realize that he was not mistaken: someone was sitting opposite him.

Had the time finally come? He had always known that one day Satan himself would appear to him, but strangely the signs were missing. It didn't smell of sulfur, the fellow had two human feet, and the cross Kircher wore around his neck had not grown warm. Even if Kircher didn't understand how he had been able to slip in so soundlessly, it was a man sitting there. He was incredibly gaunt, and his eyes were set deep in their sockets. He wore a jerkin with a fur collar, and he was resting his feet in pointed shoes on the bench, which was a boorish impertinence.

The man leaned forward, put one hand on his shoulder in an almost tender gesture, and bolted the door with the other.

"I'd like to ask you something," he said.

"I don't have any money," said Kircher. "Not here in the coach. One of the secretaries outside has it."

"It's wonderful that you're here. I've waited for so long, I thought the opportunity would never come, but you must know: every opportunity comes, that's the wonderful thing, every opportunity comes eventually, and I thought, when I saw you, now I'll finally find out. They say that you can heal people, I can too, did you know that? The house of the dying in Mainz. Full of plague victims, there was coughing, groaning, wailing, and I said: I have a powder, I'll sell it to you, it will cure you, and the poor swine cried full of hope: Give it to us, give us the powder! I have to make it first, I said, and they cried: Make the powder, make it, make your powder! And I said: It's not so easy, I'm missing an ingredient, someone has to die for it. Now it was silent. Now they were astonished. Now no one said anything for the time being. And I exclaimed: I have to kill someone, I'm sorry, you can't make something out of nothing! For I am an alchemist too, you know. Just like you, I know the secret powers, and the healing spirits obey me too."

He laughed. Kircher stared at him. Then he reached for the door.

"Don't do it," the man said in a voice that made Kircher withdraw his hand. "So I said: Someone has to die, and I will not determine who it shall be, you have to sort it out among yourselves. And they said: How are we supposed to do that? And I said: If it were the sickest, that would be the least regrettable, so see who can still run, take your crutches, start running, and whoever is the last one in the house, I'll disembowel. And before you could blink, the house was empty. Three corpses were still inside. No living people. You see, I said, you can walk, you aren't dying, I cured you. Don't you recognize me, Athanasius?"

Kircher stared at him.

"A long time ago," said the man. "Many years, a lot of wind in one's face, a lot of frost, one is burned by the sun, the hunger burns too, in the meantime one looks different. Except here you are, looking exactly the same with your red cheeks."

"I know who you are," said Kircher.

From outside the music blared. Kircher wondered whether he should cry for help, but the door was bolted. Even if they heard him, which was unlikely, they would have to break open the door, and one didn't want to imagine what the fellow could do to him in that time.

"What the book said. He would have so liked to know. He would have given his life for it. And he did. And yet he never found out. But now I could get the answer. I always thought, perhaps I will see the young doctor again, perhaps I will find out, and here you are. Well? What did the Latin book say?"

Kircher began to pray soundlessly.

"It had no binding, but it had pictures. One was of a cricket, another of an animal that doesn't exist, with two heads and wings, or perhaps it does exist, what do I know. One was of a man in a church, but it had no roof, there were columns above it, I remember that, above the columns were other columns. Claus showed it to me and said: Look, this is the world. I didn't understand, I don't think he did either. But if he couldn't know it, I at least want to know it, and you looked at his things, and you understand Latin too, so tell me—what sort of book was that, who wrote it, what is it called?"

Kircher's hands trembled. The boy from back then was

vividly preserved in his memory, as vividly as the miller, whose final croaks on the gallows he would never forget, as vividly as the confession of the miller's weeping wife, but in his life he had held so many books in his hands, leafed through so many pages, and seen so much in print that he could no longer keep it all apart. The man must have been referring to a book that the miller had possessed. But it was no use, his memory failed him.

"Do you remember the interrogation?" the thin man asked gently. "The older man, the Father, he kept saying: Don't worry, we won't hurt you if you tell the truth."

"Well, you did so."

"And he didn't hurt me either, but he would have if I hadn't run away."

"Yes," said Kircher, "you made the right choice."

"I never found out what became of my mother. A few people saw her departing, but no one saw her arrive anywhere else."

"We saved you," said Kircher. "The devil would have seized you too, one cannot live near him and remain unscathed. When you spoke against your father, he lost his power over you. Your father confessed and repented. God is merciful."

"I just want to know. The book. You have to tell me. And don't lie, for I'll be able to tell. That's what he kept saying, your old Father: Don't lie, for I'll be able to tell. Meanwhile, you were constantly lying to him, and he couldn't tell."

The man leaned forward. His nose was now only a hand's breadth from Kircher's face; he seemed to be not so much looking at him as smelling him. His eyes were half closed, and Kircher thought he heard him inhaling with a sniff.

"I don't remember," said Kircher.

"I don't believe that."

"I have forgotten it."

"But if I still don't believe it?"

Kircher cleared his throat. "Sator," he said softly. Then he fell silent. His eyes closed, but they twitched under the lids as if he were looking this way and that. Then he opened them again. A tear ran down his cheek. "You're right," he said tonelessly. "I lie a great deal. I lied to Dr. Tesimond, but that's nothing. I have also lied to His Holiness. And His Majesty the Kaiser. I lie in my books. I lie all the time."

The professor kept speaking, his voice cracking, but Tyll could not understand him. A strange torpor had come over him. He wiped his forehead, cold sweat ran down his face. The bench in front of him was empty, he was alone in the coach, the door was open. Yawning, he climbed out.

Outside there was thick fog. Billows rolled past, the air was saturated with white. The musicians had stopped playing, shadowy figures loomed—it was the professor's companions, and that silhouette there must have been Nele. Somewhere a horse whinnied.

Tyll sat down on the ground. The fog was already thinning, a few rays of sun broke through. The coaches and a few tents and the contours of the spectator benches could now be made out. A moment later it was broad daylight. Moisture steamed from the grass, the fog was gone.

The secretaries looked at each other in confusion. One of the two coach horses was no longer there; the drawbar jutted into the air. While everyone was wondering where the fog had suddenly come from, while the acrobats did cartwheels because they couldn't go long without doing them, while the donkey plucked blades of grass, while the old woman resumed reciting to Fleming, and while Olearius and Nele talked to each other, Tyll sat there motionless, with his eyes narrowed and his nose raised into the wind. And he did not stand up even when one of the secretaries approached and told Olearius that His Excellency Professor Kircher had apparently ridden away without farewell. He had not even left a message.

"We won't find the dragon without him," said Olearius.

"Shall we wait?" asked the secretary. "Perhaps he will come back."

Olearius cast a glance at Nele. "That would probably be best."

"What's wrong?" asked Nele, who had walked over to Tyll.

He looked up. "I don't know."

"What happened?"

"I've forgotten."

"Juggle for us. Then it will be better."

Tyll stood up. He groped for the pouch that hung at his side and took out first a yellow leather ball and then a red one and then a blue one and then a green one. Carelessly he began to throw them into the air, and he took out even more balls, another and another and another, until there seemed to be dozens of them leaping over his spread hands. Everyone was watching the rising, falling, rising balls, and even the secretaries couldn't help smiling.

It was early in the morning. Nele had been waiting for quite a while outside the tent. She had been thinking, had been walking up and down, had prayed, torn out grass, wept silently, wrung her hands, and, at length, had pulled herself together.

Now she slipped into the tent. Tyll was asleep, yet as soon as she touched his shoulder, he was wide awake.

She told him that she had spent the night with Olearius, the courtier from Gottorf, out in the field.

"So what?"

"This time it's different."

"Didn't he give you anything nice?"

"Yes, he did."

"Well, then it's the same as always."

"He would like me to come with him."

Tyll raised his eyebrows in feigned astonishment.

"He wants to marry me."

"No."

"Yes."

"Marry?"

"Yes."

"You?"

"Me."

"Why?"

"He means it. He lives in a castle. It's not a beautiful castle, he says, and in the winter it's cold, but he has enough to eat and a duke who provides for him, and for this he doesn't have to do anything but teach the duke's children and sometimes calculate something and keep an eye on the books."

"Will they run away otherwise, the books?"

"As I said, he has it good."

Tyll rolled off his straw sack, got to his feet, stood up. "Then you have to go with him."

"I don't like him very much, but he is a good person. And very lonely. His wife died, when he was in Russia. I don't know where Russia is."

"Near England."

"Now we never did make it to England."

"In England it's the same as here."

"And when he came back from Russia, she was dead, and they didn't have children, and ever since he has been sad. He is still fairly healthy, I could tell, and I think he can be trusted. Someone like this won't come to me again."

Tyll sat down next to her and put his arm around her shoulders. Outside the old woman could be heard reciting a ballad. Evidently, Fleming was still sitting with her and having her perform again and again so that he could commit it to memory.

"Someone like this is certainly better than a Steger," she said.

"Probably he won't even hit you."

"It's possible," Nele said thoughtfully. "And if he does, I'll hit back. That will take him by surprise."

"You can even still have children."

"I don't like children. And he is already old. But he will be grateful, with children or without."

She was silent. The wind rustled the tent, and the old woman started from the beginning.

"I don't actually want to."

"But you have to."

"Why?"

"Because we are no longer young, sister. And we're not getting any younger. Not by one day. No one who is old and homeless has it good. He lives in a castle."

"But we belong together."

"Yes."

"Perhaps he'll take you along too."

"That won't work. I can't stay in a castle. I wouldn't be able to stand it. And even if I could stand it, they wouldn't want to have me there for long. Either they will chase me away, or I'll burn the castle down. One or the other. But it would be your castle, so I must not burn it down, so nothing will come of it."

For a while they were quiet.

"Yes, nothing will come of it," she then said.

"Why does he want you anyway?" asked Tyll. "You're not even especially beautiful."

"In a moment I'm going to smack you in the mouth."

He laughed.

"I think he loves me."

"What?"

"I know, I know."

"Loves you."

"These things happen."

Outside the donkey made a donkey sound, and the old woman began another ballad.

"If it hadn't been for the marauders," said Nele. "That time in the forest."

"Don't talk about it."

She went silent.

"People like him don't usually take people like you," he said. "He must be a good man. And even if he's not a good man—he has a roof overhead and coins in his pouch. Tell him that you'll come with him, and tell him before he changes his mind."

Nele began to weep. Tyll took his hand off her shoulder and looked at her. Shortly thereafter, she calmed down.

"Will you come visit me?" she asked.

"I don't think so."

"Why not?"

"Look, how is that supposed to work? He won't want to be reminded of where he found you. In the castle no one will know, and you yourself won't want people to know. The years will pass, sister, soon all this will be a distant memory, only your children will be amazed that you can dance and sing so well and catch anything they throw."

She gave him a kiss on the forehead. Hesitantly she slipped out of the tent, stood up and went over to the coaches to inform the court mathematician that she would accept his offer and move with him to Gottorf.

When she came back, she found Tyll's tent empty. With lightning speed he had set off and had taken nothing with him but the juggling balls, a long rope, and the donkey. Only Magister Fleming, who had encountered him out in the meadow, had spoken with him. But what Tyll had said he would not reveal.

The circus scattered in all directions. The musicians headed south with the acrobats, the fire eater went west with the old woman, the others turned northeast, in the hope of getting far away from war and hunger. The freak was admitted to the Elector of Bavaria's cabinet of curiosities. Three months later, the secretaries reached the city of Rome, where Athanasius Kircher was impatiently waiting for them. He never again left the city, carried out thousands of experiments, and wrote dozens of books, until he died in high esteem forty years later.

Nele Olearius survived Kircher by three years. She had children and buried her husband, whom she had never loved but always appreciated, because he had treated her well and expected nothing more from her than some kindness. Before her eyes Gottorf Castle blossomed into new splendor, she saw her grandchildren grow up and rocked even her first great-grandson on her lap. No one had an inkling that she had once roamed the land with Tyll Ulenspiegel, but just as he had predicted, her grandchildren were amazed that even in her old age she could still catch anything you threw to her. She was well liked and respected; no one would have suspected that she had ever been anything but an honorable woman. Nor did she tell anyone that she still had the hope that the boy with whom she had once set off from her parents' village might come back and take her with him.

Only when death was clutching at her, only in the confusion of the final days, did it seem to her as if she could see him. Thin and smiling, he stood by the window; thin and smiling, he came into her room; and smiling, she sat up and said: "It took you a while!"

And the Duke of Gottorf, a son of the duke who had formerly employed her husband, having come to her deathbed to say goodbye to the oldest member of his household, understood that now was not the moment to correct errors, took the stiff little hand that she held out to him, and gave the reply that his instinct provided him: "Yes, but now I am here."

That same year, on the Holstein plain, the last dragon of the north died. He was seventeen thousand years old, and he was tired of hiding.

Thus he buried his head in the heather, lay his body, which had adapted so completely to its background that even eagles could not have made it out, flat in the softness of the grass, sighed, and briefly regretted that it was now over with scent and flowers and wind and that he would no longer see the clouds in a storm, the rising sun, or the curve of the earth's shadow on the copper-blue moon, which had always especially delighted him.

He closed his four eyes and still growled softly when he felt a sparrow alight on his nose. All was fine with him, for he had seen so much, but still he didn't know what would happen to someone like him after death. With a sigh, he fell asleep. His life had lasted long. Now it was time to transform.

In the Shaft

"GOD ALMIGHTY, LORD JESUS CHRIST, HELP US," MATTHIAS said just a short while ago, and Korff replied: "But God is not here!" and Iron Kurt said: "God is everywhere, you swine," and Matthias said: "Not down here," and then everyone laughed, yet then there was a bang and a blast so sharp and hot that it flung them to the floor. Tyll fell on Korff, Matthias on Iron Kurt, and then it was pitch-black. For a while no one moved, they all held their breath, each man wondered whether he was dead, and only gradually did they all grasp, because you simply never grasp such a thing immediately, that the shaft had caved in. Now they know that they must not make a sound, for what if the Swedes have broken through, if they are standing over them in the darkness, knives drawn—then not the slightest peep, not a breath, not a sniffle or groan or cough.

It is dark. But dark in a different way than up above. For when it's dark, you usually still see something. You don't quite know what you're seeing, but there's not nothing; you move your head, the darkness is not the same everywhere, and once you have grown accustomed to it, outlines emerge. But not here. The darkness remains. Time passes, and when more time has passed and they can no longer hold their breath, and cautiously begin to breathe again, it is still as dark as if God had extinguished all the light in the world.

Finally, because apparently no Swedes with knives are standing over them, Korff says: "Men, report!"

And Matthias: "Since when are you the boss, you drunkard?"

Korff: "Since yesterday, you dirtbag, when the lieutenant kicked the bucket. Now I have seniority."

Matthias: "Up there maybe, but not down here."

Korff: "Report, right now, or I'll kill you. I have to know who's still alive."

And Tyll: "I think I'm still alive."

The truth is that he's not sure. When you're lying flat and everything is black, how can you tell? But now that he has heard his voice, he realizes that it's so.

"Then get off me," says Korff. "You're lying on me, you bag of bones!"

When he's right, he's right, thinks Tyll, it is really not so good to be lying here on Korff. So he rolls to the side.

"Report, Matthias," says Korff.

"Fine, I report."

"Kurt?"

They wait, but Iron Kurt, as they all call him because of his iron right hand, or perhaps it was the left, no one quite remembers and it's too dark to check, doesn't report.

"Kurt?"

It's quiet, not even any explosions are to be heard anymore. A moment ago they could still be heard, distant peals of thunder from above, which made the stones tremble; it was the Swedes under Torstensson trying to blow up the bastions. But now there's only breathing, Tyll's and Korff's and Matthias's, but Kurt cannot be heard.

"Are you dead?" cries Korff. "Kurt, did you bite the dust?"

But Kurt still says nothing, which is not like him at all; ordinarily you can hardly shut him up. Tyll hears Matthias groping. He must be feeling for Kurt's neck, to see whether his heart is beating, then for his hand—first the iron one, then the real one. Tyll has to cough. It's dusty, and stifling, the air feels like thick butter.

"Yes, he is dead," Matthias finally says.

"Are you sure?" Korff asks. They can tell by his voice how it irks him—he only just got seniority yesterday, when the lieutenant was killed, and already he's down to two subordinates.

"He isn't breathing," says Matthias, "and his heart isn't beating, and he won't talk either, and here, you can feel it, half of his head is gone."

"Shit," says Korff.

"Yes," says Matthias, "shit. Although, look, I didn't like him. Yesterday he took my knife, and when I said to give it back, he said: I'll give it back all right, between your ribs. He had it coming."

"Yes, he had it coming," says Korff. "God have mercy on his soul."

"It won't get out of here," says Tyll. "How's a soul supposed to find its way out?"

For a while there's an uneasy silence, because they are all thinking about the possibility that Kurt's soul might still be here, cold and slippery and most likely angry. Then they hear a scraping, a pushing, a grinding.

"What are you doing there?" asks Korff.

"I'm looking for my knife," says Matthias. "I'm not leaving it to that dirty pig."

Tyll has to cough again. Then he asks: "What happened? I'm fairly new to this, why is it dark?"

"Because no sun is getting through," says Korff. "There's too much earth between it and ourselves."

Serves me right, thinks Tyll, it really was not an intelligent question. And to ask a better one, he says: "Are we going to die?"

"Absolutely," says Korff. "Us and everybody else."

He's right again, thinks Tyll, although, who knows, I, for one, have never died yet. Then, for the dark can be very confusing, he tries to remember how he ended up in the shaft.

First of all, because he came to Brno. He could have gone elsewhere, but in hindsight you always know better, and he came to Brno because they said the city was rich and safe. And no one suspected, after all, that Torstensson would march here with half the Swedish army. They always said he would go to Vienna, where the Kaiser is hunkering down, only you just don't know what goes on in men's heads underneath their big hats.

And then there was the town commandant, with his bushy eyebrows, his little pointed beard, his greasy cheeks, and that haughtiness in his every splayed finger. On the main square he watched Tyll, apparently with difficulty, because his eyelids drooped so nobly low and because someone like him undoubtedly thought he deserved more to look at than a fool in a pied jerkin.

"Can't you show us something better?" he grumbled.

As it happens, Tyll rarely loses his temper, but when he does, then he is better at insulting than anyone, then he says something that someone like that will never forget. What was it that he said? The darkness really does muddle your memory. The stupid thing was that they were currently recruiting men for the defense of the Brno fortress.

"Just you wait. You will do your part, you will join the soldiers! You can choose a unit for yourself. Only make sure, everyone, that he doesn't run away!"

Then he laughed, the town commandant, as if it had been a good joke, and to be fair, it wasn't bad, for that's the point of a siege, after all, that no one can run away; if you could run away from a siege, it wouldn't be a siege.

"What do we do now?" Tyll hears Matthias ask.

"Find the pickax," replies Korff. "It must be lying around here someplace. If not, I tell you, we can save ourselves the trouble. Then we're done for."

"Kurt had it," says Tyll. "It must be under Kurt."

He hears the two of them scraping and pushing and groping and cursing in the dark. He remains sitting—he doesn't want to be in their way, and above all he doesn't want them to remember that it wasn't Kurt who had the pickax but he himself. He is not entirely certain, because you grow more and more muddleheaded here. You can still remember distant events clearly, but the closer something was to the bang a short while ago, the more soupy and runny it is in your mind. He is in fact fairly sure that he had the pickax but that, because it was heavy and kept dangling between his legs, it is now lying somewhere in the shaft. He doesn't say a word about this, though. It's better if the two of them think that the pickax is with Iron Kurt, for he has moved on; however angry they get, it doesn't matter to him.

"Are you helping, bag of bones?" asks Matthias.

"Of course I'm helping," says Tyll, without budging. "I'm searching and searching! I'm searching like mad, like a mole, can't you hear?"

And because he is a good liar, this satisfies them. His aversion to moving is due to the air. It is suffocating, nothing is flowing in, nothing out, you could easily pass out and never wake up. In air like this it's better not to move and to breathe only as much as absolutely necessary.

He shouldn't have joined the miners. That was a mistake. The miners are deep down below, he had thought, and the bullets fly up above. The miners are protected by the earth, he had thought. The enemy has miners to blow up our walls, and we have miners to blow up the shafts the enemy digs under our walls. Miners dig, he had thought, while up above there's hewing and stabbing. And if a miner pays attention, he had thought, and takes advantage of the moment, then he can also simply keep digging and dig himself a tunnel and pop up somewhere outside, he had thought, beyond the fortifications, and make off before anyone's the wiser. And because Tyll had thought this, he told the officer holding him by the collar that he wanted to join the miners.

And the officer: "What?"

"The commandant said I can choose!"

And the officer: "Yes, but . . . really? The miners?"

"You heard me."

Yes, that was stupid. Miners almost always die, but they didn't tell him that until he was underground. For every five miners, four die; for every ten, eight die; for every twenty, sixteen; for every fifty, forty-seven; and for every hundred, all of them die.

At least Origenes got away. It was due to their quarrel, just last month, on the way to Brno.

"In the forest there are wolves," the donkey said, "hungry wolves, don't leave me here."

"Don't worry, the wolves are far away."

"They're so close I can smell them. You're climbing a tree, but I'm standing down here, and what do I do when they come?"

"You do what I say!"

"But what if you say something stupid?"

"Even then. I'm the human. I should never have taught you to speak."

"They shouldn't have taught you to speak either, you almost never make any sense, and your juggling is not what it was. Soon you'll be slipping off your rope. You can't order me around!"

And then Tyll simply remained angrily in the tree and the donkey remained angrily down below. Tyll has slept so often in trees that it's no longer hard for him—you need a thick branch and a rope to tie yourself up, and a good sense of balance, and as with everything else in life you need practice.

For half the night he heard the donkey cursing. Until the moon rose he grumbled and muttered, and Tyll did feel sorry for him, but it was late, and at night you cannot move on, what could you do. So Tyll just fell asleep, and when he woke up, the donkey was gone. No wolves had come, he would have noticed; apparently the donkey decided that he could make it on his own and didn't need a ventriloquist.

And Origenes was right about the juggling. Here in Brno, in front of the cathedral, Tyll blundered and a ball fell to the ground. He pretended it had been intentional, made a face that made everyone laugh, but something like that is no joke, it can happen again, and if next time it really is the foot on the rope, what then?

Well, that's one less thing to worry about. It doesn't look like they're going to get out of here.

"It doesn't look like we're going to get out of here," says Matthias.

Yet it must have been Tyll, those were his thoughts that strayed into Matthias's head in the darkness, but perhaps it was the other way around, who could tell. Now they also see little lights, buzzing like glowworms, which, however, are not really there either, Tyll knows that, for although he sees the lights, he also sees that it is still completely dark.

Matthias groans, and then Tyll hears a thud, as if someone had punched the wall. Then Matthias utters a wild curse—one that Tyll never heard before. Have to remember that, he thinks, but then he has immediately forgotten it nonetheless and wonders whether he only imagined it, but what was it anyway, what did he imagine? Suddenly he no longer knows.

"We're not going to get out of here," Matthias says again.

"Shut your stupid trap," says Korff, "we'll find the pickax, we'll dig ourselves out, God will help."

"Why should he?" asks Matthias.

"He didn't help the lieutenant," says Tyll.

"I'll bash your heads in," says Korff. "Then you definitely won't get out."

"What are you doing here, anyway?" asks Matthias. "You are Ulenspiegel, aren't you?"

"They forced me. You think I'd volunteer? And what are *you* doing here?"

"I was forced, too. Stole bread, was put in chains, bim bam

boom. But you? How did that happen? You're famous, aren't you? Why would they force someone like you?"

"Down here no one is famous," says Korff.

"Who forced *you*, then?" Tyll asks Korff.

"No one forces me to do anything. Anyone who tries to force Korff, Korff kills. I was with the drummers under Christian von Halberstadt, then I went to the French as a musketeer, then to the Swedes, but when they didn't pay, I went back to the French as an artilleryman. Then my battery was hit, you've never seen anything like it, direct hit with heated shot, all the powder blows up, fire like the end of the world, but Korff threw himself into the bushes and survived. Then I went over to the imperial forces, but they didn't need cannoneers, and I didn't want to be a pikeman anymore, so I came to Brno, and because I didn't have any money left and no one gets paid as well as the miners, I mined. Been doing it for three weeks now. Most don't survive that long. I was just with the Swedes, now I kill the Swedes, and you two dirtbags are lucky that you've been buried alive with Korff, because Korff is hard to kill." He wants to say more, but now he is running out of air, and he coughs, and then he is quiet for a while. "You, bag of bones," he finally says. "Have any money?"

"Not a penny," says Tyll.

"But you're famous. Can someone be famous and have no money?"

"If he's stupid, he can."

"And you're stupid?"

"Brother, if I were smart, would I be here?"

Korff can't help laughing. And because Tyll knows that no one can see it, he pats down his jerkin. The gold pieces in the collar, the silver in the button border, the two pearls, securely sewn into the bottom of the lapel—all still there. "Honestly. If I had anything, I would give it to you."

"You're just a poor wretch too," says Korff.

"Forever and ever, amen."

All three of them can't help laughing.

Tyll and Korff stop laughing. Matthias keeps laughing.

They wait, but he is still laughing.

"He's not stopping," says Korff.

"He's going mad," says Tyll.

They wait. Matthias keeps laughing.

"I was there outside Magdeburg," says Korff. "I was with the besiegers, it was before I was with the Swedes, at the time I was still with the imperial troops. When the city fell, we took everything, burned everything, killed everyone. Do what you want, the general said. It's hard to get the hang of it, you know, you have to get used to it first, that you really are allowed. That it's possible. To do what you want to people."

Suddenly it seems to Tyll as if they were outside again, as if the three of them were sitting in a meadow, the sky blue above them, the sun so bright that you had to squint. But while he is narrowing his eyes, he also still knows that it isn't so, and then he no longer knows what it was that he just knew wasn't so, and then he has to cough, because of the bad air, and the meadow is gone.

"I think Kurt said something," says Matthias.

"He didn't say anything," says Korff.

He's right, thinks Tyll, who didn't hear anything either. Matthias is imagining it, Kurt didn't say anything.

"I heard it too," says Tyll. "Kurt said something."

Immediately they hear Matthias shaking the dead Iron Kurt. "Still alive," he cries, "still there?"

Tyll remembers yesterday, or was it the day before yesterday? The attack when the lieutenant was killed. Suddenly the hole in the wall of the shaft, suddenly knives and screaming and banging and crashing, he pressed himself very deep into the dirt, someone stepped on his back, and when he lifted his head again, it was already over: A Swede stabbed the lieutenant in the eye, Korff slit the Swede's throat, Matthias shot the second Swede in the belly with his pistol, making him scream like a stuck pig, for nothing hurts like a shot in the belly, and the third Swede beheaded one of theirs, whose name Tyll never learned, for he was new, and now it doesn't matter, now he no longer needs to know the name, with his saber, making him spray like a fountain of red water, but the Swede couldn't rejoice for long, for Korff, whose pistol was still loaded, now shot him in the head, clip-clop, zip-zop, it took no longer than that.

Things like that never take long. Even that time in the forest it went quickly. Tyll can't help it, he has to think about it, because of the darkness. In the darkness everything gets muddled, and what you have forgotten is suddenly back. That time in the forest he was closest to Godfather Death, he felt his hand—that's why he knows so well how it feels, that's why he recognizes it now. He has never spoken of it, has never thought about it again either. For it's possible to do that: simply not think about something. Then it's as if it never happened.

But now, in the dark, everything wells up. Closing your eyes helps as little as opening your eyes wide, and to fend it off he says: "Shall we sing? Perhaps someone will hear us!"

"I don't sing," says Korff.

Then Korff begins to sing: There is a reaper, they call him Death. Matthias sings along, then Tyll joins in too, whereupon the other two go silent and listen to him. Tyll's voice is high, clear, and forceful. His power's from God on high. He'll come and steal away our breath, no matter how we cry.

"Sing along!" says Tyll.

And they do so, but Matthias immediately stops again and laughs to himself. Fair flower, beware. So fresh and green, so bonny and bright today, tomorrow with his scythe so keen, he'll cut your life away. Now Kurt can be heard singing along too. He doesn't manage it very loudly and is hoarse and doesn't hit the right notes, but he shouldn't be judged too severely; when someone is dead, singing can certainly be hard for him too. You roses red and you lilies white that gladden the meadows and hills, you lilacs that fill the air with delight, you hyacinths and you daffodils. Fair flower, beware.

"My goodness," says Korff.

"I told you he's famous," says Matthias. "It's an honor. A respected man is dying with us."

"I am indeed famous," says Tyll, "but I have never been respected in all my life. Do you think anyone heard it, the singing, do you think anyone's coming?"

They listen. The explosions have resumed. A rumbling, a trembling in the ground, silence. A rumbling, a trembling, silence.

"Torstensson is blasting away half our city wall," says Matthias.

"He won't succeed," says Korff. "Our miners are better than his. They'll find the Swedish shafts, they'll smoke them out. You've never seen Tall Karl angry."

"Tall Karl is always angry, but also always drunk," says Matthias. "I could strangle him with one hand behind my back."

"Your brain has gone to the dogs!"

"Shall I show you? You think you're a great man because of Magdeburg and wherever you've been!"

Korff is quiet for a moment. Then he says softly: "I'll beat you to death."

"Yeah?"

"I'll do it."

Then they are silent for a while, and they hear the bangs of the explosions from above. They also hear stones trickling. Matthias says nothing, because he has understood that Korff means it seriously; and Korff says nothing, because all at once he is overwhelmed by longing, as Tyll is well aware, for due to the darkness your thoughts don't stay with you alone, you overhear those of the others, whether you want to or not. Korff feels the longing for air and light and the freedom to move wherever he pleases. And then, because this reminds him of something else, he says: "Fat Hanna!"

"Oh, yes," says Matthias.

"Those thick thighs," says Korff. "That behind."

"My God," says Matthias. "Her behind. Her arse. Her arse behind."

"You had her too?"

"No," says Matthias. "I don't know her."

"And the tits on her," says Korff. "At Tübingen I knew another one with such tits. You should have seen her. She did anything you wanted, as if there were no God."

"Have you had many women, Ulenspiegel?" asks Matthias. "You had money once, you must have indulged yourself, tell us."

Tyll is about to reply, but all at once it is no longer Matthias next to him but the Jesuit on his stool, whom he sees as clearly as back then: You must tell the truth, you must tell us how the miller summoned the devil, you must say that you were afraid. Why must you say it? Because it's true. Because we know it. And when you lie, look, there's Master Tilman, look what he has in his hand, he will use it, so speak. Your mother spoke too. She didn't want to at first, she had to feel it, but then she felt it and spoke, that's how it always is, everyone speaks when they feel it. We already know what you will say, because we know what's true, but we must hear it from you. And then he says, whispering, leaning forward, almost kindly: Your father is lost. You will not save him. But you can save yourself. He would want that.

Yet the Jesuit is not here, Tyll knows that, only the two miners are here, and Pirmin over on the forest path, they have just left him behind. Stay here, Pirmin cries, I'll find you, I'll hurt you! And that is a mistake, for now they know that they must not help him, and the boy runs back again and fetches the pouch with the balls. Pirmin screams his head off and swears like a coachman, not only because the balls are the most valuable thing he has, but also because he realizes what it means that the boy is taking them with him: I curse you, I'll find you, I won't cross over, I'll stay to search for you! It's frightening to see him lying like that, so contorted. Thus the boy runs and still hears him from a distance and runs and runs, Nele alongside him, and they still hear him. It's his own fault, she gasps, but the boy senses Pirmin's curses working and something bad coming toward them, in the middle of the bright morning, help, King, get me out of here, undo it, back then in the forest.

"Well, go on, tell us," someone says. Tyll recognizes the voice, he remembers, it is Matthias. "Say something about arses, say something about tits. If we're going to die, at least give us some tits."

"We're not going to die," says Korff.

"But tell us," says Matthias.

Tell us, the Winter King says too. What was there in the forest, remember, what was it?

But the boy doesn't tell. Not him and not anyone else and especially not himself, for if you don't think about it, it's as if you have forgotten it, and if you have forgotten it, it did not happen.

Tell us, says the Winter King.

"You dwarf," says Tyll, because he is beginning to get angry. "You king without a country, you nothing, and besides, you're dead. Leave me alone, crawl away."

"You crawl," says Matthias. "I'm not dead, Kurt is dead. Tell us!"

But the boy cannot tell, for he has forgotten. He has forgotten the path in the forest, and he has forgotten Nele and himself there on the path, he has forgotten the voices in the leaves, go no farther, but it was not actually true, they didn't whisper that, the voices, if they had, Nele and he certainly would have listened, and all at once standing in front of them are the three men, whom he no longer remembers, he no longer sees them, he has forgotten them, standing there in front of them.

Marauders. Disheveled, angry, without knowing at what. Well, well, says one of them, children!

And Nele thinks of it, fortunately. Of what the boy told her: We are safe as long as we are faster. When you run faster than the others, nothing can happen to you. And so she darts sideways and runs. Later the boy doesn't remember—and how should he remember, for he has forgotten everything—why he didn't run too. But that's just the way it is, one mistake is enough: don't understand something one time, goggle for too long one time, and already he is putting his hand on your shoulder. He bends over him. He smells of brandy and mushrooms. The boy wants to run, but it's too late, the hand remains where it is and the other man is standing next to him, and the third has run after Nele, but now he is coming back, panting—of course he didn't catch her.

The boy tries to make the three of them laugh. He learned that from Pirmin, who is lying an hour from here and is perhaps still alive and would have guided them better, for with him they never encountered wolves or evil people, not once in all this time. So he tries to make them laugh, but it doesn't work, they won't laugh, they are too angry, they're in pain, one of them is injured, he asks: Do you have any money? And he actually does have a little bit of money and gives it to him. He tells them that he could dance for them or walk on his hands or juggle, and they almost become curious, yet then they realize that they would have to let go of him, and the one who is holding him says, We're not that stupid.

And now the boy grasps that there's nothing he can do, except to forget what happens, forget it even before it has finished happening: forget their hands, their faces, everything. Not be here where he is now but rather next to Nele as she runs and finally stops and leans against a tree and catches her breath. Then she creeps back, holding her breath and taking care that no branch cracks under her feet, and she ducks into the bushes, for the three are coming. They stagger past her and don't notice her and soon they're gone. But still she waits awhile before she ventures out and walks along the path that she was just taking with the boy. And she finds him and kneels beside him, and both of them grasp that they must forget it and that the bleeding will stop, for someone like him does not die. I'm made of air, he says. Nothing will happen to me. There's no reason to moan. All this is still fortunate. It could have been worse.

To be stuck here in the shaft, for example, this is probably worse, for here not even forgetting helps. If you forget the shaft in which you're stuck, you're still in the shaft.

"I'm going into the monastery," says Tyll. "If I get out of here. I mean it."

"Melk?" asks Matthias. "I was there once. It's grand."

"Andechs. They have strong walls. If it's safe anywhere, then in Andechs."

"Will you take me with you?"

Gladly, is what Tyll thinks, if you get us out of here, we'll go together. But what he says is: "No way they'll let you in, you gallows bird."

He realizes it's come out the wrong way around, because of the darkness. I was only joking, he thinks, of course they'll let you in, but says: "I'm a good liar!"

Tyll stands up. It's probably better if he shuts his mouth. His back hurts, he can't stand on his left leg. You have to protect your feet, you only have two of them, after all, and if you injure one, you can't get back up on the rope.

"We kept two cows," says Korff. "The older one had good milk." He must have been caught up in a memory too. Tyll can see it before his eyes: the house, the meadow, smoke over the chimney, a father and a mother, everything poor and dirty, but Korff didn't have any other childhood.

Tyll feels his way along the wall. Here is the wooden frame that they mounted earlier. A piece has broken off on top, or is that the bottom? He hears Korff weeping softly.

"It's gone," Korff moans. "Gone, gone! All the good milk!"

Tyll jiggles a piece of rock on the ceiling. It's loose and comes off. Stones trickle.

"Stop," cries Matthias.

"It wasn't me," says Tyll. "I swear it."

"Outside Magdeburg I lost my brother," says Korff. "A shot in the head."

"I lost my wife," says Matthias. "At Braunschweig, she was with the supply train, the plague took her, our two children too."

"What was her name?"

"Johanna," says Matthias. "My wife. I can't remember the names of the children."

"I lost my sister," says Tyll.

Korff stumbles around. Tyll hears him next to him and draws back. Better not to bump into him. Someone like Korff won't put up with that, he won't hesitate to attack. Another explosion. Again stones trickle. The ceiling won't hold much longer.

You'll see, says Pirmin, being dead isn't so bad. You get used to it.

"But I'm not dying," says Tyll.

"That's the spirit," says Korff, "that's right, bag of bones!"

Tyll steps on something soft, it must be Kurt, then he bumps into a wall of coarse debris, this is where the shaft caved in. He wants to dig with his hands, for now it doesn't matter, now there's no need to conserve air, but immediately he has to cough, and the rock won't move, Korff was right, it's impossible without a pickax.

Don't worry, you will hardly notice it, says Pirmin. You've already lost half your mind, soon the rest will abandon you too. Then you will pass out, and when you wake up, you'll be dead.

I will think of you, says Origenes. I will make something of myself, I'll learn to write next, and if you like, I'll write a book about you, for children and old people. What do you think of that?

And don't you even want to know how I've fared? asks Agneta. You and me and me and you—how long has it been? You don't even know whether I'm still alive, little son.

"I don't even want to know," says Tyll.

You betrayed him as I did. You don't need to be angry with me. You called him a servant of the devil as I did. A warlock as I did. What I said, you said too.

She's right again, says Claus.

"Maybe if we find the pickax after all," Matthias says with a groan. "Maybe we can loosen it with the pickax."

Alive or dead, you attach too much weight to the difference, says Claus. There are so many chambers in between. So many dusty corners in which you are no longer the one and not yet the other. So many dreams from which you can no longer awake. I've seen a cauldron of blood, boiling over hot flames, and the shadows dance around it, and when the Great Black One points to one of them, but he does so only every thousand years, then there's no end to the shrieking, then he dips his head into the blood and drinks, and you know, that was still far from hell, it was not even the entrance to it yet. I've seen places where the souls burn like torches, only hotter and brighter and for eternity, and they never stop screaming, because their pain never stops, and still this is not it. You think that you have an inkling, my son, but you don't have the slightest inkling. To be confined in a shaft is almost like death, you think, war is almost hell, but the truth is that anything, anything is better, it's better down here, it's better out there in a bloody ditch, it's better in the torture chair. So don't let go, stay alive.

Tyll can't help laughing.

"Why are you laughing?" asks Korff.

"Well, then divulge a spell to me," says Tyll. "You were not a good sorcerer, but perhaps you've learned more."

Who are you talking to? asks Pirmin. There's no ghost here except me.

Another explosion. Then there's a crack and a boom. Matthias lets out a howl. Part of the ceiling must have collapsed.

Pray, says Iron Kurt. I was the first to go, now it's Matthias's turn.

Tyll squats down. He hears Korff shouting, but Matthias no longer responds. Something tickles his cheek, his neck, his shoulder, it feels like a spider, but there are no insects here, so it must be blood. He feels around and finds a wound on his forehead, beginning up by his hair and going down to the root of his nose. It is very soft to the touch, and the trickle of blood keeps growing. But he feels nothing.

"God have mercy on me," says Korff. "Lord Jesus Christ, have mercy. Holy Ghost. I killed a comrade for his boots. Mine had holes in them, he was fast asleep, it was in the camp at Munich, what should I have done, I do need boots! So I struck. I strangled him, he opened his eyes, but he couldn't scream. I just needed some boots. And he had a medallion that wards off bullets, I needed that too, thanks to the medallion I have never been hit. It didn't help him against strangling."

"Do I look like a priest?" asks Tyll. "You can confess to your grandmother, leave me alone."

"Dear Lord Jesus," says Korff. "In Braunschweig I freed a woman from the stake, a witch. It was early in the morning, she was supposed to burn at noon. She was very young. I was passing. No one saw it, because it was still dark. I cut through the fetters, said: Quickly, run with me! She did it, she was so grateful, and then I took her as often as I wanted to, and I wanted to often, and then I slit her throat and buried her."

"I forgive you. This very day you will be with me in paradise."

Another explosion.

"Why are you laughing?" asks Korff.

"Because you will not get into paradise, not today and not later either. Not even Satan will touch a gallows bird like you. And I'm also laughing because I'm not going to die."

"Yes, you are," says Korff. "I didn't want to believe it, but we're never getting out. It's all over for Korff."

Another bang. Again everything shakes. Tyll holds his hands over his head as if that could do any good.

"Perhaps it's all over for Korff. But not for me. I'm not going to die today."

He takes a leap as if he were standing on the rope. His leg hurts, but he stands firmly on his feet. A stone falls on his shoulder. More blood runs down his cheek. Again there is a crash, again stones fall. "And I'm not going to die tomorrow or any other day. I don't want to! I'm not doing it, do you hear?"

Korff doesn't respond, but perhaps he can still hear.

So Tyll shouts: "I'm not doing it, I'm leaving now, I don't like it here anymore."

A bang, a trembling. Another stone falls and grazes his shoulder.

"I'm leaving now. This is what I've always done. When things get tight, I leave. I'm not going to die here. I'm not going to die today. I'm not going to die!"

Westphalia

I

SHE STILL WALKED ERECT AS IN THE PAST. HER BACK almost always hurt, but she didn't let it show and held the cane on which she had to prop herself up as if it were a fashionable accessory. She still resembled the paintings from long ago; indeed, enough of her beauty remained to fluster people who unexpectedly found themselves in her presence—as now, when she threw back her fur hood and looked around the anteroom with a firm gaze. At the arranged signal her lady's maid behind her announced that Her Majesty the Queen of Bohemia wished to speak with the imperial ambassador.

She saw the lackeys casting glances at each other. Apparently the spies had failed this time, no one was prepared for her arrival. She had left her house at The Hague under a false name; her pass, issued by the States General of the United Dutch Provinces, identified her as Madame de Cournouailles. In the company of only the coachman and her lady's maid she had traveled east through Bentheim, Oldenzaal, and Ibbenbüren, over fallow fields and through villages destroyed by fire, cleared forests, the never-changing landscapes of the war. There were no inns, so they had spent the nights in the coach, stretched out on the bench, which was dangerous, yet neither wolves nor marauders had taken an interest in the small coach of an old queen. And so they had reached the road from Münster to Osnabrück unmolested.

Immediately everything had been different. The meadows grew high. The houses had intact roofs. A stream turned the wheel of a mill. There were guard huts on the roadside, well-fed men with halberds standing outside them. The neutral zone. Here there was no war.

Outside the walls of Osnabrück a guard had come up to the coach window and had asked what their desire was. Wordlessly, Fräulein von Quadt, her lady's maid, had handed him the pass, and without great interest he had looked at it and waved them on. The very first citizen on the roadside, a tidily dressed man with a well-trimmed beard, had shown them the way to the quarters of the imperial ambassador. There the coachman had lifted her and her lady's maid out of the coach, carried them over the mucky ground, and put them down in front of the portal, their clothing unscathed. Two halberdiers had opened the doors for them. With an assurance as if she had rights over this household—according to ceremony established throughout Europe, even a visiting monarch was the master of the household everywhere—she had entered the antechamber, and her lady's maid had demanded the ambassador.

The lackeys whispered and gave each other signs. Liz knew that she had to take advantage of the surprise. The thought must not form in any of these heads that it would be possible to turn her away.

She had not made a royal appearance in a long time. When you lived in a small house and were visited by no one but merchants trying to settle their bills, you didn't often have the opportunity. But she was the grandniece of the Virgin Queen Elizabeth, the granddaughter of Mary, Queen of Scots, the daughter of James, the ruler of both kingdoms, and she had been trained since childhood in how a queen was to stand, to walk, and to look. This too was a craft, and once you'd learned it, you never forgot it.

The most important thing: don't ask questions and don't hesitate. No gesture of impatience, no movement that looked like doubt. Her parents and her poor Friedrich, who had now been dead so long that she had to look at portraits to remember his face, had stood so straight that it seemed as if no rheumatism, no weakness, and no worry could ever touch them.

After she had stood straight for a little while, surrounded by whispering and astonishment, she took one step and then another toward the gilded double doors. There were no other doors like this in the Westphalian provinces, someone must have brought them here from far away, just like the paintings on the walls and the carpets on the floor and the curtains of damask and the silk wallpaper and the many-armed candelabra and the two chandeliers, heavy with crystals, in which, even though it was broad daylight, every single candle burned. No duke and no prince, indeed not even Papa, would have transformed a residence in a small city into such a palace. It was the sort of thing only the King of France or the Kaiser did.

Without pausing, she walked toward the doors. Now she could not afford to hesitate. The briefest hint of uncertainty would be enough to remind the two lackeys standing to the right and the left of the doors that it was also entirely conceivable not to open them for her. If that should happen, her advance would be staved off. Then she would have to sit down on one of the plush chairs and someone would appear and tell her that the ambassador unfortunately had no time, but that his secretary would be able to see her in two hours, and she would protest, and the lackey would say coolly that he was sorry, and she would raise her voice, and the lackey would repeat it unimpressed, and she would raise her voice further, and more lackeys would gather, and thus she would all at once no longer be a queen but a complaining old woman in the anteroom.

That was why it had to work. There would be no second attempt. One had to move as if the door weren't there, not be slowed down by it; one had to walk in such a way that if no one opened the doors, one would crash into them at full force, and since Quadt was following her at two paces' distance, her lady's maid would then crash into her back, and the humiliation would be unbearable—for that very reason, they would open them; that was the whole trick.

It worked. With confused expressions the lackeys reached for the handles and heaved open the doors. Liz stepped into the reception room. She turned around and gestured to Quadt with her hand not to follow any farther. That was unusual. A queen did not make visits unaccompanied. But this was not a normal situation. Taken aback, her lady's maid stopped, and the lackeys closed the doors in front of her.

The room seemed huge. Perhaps it was due to the skillfully arranged mirrors, perhaps it was a trick of the Viennese court magicians. The room seemed so large that one couldn't quite comprehend how the house could contain it. It stretched like a hall in a palace, and a sea of carpets separated Liz from a distant desk. Far beyond, open damask curtains revealed a suite of rooms, even more carpets, even more golden candleholders, even more chandeliers and paintings.

Behind the desk rose a gentleman of small stature with

a gray beard, who looked so inconspicuous that it took Liz a moment to notice him. He took off his hat and gave a courtly bow.

"Welcome," he said. "May I hope, madame, the journey was not arduous?"

"I am Elizabeth, Queen—"

"Forgive the interruption, it is only to spare Your Highness the trouble. Explanations not necessary; I am informed."

It took her a while to understand what he had said. She drew a breath to ask him how he knew who she was, but again he was quicker.

"Because it is my profession, madame. To know things. And my duty to understand them."

She furrowed her brow. She felt hot, which was partly due to the thick fur coat and partly due to the fact that she was not used to being interrupted. He now stood bent forward, one hand on the desk, the other on his back, as if afflicted by a sudden pain there. Quickly she walked toward one of the chairs in front of the desk. But as in a dream the room was so large and the desk so far away that it would take a long time before she reached it.

His addressing her as Your Highness meant that he did acknowledge her status as a member of the English royal family, but did not recognize her as Queen of Bohemia, for otherwise he would have had to address her as Your Majesty; indeed, he did not even recognize her as an electress, for then he would have called her Your Serene Highness, which might not be worth much at home in England but here in the Empire was worth more than even the royalty of a king's child. And precisely because this man knew his trade, it was essential that she sit down before he invited her to, for whereas he naturally had to offer a princess a chair, in the case of a queen it was not his place to do so. Monarchs sat down uninvited, and everyone else stood until the monarch permitted them to sit.

"Would Your Highness—"

But since the chair was still far away, she interrupted him. "Am I speaking with him who I assume he is?"

This brought him up short for a moment. For one thing, because he had not expected her German to be so good. She had made good use of her time, she had not been idle over the years, she had taken lessons with a kind young German whom she had liked and with whom she almost could have fallen in love—often she had dreamed of him and once even drafted a letter to him, but such a thing was not possible, she could not afford a scandal. For another thing, he was silent because she had affronted him. An imperial ambassador was to be called Your Excellency—by everyone but a king or queen. He thus had to insist to her on a form of address that she could under no circumstances grant him. For this problem there was only one solution: someone like her and someone like him must never encounter each other.

When he began to speak, she darted sideways, went to a stool and sat down; she had beaten him to it. She enjoyed this small victory, leaned her cane against the wall, and interlaced her fingers in her lap. Then she saw his look.

She went icy cold. How could she have made such a mistake? It must have been because she had been out of practice for years. Of course she could neither remain standing nor let him invite her to sit, but a chair without a backrest, that should not have happened to her under any circumstances. As a queen, she was entitled to sit on a chair with a backrest and armrests even in the presence of the Kaiser, a mere armchair would be an indignity, but a stool was out of the question. And he had deliberately placed stools all around the reception room, yet only behind his desk was there an armchair.

What should she do? She smiled too and decided to pretend it was of no consequence. But he now had the advantage: All he needed to do was to call in the people from the anteroom, and word that she had sat on a stool in his presence would spread through Europe like wildfire. Even at home in England they would laugh.

"That depends," he said, "on what Your Highness deigns to assume, but since it is not the place of Your Highness's humble servant to assume that Your Highness could make anything but the correct assumption, I in turn do not hesitate to answer Your Highness's question with yes. It is I, Johann von Lamberg, the Kaiser's ambassador, at Your Highness's service. A refreshment? Wine?"

This was another skillful injury of her royal dignity, for one offered nothing to a monarch—he had rights over the household, it was up to him to demand what he wanted. Such things were not unimportant. For three years the ambassadors had negotiated only matters of who had to bow before whom and who had to take off his hat first before whom. He who made a mistake in etiquette could not win. So she ignored his offer, which was not easy for her, because she was very thirsty. She sat motionless on her stool and gazed at him. She was good at that. She had learned to sit calmly, she was practiced in it—in this, at least, no one surpassed her.

Lamberg was still standing bent forward, one hand on the desk, the other on his back. He was doing so apparently so that he would not have to decide whether to sit down or remain standing: In the presence of a queen he would not be permitted to sit, but before a princess it would be a violation of etiquette for an imperial ambassador to stand when she was sitting. Since, as the Kaiser's ambassador, he did not recognize Liz's royal title, it would be consistent to sit down—but at the same time also a severe insult, which he avoided in this way, out of politeness and because he did not yet know what weapons and offers she had in her hands.

"With Your Highness's kind permission, a question."

All at once his manner of speaking was just as unpleasant to her as his Austrian intonation.

"As Your Highness knows very well, we are in the midst of a diplomatic congress. Since the beginning of the negotiations, no royal personage has set foot in Münster and Osnabrück. As delighted as Your Highness's faithful servant is to have the privilege of welcoming Your Highness's gracious visit to his poor domicile, he nonetheless fears just as much—" he sighed as if it caused him great sorrow to say so—"that it is not proper."

"The count means we should have sent an ambassador too."

He smiled again. She knew what he was thinking and she knew that he knew that she knew it: you are no one, you live in a small house, you're buried in debt, you're not sending any ambassadors to congresses.

"I'm not even here," said Liz. "That way we can talk to each other, can't we? The count can imagine he is talking to himself. He is speaking in his head, and in his head I reply to him."

She felt something she had not expected. For so long she had been making preparations for this encounter, mulling it over, fearing it, and now that the day had arrived, something strange was happening: she was enjoying it! All those years in the small house, far from notable people and important events—all at once she was again sitting as if on a stage, surrounded by gold and silver and carpets, and speaking with a clever person before whom every word counted.

"We all know that the Palatinate is a perpetual point of contention," she said. "As is the Palatine electoral dignity, which was held by my late husband."

He chuckled.

This flustered her. But that was his aim, of course, and for that very reason she had to persevere.

"The electors of the Empire," she said, "will not accept the Bavarian House of Wittelsbach keeping the electoral dignity of which the Kaiser wrongfully stripped my husband. If Caesar can dispossess one of us, they will say, then he can do it to all of us. And if we—"

"With Your Highness's kind permission, they have long since accepted it. Your Highness's husband was placed, along with Your Highness yourself, under the imperial ban, which, incidentally, anywhere else would obligate me to have Your Highness arrested."

"Which is why we have come here and not anywhere else."

"With Your Highness's kind permission—"

"We grant it, but first we shall be heard. The Duke of Bavaria, who calls himself Elector, illegally bears our husband's title. The Kaiser has no right to revoke an electoral dignity. The electors elect the Kaiser, the Kaiser does not elect the electors. But we understand the situation. The Kaiser owes the Bavarians money; the Bavarians, in turn, have the Catholic estates firmly in their hands. That is why we are making an offer. We are the crowned Queen of Bohemia, and the crown—"

"With Your Highness's kind permission, for one winter thirty—"

". . . will pass to our son."

"Bohemia's crown is not hereditary. If it were, the Bohemian estates would not have been able to offer the throne to the Palsgrave Friedrich, Your Highness's husband. The fact that he accepted the crown means that he knew that Your Highness's son could assert no claim."

"One can see it that way, but must one? Perhaps England will not see it that way. If he asserts claims, England will support them."

"There's a civil war in England."

"There is, and if our brother is deposed by the parliament, the English crown will be offered to our son."

"That is unlikely at best."

Outside, trombones blared: a tinny call, which rose, hung for a while in the air, and died away. Liz raised her eyebrows questioningly.

"Longueville, my French colleague," said Lamberg. "He has them blow a fanfare when he sits down to eat. Every day. He is here with a retinue of six hundred men. Four portrait painters are entrusted with the sole task of painting him. Three wood-carvers are crafting busts of him. What he does with those remains a state secret."

"Has the count asked him?"

"We are not authorized to speak to each other."

"Is that not a hindrance to negotiation?"

"We are not here as friends, nor to become friends. The ambassador of the Vatican mediates between us, just as the ambassador of Venice mediates between me and the Protestants, for the ambassador of the Vatican is in turn not authorized to speak to Protestants. I must now take my leave, madame, the honor of this conversation is as great as it is undeserved, but pressing duties make demands on my time."

"An eighth electoral dignity."

He looked up. His eyes met hers for only a moment. Then he looked at the desk again.

"The Bavarian shall keep his electoral dignity," said Liz. "We formally relinquish Bohemia. And if—"

"With Your Highness's kind permission, Your Highness cannot relinquish something that does not belong to Your Highness."

"The Swedish army is standing outside Prague. The city will soon be back in the hands of the Protestants."

"Should Sweden take the city, Sweden will certainly not give it to you."

"The war is nearly over. Then there will be an amnesty. Then the breach . . . the alleged breach of the imperial peace by our husband will be pardoned."

"The amnesty has long since been negotiated. All acts of the war will be pardoned with the exception of one person's."

"I can guess whose."

"This endless war began with Your Highness's husband. With a palsgrave who set his sights too high. I'm not saying that Your Highness is to blame, but I can imagine that the daughter of the great James did not exactly try to urge her ambitious husband to be modest." Lamberg slowly pushed his chair back and straightened up. "The war has been going on so long that most people alive today have never seen peace. That only the old can still remember peace. My colleagues and I—yes, even the idiot who has fanfares played when he sits down to eat—are the only ones who can end it. Everyone wants territories that the others would under no circumstances part with, everyone demands subsidies, everyone wants mutual-assistance pacts terminated that the others consider permanent, so that instead new pacts result that others find unacceptable. All this is beyond the abilities of any human being. And yet we must succeed. You and your husband began this war, madame. I shall end it."

He pulled a silk cord over the desk. Liz heard the sound of a bell from the next room. Now he is summoning a secretary, she thought, some gray cipher who will usher me out. She felt dizzy. The room seemed to rise and sink as if she were on a ship. Never before had someone spoken to her that way.

A ray of light captivated her. It fell through a thin crack between the curtains, specks of dust whirling in it, a mirror on the opposite wall catching it and casting it to the other wall, where it made a spot on a picture frame gleam. The painting was by Rubens: a tall woman, a man with a lance, above them a bird in the azure. A hovering serenity emanated from it. She remembered Rubens well, a sad man, who audibly had difficulty breathing. She had wanted to buy one of his paintings, but it had been too expensive for her; nothing seemed to interest him except money. But how had he been able to paint like that?

"Prague was never for us," she said. "Prague was a mistake. But it is for the sake of the Palatinate that I did not go back to England. My brother invited me time and again, but Holland is formally still part of the Empire, and as long as I live there, our claim endures."

A door opened, and a corpulent man with a kind face and shrewd eyes came in. He took off his hat and bowed. Although he was young, he had hardly any hair left on his head.

"Count Wolkenstein," said Lamberg. "Our *cavalier d'ambassade*. He will provide you with accommodations. There are no rooms left in the inns here, every corner is packed with the envoys and their retinues."

"We don't want Bohemia," said Liz, "but we will not cede the electoral dignity. My firstborn, who was clever and lovable and on whom everyone would have been able to agree, died. The boat overturned. He drowned."

"I'm sorry," Wolkenstein said with a plainness that touched her.

"My second son, the next in the line of succession, is neither clever nor lovable, but the electoral dignity of the Palatinate is rightfully his, and if the Bavarian simply won't hand it over, an eighth must be created. The Protestants will not tolerate anything else. Otherwise I will go back to England, where the parliament will depose my brother and make my son king, and from high upon the English throne he will then demand Prague, and the war will not end. I will prevent it. All by myself."

"We don't need to get worked up," said Lamberg. "I will pass on Your Highness's message to His Imperial Majesty."

"And my husband must be included in the amnesty. If all acts of the war are to be pardoned, then his too must be pardoned."

"Not in this life," said Lamberg.

She stood up. She was boiling with anger. She sensed that she had turned red, but she still managed to draw up the corners of her mouth, set her cane on the floor, and turn to the doors.

"A great and unexpected honor. A splendor in this poor house." Lamberg took off his hat and bowed. Not a hint of mockery could be heard in his voice.

She raised her hand for the careless royal wave and walked on without a word.

Wolkenstein overtook her, reached the doors, and gave a

knock—immediately the lackeys outside pulled them open. Liz stepped into the anteroom, followed by Wolkenstein. With her lady's maid behind them, they walked to the exit.

"As for Your Royal Highness's accommodations," said Wolkenstein, "we could offer—"

"The count shouldn't trouble himself."

"It's no trouble, but rather a great—"

"Does the count seriously believe I would wish to lodge somewhere that is teeming with imperial spies?"

"If I may speak plainly: Wherever Your Royal Highness finds accommodation, the place will be full of spies. We have so many of them. We're losing on the battlefields, and there are not many secrets left. What are our poor spies to do all day?"

"The Kaiser is losing on the battlefields?"

"I was just there myself, down in Bavaria. My finger is still there!" He raised his hand and moved his glove to show her that the sheath of the right index finger was empty. "We have lost half the army. Your Royal Highness has not chosen a bad moment. As long as we are strong, we never make concessions."

"It is a favorable time?"

"It is always a favorable time, when you begin correctly. Take pleasure in yourself and do not bow to sorrow, though fortune, place, and time may be in league against you."

"Pardon me?"

"That is by a German poet. There's such a thing now. German poets! His name is Paul Fleming. His works are so beautiful that they bring tears to one's eyes; unfortunately he died young, from disease of the lung. One doesn't dare to imagine what might have become of him. Because of him I write in German."

She smiled. "Poems?"

"Prose."

"Really, in German? I once gave Opitz a try—"

"Opitz!"

"Yes, Opitz."

Both of them laughed.

"I know, it sounds like a folly," said Wolkenstein. "But I think it's possible, and I have decided to one day write my life in German. That's why I'm here. Some day people will want to know what it was like at the great congress. I brought a traveling entertainer from Andechs to Vienna, or actually he brought me to Vienna—without him I would be dead. But when His Imperial Majesty then sent him to appear before the envoys, I seized the opportunity and came here with him."

Liz gave her lady's maid a sign. She hurried out to have the coach drive up. It was a beautiful carriage, fast and to some extent befitting her station. Liz had spent her last savings to rent it for two weeks along with two strong horses and a reliable coachman. This meant that she could remain in Osnabrück for three days, after which she had to set off for home.

She stepped outside and pulled her fur hood over her head. Had it gone well? She didn't know. There was so much more she would have liked to say, so much else she would have liked to bring up, but that was probably how it always was. Papa had once said that one could always deploy only a fraction of one's weapons.

Rumbling, the coach drove up. The driver climbed down. She looked around and realized with a peculiar regret that the fat *cavalier d'ambassade* had not followed her farther. She would have liked to speak a little more with him.

The coachman clasped her around the hips and carried her to the carriage.

II

The next morning Liz called on the Swedish ambassador. This time she had announced her visit. Sweden was a friendly power and the element of surprise unnecessary. The man would be glad to meet her.

The night had been terrible. After searching for a long time, she had found a room in an especially filthy inn: no window, brushwood on the floor, instead of a bed a narrow straw sack, which she had to share with her lady's maid. When she had after several hours finally fallen into a restless sleep, she had dreamed of Friedrich and their days in Heidelberg, before people with unpronounceable names had pressed Bohemia's crown on them. They had walked side by side through one of the stone corridors of the castle, and she had felt to the core of her soul what it meant to belong together. When she had woken up, she had listened to the snoring of the coachman sleeping outside the door and thought about how she had now lived almost as long without Friedrich as she had formerly been married to him.

When she entered the envoy's anteroom, she had to suppress a yawn; she had slept far too little. Here too there were carpets, but the walls were bare in Protestant fashion; only on the side wall hung a cross adorned with pearls. The room was full of people: some were studying files, others walking restlessly up and down. They had apparently been waiting for some time. How did it happen anyway that Lamberg's anteroom had been empty? Did he have another, perhaps even several?

All eyes turned to her. Silence fell. As on the previous day she walked with a firm step toward the door, while Quadt behind her called out in a loud, though somewhat shrill, voice: "The Queen of Bohemia!" Suddenly she worried that it would not go well this time.

And indeed, the lackey did not reach for the doorknob.

With an inelegant half-step she stopped, so abruptly that she had to support herself with her hand against the door. She heard her lady's maid behind her nearly stumbling. She felt hot. She heard murmuring, she heard whispering, and yes, she heard snickering too.

Slowly she backed up two paces. Fortunately, her lady's maid had the presence of mind to back up too. Liz clenched her left hand around the cane and looked at the lackey with her most pleasant smile.

The fellow goggled stupidly. Of course, no one had told him that there was a Queen of Bohemia, he was young, he didn't know anything, and he didn't want to risk making a mistake. Who could blame him?

But she couldn't just sit down either. A queen didn't wait in the anteroom until someone had time for her. There were indeed good reasons for crowned heads not to travel to a diplomatic congress. But what else should she have done? Her son, for whose electoral dignity she was fighting, was far too imperious and naive, he would certainly have ruined everything. And she didn't have diplomats.

She stood as motionless as the lackey. The murmuring swelled. She heard loud laughter. Do not turn red, she thought, not under any circumstances. Just do not turn red!

She thanked God with all her heart when someone opened the door from the other side. A head slid through the crack. One eye was higher than the other, the nose was set below them at a strange angle, the lips were full but did not quite seem to fit together. From his chin hung a stringy goatee.

"Your Majesty," said the face.

Liz stepped in, and the uneven man quickly closed the door again, as if he wanted to avoid others pressing after her.

"Alvise Contarini, at your service," he said in French. "Ambassador of the Republic of Venice. I am the mediator here. Come with me."

He led her through a narrow corridor. Here too the walls were bare, but the carpet was exquisite and—Liz could tell; she had, after all, furnished two castles—of inestimable value.

"A word in advance," said Contarini. "The greatest difficulty is still that France demands that the imperial line of the House of Austria no longer support the Spanish line. This would not matter to Sweden, but because of the high subsidies that Sweden has received from France, the Swedes must adopt the demand as their own. The Kaiser remains categorically against it. As long as this has not been settled, we will obtain no signature from any of the three crowns."

Liz tilted her head and smiled inscrutably, as she had done all her life when she didn't understand something. Probably, she thought, he didn't want anything in particular from her and was simply used to talking. There were people like that in every court.

They reached the end of the corridor. Contarini opened the door and, with a bow, let her go first. "Your Majesty, the Swedish ambassadors. Count Oxenstierna and Dr. Adler Salvius."

Disconcerted, she looked around. There they sat, one in the right corner of the reception room, the other in the left, in armchairs of equal size, as if placed by a painter. In the middle of the room was another chair with armrests. When Liz stepped toward it, both men rose and bowed deeply. Liz sat down. The men remained standing. Oxenstierna was a heavy man with full cheeks. Salvius was tall and thin and looked above all very tired.

"Your Majesty paid Lamberg a visit?" Salvius asked in French.

"You know that?"

"Osnabrück is small," said Oxenstierna. "Your Majesty knows that this is a diplomatic congress? No princes, no rulers, and—"

"I know," she said. "I'm actually not here either. And the reason I'm not here is the electoral dignity that rightfully belongs to my family. If I am correctly informed, Sweden supports our claim to a restitution of the title." It did her good to speak French. The words came more quickly, the phrases strung themselves together. It seemed to her as if the language itself were forming the sentences. She would have liked best to speak English, of course, the rich, supple, and singing language of her home, the language of theater and poetry, but almost no one here understood it. Nor was there an English ambassador in Osnabrück; ultimately Papa had sacrificed her and Friedrich to keep his country out of the war.

She waited. No one spoke.

"Isn't that right?" she finally asked. "That Sweden supports our claim, it's true, isn't it?"

"In principle," said Salvius.

"If Sweden insists on a restitution of our royal title, my son for his part will offer to relinquish this very restitution, provided that in return the imperial court promises us in a secret agreement to create an eighth electoral dignity."

"The Kaiser cannot create a new electoral dignity," said Oxenstierna. "He has no right to."

"If the estates give it to him, he has it," said Liz.

"But they are not permitted to," said Oxenstierna. "Besides, we want much more."

"A new electoral dignity would be in the Catholic interest, because Bavaria would keep the electoral dignity. And it would be in the Protestant interest, because our side would get an additional Protestant elector."

"Perhaps," said Salvius.

"Never," said Oxenstierna.

"The lords are both right," said Contarini.

Liz looked at him questioningly.

"It can't be helped," Contarini said in German. "They must both be right. The one is close to his father, the chancellor, and wants to keep waging war, the other was sent by the queen to make peace."

"What did you say?" asked Oxenstierna.

"I quoted a German saying."

"Bohemia is not part of the Empire," said Oxenstierna. "We cannot include Prague in the negotiations. That would have had to be negotiated first. Before you negotiate, you always have to negotiate what you are actually going to negotiate."

"On the other hand," said Salvius, "Her Majesty the Queen of Sweden—"

"Her Majesty is inexperienced, and my father is her guardian. And he says that—"

"Was."

"Excuse me?"

"The queen is of age."

"Has just come of age. My father, the chancellor, is Europe's most experienced statesman. Ever since our great Gustav Adolf drew his last breath in Lützen—"

"Since then we have hardly won anymore. Without the help of the French we would have been lost."

"Do you mean to say—"

"Who am I to diminish the merits of His Excellency your father, the Lord High Chancellor and Count, but I am of the opinion—"

"But perhaps your opinion doesn't count for much, Dr. Salvius, perhaps the opinion of the second ambassador is not—"

"The chief negotiator."

"Appointed by the queen. Whose guardian, however, is my father!"

"*Was*. Your father *was* her guardian!"

"Perhaps we can agree that Her Majesty's proposal is worthy of consideration," said Contarini. "We do not have to say that we will accept it, we do not even have to promise to consider the proposal, but we can still all agree that the proposal might be worthy of our consideration."

"That's not enough," said Liz. "As soon as Prague is conquered, an official demand must be issued to Count Lamberg to restore my son to the Bohemian throne. Then my son will immediately make a secret agreement with him to the effect that he relinquishes it, provided that he in turn makes a secret agreement with Sweden and France regarding the eighth electoral dignity. This must happen quickly."

"Nothing happens quickly," said Contarini. "I have been here since the beginning of the negotiations. I thought that I would not be able to stand one month in this horrible rainy backwater. In the meantime, five years have passed."

"I know what it's like to grow old while waiting," said Liz. "And I will wait no longer. If Sweden does not demand the Bohemian crown, so that my son can relinquish it in exchange for the electoral dignity, we will relinquish the electoral dignity. Then you will have nothing left with which to gain an eighth electoral dignity. It would be the end of our dynasty, but I would simply go back to England. I would like to be home again. I would like to go to the theater again."

"I would like to be home in Venice too," said Contarini. "I would like to be doge one day."

"If Your Majesty would permit me to inquire," said Salvius. "So that I may understand. You have come here to demand something that we would never have pursued on our own. And your threat is: if we don't do what you want, then you will retract your demand? What is one to call such a maneuver?"

Liz smiled her most mysterious smile. Now she really was sorry that she wasn't standing at the edge of a stage, facing the semidarkness of an auditorium, where the audience listened spellbound. She cleared her throat, and even though she already knew her reply, for the sake of a stronger effect on the spectators who weren't there, she pretended she had to think.

"I suggest," she finally said, "you call it politics."

III

The next day, the last of her stay in Osnabrück, Liz left her room at the inn early in the afternoon to make her way to the bishop's reception. No one had invited her, but she had heard that everyone who mattered would be there. Tomorrow at this time she would already be on the way back, through ravaged landscapes, to her small house at The Hague.

She could not prolong her stay. She had to depart, not merely due to the lack of money, but also because she knew the rules of a good drama: a deposed queen who suddenly appeared and then disappeared—something like that made an impression. But a deposed queen who appeared and then stayed until people got used to her and began to make jokes about her—that would not do. She had learned this in Holland, where she and Friedrich had once been so kindly welcomed and where in the meantime the members of the States General were always otherwise engaged just when she asked for a meeting.

This reception would be her last appearance. She had made her proposals, had said what she had to say. There was nothing more she could do for her son.

Unfortunately, he came after her brother and was a real lout. Both of them resembled Papa, but they had nothing of his sly intelligence. They were space-filling, self-important men with deep voices and broad shoulders and sweeping movements, who were mad about hunting. Over in her native land her brother would probably lose his war against the parliament, and her son, should he actually become elector, would hardly go down in history as a great ruler. He was already thirty years old, thus no longer young, and currently he was roaming around somewhere in England, probably hunting, while she was negotiating for him in Westphalia. His rare letters to her were brief, with a coolness that was not far from hostility.

And as always when she thought of him, the image of the other one took shape in her: her beautiful son, her clever and radiant firstborn, who had had his father's kind soul and her intellect—her pride, her joy and hope. When his image arose in her, it bore various faces, all at the same time: she saw him as he had been at three months old, at twelve years old, at fourteen. And then she felt that other image looming up, which every thought of him brought with it and because of which she strove to think of him as little as possible: the capsizing boat, the black maw of the river. She knew how it felt to swallow water by mistake when swimming, but drowning? She couldn't imagine it.

Osnabrück was tiny, and she could have walked from the inn. Yet the streets were dirty even by German standards, and besides, how would it have looked?

So she had herself lifted into the coach again, leaned back, and watched the narrow gabled houses jerking past. Her lady's maid sat silently beside her. She was used to being ignored by Liz and never spoke to her unless spoken to. To act like a piece of furniture was the only thing a lady's maid really had to be able to do. It was cold, and a fine drizzle fell. Nonetheless the sun could be made out as a pale spot behind the clouds. The rain cleared the air of the smell of the streets. Children ran by. She saw a group of city soldiers on horses, then a donkey cart with sacks of flour. Now they were turning toward the main square. Over there was the residence of the imperial ambassador where she had been the day before. In the middle of the square was a block the height of a man with holes for head and arms. Just last month, the innkeeper had told her, a witch had stood here. The judge had been lenient: she was granted her life and after ten days in the pillory driven from the city.

The cathedral was bulky and German, a disastrous monstrosity, one tower thicker than the other. Attached to its side was an oblong house with massive cornices and a pointed roof. Several coaches were blocking the square, so that Liz could not drive up. Her coachman had to stop at some distance and carry her to the entrance portal. He smelled bad, and the rain wet her fur coat, but at least he didn't drop her.

Somewhat ungently he put her down. She leaned on her cane so that she wouldn't lose her balance. At moments like this she felt her age. She threw back her fur hood and thought: my last appearance. A tingling excitement filled her, as it hadn't in years. The coachman went back to get her lady's maid, but Liz didn't wait, instead entering alone.

Even in the entrance hall she could hear music. She stopped and listened.

"His Imperial Majesty has sent us the best string players of the court."

Lamberg was wearing a cloak of dark purple. Around his neck he had the necklace of the Order of the Golden Fleece. Beside him stood Wolkenstein. The two of them took off their hats and bowed. Liz nodded to Wolkenstein. He smiled at her.

"Your Highness is departing tomorrow," said Lamberg.

It irritated her that it didn't sound like a question but like an order.

"As always, the count is well informed."

"Never as well as I would like to be. But I promise Your Highness that you will not easily hear music like this elsewhere. Vienna would like to show the congress its favor."

"Because Vienna is losing on the battlefield?"

He acted as if he hadn't heard the question. "And so the court has sent its best *musici* and eminent actors and its best entertainer. Your Highness paid the Swedes a visit?"

"The count really knows everything."

"And now Your Highness also knows that the Swedes are at odds with each other."

Outside, trombones were played. Lackeys flung open the doors. A man flashing with jewels came in, a woman with a long train and a diadem on his arm. As he passed, the man cast Lamberg a not unfriendly glance. Lamberg inclined his head so slightly that it was not quite a nod.

"France?" asked Liz.

Lamberg nodded.

"Has the count sent our proposal to Vienna?" she asked.

Lamberg did not answer. She couldn't tell whether he had heard her question.

"Or is that not necessary? Does the count have the authority to decide on his own?"

"A decision of the Kaiser is always a decision of the Kaiser and no one else. And now I must take my leave of Your Highness. Even under the protection of a false name it is not proper for your faithful servant to continue to converse with Your Highness."

"Because we are under the imperial ban, or because your wife will be jealous?"

Lamberg chuckled. "With Your Highness's permission, Count Wolkenstein will escort you into the hall."

Wolkenstein bent his arm, Liz laid her hand on the back of his hand, and they went in with measured steps.

"Are they all ambassadors here?" she asked.

"All of them. Only not everyone is permitted to greet everyone, let alone talk to everyone. Everything is strictly regulated."

"Is Count Wolkenstein permitted to talk to me?"

"Absolutely not. But I am permitted to walk with you. And I will tell my grandchildren about it. And I will write about it. The Queen of Bohemia, I will write, the legendary Elizabeth, the . . ."

"Winter Queen?"

"*Fair phoenix bride*, I was about to say."

"The count can speak English?"

"A little."

"And has read John Donne?"

"Not much. But I have read the beautiful song in which

he urges Your Highness's father to finally support the King of Bohemia: *No man is an island.*"

She looked up. The reception hall had the amateurish ceiling frescoes commonly seen in German lands—usually the work of a second-class Italian artist who had never made it in Florence. A ledge bore statues of serious-looking saints. Two of them held lances, two held crosses, one clenched his fists, one held a crown. Below the ledge, torches were mounted, and in four large chandeliers burned dozens of candles, multiplied by mirrors. At the rear wall stood six musicians: four violinists, one harpist, and one holding a strange horn unlike any Liz had ever seen before.

She listened. Even in Whitehall she had heard nothing like it. One violin made a melody rise from the depths, another violin took it up, gave the melody clarity and force, and passed it on to the third, while the fourth violin played around it with a second, lighter melody. Suddenly the two melodies merged and were taken up by the harp, which now came to the fore, while the violins, as if in a quiet conversation, had already found a new melody—and at that very moment the harp gave them back the other melody, and the two melodies coalesced, and above them soared the joyful cry of a third melody, steely and pulsating, the voice of the horn.

Then it was silent. The piece had been short, but it felt as if it had lasted much longer, as if it had borne its own time in itself. A few listeners clapped hesitantly. Others stood still and seemed to have turned their ears inward.

"On the way here they played for us every evening," said Wolkenstein. "The tall one there is named Hans Kuchner, he comes from the village of Hagenbrunn, he never went to school and can hardly speak, but the Lord has blessed him."

"Your Majesty!"

A couple had come up to her: a gentleman with an angular face and a large jaw, a lady on his arm who looked as if she were freezing.

Liz was sorry to see that Wolkenstein, who was apparently forbidden even to take notice of the man's presence, took a step back, folded his hands behind his back, and turned away. The man bowed, the woman gave a courtly curtsy.

"Wesenbeck," he said, pronouncing the crack at the end of his name so harshly that it sounded like a small explosion. "Second envoy of the Elector of Brandenburg. At Your Majesty's service."

"How nice," said Liz.

"Demanding an eighth electoral dignity. Quite bold!"

"We have demanded nothing. I am a weak woman. Women do not negotiate and do not make demands. My son for his part currently has no title that would permit him to demand anything. We can only relinquish. I have offered this in all humility. No one else can relinquish Bohemia's crown, we alone can do that, and we will do it in exchange for the electoral dignity. Demanding the crown for us is what the Protestant imperial estates must do."

"Us, that is."

Liz smiled.

The envoy nodded thoughtfully.

And all at once the thought came to her that she had not yet dared to think. It would work! When she had had the idea of renting the coach, traveling to Osnabrück, and intervening in the negotiations, it had at first struck her as a completely absurd whim. It had taken her almost a year to begin to trust herself and a further year to really set it in motion. But at bottom she had expected all along that they would laugh at her.

Now, however, standing opposite the man with the large jaw, she realized confusedly that it could actually succeed: the electoral title for her son. I was not a good mother to you, she thought, and I probably loved you scarcely as much as I should have, but there is one thing I have done for you: I did not go back to England, I stayed in the small house and pretended it was a royal court in exile, and I have refused all men after the death of your poor father, although many wanted me, even very young ones, for I was a legend and beautiful to boot—but I knew that there must be no scandal, for the sake of our claim, and I never forgot it for a moment.

"We're counting on you," she said. Had she struck the right tone, or was that too solemn? But he had such a large jaw, and his eyebrows were so bushy, and when he had said his name, tears had almost come to his eyes. For him the lofty tone was probably appropriate. "We're counting on Brandenburg."

He gave a bow. "Then count on Brandenburg."

His wife was regarding Liz with an icy gaze. In the hope that the conversation was now over, Liz looked around for Wolkenstein, but he was no longer to be seen. And now the Brandenburg couple too had moved on with deliberate steps.

She was standing alone. The musicians began anew. Liz counted the beats and recognized the latest fashionable dance, a minuet. Two lines formed, the gentlemen here, the ladies over there. The lines moved away from each other, then they walked toward each other. Partners took each other by the gloved hands. After a spin, they separated, the lines moved away from each other, and everything was repeated, while the music varied the previous theme lightly and liltingly: apart, together, spin, apart. In the notes vibrated longing, which you could feel without understanding whom or what it was directed at. There was the French ambassador stepping beside Count Oxenstierna: the two of them did not look at each other, but they moved, carried by the beat, in step. There was Contarini, whose lady was very young, an enchantingly slender beauty, and there was Wolkenstein, his eyes half closed, abandoning himself to the music, and apparently no longer thinking about her.

She was sorry that she could not participate. She had always liked to dance, but all she had left was her rank, and it was too high to fit into one of the lines. Besides, she could hardly move, her fur coat was too thick for a hall heated up by so many torches, nor could she take it off easily, because the dress she was wearing underneath was too simple. This ermine coat was all that remained of her old wardrobe, everything else having been pawned and sold. She had always wondered why she had kept it. Now she knew.

The lines came back together, but all at once there was disorder. Someone was standing in the middle of the hall and apparently making no move to get out of the dancers' way. At the edges they were still moving to the music—there was Salvius, over there the Brandenburg envoy's wife—yet in the middle the lines could no longer merge: Dancers crashed into each other, dancers lost their balance, everyone was trying to get past the standing man. He was scrawny, his cheeks hollow, his chin very sharp, a scar on his forehead. He was wearing a pied jerkin and baggy breeches and fine leather shoes. On his head was a colorful cap and bells. Now he began to juggle too: steel things flew into the air, first two, then three, then four, then five.

It took a moment, but then everyone realized at once: those were blades! People shrank back, men ducked, ladies covered their faces protectively with their hands. But the curved daggers kept returning to his hands, right side up, always with the handle at the bottom, while he now began to dance too—with small steps, forward and back, at first slowly, then more quickly, which in turn changed the music, for he did not follow it but it him. No one else was dancing anymore, they had made room to see better how he whirled around himself, while the flashing blades flew higher and higher. This was now no longer a deliberate, elegant dance, but a wild hurtling toward a breathless, galloping beat, which grew faster and faster.

Then he began to sing. His voice was high and tinny, but he hit the right notes and did not lose his breath. His words could not be understood. It was probably a language he had invented. And yet it seemed as if you knew what it was about: you understood it even though you could not have put it into words.

Now there were fewer daggers in the air. Only four left, now only three—one after the other was stuck in his belt.

A scream went through the hall. The green skirt of a lady, it was Contarini's wife, was suddenly speckled with red. Apparently one of the blades had grazed the palm of his hand, but you could see nothing of it in his face. Laughing, he hurled the last dagger so high that it flew through the arms of a chandelier without touching a single crystal, and as it whirled down, he caught it and put it away. The music stopped. He bowed.

Applause broke out. "Tyll!" someone shouted. "Bravo, Tyll!" someone else exclaimed. "Bravo! Bravo!"

The musicians began to play again. Liz felt dizzy. It was so hot in the hall, due to the many candles, and her fur was much too thick. On the right side of the entrance hall a door was open. Behind it a spiral staircase led upward. She hesitated. Then she went up.

The staircase was so steep that she stopped twice, gasping for breath. She propped herself up against the wall. Briefly, everything went black, her knees were weak, and she thought she would fall down. Then she recovered her strength, pulled herself together, and continued climbing. Finally she reached a small balcony.

She threw back her hood and leaned against the stone balustrade. Down below was the main square. To her right, the towers of the cathedral rose into the sky. The sun must have just set. A fine drizzle still filled the air.

Down below in the twilight a man crossed the square. It was Lamberg. He walked bent forward, with small, dragging steps, toward his residence. The purple cloak flapped languidly around his shoulders. For a moment he stood slumped outside the door. He seemed to be reflecting. Then he went in.

She closed her eyes. The cold air did her good.

"How is my donkey?" she asked.

"He's writing a book. And you, little Liz?"

She opened her eyes. He was standing next to her, resting on the balustrade. A cloth was tied around his hand.

"You are well preserved," he said. "You've grown old, but your mind is not yet weak, and you even still make a good impression."

"You too. Only the cap doesn't suit you."

He raised his unwounded hand and played with the little bells. "The Kaiser wants me to wear it, because that's how I was drawn in a brochure he likes. I had you brought to Vienna, he said to me, now you should also look the way people know you."

She pointed questioningly at his wrapped-up hand.

"In front of distinguished lords and ladies I always miss. Then they give more money."

"What is the Kaiser like?"

"Like everyone. At night he sleeps, and he likes when people are nice to him."

"And where is Nele?"

He was silent for a moment, as if he had to remember whom she was talking about. "She got married," he said. "A long time ago."

"Peace is coming, Tyll. I will return home. Across the sea, to England. Do you want to come with me? I'll give you a warm room, and you won't go hungry. Even when you one day are no longer able to perform."

He said nothing. So many flakes had mingled with the raindrops that there was no longer any doubt—it was snowing.

"For old times' sake," she said. "You know as well as I do that the Kaiser will sooner or later grow annoyed with you. Then you will be on the street again. You'd have it better with me."

"Are you offering me charity, little Liz? A daily soup and a thick blanket and warm slippers until I die in my bed?"

"That's not so bad."

"But do you know what's better? Even better than dying in one's bed?"

"Tell me."

"Not dying, little Liz. That is much better."

She turned to the staircase. From the hall below she heard shouts and laughter and music. When she turned back to him, he was gone. Astonished, she bent over the balustrade, but the square lay in darkness, and Tyll was nowhere to be seen.

If it kept snowing like this, she thought, tomorrow everything would be covered with white, and the return journey to The Hague might be difficult. Wasn't it far too early in the year for snow? Probably some unfortunate person would soon be standing in the pillory down there for this.

And yet it's because of me, she thought. I am the Winter Queen!

She leaned her head back and opened her mouth as wide as she could. She hadn't done this in a long time. The snow was still as sweet and cold as it had been when she was a girl. And then, to taste it better, and only because she knew that in the darkness no one could see her, she stuck her tongue out.